Blitzing Emily

By Julie Brannagh

Blitzing Emily
Coming Soon:
Rushing Amy
Catching Cameron

Blitzing Emily

A LOVE AND FOOTBALL NOVEL

JULIE BRANNAGH

AVONIMPULSE
An Imprint of HarperCollinsPublishers

Excerpt from *Rushing Amy* copyright © 2014 by Julie Revell Benjamin.

Excerpt from *Santa, Bring My Baby Back* copyright © 2013 by Cheryl Harper.

Excerpt from *The Christmas Cookie Chronicles: Grace* copyright © 2013 by Laurie Vanzura.

Excerpt from *Desperately Seeking Fireman* copyright © 2014 by Jennifer Bernard.

EPub Edition JANUARY 2014 ISBN: 9780062279712

Print Edition ISBN: 9780062279743

JV 10 9 8 7 6 5 4 3 2

To my husband, Eric
To have and to hold, from this day forward
For better, for worse, for richer or for poorer
In sickness and in health
To love and to cherish
As long as we both shall live
You are my happily ever after.

Acknowledgments

WRITING A BOOK might seem like a solitary activity. It's actually anything but. I have lots and lots of thank yous, so let's get started.

Thank you to my wonderful agent, Sarah E. Younger of Nancy Yost Literary Agency, who went above and beyond to make sure my dream of being a published novelist became a reality. I could never thank her enough.

Amanda Bergeron is my equally terrific editor at Avon Impulse. I am so lucky she chose me. She makes my work sparkle. Plus, she doesn't laugh at my (many and egregious) grammatical errors. Thank you so much!

This book started as the result of a "writing exercise" at Susan Elizabeth Phillips' former message board. She wrote the first contemporary romance I ever read. I'm thrilled to be following in her footsteps. Thank you, SEP.

Thank you to Kristan Higgins for beta reading and early edits of this manuscript. She offered great help and advice.

My husband Eric encourages me, reads manuscript pages, listens and helps with plotting issues, and supports our family so I can follow my dream. Thank you, honey. I love you.

Thanks to the brilliant Susan Mallery, who cares enough to tell me the truth. I could never repay you for everything you have done for me.

Thank you to my fantastic critique group, the Cupcake Crew, who also cares enough to be honest. Amy Raby and Jessi Gage, you want my best work, and I am grateful for that. The cupcakes are on me today!

Thanks to the Bellevue, WA Cupcake Royale for harboring the Cupcake Crew each week.

I'd like to thank both the Greater Seattle and Chicago-North chapters of Romance Writers of America who encourage me, instruct me, and share their chocolate with me.

I'd like to thank Gari for suggesting a wonderful title. Thank you so much!

Thanks to the public relations department of Seattle Opera, especially Jonathan Dean. They were more than generous with research and answering my (endless) questions.

I would be remiss if I did not thank several of the Seattle Seahawks (past and present) for interviews they've given in multiple media sources which were a huge help with my research, especially Patrick Kerney.

Last but not least, I'd like to thank the real-life Dr. Su of Evergreen Hospital Sleep Disorders Clinic, who saved my life.

Brandon is a character created in my imagination. I did not base him on any person currently or formerly playing in the NFL. Any mistakes in the research are mine. Any artistic license is mine as well.

I hope you'll enjoy Blitzing Emily! If you'd like to visit my website, I'm at www.juliebrannagh.com. I'm also @julieinduvall on Twitter.

Chapter One

EMILY HAMILTON PLANNED to kill her sister. She just had to figure out where to hide the body. After that, she'd have to explain to Mom and Dad why Amy didn't attend Sunday dinners anymore. Right now, though, that was all secondary.

Emily parked in front of the Seattle Sharks' headquarters on a cold, windy Valentine's Day afternoon, wrestling the biggest balloon bouquet known to mankind from the back of her Ford Escape.

Couldn't this guy's girlfriend choose a better method of saying "I wuv you" than seventy-five personalized Mylar balloons, five pounds of Fran's Chocolates, and a teddy bear the size of Sharks Stadium? A greeting card would work. They're portable. They're tasteful. Well, most of them are. The mailman would even pay a visit to one's very own mailbox to ensure that the Valentine in question found its way into the paw of some neckless, muscle-bound football player in plenty of time for the big day. Then again, Emily didn't actually know any football players, and maybe she was being a little harsh.

She gazed at the profusion of balloons reading "I love you, Brandon." Brandon would also be the only man in America who might find such an over-the-top display compelling.

Emily carefully tugged, rearranged, coaxed, and swore under her breath for what felt like a half-hour, and the balloons wrapped themselves around the bear. The bear wedged under the huge box of chocolates. She'd opened all four car doors in an attempt to push or pull the whole thing out. Moving the box was frightening. Even better, it had been an unseasonably cold February in Seattle. The parking lot resembled an ice skating rink courtesy of the last (surprisingly deep) snowfall. Replacing a five-pound box of expensive Fran's Chocolates meant one less pair of Jimmy Choos in her closet, which was always unacceptable.

Emily pulled on the balloons again as she slid around on pavement that felt like it was greased. She wasn't exactly dressed for balloon wrangling. The stiletto-heeled boots she'd bought during her last trip to Rome and couldn't wait to wear looked great at rehearsal. But they didn't work well in an icy parking lot by any stretch of the imagination. The dress trousers and lacy silk cardigan she had on today weren't made for flexibility, either.

Emily wasn't a floral delivery driver by profession. She typically spent her days, and several evenings a week, being rescued from evil spirits, pursued by noblemen, or falling in love with *entirely* inappropriate scoundrels as an opera singer. Rehearsal was done for the day, however, and she was helping her sister out. Amy's floral shop had opened less than six months ago, and Valentine's Day was the biggest delivery day so far. Amy needed the money. After all, her business loan balance was the financial equivalent of Shock and Awe.

Emily needed a stiff drink and an evening with George Clooney, but she didn't see either materializing anytime soon.

She could free the bear, but that would send the candy box flying. She couldn't get through the mass of balloons to push the candy box aside. The bear watched her through beady and unmoving eyes as she stopped swearing and started praying. She wasn't Catholic, but reciting a couple of Hail Mary's wouldn't hurt.

Maybe she imagined devil horns sprouting through the bear's thick plush.

Valentine's Day was the first night off she'd had in quite some time. Even more than a date or any extravagant Valentine's observance, Emily wanted a peaceful evening alone in her cozy, early 2000's up-market townhouse. Besides, she had no use for the holiday. She'd learned long ago that men really couldn't be trusted. Instead of getting winged by Cupid's arrow, she'd take a bubble bath with the expensive French freesia-scented bath gel she bought but never had time to use, she'd read her copy of last year's hottest bestseller, still gathering dust on the nightstand in her room—better late than never—and she'd open a split of Perrier-Jouet champagne. It sounded perfect. All she had to do was finish this, make sure Amy didn't need any more help, and she could go home. The thought cheered her.

Five sweaty-looking, disheveled men gathered around the front door of the square, three-story team facility, watching Emily's every movement. Each wore multiple items of clothing bearing the Seattle Sharks' logo. Did they offer to help her? Hell, no. She saw cash change hands. Of course, she could only imagine what they were betting on: who this crap was for. Whether or not the gigantic balloon bouquet would propel her into the flight pattern at Sea-Tac Airport.

She braced one foot against the car's back bumper, gingerly tugging yet one more time. She resisted the impulse to cross herself before heaving the box of candy under one arm. She wrestled the evil red teddy bear into a headlock under her other arm.

She extracted the balloons from the back of her car with sheer force of will, gripping them in three-and-a-half fingers, and minced toward the staircase leading to the front door of the facility.

The ice crunched under Emily's feet. Only a couple more steps to that staircase, which appeared to rival the slickness of Vaseline. She hitched the candy box a little higher against her side. The teddy bear would survive a spill, but the candy wouldn't. Every step proved she'd make it up those damn stairs, delivery intact. A little frostbite wouldn't be that big of a deal.

She braced the candy box against the metal stair railing. If she wrapped her arm around it, she could slide her way up. Perfect.

"Get that the hell out of here!" an obviously angry male shouted.

It felt like slow motion. The stiletto heel on her boot snapped off as she jumped. The candy box slipped from her grasp. She let go of the railing as she tried to grab it. Both feet slid out from under her, and she had the sickening realization that she was falling. Adrenaline shot through her system. This would leave a mark. Emily tried to grab on to anything at all. The only thing to hang on to was the huge bunch of balloons.

She landed flat on her back. The candy flew in all directions, the bear landed squarely in the middle of her chest, and she heard a loud *thunk* as everything went black.

EMILY HEARD A voice as she came to. He was close, and he was murmuring to himself. "Shit. Please don't be dead."

She felt a weight resting on her chest. She wriggled her toes. They worked. She spread her fingers. They worked, too. She tried to take a breath.

"I didn't mean to scare you. This is all my fault. I don't want any more crap from—oh, hell."

Oh, God. Imagining how she would explain this to Amy hurt worse than her headache.

"Hey." He patted her cheek. "Are you okay?"

She couldn't speak. Whoever he was, his Southern drawl dripped like thick, sweet, warm honey into her ear. She smelled magnolias and fresh beignets. She must have been dreaming.

"You hit your head. Let me feel for bumps." Emily felt the back of her head cradled in a very large hand. Long, warm fingers slipped through her hair and over her scalp, moving effortlessly. "You got the wind knocked out of you. Take a breath."

"Mmph," Emily mumbled.

"There. You're breathing." He continued rubbing her head, his fingertips roaming as he spoke. The ice and snow burned against her back and legs, but she'd give him an hour to stop. "And you have a cut on your head. It's bleeding."

Oh, God.

"It's pretty dumb to wear spike heels in an icy parking lot." He sounded angry. She heard the balloons rustle. He must have grabbed one to look at it. "How the hell did she get my name on them?"

Emily opened her eyes to see the evil red bear sitting on her chest, and the puckered brow and concerned blue-green eyes of the most handsome man she'd ever seen.

Amy would kill her when she found out how messed up the delivery was, unless she expired on the spot from sheer embarrassment first.

He studied her. He still knelt beside her. "What's your name, sugar?"

Any other man would have gotten the full force of her offended feminist sensibilities at that point, but all she could manage to breathe was, "Emily, but not for long."

She still clutched the balloons. They'd been threaded through a metal weight that looked like an oversized Hershey's Kiss, but the sheer amount of helium involved threatened to pull her off the ground. Thank God the wind had died down a bit.

Brandon slipped his arm around her shoulders and helped her sit up. "Emily. Let me take those." He pried her fingers off the tangled, several-inches-thick bundle of ribbon, and put his foot down on it while he spoke. He didn't have to work very hard. Her fingers went slack at his touch.

"You might need to see a doctor for that cut," he suggested.

"Looks like it was for you, McKenna," yelled one of the five guys who'd been watching. They crossed the sidewalk to see what was happening. Emily found herself surrounded by six sweaty and disheveled men, one of whom still checked her for injuries.

"A little help?" A tall guy—hell, they were all tall, but this one had close-cropped black curls—said: "Hey, baby, what's your name?"

"I've got this," Brandon told them. He still supported her with one arm. "Back off."

"Ooh, I'm scared of you," the dark-haired one shot back.

Brandon gave him a look that should have liquefied the parking lot. "You should be." He shielded her from the other men with his body.

"Emily, I hope you won't be mad about this, but it's for the best."

He stripped the weight off the huge bunch of balloons and let them go. They shot what she imagined to be several hundred feet into the air. The bear on her lap started to spin. Now she was dizzy as well.

"I . . . You can't do that!" she cried and clutched her pounding head. "Do you know how long it took my sister to inflate those balloons? The customer wanted them delivered."

"I probably should have donated them to Children's Hospital or something. I wanted them gone. Sick kids don't need some stupid balloon that reads, 'I love you, Brandon.'"

"The FAA's scrambling jets as we speak," one of the guys said. They continued staring at Emily as if they hadn't seen a woman sprawled on her back in a public parking lot before.

"Hey, pretty lady," one of the guys said as he stepped forward. Brandon glared at him, and he rapidly stepped back.

"I said, I've got this," Brandon told him. "Show's over. Get lost." He picked up the evil red teddy bear and threw it at them. This brought on a chorus of responses from the guys still standing around her.

"McKenna, you cranky bitch," one of them said. "That's what happens when you go without."

"Dawg, I like her better than the last one."

"At least she's got curves. Junk in the trunk. Hey, pretty lady, have dinner with me." The guy with the black curls, eyes like a melted Hershey's bar, whipped out his smart phone. "I'll get us a table at Seastar at eight."

"Go fu— She's not going anywhere with you, dirtbag," Brandon snapped. He took her elbow and helped her up.

She swayed toward him, still dizzy. All she had to do was get in her car and drive away. She would put a Band-

Aid on whatever was bleeding. Lying in a bubble bath would fix it all. She'd explain to Amy later.

She couldn't seem to move.

"You're not okay," he said. "I broke it, now I have to fix it." To her amazement, he scooped Emily up in his arms. "Do you feel sleepy? Dizzy? How about double vision, or a headache? Nausea?"

He was walking away with her. She could hear voices as the guys followed them.

"Well, that's one way to get a date for Valentine's Day."

"Me Tarzan, you Jane."

"Hey, Balloon Girl, I'll give you a ride."

Brandon's lips compressed into a thin line, and a flush spread over his cheeks and the tops of his ears. "Sorry about that," he told her. "They don't know any women they can actually be seen with in public."

Her stomach lurched and rolled with each footstep Brandon took. She was not going to throw up. She tried not to think about how much she weighed as Brandon carried her. He did not slip and slide on the ice. He wasn't even breathing hard as he settled Emily on the passenger seat of her Escape.

"Hang on." He hurled himself into the driver's seat.

"What are you doing? You can't drive my car. The insurance—" she cried out. She clutched her aching head in both hands.

"You need to get looked at, and you're not driving yourself to the hospital."

He pulled away from the curb. Emily saw the other five guys on the sidewalk, debris at their feet, receding in the rear-view mirror. All that chocolate . . . Somebody was going to have a mess to clean up.

She leaned back against the seat and closed her eyes.

Brandon's voice was sharp. "Don't go to sleep. You have to stay awake till we get to the emergency room."

He held the steering wheel as he reached out and shook her shoulder. He glanced over at Emily as he maneuvered in and out of traffic. "Emily, I mean it. Open your eyes and look at me."

Obviously he was great at multi-tasking. She forced her eyes open.

"Good girl," he said.

Her car would need a detailing when this was all over. She was bleeding. The t-shirt and shorts he wore were drenched in sweat from what must have been his workout. Even sweaty, he smelled wonderful. Clean, with the faint scent of Old Spice. It was surprising to her he wore such an old-fashioned aftershave, but it fit him.

"Keep talking to me, sugar. You don't look like any delivery person I've ever seen."

She'd have to marshal enough brainpower to answer. It was all she could do not to close her eyes. "My sister Amy owns a flower shop. She needed a driver. It beats the hell out of sitting around at home watching reality TV."

"That's nice of you. What's her shop called?" The dimple in his left cheek flashed as he grinned at Emily. He turned into the emergency room's driveway.

"Crazy Daisy. It's on Broadway," she said.

"I'll have to remember that." He came to a halt in

front of the sliding front doors, threw the car into park, hopped out, and hurried around to open Emily's door.

"Easy," he said, and reached in to unsnap her seat belt. He also grabbed her handbag off the floorboard.

Brandon was all business. "Here. Take my hand." Emily clutched his bigger, slightly rougher hand. He eased her out of the seat. She tried to stand on her own but swayed again. He glanced around, frowned a little, and told her, "No wheelchairs, damn it. I think you need a ride." He scooped her up once more.

"I can do this myself." She could barf on his shoes, too.

"And have you pass out on the sidewalk and hit your head again? My mama taught me better than that. I'm already in enough trouble."

Brandon strode into the emergency room. Every time Emily had visited a hospital emergency room in the past, no one had rushed unless a patient was bleeding from multiple places. Maybe the key was being carried in by a big jock in sweaty workout clothes. Nurses scurried toward her.

"What do we have here?" one of them asked Brandon.

"She decided to try ice skating in stiletto heels. She's bleeding a little."

"We've got a room with her name on it."

They were shown to a dimly lit room painted the shade of Silly Putty and dominated by monitors, IV medication pumps, a rolling cabinet with clean linens, and a computer setup. Brandon laid Emily down on a narrow bed. He dropped her purse next to her.

"No sleeping," he warned again, pulling a chair up

beside her. He threw himself down in it. They didn't have long to wait. A doctor breezed through the doorway.

"Hi, there. I'm Dr. Su. What have we got?"

"This is Emily. She wiped out on some ice in the parking lot," Brandon explained.

The doctor moved closer and pulled a small flashlight out of his breast pocket. "Emily." He sat down on a rolling examination chair as he took her hand. "I'll bet you think you're the first person I've seen today who had an encounter with some ice."

Emily glanced over at Brandon, and he gave her a reassuring smile. She tried to look pitiful in response. She turned her head and focused on the doctor again.

"I'll bet none of them were wearing a thousand dollars' worth of Italian leather boots at the time."

While she spoke, the doctor examined the back of her head, shone a light in her eyes, and said, "How many fingers, Emily?" He held up two.

"Three," Emily responded. Brandon let out what sounded like a groan.

"That's never happened to me before," he muttered.

"Are you sleepy? Nauseated? Have a headache? Follow my fingers, okay?" He asked the same questions Brandon did. They didn't sound any better the second time.

"I mostly feel stupid."

She glanced over to see Brandon eying the clock on the wall in the opposite corner of the room. His eyes slid back to her, but he seemed distracted.

"I'll be fine. It's okay if you leave," she said.

"No, no," Brandon insisted, but he looked at the clock once more. "Don't worry about it."

"Just to be safe, Emily, I'm ordering a CT scan. We're also going to stitch that cut. Sit tight for a few minutes, and I'll send the nurse in to start this process."

Emily tried to sit up. "I'm fine. I have to make some other deliveries for Amy. I . . ." The room spun around. The doctor caught her just before she fell off the side of the narrow bed.

Brandon jumped out of the chair and arrived at her bedside in one long stride. He pulled up the bedside railings. "Doctor, may I talk with you in the hallway for a moment?"

Emily heard only broken bits of their discussion. It didn't sound positive. Brandon gestured toward the room a few times with his hand while they talked. The noise in the hallway finally dropped a little and she could listen in.

"Look, Doc, I'm late. I want to stay, but I really can't," Brandon said.

"Emily needs . . ." but whatever it was the doctor thought she needed was drowned out by yet more voices, one high-pitched and panicky, from an adjoining room.

"If you tell us what you took, we won't tell anyone else. We need to know before we can treat you."

"I can't talk about it."

"You're going to have to talk about it at some point. You're not the first guy that showed up at this hospital after an erection of more than four hours. Did you take something besides an ED drug? Recreational drugs? Did you drink alcohol tonight? This isn't a joke."

"It's Valentine's Day. My girlfriend expected something special."

"She'd like it better if you both were around next Valentine's Day, too."

A nurse shut the sliding glass door in Emily's room, pulling a floor-to-ceiling cloth curtain around the bed Emily lay in.

"The admitting person will be here shortly, but let's get you into a stylish hospital gown while we wait."

The nurse was tall and stocky. She wore her hair in a long, dark pigtail. She had what appeared to be a permanent grin, and her nametag read "Cheryl." She undressed Emily with a speed and gentleness that showed many years of practice. Emily pushed her arms through the hospital gown sleeves, and the nurse draped a warm, fluffy cotton blanket over her as she lay down again.

"It's just like the day spa."

"Those boots must have been gorgeous before the heel snapped off."

"Thinking about how much they cost makes my headache worse."

"So, Emily, how's your pain level on a scale of one to ten?"

"My head's a seven. The boots are a twenty."

"Isn't that Brandon McKenna of the Sharks?"

"I picked him up in the parking lot," Emily sighed.

It was increasingly evident that Emily needed a ride home. After hearing a little of Brandon's conversation, he wasn't going to be around. There were signs all over the hospital stating that the use of cell phones was not allowed. The TV remote control fastened to the side of the bed didn't have texting capability, either.

"I'd like to call a friend. Is there a telephone I can use?"

Cheryl must have misheard her. "We don't allow non-family members in here, unfortunately. Your valentine is on his way to the waiting room."

Family member, Emily thought. "Valentine" wasn't exactly a family member, but she needed to get Brandon back in here. If she could find someone to pick her up, he'd be able to leave.

"Is there anything else I can do for you?"

"You know," Emily said, "You're right. It's a special day, and I really want to spend some time with him. Is there any possible way he could sit with me while I'm waiting?"

Cheryl winked at her. "For today, I'll make an exception. To the rest of the hospital, he's your fiancé. You just relax. He'll be here in two shakes of a lamb's tail."

Cheryl sped out of the room. Emily craned her neck to glimpse Brandon standing at the nurse's station in the midst of a crowd of people, signing autographs.

Moments later Brandon walked into the room. To Emily's relief, he was grinning like everything and everyone existed solely to amuse him. He sat down on the rolling examination chair the doctor had vacated.

"Well. Aren't you the shameless hussy. We haven't even had dinner yet, and you told the nurse we were engaged." He raised an eyebrow. "What do you do on the second date? File for divorce?"

"I should have told her you were my baby daddy . . ."

"And here I thought I was so irresistible." He twirled a lock of her hair around his finger. "Mmm. Red."

Speaking hurt, but Emily had to make him understand. "I really appreciate your driving me over here, but let's get real. You obviously have other plans tonight, and I need to call someone to come and get me. You've been looking at the clock since we got here."

Brandon looked a bit uncomfortable and shifted on the chair. "You've got me. I have plans. I could cancel them, but I left my phone in my locker."

Emily produced her iPhone from her purse and handed it to him. "If you make a call for me, you can go. Here, just a minute." She took the phone out of his hand and scrolled through her contacts list. "My sister is busy, but one of my friends might be available. If you'll call Sarah—I work with her—she doesn't live far away, and she might be able to pick me up and drop me off at home." She nodded at the sign. "You'll need to go outside."

"Got it." He fiddled with the phone for a few seconds, and handed it back to her. "I have a BlackBerry. How do you use this thing again?"

It was a good thing he was handsome, because he evidently wasn't that smart. Emily hit the keys on the display again. "If you push this, the phone will dial. Ask Sarah to come and get me." She closed her eyes for a moment. "That whole joking about being engaged thing is not going to be a problem for you, is it?"

He shrugged. "Only on a slow news day. Plus, if anything weird happens, I can deal with it."

Emily tried to shake her head and winced. Obviously

she was a public person, too. There'd be a little interest in Emily's engagement, but Brandon was evidently some kind of big deal. This was a hospital, though. That stuff was confidential.

"I'm betting you have one hell of a headache. Rest." He reached out to pull the blanket up beneath her chin. "I'll get you some water."

"I'm so sleepy," she told him. "I don't understand why you're still here."

"You fell down. It's my fault. I want to make sure you're safe."

"I'll be fine. You can go," she insisted. "Isn't that what you want?"

Emily wanted to go home and soak in a hot bath. That bath was assuming mythical proportions by this point.

"I'll tell you what. I'll be back in a few minutes." Brandon rose from the chair, stroked her cheek, tossed a "See ya" over his shoulder, and loped out of the room.

Brandon reappeared less than five minutes later.

"Sarah's busy. Her boyfriend answered the phone. I believe the message was 'She'd have to get out of my bed for that, and it's not happening tonight.' So, I cancelled my plans, and I will chauffeur you home."

"Let me see if I can find someone else."

"Not going to happen, sugar. Everyone is out with their valentine, or they're staying in and not answering the phone."

"I can do this." She took the phone out of his hand and started scrolling through names. "I . . . Stop calling me sugar."

He laughed. It wasn't that damn funny.

Two male nurses walked into the room. "Emily, we're here to take you upstairs for some tests. I'm Kevin, and this is Jeff." Kevin glanced at the phone in Emily's hand. "You'll need to put that away," he scolded.

Emily didn't remember much of the tests she had. She did remember, however, the stitches she received in the cut on her head. Cheryl the nurse produced two ibuprofens and a cup of cold water as a reward. Emily awoke once more in the dimness of the emergency room cubicle Brandon still sat in. The doctor was talking with him.

"I was at the Minutemen's game last season," he told Brandon. "That was quite a sack at the end of the third."

"What's a sack?" Emily murmured to Brandon.

His brows drew together, his lips twitched into a smile, but he didn't answer her.

"I enjoyed it, that's for sure." Brandon told him. "I'd like to take my girl home, if that will work for you."

He set a Styrofoam cup and the newspaper sports page he held on a low rolling table and waited expectantly.

"Shall I tell you the good news or the bad news first?" Dr. Su grinned with what he probably thought was quite a joke.

"Let's go with the good news." Brandon patted Emily's hand as he spoke.

"Hospital cuisine has improved." Everyone was a comedian. "However, Emily is going to have to stay overnight with us."

Chapter Two

"DOCTOR, I CAN'T do that. Since the tests are fine, I'd like to go home." Emily was having no part of the doctor's orders. She looked like someone ran over her skateboard. She even managed to work up a couple of tears, which glistened in her amber-brown eyes. Brandon had spent less than two hours with this woman, and he already knew the doctor didn't stand a chance. In the dictionary under the word "intractable" there was a photo of Emily.

"We'd rather you stayed here." Dr. Su was still talking. Well, perhaps it should have been called "negotiating." Maybe Emily was available for Brandon's upcoming contract discussions. He'd love to see what would happen when she went up against the Sharks' owners. Then again, it wouldn't be a fair fight. Emily was as lovely as she was hard-headed.

"I live in Redmond. It's ten miles away or so," she said.

The doctor caved. "If you really want to go home, you

can. But you'll need to be watched by another adult for the next twelve to twenty-four hours. This is non-negotiable. You won't be able to do anything but relax. No driving, no working, no nothing."

"We could call your sister," Brandon told Emily. "She'll come over."

"This is the busiest day of the year for her. She *can't* come over . . ."

Emily was clutching her head again. Brandon knew she had to have one hell of a headache. If there was one thing all football players had in common it was the fact that every one of them, at one time or another, had suffered a concussion. She looked at him pleadingly. He could never resist a somewhat helpless female. Emily really couldn't be called helpless, though. One minute she was tougher than Dallas's defense; a minute later she was all sad golden eyes, fluttering lashes, and quivering lips. There wasn't a man in the universe that could hope to withstand what she dished out.

"No problem," Brandon interrupted. "I'll just stay over."

Emily's eyes got huge, but she said nothing. She opened her mouth, quickly clamping it shut when he caught her eye and gave her a barely noticeable head shake.

He'd spend a couple of hours doing the gentlemanly thing. If he moved his ass, he could salvage his evening's plans as well. It was a win-win. If it got him laid in the next twenty-four hours, even better.

Dr. Su shook Emily's hand. "It was nice to meet you both. I'll send the nurse in with discharge instructions. Take it easy. You'll feel much better in a day or so."

Emily waited until the doctor left the room before glancing up at Brandon. "If you'll get me home, I can take care of the rest."

She evidently wanted to get away from him as much as he wanted to leave, so at least they were even. Another commotion in the doorway revealed Cheryl, the nurse. The discharge instructions were given more to him than to Emily, verbally and in print. Lucky him.

"Emily can have ibuprofen for her headache every four to six hours," she said. "She had some an hour ago. You'll need to wake her up every couple of hours and talk with her. If she has double vision, if you can't wake her up easily, or if she is not making sense when she speaks, she will need to come back to the hospital immediately."

Brandon was nodding as if he actually planned on staying with her. Mostly, he wanted to leave. Hospitals reminded him of injuries, and injuries were something he didn't want to be reminded of at all.

"Let's get you ready to go," Cheryl said to Emily.

She pulled Emily's clothing off a hanger in a concealed closet. Brandon ducked behind the sports page once more, but Emily gave him a glare that could melt steel.

"Don't look," she said.

"Oh, I'm not," but it was all he could do not to laugh.

Brandon had known a lot of women since he was old enough to notice. He loved them, and they loved him back. It was as certain in his life as the sunrise each morning. At the same time, Emily was an odd combination of vulnerability and drill sergeant. He wasn't sure what to think of her.

The nurse was getting in on the act, too: "No funny business. She needs rest."

Brandon was a little stunned. Here he was doing his Boy Scout good deed for the day, but it still didn't vouch for either his character or his upbringing. Then again, his mama would be doubled over with laughter right now.

"I don't know what you're talking about, ma'am." He arched one brow.

"Don't start with me." Cheryl wagged one finger in his general direction, and indicated the wheelchair by the door. "Let's go for a little ride, Emily. Mr. McKenna, please get your vehicle."

Brandon sprinted down the hallway and vanished through the double doors leading to the waiting room. Get in Emily's car, get on the road, and he could call his date for the evening from the cab he'd be leaving Emily's place in.

Emily waited on the sidewalk with the nurse.

"Thank you, Cheryl." Brandon extended his hand to her. "I'll take it from here."

"You *will* drive safely on the way home," Cheryl said.

"My mama must have called you." He took Emily's elbow as he led her to her car. "Come on, sugar. Let's go."

"I NEED SOME directions to your place," Brandon said.

Emily was fiddling with her phone, and frowning a little.

"Oh, you can just drop me off—"

"There will be no 'dropping off.'" His voice was stern. "You're doing exactly what Cheryl and the doctor told us. You have to go straight to bed. Let's get you there."

"I can't figure out why you are doing this. Yeah, I fell down, but it wasn't like you did it. I'm not mad at you. Plus, you have other pla—"

"Give me the address."

"I'm on Alder Crest Road in Redmond Ridge. My townhouse is the first one on the corner." Emily had the phone up to her ear. "Simone, it's Emily Hamilton." She listened intently for a few moments. "Not a good time?" He heard a peal of laughter. "Have a great evening with him. I'll talk to you tomorrow."

Emily punched the "end" button, and appeared to be thinking. She dialed her phone once more.

"Janey, it's Emily. Hey, are you busy right now?" She was nodding like Janey was in the car with them. "I understand. Happy Valentine's Day. I'll see you soon." She disconnected her call, and glanced over at Brandon.

"Remember that conversation we had about how everyone you know has plans tonight?" He gave her what he hoped was a sympathetic smile. "It might be a pretty tall order to find someone available."

Brandon listened while Emily made call after call.

"I'm screwed. Actually, I'm the only one who's not, according to everyone who's actually answering their phone." Her phone rang; Brandon had to smile at the excitement in her voice. "Tristan. How are you doing?"

Brandon couldn't hear how Tristan was doing, but he heard Emily's sharp intake of breath.

"Oh, no. I really need your help. I had an accident, and I can't be left alone tonight. No, no. I'm okay, I just . . . Is there any way that you and Jason could possibly come over? I know it's a huge imposition." She listened for a moment, said, "Don't worry about it. I'll call my mom and dad. You two have a great evening."

Emily sagged against the passenger seat. So, Tristan *wasn't* her boyfriend.

"Tristan said that unless I wanted to witness him performing acts on Jason that are illegal in thirty-seven states, it probably was not going to happen tonight." She let out a sigh, and intoned, "It's time to call my parents."

"Sounds like a rugged phone call, sugar."

Emily rolled her eyes. The movement must have hurt because she flinched.

"It's not that I don't want to see them. They're going to freak out. I'd rather avoid it." She fiddled with her phone again, and listened for a few minutes. "Mom, it's Emily. I spent the afternoon at Evergreen, and I need your help. Love you. Bye."

"Let me guess. They're not home, either." Brandon turned onto Alder Crest Road, and Emily pointed to the townhouse on the corner.

"That's mine."

He pulled into the driveway, shut off the ignition, and turned to her expectantly. "So, invite me in."

"Look," Emily dropped the phone back into her purse. "I really appreciate your taking me to the hospital, staying with me, and driving me home, but I was wondering if I could ask you for one more favor."

He got out of the car, crossed to the passenger door, and opened it. "Let's have this conversation inside."

AFTER A SHORT tutorial on which key fit in the front lock, Brandon followed Emily into her house. She promptly tripped on the luggage left in the entryway. He reached out, caught her around the waist, and set her back on her feet.

"Your roommate should clean up more often."

Emily wriggled out of his grasp and bent down to unzip her boots. She clutched her head. "No roommate," she said.

"Maybe you should sit down before trying that."

She limped across the living room to a pair of leather couches. "I just got home from San Jose. I'll drag them upstairs to unpack at some point."

"That's the least of your problems right now."

"I have to be onstage at McCaw Hall at ten o'clock tomorrow morning," Emily told him. "I don't have time for this." She dropped both boots on the carpeting and leaned back against the couch. She pushed a curtain of strawberry-blonde curls out of her eyes with one hand. "Please sit down."

"You might want to reschedule," he told her.

"I have to go. I have rehearsals. I'm performing in *The Marriage of Figaro* in two weeks," Emily said. "It's an opera."

"You're an *opera singer?*" Brandon realized his mouth was hanging open. He blurted his question out in the same tone of voice he might have used to say, "You're a *convicted felon*?" or "You were *raised by wolves*?"

"The technical term is 'diva.'"

He was having a rough time wrapping his brain around this. "But you're not fat. Opera singers are . . . larger. They wear headgear with horns sticking out on either side."

"That's only for *The Ring*," Emily said.

"I saw that movie. That little girl's eyes . . . She freaked me out," he muttered.

"Most opera singers now are normal weight," she continued. "I have to have the physical strength to lift my voice past a sixty-person orchestra without a microphone, though, so I work out, and I practice every day."

"How long have you been doing this?"

Emily propped two stockinged feet on a wood-and-glass coffee table. "Most of my life. I started ballet at three. I entered a training program with a former diva in my teens. After that, I went to a conservatory. I've been performing with opera companies in the US and Europe ever since."

"This isn't like finding a job on Craigslist. You have someone representing you, like an agent."

His interest surprised Emily. Usually, guys outside of her little world ran away when they heard the word "opera."

"Yes. It depends on what operas the company is presenting each year, that kind of thing."

"Do you listen to other types of music?"

"Sometimes." She gestured toward the iPod stereo

system on a nearby table. "You can take a look at what's on my playlists if you'd like. Have you heard an opera before?" *Opera?* He considered himself a pretty open-minded guy, but he drew the line at that kind of thing. "Oh, all the time."

She closed her eyes, but he saw her lips curve into a smile. "You might like it," she teased. "It's a play, set to music."

"And you act as well as sing." He sat up and leaned toward her. "And you have to be there tomorrow."

She heaved a long sigh. "I have a substitute—actually she's called a 'cover'—but I really can't miss the rehearsal. It's only two weeks till we debut. There's a lot to get done."

She wasn't meeting his eyes. She was twisting her hands in her lap. Obviously there was something else going on here, but he'd deal with the more immediate issues first.

"You know, it's fairly typical for NFL players to gut it out and play hurt, but other industries frown somewhat on that kind of thing. Take a couple of days off and heal up."

She rubbed one hand over her face. "I . . . I'll be fine. I need to work. I'm sure this will go away by morning, and everything will be perfect." She struggled to her feet. "Let me get you something to drink. What would you like?"

She was swaying again, and he grabbed her elbow. This woman did not know when to give up. He wondered if she ever relaxed.

"I can get it," he said.

She collapsed on the couch in a heap, leaning back

against the dark leather. He finally figured out the décor as he glanced around the room: corporate hotel. He'd never seen a house so sterile. Emily might own the place, but she didn't live here. He wondered where she spent most of her time.

"I'll rustle us up a bite to eat—"

"Uh—wait." She sounded a bit panicked. "There's not a lot of food here," she admitted. "I eat out a lot."

"I do amazing things with a telephone and a delivery menu. Take it easy."

"I'm so sorry, Brandon, but I should go lie down."

She pushed herself off the couch again. Before she could take another uneven step he slipped his arm around her waist and took her other hand. Her forehead drooped onto his chest like one of the wilted daffodils in his mother's garden.

She dropped his hand. Her arms clasped loosely around him. He knew she was only trying to keep her balance, but a jolt of attraction sizzled through every nerve in his body. She rubbed her face against his shirt front like a cat.

"Let me find a pillow and a blanket for you. I'll be back in a jiffy."

"If you decide to let yourself out, please lock the front door and put the key under the mat. There's a key hanging up in the kitchen by the calendar."

"You're trying awfully hard to get rid of me. I think my feelings are hurt." He kept his voice light.

"Thank you for taking care of me. It was nice to meet you."

"I'll be here when you wake up," he said.

After a quick search, Brandon spread a blanket over her. He tucked a pillow beneath her head, too. Her eyelids fluttered closed. A few minutes later, her even breathing told him she was asleep.

A GENTLE HAND shook Emily's shoulder and a sweetly accented voice in her ear said, "Hey, sugar. Talk to me for a few minutes."

"Not interested." She pulled a pillow over her face. He took it away from her. "That is *mine*." She tried to scowl at him.

"It's mine now," Brandon joked. "How are you feeling?"

"Sleepy. Need to sleep," she mumbled.

"Do you know where you are right now?"

She shook her head. "You're waking me up. I want to sleep. I can't believe you're still here."

Emily's outrage was surprisingly funny. He perched on the edge of the couch.

"Let's see if I can torment you some more."

She tried to push him away. "Noooo. I want to sleep. Leave me alone."

She let out a contented sigh as she snuggled into her pillows again.

"See you in two hours. I'll be the hot guy you can't resist."

"No," she protested. He couldn't stop laughing.

"Damn, you're cranky when you first wake up."

Emily definitely wouldn't be starring in *Sleeping*

Beauty. He knew she was probably in pain and a little cranky as a result, but he couldn't resist teasing her a bit.

She let out an irritated groan.

"How would you feel . . ." Her words trailed off as she turned into the pillow once more.

BRANDON TRIED TO adhere to the doctor's schedule, but Emily was surprisingly resistant to his efforts.

"Hey, it's time for you to talk with me again," he said.

"Don't wanna." This time, she pulled the blanket over her head. Brandon pried them away from her face. She rewarded him with a glare that should have melted flesh.

"You said that last time. You're going to have to come up with something more original. Dazzle me."

"Bite me."

"The kitten has claws."

She let out a long, tortured sigh. "You're really enjoying this."

"I'm wounded, sugar. And here I thought you liked me."

"Oh, yeah. Just like a cold sore." He saw her lips curve into a smile. She shoved herself into a sitting position. "Did anyone call?"

"It's been quiet."

He was surprised her mother hadn't called. His parents would have been on the next flight out if he left a message like that on their voice mail. Then again, he hadn't asked them for help for several years now. Maybe her parents were out of town.

THE NEXT TIME she opened her eyes, Emily decided she could stand up without falling over. She needed to make a few phone calls. The sound of the television from upstairs told her Brandon was otherwise occupied, at least temporarily.

Emily's manager David took the news of the spill in the parking lot much better than she thought he would. David never missed an opportunity to panic. Today he seemed somewhat calm.

"I'm assuming you think you're going to rehearsals tomorrow," he said.

"There is no way Anna will be singing this role."

"Let me call the floor director. Nobody would call anyone with a concussion 'difficult,' so don't worry about it. Just get better. Amy must be there with you."

He'd always been a little sweet on Emily's sister. Of course, Amy thought he was a mutant.

"She's at the shop today, David." Maybe Amy should tell David to buzz off. Again. Emily got tired of relaying his messages.

"Be sure and tell her I said 'hello.' "

"I'll keep you updated."

Moments after she hung up with David the phone rang. Amy didn't even bother to say "hello."

"You never called me."

"There was a little accident," Emily told her.

"That's awful. Are you okay?" Amy paused, but only for a moment. "There was something on the news about a huge bunch of Mylar balloons that are now tangled in the grid work on top of Sharks Stadium." Emily was silent. "Please tell me they are not the balloons that were supposed to go to Brandon McKenna."

With more than a little trepidation, Emily told Amy her tale of woe. For once Amy listened without interrupting, except the few times that she gasped.

"Brandon drove me home."

"Brandon. *Brandon McKenna?*"

"That's what I said. Please don't yell."

"Where is he now?"

Emily knew that if she didn't confess, Amy would get in the car and come over to find out for herself.

"Upstairs watching TV," she finally admitted.

Amy let out an "Oh, my God" Emily was sure they heard in the next county. She couldn't believe she was the only one with a sister whose volume was stuck on "shout." It left her clutching her head.

"Ame, knock it off. That hurts."

"Sorry." She didn't sound sorry at all in Emily's opinion. "So, he's still there. What's going on?"

"Nothing."

"Sure." Sarcasm dripped from every syllable.

"Yes, I'm totally lying to you. I'm having hot monkey sex with a guy I met oh, maybe four or five hours ago, while my head feels like it's going to pop right off my body," Emily said.

"Okay, okay, okay. I get it." Amy paused. "So, how hot is he?"

"He'll come back downstairs at any time. Do we need to talk about this now?"

"Come on," her sister wheedled. "Throw me a bone."

"David's looking for you."

"David is a money-grubbing moron. I can't believe I didn't go over there myself. You probably saw other Sharks there, too."

"I wouldn't know. I'm not the football fan."

"Okay. There are a few things I need to tell you about."

Emily heard the toilet flush in the master bathroom.

"I gotta go."

"Call me if you need me," Amy said, and she hung up.

Chapter Three

EMILY HAD BARELY enough time to hang up the cordless and flip on the TV before Brandon wandered down the stairs.

"Hey," he said, and he threw himself down on the couch next to her.

His blond curls were tangled, his eyes sleepy, and she saw a pillowcase crease on his cheek. He looked completely innocent, until she saw the wicked twinkle in his eyes. Even in dirty workout clothes, he was breathtaking. She wondered if it was possible to ovulate on demand.

"I'm guessing you took a nap," she said.

"I was supposed to be watching you." He tried to look penitent. It wasn't working.

"Glad to know you're making yourself comfortable," she teased.

He stretched his arm around the back of the couch.

"Everything in your room smells like flowers, and

your bed's great." He pulled up the edge of his t-shirt and sniffed it. Emily almost drooled at a glimpse of his rock-hard abdomen. Evidently, it was possible to have more than a six pack. "The guys will love my new perfume. Maybe they'll want some makeup tips," he muttered, and grabbed for the remote Emily left on the coffee table.

He clicked through the channels at a rapid pace.

"Excuse me. I had that." She lunged for it. No such luck. Emily ended up sprawled across his lap.

"The operative word here, sugar, is 'had.'" He held it up in the air out of her reach while he continued to click. He'd wear a hole in his thumb if he kept this up. "No NFL Network." She tried to sit up again, which wasn't working well. Of course, he was chuckling at her struggles. "Oh, I get it. You're heading for second base."

"Hardly." Emily reached over and tried to push off on the other arm of the couch. One beefy arm wrapped around her. "I'm not *trying* to do anything. Oh, whatever."

"You know, if you want a kiss, all you have to do is ask."

She couldn't imagine how he managed to look so innocent while smirking.

"I haven't had a woman throw herself in my lap for a while now. This could be interesting," he said.

Emily's eyebrows shot to her hairline. "I did not throw myself in your lap."

"Could've fooled me. Which one of us is—"

"Let go of me." She was still trying to grab the remote, without success.

"You'll fall," he warned.

"What's your point?"

"Here." He stuck the remote down the side of the couch cushion so Emily couldn't grab it. He grasped her upper arms, righted her with no effort at all, and looked into her eyes. "All better. Shouldn't you be resting, anyway?"

Emily tried to take a breath. Their bodies were frozen. He held her, and she gazed into his face. His dimple appeared, vanished, appeared again. She licked her lips with the microscopic amount of moisture left in her mouth. He was fighting a smile, but even more, he dipped his head toward her. He was going to kiss her.

"Yes," she said.

Her voice sounded weak, but it was all she could do to push it out of lungs that had no air at all. He continued to watch her, and he gradually moved closer. Their mouths were inches apart. Emily couldn't stop looking at his lips. After a few moments that seemed like an eternity, he released her and dug the remote from the couch cushion. She felt a stab of disappointment. He had changed his mind.

"Turns out you have the NFL Network, so I think I can handle another twenty-four hours here," he announced as he stopped on a channel she'd never seen before.

"You might not be here another twenty-four minutes. Don't you have a TV at home?" She wrapped her arms around her midsection. She wished she could come up with something more witty and cutting to say. She was so sure he would kiss her, and then he hadn't.

"What's a 'sack'?" he mimicked, referring to her question at the hospital. "My work's cut out for me, sugar. You know nothing about football. You need some help, and I'm the man for the job." He turned the volume up a bit. "Finally. I feel right at home."

"Well, good for you, Brandon. I can take care of myself now. Thanks for coming over."

"Sure you can. There's nothing in your refrigerator except beer and soda, a few condiments, a box of baking soda, and some kind of science project in a Chinese food container." He shook his head. "I'm guessing you don't cook."

"I wouldn't say that."

He laughed. The sound bounced around her living room. She had to laugh, too. The sudden explosion of joy on his face, the way his entire body shook, made her wonder what else she could say to make him laugh again.

He used the remote like a laser pointer.

"Okay. Here's a prime teaching opportunity. It's the Sharks versus the Minutemen from last year. We kicked their as— We beat them, badly. We can watch this, and then you can figure out what you're making me for dinner."

Emily found herself temporarily speechless again. He seemed to delight in saying whatever it might be that left her completely bewildered.

"We're not getting into a restaurant tonight," he said. "I'm hungry, and I'm stuck here."

"You're not *stuck* anywhere!" She clutched her head. God, it hurt.

"Your head wouldn't hurt if you didn't yell," he said solicitously, wagging his finger. He seemed to be using

Emily's last nerve as a trampoline. The only thing that saved him at that moment was the fact she preferred staying out of prison.

"I could pay your cab fare back to your car, and you can go wherever you'd like," she pointed out.

His dimple flashed as he gave her an unrepentant grin. "That's not going to work for me."

He got to his feet, pulled her cordless phone off its base, and wandered into the kitchen. Emily wondered if he was always this exasperating. She should have walked over to the front door, pulled it open, and ordered him out, but she knew she probably wouldn't be able to stand up that long.

He returned to the living room a few minutes later with a soda for her and a beer for himself. She wasn't watching football anymore.

"I can't believe you changed the channel," he informed her in mock outrage. "This is a chick flick."

"It's *Pride and Prejudice*. That's Colin Firth." Emily pointed at the television. "Don't tell me you don't know who Colin Firth is."

Brandon looked adorably confused. "Maybe he played for the Canadian Football League."

"No. He's a classically trained actor."

Now it was his turn to rub his face with both hands. She heard him muttering something almost unintelligible that contained the phrases "women," "Valentine's Day," and "girly men with lace sleeves."

"He's the definitive Mr. Darcy, you know."

"Definitive. What the fu—" He sent one hand through

his mop of blond curls like he wanted to pull them out by the fistful. "My ex-girlfriend used to try to get me to watch this crap. Let's watch something on the Speed Channel. Now *there's* some good television."

She let out a groan. "Nonstop Darwin Awards contestants are more valuable than a literary classic to you?"

He glared at her. One eyebrow went up.

"Make fun of me all you want, Opera Girl. I'm doing this for your own good." Emily realized she would have to take up professional wrestling to recover control over her TV, and she was too hungry to keep squabbling with him at the moment. He clicked through channels at lightning speed. He settled on the NFL Network again. "Pizza is on its way. You can thank me later."

"Let me give you some cash." She tried to rise from the couch. He pulled her back down by one elbow.

"You're going to hurt yourself." He gestured toward the television. "Listen and learn, sugar. First of all, these are the special teams guys. They're the toughest guys on any football team. They have no fear of giving up the body."

"I'm not sure why you're telling me this."

"Watch the guy at the back, by the end zone. He wants to run to the opposing end zone, so he can score. All those guys want to rip his head off and shi— They want to stop him."

Emily watched a bunch of guys jump on the guy with the ball, grinding his face into the grass. Surprisingly, he didn't seem to care. Maybe it wasn't as painful as it looked.

"He just got up and ran away."

"He made it to the forty. He's the man."

"They were trying to hurt him."

"Okay. Here comes the offense."

Brandon spent the next hour attempting to explain the intricacies of the NFL, and its endless rules to Emily. He was surprisingly patient. His tutorial was interrupted by the arrival of food, which he wouldn't allow Emily to pay for.

"There's cash in my wallet," she argued.

"And your point would be?"

"I can at least buy your dinner. You brought me home."

"Maybe other guys will let you do that, but I won't."

After only a few bites of pizza, Emily leaned back against the couch. Her eyelids drooped. He took the plate out of her hand.

"You need to go to bed. Come on, sugar."

"I don't understand why you're still calling me that, either."

Brandon didn't answer. He helped her up, offering his arm. Emily felt a little steadier than earlier, but she took it. They crossed the living room at a glacial pace and climbed the stairs one at a time.

"I think I need more medicine, too. My head—"

"Hang on."

He swept her up in his arms. This time, though, she clasped her arms around his neck.

"Last door on the left," she said sleepily. She laid her cheek against his shoulder. "Thanks for the ride."

He put her down on the bed and threw the blanket from the foot of the bed over her.

Emily's room was a confection of lace, ruffles, and a rainbow of pink. Besides the four-poster bed, which was dressed with ruffles and flounces and lacy pillows, and the overstuffed easy chair and ottoman, which was covered with a print festooned with huge cabbage roses, she lay on a custom-made, floral-print quilt. She was exhausted, but she could only imagine his thoughts. Brandon had stumbled into some kind of parallel universe. Girly World: No Boys Allowed. She could only imagine how shocking it was in comparison with what he'd seen of the rest of her house.

"Everything's so soft," he muttered.

EMILY OPENED HER eyes to see Brandon sitting in her bedroom chair and watching CNN. He wore her coral pink silk bathrobe. It didn't come close to fitting him. His damp hair and a wave of what she now knew as Brandon's scent—clean male skin, a bit musky, and a hint of old-fashioned aftershave—announced he'd been in the shower.

"My clothes will be done in the dryer pretty soon."

"I was wondering if pink silk was a new look for you."

"There isn't a pair of sweats in this house," he complained. "It's not like I could go naked."

He propped his crossed ankles on the edge of Emily's bed. She tried not to stare at the sculpted chest covered in darker blond curls or let her eyes stray further down.

"You went through my closet. That's private. What are you still doing here?" she said.

"You were out for a while."

"Brandon, I'm fine. You don't have to stay. Your girlfriend must be crazy mad. You should call her."

"I don't have a girlfriend."

"Well, then, who sent you all the stuff I dropped off today?"

"Not a big deal—"

Emily interrupted him. "Let's go back to my original question."

"The doctor told me to watch you. Apparently, I'm the only person in the country who doesn't have a date tonight," he joked. "I have to be here."

She craned her neck to look at the clock radio, which he was currently blocking. "It's eleven-thirty. I'm imposing on you."

"I wouldn't be here if I didn't want to be," he responded. He didn't meet her eyes. Emily resolved that when his clothes were done he was leaving, whether he knew it or not.

She pushed herself out of bed. She was still a little woozy, but she needed to get up and do some things. She headed toward the staircase, bracing herself against the wall with one hand.

He hurried into the hallway. His arm snaked around her waist.

"Let's go together."

Emily resisted the impulse to melt into his side. She reminded herself that she didn't know him. He wasn't part of her life. He'd go back to the Victoria's Secret models or whoever else he dated, and she would still be alone.

"I'm fine. I can do this." She missed a step. He caught her before she fell. "Oops."

"That's right. You're just fine." he scolded. "You're going back to bed before you kill yourself. I'll get whatever it is you were after."

She climbed back into her pink paradise a few moments later. He brought the Coke she requested and a beer for himself. He also ditched her silk bathrobe in favor of his own clean clothes. He sat down in the chair across from her bed again.

"So, let's talk about the woman who sent you all the stuff earlier." Emily hoped she sounded chipper.

He groaned. "Let's not."

"It was a pretty nice valentine."

The beer bottle dangled from his fingertips as he leaned forward.

"I can see that you aren't going to let this go until we talk about it, so here are the facts. There is no girlfriend. She and I broke up a couple of weeks ago. It wasn't working. She seems to think that if she follows me around, sends me stuff, and pesters me enough, I'll change my mind. I won't. I've told her this. She's not listening." He blew out a breath, and took a long swig of beer. "Happy now?"

"She must make the big bucks. Just the candy cost a fortune."

"She's a model."

Emily put her empty glass down on the nightstand and chewed her lower lip. She couldn't even look at him.

"Do you ever date anyone, well, *normal?*"

"Please explain."

"Non-models."

"Not recently."

This could not be the same guy that took care of her for the past several hours. Shallow, and well, shallow. Warning alarms went off in her head. Well, in the part of her head that wasn't dazed because of his nearness, and the part that wasn't still feeling woozy.

Emily saw him studying her from the corner of her eye. She revised her earlier impression—Brandon might have been a lot of things, but stupid didn't seem to be one of them. He leaned back in the chair once more, and crossed his arms.

"Let's talk about your love life."

"Oh, let's not." She resisted the impulse to pull the blankets over her head till he was gone.

"Maybe I need to call your Valentine's date, and tell him you're unavoidably detained."

Considering the fact that a boyfriend would have made his appearance long before now, Emily decided to go with the truth.

"No such luck." She tried to make her voice light.

"I'm surprised at that, sugar." Emily shrugged her shoulders, and he continued. "It seems to me there would be a line around the block."

Speaking of lines, she wondered if that one had worked for him lately.

"I'm pretty busy. There isn't a lot of time to date," she pointed out.

He didn't need to know she hadn't had a date in a year, and that before James she had hardly dated at all. She was too busy with her career. There was also the added benefit that by not dating, nobody got close enough to hurt her again.

"I might have to take a page out of your playbook."

The stretch and yawn she gave him was Oscar-worthy.

"Ah. You're tired," he said.

Emily wasn't at the moment, but it would get her out of this conversation. She scooted down in the bed and pulled the blankets up to her nose.

"When you leave, please lock up after yourself." He was watching her again. The look on his face was inscrutable. "Thank you so much for taking care of me. Goodnight."

"I heard that speech a while ago. I'm not going anywhere, sugar."

A FEW HOURS later, Brandon shook Emily's shoulder and spoke into her ear. "Wake up." He sat down next to her on the bed.

"Absolutely not." She sounded outraged. She tried to pull the blankets over her head again, but he was too fast for her.

"Let's get you some medication. Sit up."

He gave her a dose, and set the glass and bottle of pain reliever on the nightstand. He tugged the blankets up around her shoulders and fluffed the pillows around her head. "Now you can sleep."

"Aren't you going to tell me a story?" He heard the slight note of sarcasm in her tone, but he found himself chuckling again.

"Maybe I should." He took one of her hands in both of his. "Once upon a time, there was a diva who knew nothing about football."

"That's not true. I know what a runback is."

"Yes, you do." His voice was quiet in the dimness of her room. "You're practically an expert. Back to the story." He thought for a moment. "The diva had a bad experience with a huge bunch of Mylar balloons, and she needed the handsome prince's help."

Emily let out a snort. He ignored it.

"Of course, the handsome prince was exhausted after a brutal workout with his teammates, but a few balloons didn't scare him. Oh, no. He managed to save the diva from herself, even though she fought him all the way. She argued, and was generally disagreeable about the whole thing. He, of course, overlooked this."

"I was not."

"You just proved my point."

"That's not true."

"Shh. You'll make your headache worse," he soothed.

"Like I can sleep now," Emily muttered darkly.

"Of course you can. Close your eyes."

She was falling asleep, but she had a few more things to say to him.

"You should go home and get some sleep. I'll be fine. Thank you again."

"Don't you worry about me. You get better," he said.

"Happy Valentine's Day," she said.

"You, too, sugar."

He walked to the other side of her room, settled into the chair, and threw the pink cashmere blanket from the foot of her bed over himself. She snuggled further into her blankets. Tomorrow morning, he'd be gone.

EMILY AWOKE WITH a gasp. She wasn't alone.

It took a few seconds, but her eyes adjusted enough to the pearly light of dawn peeking through the blinds to spot Brandon, asleep in her bedroom chair. The cashmere blanket he'd thrown over himself didn't come close to covering him. He'd curled himself into the chair, resting his head at a weird angle against the upholstery. His neck would be sore when he woke up. His feet hung over the edge of the ottoman. He didn't look especially comfortable. She'd spent the night in her warm, soft, cozy bed, and he'd slept sitting up. For her.

To say it was a surprise that he was still there was an understatement. Even more, she was touched. Anyone else on the planet would have decided she was going to live and gone home to a much more comfortable bed, but he'd stayed.

She couldn't figure it out. He didn't know her. He owed her nothing. Actually, she owed *him*. He shifted a little in his sleep and pulled the blanket higher around himself. He was probably cold. She could at least do something about that.

She shoved herself out of bed, pulling the blankets off

as she went. She extracted a sand-colored woven-cotton blanket from the pile. It was still warm from her body heat. She tiptoed across the room.

She draped the blanket over him as carefully as she could. He stirred a little, but he didn't open his eyes. She watched him sleep for a few moments. Maybe she should wake him up and tell him to go back to sleep in the bed for a while.

Maybe she needed to go downstairs, make some coffee, and get a grip on herself.

A short time later Emily was nibbling on a bagel and cream cheese she had found in the refrigerator when heavy footfalls sounded on the staircase.

"Good morning."

"Morning," he mumbled. He looked a bit dazed. "Coffee."

"It'll be done in just a few minutes," she reassured him. "How's your neck?"

He rubbed it a little. "Don't worry about it. I'm fine."

He invaded the kitchen, found a mug in the cupboard over the sink, pulled the carafe out of the coffee maker, and stuck his mug under the stream. He replaced the carafe without spilling a drop. He sauntered to the other side of the kitchen. He wore a pair of navy-blue shorts, which matched his navy blue boxer briefs. She looked anywhere but at his bare chest, the vertical line of hair on his abdomen that vanished under the waistband of the shorts, and a six pack she wanted to lick.

"Navy blue?" she asked.

"I like blue." He rubbed his eyes.

"Oh."

"Billowing white cotton." He indicated her nightgown. "I like it."

"It's kind of . . . virginal." He glanced at the kitchen floor, and a faint flush spread over his cheekbones. "And much hotter than most of the lingerie I've seen," he said.

He avoided Emily's eyes. She walked away from him.

"Want to sit down?" She tossed the words over her shoulder.

"Hey, let's get the news," he said, and flipped to ESPN.

"Excuse me," she said. "*SportsCenter* is not news." Despite his commandeering the remote again, she had to smile.

"It's the most important news." He laughed, and turned up the volume on the television. There was a photo of Brandon on the screen, and one of her.

"It's the end of an era this morning," the announcer said. "Our sources tell us that Brandon McKenna, the Seattle Sharks' All-Planet defensive end and ladies' man, is off the market. McKenna's engaged to opera diva Emily Hamilton. Wedding plans are pending. Our congratulations go out to the happy couple."

Emily turned to Brandon in shock. He grinned in response. Her home phone and cell phone both started ringing.

Chapter Four

EMILY'S MOUTH OPENED and shut, and opened again.

Brandon just sipped his coffee. The phones were still ringing. They stopped, and then started again. Emily's voicemail was going to be full if she didn't pick one of them up. Right now, though, it was the last thing she intended to do.

She took the deepest breath she could. "This is an *accident*. They think we're engaged?" She gasped. "We—we're not engaged. We're not even dating. I met you *yesterday*. Why are they— Oooh!" Emily pointed at the television screen. "We have to *do* something about this."

Brandon didn't seem upset by this development. His body shook with laughter, and he put his cup down on the table in front of them. "Not dating? We could change that." Emily's glare was lethal. He ignored it, and stretched his arm out across the back of the couch, his fingers brushing her shoulders. "According to ESPN, you're my betrothed. I'm thinking this could work out well for me." His smile was confident. "How about making me some breakfast, sugar?"

Emily's mouth dropped open. In the meantime the bare skin he was touching was starting to tingle just a bit. She was spellbound by her head shot on the television screen and she didn't answer.

His voice dropped to a murmur. "Of course you want to do this for me." Emily swallowed hard. She could feel the hot flush spreading over her cheeks. Even more, things were—liquefying. Yeah. She knew she owed him something for making sure she was still amongst the living, but cooking wasn't one of her talents.

She shouldn't be reacting to him this way. She knew better than that. "Player, player, player," she mentally chanted. He could charm a rock, though.

He abruptly shoved himself off the couch. "I need to use your phone." He grabbed the cordless as he strolled away from her. It rang again before he could hit "talk." Brandon answered it.

"McKenna." He turned back to Emily. "Just one moment." She took the receiver from him. "It's your manager," he said.

"Hi, David." She got up from the couch, walked to the kitchen table, and dropped into a chair.

"That must be your fiancé."

"David, there's been a—"

"Congratulations, Emily," he interrupted. "The phone's been ringing like mad. I've had five booking requests this morning already. *Five*. What are you, Renée Fleming?" he teased. "Reporters are calling me as well. When did you start seeing this guy?"

"Well, uh—It's pretty recent. It took me by surprise, too," Emily stammered.

"Must be. What would you like me to tell the press?"

"I'm not sure what we should tell them yet."

"That's not going to work."

She closed her eyes. She was developing a throbbing headache. She wondered if it was possible to have two headaches at once. "David, let's discuss something else right now."

"Sure, Em. I'll make a statement to the effect that you're very happy, the wedding date is forthcoming, et cetera. The publicity's already helping your career." David sounded positively orgasmic about it all.

"Not yet. Let's hold off on that statement."

David let out a laugh. "Oh. I see—playing hard to get. How about 'They're just friends'? While you're thinking, Emily, Santa Fe Opera called. They're doing *The Magic Flute*. They're offering Pamina. I think you'll be happy with the compensation. Their lead soprano's evidently got a scheduling conflict."

Brandon emerged from the kitchen with the coffeepot and an evil-looking gleam in his eye.

Unbelievable. *The Magic Flute*, one of the most challenging pieces for sopranos ever, and in Santa Fe, an opera company famed for the quality of their productions. She felt like she was dreaming.

"Oh . . . of course. Yes, yes, I'll go. Thank you, David."

Emily said goodbye to David and hung up, dumbfounded.

Brandon poured them both another cup of coffee, and picked up the cordless again. He dialed a number, listened to it ring a few times, and said, "Hey, dawg." Whoever was at the other end sounded agitated. "I forgot my phone in my locker. Everything's fine, but I won't be in the weight room today or tomorrow." He listened for a few moments more and said, "No. I'm taking care of a very argumentative woman for a couple of days." Emily let out an exasperated sigh. "They what? Is that so? I'll give him a call." She saw his lips twitch into a smile. "Coach is happy about this? Thanks. I'll send you an invitation."

"What?" she prompted.

He shot her a playful grin. "Okay. I gotta go. I'll call y'all later. Bye." He hung up, still chuckling to himself over something.

"'A very argumentative woman.'" Emily said. "Oh, that's rich. I can't believe you would think—"

"Sugar, darlin', there's something we need to talk about. Right now."

"I don't think we're talking about anything right now. I think—"

He interrupted her again. "Listen. We're going to have to deal with this." He leaned over the table and grasped her hand. "I know what happened." He leaned even closer. Emily shifted away from him, but he didn't let go of her hand. "There was a whole crowd of people standing around that nurse's station when I was signing autographs yesterday. Evidently, they couldn't tell she was kidding about the whole 'your fiancée is looking for you' thing."

She shook her head. "It was a joke."

"You don't understand," he said patiently. "I'm—well, when stuff happens, it makes the papers, it makes the national media, and then I have to deal with it. My roommate Greg says it's hit the national wires. My agent has been trying to call me, and the press has been calling my house trying to confirm the story since last night. What did your manager say to you?"

"He said he wants to make a statement. He said people are calling that want to book me as a result."

Another broad smile spread over Brandon's lips. He picked up his coffee cup, and took a swallow. In the meantime, an idea was beginning to dawn on her. He'd never go for it. She should just forget it—

The phone rang again, and Emily snatched it up.

"Hello?"

"Emily."

She couldn't believe she didn't check the caller ID before she picked up. It was James, and she wasn't in the mood. She was sure she wouldn't be in the mood for the rest of her life.

"Long time no talk. How are you doing?"

"Fine," Emily said.

"I had to call and congratulate you on your engagement. This is wonderful news." The coffee instantly turned into burning acid in her stomach. She was trembling. "I hope you and your fiancé will be very happy."

Brandon's brows knit together as Emily rubbed her face with a shaking hand.

"Thank you," she managed to get out. "How is Heather?"

"She's great. We're both very happy for you. We look forward to meeting—Brandon, isn't it? A pro football player. That's interesting." His voice was mild, but she felt the chill beneath it. Of course, he found it amazing that anyone would want Emily. He'd made that clear before.

"Yes. Yes, it is. James, I have to go—"

"I hope you'll be able to let go of the bitterness and we can finally become friends, Emily. After all, it's the adult thing to do. This was one of those things. Are you going to continue punishing both of us for it?"

Emily gripped the coffee mug so hard it should have shattered. Sure. She couldn't wait to be friends with a guy who slept with her former best friend and voice teacher. When he wasn't doing that, he'd spread rumors about Emily's being "difficult" during productions throughout the entire industry. He put a serious dent in her career as a result. *Friends?* If she never saw James again, it would be too soon.

Brandon's face turned into a thundercloud as he watched her shake like a leaf. Her stomach was churning, and she needed to get off the phone before she threw up.

"Let's talk about that later, James. Bye." She hung up, tossed the phone down on the table, and hurried to the staircase leading to her room. She had to get dressed for rehearsals today, but even more, she needed to get somewhere she could be alone.

"What happened, sugar?" Brandon called out to her. "Who was that?"

Emily stopped at the top of the stairs, took a deep breath, and told herself to buck up. James was the only person who could get under her skin like this, and it was time it stopped. She couldn't believe she was still allowing him free rent in her head. She was so vulnerable with him, and it was such a mistake. She couldn't believe she was stupid enough to think he ever loved her at all. She couldn't believe she spent one minute of her life caring what he thought.

She wasted her last tear on him. She bit her lower lip, hard. All she needed was a couple of minutes to compose herself.

Brandon's heavy footsteps moved up the staircase. He waited till she turned to face him and said, "Who was that on the phone?"

"Nobody." The headache was now worse than ever. She needed to take a breath. More than that, she needed to cry, but she wasn't doing that around anyone else.

"Maybe you should tell me the truth."

"I'd prefer not to."

"Let me guess. Your ex-boyfriend." Brandon's eyes bored into hers. "Wanted to chat, huh?" He braced one hand against the wall over Emily's head. "News travels fast."

His lips formed a bloodless line. She remembered a negotiation tactic she had heard many times before: The first to speak, loses. She swallowed hard. She stood up straight, threw her shoulders back, and tilted her chin a bit. He continued to watch her silently. She felt her chin quiver. She blinked rapidly in any attempt to hold back the tears blurring her vision.

"He really did a number on you." Brandon's voice was soft, and he brushed another tear away with his thumb. She closed her eyes for a moment. "He's not worth your tears."

She swallowed hard. "Thank you."

"Well, sugar, I know I'm hungry. Let's get another cup of coffee."

Emily was doing everything in her power to pull herself together. He gave her a nod. He took her arm and led her down the stairs again.

BRANDON COULDN'T FIGURE out what had happened. Her indignation over the news of a nonexistent engagement being announced on national TV was pretty comical. Directly after that, though, the seemingly confident, self-possessed Emily crumpled like a wet paper towel over a five-minute phone call from a guy that had to be one of the more stupid people walking the planet, in his opinion.

She could be a handful. He wasn't used to the women in his life arguing with him about anything. The more time he spent with her, though, the more intrigued he was. Obviously, she was beautiful. She had the kind of understated, bone-deep beauty that guys in his profession were quick to pass over in favor of women who paid good money for perfect faces and bodies. Emily wasn't NFL cheerleader or Playmate of the Month material, but he'd have to be blind *and* dense to not enjoy the view. His mama didn't raise stupid children, either. He'd wanted to meet someone like Emily for a while now. Even suffering the aftereffects of a concussion, she was smart, funny, and interesting. He appreciated the fact she didn't collapse into helplessness and let him take care of everything. Plus, an idea had taken root that would help them both, and it was time to discuss it.

"Let's sit down for a few minutes," he interrupted, and he tugged her over to the living room couch. He instinctively grabbed for the remote, and then dropped it on the couch cushion. "I take it you didn't want to talk to him."

"No. No, I didn't." Emily shook her head, and flinched. Evidently, the headache was still there. "Now I'll have to go back to all these people I work with and tell them I'm not engaged, that it's not true, and I—I—"

She turned her face away, but she wasn't fast enough. He saw more tears splash off the hands she clenched together in her lap. He knew women who manipulated him and everyone else with their tears, but Emily wasn't one of them. She was trying so hard to be brave. All he wanted to do was comfort her, but he knew she wouldn't accept it at that moment.

He took both her shoulders in his hands and gently turned her toward him. "Don't cry. It's all right. We'll think of something."

"I'm not usually such a baby." She started to rise from the couch; he caught her hand and pulled her back down.

"Wait." He studied her for a few moments. It was time to man up, although she was probably going to slap his face off. "I have an idea."

"Okay." Her expression was cautious. Brandon hadn't let go of Emily's hand. He gave it an experimental squeeze.

"Here's the thing. Let's stay engaged for a little while."

"We're not really engaged in the first place." Emily shook her head. "We can't do that, can we?"

"Of course, we can. It's between you and me. This works for both of us. It's positive publicity for everyone. The team's happy with me, my ex-girlfriend will finally get the hint, and your ex-boyfriend will be jealous as hell. There's no downside to this." Okay, so far so good. She looked more shocked than angry. He hadn't gotten away scot-free, though: Emily's eyes were narrowing. Uh-oh.

"The team would be happy about this? Why would they even care?"

This ought to be fun, he told himself. He folded his lips and examined the ceiling for a moment. "It's a public relations thing. I'm a bit of a hell raiser. Well, I *was*." He resisted the impulse to squirm. "There's no downside," he repeated.

"Just tell me the truth. You're quite fond of that, aren't you?" Evidently her mama hadn't raised any stupid children, either. He took a deep breath.

"I'm in the middle of contract negotiations—my agent is—and there was a little problem. This will fix it. Well, it'll take the heat off." He tried to look reassuring. "Again, there's no downside for either of us."

"There is, too." It seemed that Miss Emily had a redhead's temper. "We don't know each other."

"We can pull this off," he insisted. "We'll get to know each other. Let's give it a month."

"What are we going to tell our families?"

He shrugged one magnificent shoulder. "Tell them we're engaged. They'll be fine with it."

"It's not going to work," Emily insisted. "Won't your family flip out? Mine will. They'll never believe this. You think it's okay to lie to everyone in both our lives?"

Brandon pinned her with his eyes. "Maybe you should tell me what else David had to say when he called."

Emily shrugged her shoulders, and rubbed her face a little. "What do you mean? Oh. He said he'd had five booking calls already today, which is amazing, and I'm now singing a lead role at Santa Fe Opera as a result."

"You lied to him," he pointed out. It wasn't gentlemanly, but one had to take the opportunity when it presented itself.

Her mouth dropped open, and her eyes flew wide. "I did not." She was the picture of injured outrage, and it was all he could do not to laugh. At the same time, it was high time he established who was in charge here: *Him*.

Brandon narrowed his eyes in response. "Hey, sugar, I saw your face light up when he called. You didn't exactly set him straight about us."

"I—I—" she sputtered. He leaned toward her.

"This works for both of us. You get what you want, I get what I want. No harm, no foul." He stuck out his hand. "Will you agree to be engaged to me for thirty days?"

He had a point. Emily knew he had a point. At the same time, there was one last little problem.

"What happens if someone finds out this isn't real?"

"Hey. It's not going to happen. Don't be so negative."

She let out a snort, and he continued. "Plus, you get to hang around me for another month. Remember, there are lots of women who'd love to spend more time with me."

"Is your ego always this big, or only on days ending in 'y'?" she teased.

"I know you didn't mean that," he chided. He extended his hand once more. "Are you in?"

All she had to do was pretend to be his fiancée for a month. Piece of cake. She put her hand inside of his.

"Yes."

"Thirty days."

"Yes. Thirty days." She gazed at him for a moment. He could practically see the wheels turning in her head. "What happens when the thirty days are up?"

His smile was positively mischievous, and he still held her hand. "We go our separate ways. Again, no harm, no foul."

"Fine." They shook hands, and he brought the back of Emily's hand to his lips. He barely brushed her skin, and gave her a slow smile.

"Now, go get dressed, because we have things to do today. I'll even take you out to lunch."

He was right. She had to know he was right. It would work for both of them. How bad could it be, anyway?

Chapter Five

"COME ON, SUGAR," Brandon shouted up the staircase. "Time's a-wastin'."

"Chill out," Emily yelled back, and clutched her head. *Ow.* She moved as quickly as she could. Some people had no respect for the recently concussed.

She stepped into a pair of flats. *No high heels today,* she thought mournfully as she surveyed the destroyed Italian leather boots lying on the bedroom floor, a constant reminder of how much those damn things cost.

The ponytail she'd gingerly brushed her hair into might disguise the stitches. She swallowed a couple of pain killers before pulling on a pair of pants, a soft yellow silk and cotton sweater, and a strand of pearls. She spent fifteen minutes searching her bathroom for the silver circlet of hearts ring she wore on her left middle finger. She had misplaced it somewhere.

She was off to rehearsal, whether she felt like it or

not. Of course, this brought another argument with Brandon.

"You are not going," he told her. "You are going right back to bed."

"I have to be there, even if I don't think I can sing." She pulled the car keys out of her purse. He took them out of her hand.

"You are *not* driving. Are you nuts? Did you even listen to the doctor?"

"This is my job. I—"

He cut her off, as usual. "I'll take you. If you insist on going, we'll go, but if you get worse, we're going back to the emergency room." He glanced down at himself. "We'll need to stop at team headquarters so I can change my clothes and pick up my car, too."

"Fine," she said. She shut the door hard, even if it hurt. Door-slamming hadn't been her preferred method of communication since junior high, but right now, it was working for her. She heard the soft sound of his laughter in response.

She knew he was just trying to help, but she hadn't had to answer to anyone but David regarding her life and her schedule for a while. Perhaps she could be a little more gracious right now.

Brandon wore a playful smile as he stood in the entryway of Emily's house. "There she is," he purred as she made her way downstairs. He'd evidently forgotten the argument they just had. "Shall we?"

"Absolutely."

She was still sore from yesterday. The headache was

under control, thanks to her new best friend Mr. Ibuprofen, but nobody could tell her she had wimped out by not showing up at rehearsal this morning. She grabbed her handbag. Brandon pulled the front door open, they walked out onto the porch, and she heard, "Miss Hamilton!" Emily saw flashes and TV cameras—*what the hell was going on?* She reached out for a handful of Brandon's t-shirt.

"Where did all of these people come from?" she asked as his arm slid around her waist.

"Smile," he murmured.

"Brandon, why are they here?"

"I have no idea," he insisted, but he wouldn't look at her. He looked at everything (and everyone) but her. He was lying.

Emily pretended like she was cuddling shyly in his arms. She said into his ear, "Did you call someone?"

His lips grazed her cheek. "My agent may have had something to do with this." She tried to bring her shoe down on his toes. He was too fast for her. "Be nice, sugar." Reporters were approaching them.

"Congratulations, Brandon," one of the reporters called out to him. "Another one bites the dust, huh? How about a smile?"

His arms tightened around her. "Do you know Emily?"

"Hello," she said to the people currently sticking microphones in her face.

"Miss Hamilton, Shelly Case from MSNBC. How long have you and Mr. McKenna been seeing each other?" The look on the woman's face made the hair stand up on the back of Emily's neck. "Unfriendly" was an understatement.

"A little while," Emily spoke over the din.

"How long?" Ms. Case persisted. Maybe it was better not to answer her question.

"Emily. You must be thrilled. When did he propose?" another woman called out.

"A few days ago."

"How did it happen? What did he say to you?"

She felt Brandon stiffen a little against her, but the brilliant smile hadn't left his lips. Those same lips touched her forehead. Emily resisted the impulse to gasp. Pretend or not, she was starting to wonder what it would be like to kiss him.

"We'd rather keep that private," Brandon interrupted.

"Were you surprised?" another female reporter asked Emily.

"Yes, you could say that."

Laughter rippled through the crowd. Brandon murmured, "Good one," into her ear.

"Let's have a look at the ring," someone else called out.

"We're picking it up this morning," Brandon assured the guy. Emily remembered the small silver ring she'd worn for the past couple of years, and resisted the impulse to flinch. Hopefully, it hadn't fallen down the drain in the bathroom sink.

"Anastasia Lee says that you're on the rebound, Brandon. What are your thoughts on that?"

"No comment." His expression didn't change.

"When's the wedding, Emily?"

"We're still discussing it. Maybe you could help us with that."

The reporters laughed again, and Shelly Case spoke up once more.

"What are your thoughts on Brandon's recent off-the-field incident, Emily?"

Emily shook her head. "I don't know what you're talking—"

Luckily, Brandon interrupted her. "Listen, folks, I could stand here for hours and show off my beautiful fiancée, but we have things to take care of. Thanks for coming out," he said, and walked Emily to the passenger side of her Escape. She waved goodbye to the reporters and got in. Brandon was still talking to the group outside the car, but Emily couldn't quite hear what was said. She heard another wave of laughter, though. He jumped into the driver's seat, snapped his seatbelt on, and they drove away.

Emily was stunned into silence at the sheer number of news trucks that lined both sides of the quiet street she lived on. He glanced over at her. "You okay, sugar?"

"I'm fine. Why didn't you tell me?"

"Huh?"

"Don't play dumb." She folded her arms across her chest.

"Okay. You got me." He flashed Emily a naughty-little-boy grin. "I talked to my agent while you were in the shower. He asked if we'd pose for some pictures and maybe a little interview. I thought they'd catch up with us later today, but hopefully, they'll leave us alone now. You're not mad, are you?"

"I wish you would have told me."

"Then it wouldn't be a surprise." She shook her head.

"C'mon. It wasn't too bad," he coaxed. "There'll be a nice picture of you on the news."

"I haven't even told my family."

Speaking of family, it might be nice if she gave them a call, despite their unavailability up to this point. Amy was going to freak out. Her parents were going to lose their grip—especially her dad, which was why she hadn't called him from the hospital yesterday. She loved her dad, but she didn't depend on him for help, and she hadn't for a long time now. What was she thinking? Maybe she could avoid telling them.

"Oh, they're about to find out," he interrupted. Brandon patted her thigh with one big hand. "I have to pick up my stuff, we'll go to your rehearsal, and then we'll have some lunch." His voice dropped a bit. "Are you up for this?"

"Sure." This must have been one of those "Be careful what you wish for, you might get it" moments.

Brandon pulled up in front of the team headquarters a short time later. The debris from yesterday's parking lot misadventure had been cleared away. Someone had even shoveled the lot. Maybe Emily should have waited a day.

"Listen. I don't think you want to spend time in the locker room while I'm getting dressed. I'll take you to the lobby, where you can have a seat."

"No. I'll wait out here."

"I'll be back."

He sprinted through the front doors of the facility,

and Emily pulled her phone out of her purse. She left more messages. Her mom still wasn't home, and Amy must have been sleeping in after yesterday. Even if it was cold outside the car's interior was toasty warm, and she drifted off for a few minutes.

Emily awoke to a blast of freezing cold air and Brandon's voice. "Hey. Let's get in my rig, and we'll pick yours up later." A black, late-model Land Rover was idling in the parking spot next to her. "We gotta go, or you'll be late. Come on."

They arrived at McCaw Hall after the fastest trip across the bridge to Seattle she'd ever experienced. He wasn't reckless, but he made it clear he was getting to his destination as quickly as humanly possible. He also insisted on walking her inside.

"Brandon, I am fine. I can do this myself. I've been doing it for a long time. Really."

"Let me make sure that you're going to be okay." He pulled the auditorium door open for her, and she made her way to the backstage area. Their footsteps echoed down a long parquet hallway.

Tristan, the production's lead costumer, emerged from one of the dressing rooms with an armload of costumes. He still managed to grasp both of Emily's hands.

"Ah, my diva. How are you feeling today? And who's this?" He looked Brandon up and down, lingeringly. One of Brandon's brows arched a bit.

Brandon stuck out a hand. "I'm Brandon McKenna. Nice to meet you."

If Brandon was going to flip out over this whole arrangement, he'd just been presented the best opportunity possible. Tristan enjoyed fashion, and every day was a new opportunity to give his closet a workout. Today he wore skin-tight red wet-look leather pants that laced on the outside seam from toes to hips, black leather pointy-toed high heeled boots, and a black silk t-shirt topped with a black silk jacket. His ornate silver belt buckle read "boy toy."

Tristan dropped Emily's hands to shake Brandon's, winking at him. "I'm Tristan, and the pleasure's all mine."

Emily stifled a laugh. Jason *who*? Tristan was flirting outrageously. Of course, Brandon acted like this happened to him every day. Maybe it did.

"So, Tristan, Emily insists on going through with her rehearsal. Can't divas call in sick once in a while?"

Tristan laughed like Brandon had said the wittiest thing he'd ever heard. Emily resisted the impulse to smack both of them, and settled for an eye roll.

"Well, the floor director knows she had an accident. Most of the company knows, too, and this morning, we were so thrilled with your happy news. When's the wedding?"

"I want her to have the wedding of her dreams, so it may be awhile." Brandon leaned closer, and his voice became conspiratorial. "We're planning."

"Certainly. It'll take at least a year. Plus, my diva's not getting married in some off-the-rack *schmatta*. I made some preliminary sketches this morning, and—"

It was time for Emily to break up the love fest. "Guys. I have to sit down. I'll talk to you later. Bye, Brandon."

She headed off toward the dressing room, only to hear two sets of footsteps behind her: The click of Tristan's heels, and the "thump, thump" of Brandon's heavier footsteps.

"Listen, T." Oh, now they were on a nickname basis? Emily wondered if Tristan would start skipping down the hallway. "I have a few errands this morning, but I am worried about leaving Emily. She's still not feeling well. Is there any possible way you could keep an eye on her? I'll be back to pick her up in a couple of hours or so."

She stopped in the doorway of the dressing room and whirled to face them. Suddenly dizzy, she grabbed for the doorjamb, but straightened up to fix them both with what she hoped was an intimidating stare.

"I am not a child," she enunciated. "If I am too ill to continue, I will take a cab home."

It was like she'd never spoken.

"I'll take care of everything, Brandon." The two men shook hands again. Brandon bent to brush his lips across her cheek. She resisted the impulse to turn into his kiss.

"Bye, sugar. I'll be back to pick you up in a little while."

Emily walked into her dressing room, dropped her handbag on the table, and fell onto the couch. "When Jason finds out you were flirting with him, your life won't be worth living. He'll lock you out of the house."

"Do you know who that man *is*, cherie? Jason would be flirting with him, too."

"He's a football player—"

"No. He's an *icon*." Tristan let out a sigh. "Do you know how many websites are dedicated to him? You should see his practice photos. He's beautiful. Imagine how many men would like to lick him dry."

"And you're one of them," she teased.

"Absolutely."

"Well, then, it's your lucky day. Have at it." Emily rummaged through her purse for another ibuprofen. She'd left them at home. Damn.

"What do you mean?"

Emily had known Tristan since she walked out onto a stage and auditioned to get into the conservatory. They'd been friends for almost twenty years now, and she hoped they'd be friends for the rest of their lives. Tristan never wanted to sing. He dressed those who did, and his star continued to rise. She knew he should have been dressing opera companies in New York or Europe. She also knew that she could never, ever lie to him.

"We're not dating. We're not engaged."

Tristan's mouth dropped open. "So, what was today's big announcement?"

"A mistake. We'll correct it in a month."

"I don't understand."

"It works for both of us." She studied her manicure, or what was left of it. She had to get her nails done. Maybe later.

"You're sure about this? After all, he may fall madly in love with me, cherie."

"That's a risk I'll have to take." She stood up from the couch. "I need to get out there and see if I can sing right now. God, my head hurts."

Tristan laid another armload of costumes over a table.

"I want to see how the scene three costume fits one more time before you go." He pulled it off a rolling rack and advanced on Emily. "Are you sure you're up to this?"

"Yeah. Maybe. I have no idea." It wasn't just the singing she wasn't sure of, either.

"Well, let's try this on first."

EMILY WALKED ONSTAGE a short time later to a smattering of applause. The practice pianist launched into Lohengrin's Bridal Chorus.

"That's enough," Emily joked.

"When's the wedding?" a heavily accented voice called out from the audience. That would be Johann, the baritone playing Count Almaviva. Johann had asked Emily out. Even if she were interested, she would never agree to date anyone she worked with again.

"We're still working on that."

"Miss Hamilton," the floor director called out. "How are you feeling?"

"Not great," Emily said.

He approached the lip of the stage. "Let's try Cinque, dieci, venti, trenta from The Marriage of Figaro." Johann rose from his seat and joined Emily.

"A marriage, is it? That was fast," Johann muttered to her. "Simply because you didn't want to date me?" She ignored him. The pianist began playing, and Emily tried to sing. What was typically so effortless for her now brought waves of pain. This wasn't going to work. She stopped, and everyone on stage was silent.

"I—I don't think I can do this today. I am so sorry." She closed her eyes, took a deep breath, and laid a hand on Johann's arm to brace herself. She wasn't as dizzy as she'd been yesterday, but she knew she couldn't practice until the headache subsided.

The floor director was running down the aisle from the seats. "Do you need a doctor?"

"No. I need to sit down. And some water might be nice. Again, I'm sorry." Emily was helped offstage to a front-row seat. Tristan arrived with a cold bottle of water and a couple of pain relievers. Once she was settled, the group onstage assembled once more. Anna, Emily's cover, soared into the aria Emily could not finish, and the rehearsal continued.

Other than the typical colds and flu over the past twenty years, this was the first time Emily had been unable to practice. Watching Anna was a special kind of torture. She leaned back in the seat and closed her eyes. If she wasn't well by next week she would not be singing in the performances, which would be disastrous. She wasn't sure how quickly anyone recovered from something like this, but it had to happen now. Applause—the love of an audience—was the drug she needed to survive. There was nothing else in her life but music and her career. She had worked for so long to get to where she was now.

A large, clean-smelling body sat down in the seat next to her. "Hey, sugar. Taking a little break?"

She opened her eyes. "You're here?"

"Where did you think I'd be?" Brandon wrapped one

arm around the back of her seat. "Had to come back here and pick you up."

"Thanks." She folded her hands in her lap.

"So," he continued in a stage whisper, "let me guess. You tried to sing, and it didn't work."

"No, it didn't." She stared at the floor in front of them. "What if I don't get better?" The words flew out of her mouth before she could stop them.

He leaned closer. "Now you're being silly. You bumped your head. It's going to hurt for a couple of days. The doctor didn't see anything that indicated permanent damage, or he never would have let you out of the hospital."

Emily's stomach was a cold knot of fear, but as Brandon talked the knot loosened a bit. "I've worked so hard. I really need to sing this role. I can't take a week off to recover."

He caught her chin in his fingertips. "You will be fine. I promise."

BRANDON INSTALLED EMILY in his Land Rover a few minutes later, swung himself into the driver's seat, and pulled out into traffic. "We'll get you some lunch, and then it's back home. You need some rest."

Emily was about to respond, but her phone was ringing again. At least she'd be able to find out where her parents had been last night.

"Hi, Mom."

"Emily Anne Hamilton, what have you done?" her mother cried.

"Mom?"

"You're *engaged?* My phone's ringing off the wall. Reporters are calling. They want to know when the wedding is. When did you meet this Brandon? Your father says that he's . . . What have you done!?"

She saw Brandon glance over out of the corner of her eye, grin a little, and focus on the road again.

"Mom, it's fine. Really." Emily swallowed hard. "He's a nice guy, and I—"

"This is not Las Vegas, young lady." She heard the catch of tears in her mother's voice. "I can't believe that you would take marriage so lightly. Didn't I teach you better than this? You're going to marry a man Daddy and I had no idea you were even dating. When did this *happen?*"

"Mom. Please don't cry. We'll have dinner together and you can meet him. Everything is fine. We just sped things up a little, that's all." Emily was surely going to Hell for lying to her mother, but just thinking how she was going to explain this one away made her wonder if her head would explode.

Brandon glanced over at Emily. "Sugar. What's happening?" She held up one hand to signal she'd talk with him in a moment. He reached out for the phone. "Let me talk to your mama." She turned slightly so he couldn't grab it out of her hand.

"Sweetheart," her mom finally choked out, "Are you pregnant? If you're pregnant, you know your dad and I will stand by you. You don't have to marry him. Of course, he'll want to see the baby, but we can get a custody agreement."

Emily's mother had never missed an opportunity to panic since Emily was very young. She was in rare form today. Emily closed her eyes, and took the deepest breath she could in order to calm herself. Her parents were total opposites. Her excitable, passionate, affectionate mother and her calm, controlled, stoic father complemented each other, unless they locked horns. Emily's mother took any argument as an excuse to increase the volume and dramatics. Emily's father responded with silence, which made things worse.

She'd lived away from home for the most part since she was fourteen and started her training. She'd had to grow up fast as a result. She loved her parents, but she wished at times they understood each other a little better.

"Mom. Mama. I'm not pregnant."

Brandon let out a low chuckle. Of course he'd find this hilarious.

"I could help you with that. Just let me know." His voice was so soft that Emily's mother couldn't hear him, but Emily could. She turned in the seat, giving him a look she was sure would melt flesh. His response was to raise one eyebrow.

"This is going to kill your father." Her mother heaved a huge sigh. "Will we see you before the performances start? How are you feeling today? Amy said you got hurt on that delivery."

"I have a headache, but I'll be fine," Emily said. "The opera company wants me to get a doctor's release. If I'm feeling any better, I'll be over on Sunday for dinner."

Emily could still hear her mother sniffling on the other end of the phone.

"Okay. Hopefully, we'll see you then. If we can't, we'll see you when you're back from Chicago." Mrs. Hamilton blew her nose. "Promise me you won't sneak off and get married."

Chapter Six

BRANDON STROLLED INTO Daniel's Broiler like he owned
the place. Daniel's was an institution on Seattle's Eastside,
located on the twenty-first floor of the Bank of America
Tower in Bellevue. The restaurant featured dark wood,
plush chairs, soft music, floor-to-ceiling windows that
looked out on a dazzling view of Lake Washington, and
amazing food. The service was even better than the food,
if that was possible. It wasn't cheap, but a meal at Daniel's
was something to be savored and remembered.

"We'd like to sit in a booth," he said to the hostess,
who'd just called him "Mr. McKenna" and asked if he'd
like "the usual."

"No, thank you," he said to the hostess.

"What's 'the usual'?" Emily asked him as they followed the hostess.

"A big steak and an ice-cold vodka martini with
olives. Please don't tell me you're a vegetarian," he said.

"No. I eat meat. I just don't eat that much of it." She passed a glass case with steaks the size of someone's head.

They were seated, and Brandon opened the menu. "We have to drink a little champagne to celebrate."

"I'm concussed, and you want to celebrate."

"Maybe I should rephrase that. We'll drink a little champagne. Other than that, you should order whatever you'd like." He lowered his voice. "Are you feeling better?"

"It comes and goes. What's good here, besides meat?" Emily laid her menu on the table and glanced around. Brandon had slid into the booth next to her, so they could (hopefully) talk without being overheard. It was a cold but gorgeous day, and the view of Lake Washington was breathtaking. The water looked like blue glass.

"I'm going for the penne with lemon-thyme chicken."

"I'll have some, too."

Brandon leaned against the padded back of the booth. "The server will be along any minute now. I know *I'm* hungry." Oddly enough, he appeared somewhat nervous. They'd spent the last twenty-four hours together, they'd slept in the same room, but she still knew almost nothing about him. Speaking of "knowing nothing," she dug through her purse, extracted a folded piece of paper, and handed it to him.

"This is for you."

He shook his head. "A list?"

"I wrote this while you were in the shower earlier. It's biographical information about me. Maybe you could write up a few things before we see each other again,"

Emily suggested. He unfolded the piece of paper, glanced at it a moment, and dropped it next to his silverware.

"What are you talking about?" He was obviously unconvinced.

"If we're going to pull this off, we have to know things about each other."

It seemed perfectly logical to her. Memorizing a list was easy, and it left no room for error. Obviously, he had other plans. His eyebrows smacked together, and he folded his arms across his chest.

"Isn't this a bit impersonal? Can't we get to know each other without a written checklist?"

"We have to have a plan," Emily insisted, and the server approached.

Brandon seemed to shake himself a bit and said, "Hello."

"Hi. I'm Jordan. I'm your server today. Would you like a drink to get your lunch order started?"

"Well, Jordan. Nice to meet you." Brandon flipped to the menu's wine list. "We'd like to order a good bottle of champagne. I'll leave that up to you and the sommelier, other than to say I'm not a big Dom Perignon fan, and maybe more dry than sweet. We'd both like the penne pasta with chicken for lunch, but I'd like a double order for myself. We'd like the house salad with vinaigrette dressing, and we'd like some bread and butter for the table, please."

"May I have some water with no ice?" Emily asked.

"Of course you may," Jordan said. "I'll bring the champagne, the water, the salad, and the bread right away."

"No ice?" Brandon looked quizzical.

"Bad for the vocal cords," she explained. "They need to stay nice and warm."

"Ahh. I see. So, Emily Anne Hamilton, maybe I'll burn this little piece of paper and ask you questions instead." He made a grab for the small glass oil candle at one end of the table. Emily pushed it out of his reach.

"You won't remember everything—"

"You worry too much," he assured her. He patted her hand. "Maybe we should start with something easy. What year did you graduate from high school?"

"Excuse me? You're trying to find out how old I am." Brandon didn't seem to notice, but Emily saw a few of the other diners, primarily men, gesturing toward their table and commenting. He must be used to it.

"Of course I am," he assured her with exaggerated patience.

"It's on the piece of paper." To Emily's horror, he tore her painstakingly composed list into four even squares, crumpling them in his hand. She let out a gasp of distress.

"What are you doing?" She tried to keep her voice down. More people turned around.

"There." He grinned like he'd really accomplished something. "Now we'll have to do this the old-fashioned way."

"Why can't you—" Emily felt best when there was a list, an action plan, written directions of any kind. She could follow directions. They kept her on track. She could measure her progress. Even more, being in control of herself and her surroundings was comforting, even if she was fairly positive there were many people who thought she needed to take it down several notches.

He stroked Emily's cheek with one hand. "Relax, sugar. This isn't brain surgery. We'll have lunch; we'll get to know each other. It'll be fine." If she could tell him how scary it was for her to feel like things were out of control, it might help, but she'd just met him. Maybe it should wait a little while.

He leaned a little closer "Take a breath," he prompted. He squeezed her hand. The sommelier arrived at the table. "Mr. McKenna, I thought you might like to try a bottle of Krug." The bottle was opened. Two glasses were poured, and they were alone again. Well, other than the fact that most of the restaurant seemed to be staring at them by now.

Brandon turned to her. "Let's have a toast." He handed a glass to Emily, picked up his own and said, "Toast." She may have rolled her eyes, but she couldn't help but smile at the mischievous expression in his eyes. "Seriously," he said, looking thoughtful, "Here's to a successful engagement."

"To the engagement." She took a sip. The champagne was wonderful. Brandon dug into his jacket pocket for something.

"I have a confession to make. I borrowed that ring you couldn't find this morning." He gave her what she was sure he thought was an apologetic grin. "I—you needed another ring. I stopped at Tiffany's after I dropped you off. This is for you."

He put a ring box, wrapped in robin's egg-blue paper

and tied with a white, double-faced satin bow, into her hand. She stared at it in shock for a moment. Obviously if they were supposedly engaged she'd need a ring. But she didn't realize he was serious about buying one.

"You 'borrowed' my ring? Is that what they're calling it now?" she teased.

Even though she hadn't spent that much time with him, she could see that he was nervous. She saw a faint flush on his cheekbones. His normally graceful movements were a bit jerky. He swallowed hard, and he didn't seem to know what to do with his hands. Suddenly she was nervous, too. This was pretend. It meant nothing. At the same time, how many times in any woman's life did she hold a ring box?

"I can wear the ring I already have," she said. He looked bewildered. After all, most women probably didn't argue with the giver when they saw a box from Tiffany's. "Are you sure about this?"

"Of course, I'm sure. Go ahead. Open it."

Emily pulled at one end of the bow, and the ribbon fell away. The paper the box was wrapped in spread out like a star in her hand to reveal another smaller, robin's egg-blue suede box inside the cardboard one.

"Even the box is beautiful," she sighed.

He pulled the box open, took the ring out, and slid it onto the third finger of her left hand.

"What do you think?"

He licked his lips. His hand trembled a little. The diamond was very, very large. A round center stone was flanked with pear-shaped diamonds set in platinum. The weight on her finger was unfamiliar, but not unpleasant. The diamonds sparkled like they were alive. Even more, the ring looked like it was made especially for her. It was perfect.

She'd be wearing this ring for a month. He'd lost his mind.

"Did you tell them you wanted the biggest one?" she managed to rasp out.

"A diva would *need* the biggest one."

Their eyes locked. He brought her hand to his lips and kissed it. Emily didn't know what to say. She finally repeated, "Are you sure?"

There wouldn't be any romantic words, and he didn't get down on one knee, but the look in his eyes as he lingered over the back of her hand made Emily's heart skip a beat. He brushed her knuckles with his lips again. She stifled a gasp.

"It's beautiful. Thank you, Brandon."

"Soft hands, sugar." He laid her hand back in her lap. She still clutched the little ring box. "So, where were we? You were telling me about your sister."

"I was not."

"Well, speak up. Isn't she single?" Emily's mouth dropped open. His grin was shameless.

"You're kidding me. You just gave me a ring, and now you're picking up on my sister." He put his fingertips over her mouth.

"Shh," he soothed. "All this stress and upset isn't good for your headache. You need to take it easy." She knew he was right, but she resisted the impulse to drive her fork into the back of his hand. "Relax." She took a deep breath and closed her eyes for a few seconds. "There you go. That's much better." He patted her knee. "You were telling me all about—Amy, isn't it?"

"Actually, you'd probably really like my sister. She loves football."

"I'm sure she's nice. You're more interesting, though." Emily just stared at him. "You seem surprised."

"I—"

"So, what was on your piece of paper? Why don't you tell me all about it?"

"It would have been so much easier if you would have read it before you tore it up."

"Let's try this one more time." He probably seemed mild-mannered and reasonable to the other people sitting in the restaurant. The teasing in his voice made Emily want to commit bodily harm. If he'd let her speak . . . "You have a sister named Amy. Do you have any other brothers or sisters?" She shook her head no. "Do your parents still live in the area?" She nodded. He took a deep breath, and his fingers slid away from her face. "Now, that was easy. Where do they live, sugar?"

"My mom lives in West Seattle, and my dad lives in Issaquah."

"They're no longer married." She wondered if she heard regret in his voice.

"No. They're not." She put the little suede ring box back into the bigger one, and crammed it all into her handbag. "Are your parents still married?"

"Yeah" was all he said. The teasing was gone. A gentle smile touched his mouth.

"They still love each other?"

Brandon studied her face for a few moments. Emily had the oddest feeling he had decided she could be confided in, and he didn't do this often. "They do," he said, finally. "I see what they have, and I want the same thing."

"What's that?"

"I thought we were supposed to be talking about you."

"Well, I'm curious," she insisted.

Brandon's lips twitched in amusement. "My dad was so crazy about my mama that he wouldn't take no for an answer. She was engaged to someone else when he met her. He kept pursuing her. He told me that if he hadn't married her, he would have never gotten married. She's the other half of him." He thought for a moment. "My dad's a bit rough. His daddy worked in the oil fields; they didn't have the social graces. My mama was Miss Louisiana and a Miss America runner-up, so I don't embarrass myself at a formal dinner party, for instance. She gave him polish, and he gave her the ability to be who she is."

Emily grinned back at him. "That sounds wonderful."

"It is. My dad played in the NFL when I was young. They had a hard time with all the traveling when I was a kid, but when Dad started coaching, it was even worse. They did their best to spend more time with each other and with us."

"Do you have brothers and sisters?"

"I have a younger brother, Dylan. He and Amy must be about the same age." Emily hadn't said a word about how old Amy was. She'd find out later how he knew that fact.

"Does Dylan play football?"

"Sugar, he's a doctor."

"That's interesting."

He stifled laughter. "Interesting, huh? Why don't you tell me some more about your sister?"

The food arrived while they were talking. He unwrapped the breadbasket and offered it to Emily. "Is Amy a redhead as well?"

"No. Amy's hair is blonde, and she's taller than me. When we don't want to kill each other, she's my best friend in the world. She's really outspoken, she's funny, and she's also the bravest person I know."

"What makes you say that?"

"When she wants something, she goes after it. Nothing stops her."

"It would seem to me that the two of you might have more in common than you think. You seem fairly motivated, too."

"Not that kind of motivation." Amy had opened her flower shop with no financial help from their parents or anything else besides a standard small-business loan. She had left a solid, secure career to risk everything following her dream. "I'm so proud of her."

Emily saw the dimple in his cheek deepen. She had spent only twenty-four hours with him, but she knew already that he concealed something he wasn't about to tell her. Then again, maybe he was.

"Oh, no motivation at all," he observed. His voice was as dry as the champagne he'd just taken another sip of. "You got into a highly exclusive training program as a teen. You graduated from a leading conservatory and have a grad degree from Juilliard. You've been working your ass off for the last eighteen years singing all over the world." He put the glass back down on the table. "What happens when you're motivated?"

Emily wondered if she was about to spend the next month with her mouth hanging open. "Maybe I didn't explain that well," she told him. "How do you know all this stuff, anyway?"

"It's surprising what you can find out with a Google search," he said lazily and leaned back against the booth again.

"You borrowed my ring, you searched my closets, and you used my *laptop*. Wait till we get home. I'm searching on you, too. It's on, like Donkey Kong."

"You could ask me questions instead," he observed.

"Well, that's no fun," she said. "Where am I going to get the dirt?"

"I might tell you some of that, too." He drained his glass. "Then again, maybe not. A man needs a few secrets. Speaking of secrets, I understand that Cheryl the nurse thinks I'm a horn dog." He took a large bite of salad, and gave Emily an expectant look.

"Aren't you?" He choked on the salad. She patted him on the back till he stopped coughing. She reached out for the bottle of champagne and poured him another glass. "Sorry," she teased.

"No, you're not," he said.

"How do you know that?"

"I just do."

Emily couldn't stop laughing with him. The longer they talked, the more she felt tension drain out of her. She realized with a shock that she felt safe with him, and it wasn't just because he towered over the other guys in the restaurant.

Their entrees arrived. The penne with chicken smelled heavenly. Brandon took a large bite. "It's good, sugar."

"It is." Emily pointed her fork at him. "Back to the horn dog stuff."

"Listen. I'm human. I'm a normal, healthy guy with a sex drive. Have I done things that, in retrospect, maybe I shouldn't have? Hell, yes. There isn't a man that hasn't. At the same time, you don't have to worry." He patted her kneecap again. "I promise I will not drag you under the table, tear your clothes off, and make love to you in front of Jordan and the sommelier. Then again, it beats the hell out of the dessert menu, doesn't it?" His smile was unrepentant. He took another bite of his lunch and washed it down with champagne. "You're not eating."

Emily was feeling a little warm. Maybe it was the champagne, or maybe she was going to blush herself into a coma. The thought of getting naked with Brandon wasn't exactly repulsive.

"Did you always want to be a football player?"

"Questions, questions. Do you work for ESPN?" he said, but she saw his dimple. "I wanted to be like my dad. He played football, so I played football. It helped that I fell in love with the game, too."

"What would you have done for a living if you didn't do this?"

"Interesting question." He gave her a sly smile. "I might have been a math teacher."

"You're kidding me." He loved math? He wasn't a geek. Then again, he'd thought that all opera singers were fat. Maybe it was time to retire some of these generalizations.

"No. I was a math major. I have a master's in math as well from the UW. I worked on it during the off-season for a couple of years." He chewed for a few moments. "Damn, sugar, this stuff's good." Brandon scooped a bite up on his fork, and held it in front of her mouth. "Come on, I'm going to eat all of this if you don't take a bite."

"Mmhmm," was all she could get out around the mouthful of food he fed her.

He inhaled a huge platter of pasta, all the bread, and scooped a bite off of Emily's plate. "I'm still hungry." He appeared to be eating her lunch, too. She wondered if he was always this hungry.

"What are you doing?" she asked. Then again, it was kind of cute. "Oh, okay." She shoved her plate closer to his.

"You have to eat." He scooped up a forkful of penne and chicken and said, "Open up."

"You don't have to f—" Emily began, before her mouth was full once more.

"C'mon. Finish this," he said. "You'll want dessert."

"You're going to tell me about the starving children in Third World countries next, aren't you?"

"No. I want to make sure you've got food in your stomach. You've swallowed an awful lot of medication in the past twenty-four hours, and you had some champagne on top of it."

She wondered if he was like this all the time, or just with women he had a fake engagement with. Whenever Emily would convince herself again he was probably an egotistical nightmare, he'd do something sweet, and she was totally confused. Wasn't he supposed to act like a jerk? She knew little about football players, but according to their discussions over the past twenty-four hours, he was some kind of big deal.

Emily's cell phone vibrated in her pocket. Brandon's rang as well.

"'She Works Hard for the Money'?" Emily said.

"That assho— That jerk Greg downloaded it onto my phone. It's the team headquarters. I have to take this one. I apologize." He pressed the phone to his ear.

Maybe he wouldn't mind if she checked her messages. Amy had called four times in the past hour. Her dad called. Emily hoped her family wasn't watching the news. Her mom must have put the word out to the family.

"Hey, Coach. I'm having lunch with my fiancée. Yeah, I can be there. What's going on?"

He listened for a moment while Emily listened to Amy's message on her voice mail. Her sister sounded a bit irritated. At that moment, a woman in a business suit approached the table.

"Miss Hamilton, I'm Valerie Walker from the Bellevue Informer. I was wondering if you and Mr. McKenna would answer a few questions about your engagement and how you met." She laid one hand on the edge of the table. Brandon was still listening to his caller. "I couldn't help but notice your little moment with the ring. Very sweet. Would you be willing to pose for some photos as well?"

"Just a second," Brandon told the person he'd been speaking with, and glanced at Ms. Walker. "Please call my publicist." He fumbled in his pocket with his other hand, produced his wallet, and handed her a card.

"Let's do this right here. It won't take long." She perched on the bench facing them.

"While I appreciate your interest, Emily and I would appreciate some privacy. Please call my publicist and make an appointment." He picked up his phone again and ignored her. "Let me take my girl home, and I'll be right over," he said to his caller. "Let's go," he said to Emily.

The reporter leaned over the table. "That's quite a ring, Ms. Hamilton. How about a closer look?"

Emily dutifully held out her hand. The restaurant's indirect lighting made the diamond sparkle like it was alive.

"All that for one woman." Her eyes were hard. This was the second female reporter today that had greeted the news of Brandon's engagement with thinly veiled hostility. Emily wondered what the story was.

Brandon frowned a bit. "She's worth it." He took Emily's hand. "It was nice to meet you, Ms. Walrus."

"Walker," she corrected him.

"Ms. Walker." Brandon tugged Emily out of the booth. She grabbed her purse. He handed a credit card to a passing server and said, "Please bring our bill to the hostess desk, I'll sign the slip there." He seemed to be intent on putting as much space between them and the reporter as quickly as possible.

"Don't you want to talk with her?" Emily asked, as they hurried away.

"Not really." He shook his head. "Who was on your voice mail?"

"My sister is a little upset."

"Sounds like it. Listen, sugar, I'll give you a rain check on that dessert I offered. I have to go to a team meeting this afternoon. Let's see how fast we can get out of here."

FIFTEEN MINUTES LATER, Brandon and Emily were in Brandon's Land Rover and heading toward 520, one of the floating bridges between Seattle and its Eastside. Brandon's phone rang again. "It's my mama," he sighed.

He adored his mother. He loved his dad. At the same time, he'd ducked her calls all day. He needed to figure out how he was going to explain what had happened, but it looked like there was no time like the present.

He clicked the hands free device on his car's dashboard and said, "Hey, Mama. I know I was supposed to call you. I apologize. How's my best girl?"

"Brandon James McKenna, that sweet talking might work on all those girls up there, but it doesn't work on me. You are in big, big trouble, young man. You're engaged, and your daddy and I found this out from a sports reporter. They've been calling here all morning. That woman from *Entertainment Tonight* asked me for an exclusive."

"I know. I apologize. I didn't realize they were going to announce—"

"You're going to have to try this on someone who might believe it. Since when do you get engaged to a woman we didn't know you were dating?" Brandon's mama didn't yell. She used much more lethal tactics, like guilt. It was hard to believe that Mama could still make a grown man want to hide somewhere till she settled down, but this was one of those times. "Emily Hamilton sang here last year, honey. How many times have I invited you when your daddy was out of town, and you told me you'd rather be dragged buck naked over broken glass than go to the opera?" His mother finally took a breath. "Does she know this?"

"Mama. I'm sorry." He didn't dare glance over to see the expression on Emily's face at that moment.

His mother's voice softened. "I know there's another story here, and you *will* tell me what it is." He braced himself for incoming. He spent the last thirty-four years knowing that his mama left the best for last. "You are not having a baby, are you? Please tell me you didn't get that young lady pregnant. What will her parents say?"

Oh, there it was.

"Mama. You taught me better than that," he cajoled. He glanced over at Emily, who was stifling laughter. She'd heard every word. "Where's Dad?"

"He went to hit a bucket of balls with Dylan. He says he can't believe you'd consider getting married without bringing Emily home to meet us. Honey, I'm so disappointed in you. I've waited so long for this, and—"

"Mama. _Mama_. I promise I will not marry anyone you haven't met yet." Emily was now smothering laughter with both hands. If this had been happening to anyone else, it would probably be funny, but right now, he'd appreciate a little support. He could only deal with one woman at a time, though, so that discussion would happen later.

"When are we going to meet her? We want to meet her mama and daddy, too. They'll be our family, honey. It's important." He took the exit to Emily's place and resisted the impulse to floor it.

"I know, Mama. Of course she wants to meet you, too. She has performances in Seattle, and then she's going out of town for several weeks. I'll ask her when it will work to get everyone together, and we'll do it." He pulled into Emily's driveway. "I need to scoot. Let me call you back when I'm in the car again."

"Okay. Do not think I'm going to forget about this, young man."

"I know you won't. Tell Dad and Dylan I said hey."

"I will, honey. I love you."

"Love you too." He hung up his phone. Emily was already climbing the steps to her front door, and he hurried after her.

"So, your mom was on a tear. Welcome to my world," she said.

"Oh, yeah. She's probably taking away my allowance." Emily opened the front door, and they trooped inside.

"I'd love to chat about this, but I'm going to be late. We can talk later if you'd like."

The look on Emily's face was comical. "Our parents think I'm pregnant. This should be interesting."

Suddenly, everything was a little awkward. He wasn't sure what to say, and he certainly wasn't sure what was appropriate. She wore his ring, but she wasn't his. She put her purse down on the hall table and shuffled around a little. She bit her lip and a flush moved over her cheekbones. He watched the previously smiling and relaxed Emily retreat behind a wall of uneasiness. She folded her arms in front of her.

"Thank you for taking me out to lunch, and for the beautiful ring. I could have worn my ring, you know."

No, she couldn't have. Everyone would expect her to have an engagement ring someone pulling down over twenty million dollars a year could afford to buy for her. He pulled the small silver circlet of hearts out of his jeans pocket, and put it back on the middle finger of her left hand. "You'll still wear it." He held her hand in both of his. She didn't pull away.

She took a deep breath, and tipped her face up. Her golden eyes searched his. "Do you really think this is going to work? I—I'm just not sure."

"We'll be fine." He leaned down, planted a kiss on her forehead, and told her, "I'll see you later." He felt her smaller hand gripping his.

"I'm okay. I—I'll understand if you have something else going, if you're meeting up with someone or have an appointment. I know this was sudden. You have a life you might want to get back to."

"We can cross some more stuff off your list. We'll have dinner or something."

He didn't want to leave. He turned, though, and hurried out the front door.

Chapter Seven

Despite a several-pages-long to-do list, it was apparent to Emily the best thing she could do was rest. She made it up the stairs to her room and flopped onto her bed. The unpacking would have to wait. Again. She was running out of clean underwear, but that was the least of her problems right now.

A short time later she heard the scrape of a key inserted into the lock on her front door, and Amy's voice echoed from downstairs.

"Hey, weirdo. Where are you?"

Emily tried to call out, "I'm up here," but anything above a normal tone of voice brought additional waves of pain. She heard Amy's light footsteps on the staircase. Hopefully, she'd figure it out for herself.

"There you are," Amy said. She flipped on the overhead light, which could be seen from space. Emily threw her left forearm over her eyes. She was a few seconds too late. She let out a groan.

"Don't. I have a splitting headache."

Her sister rushed across the room. "What in the hell is on your hand? Oh, my *God*," she cried out.

"Please be quiet," Emily pleaded. "My head . . ."

Amy grabbed Emily's left hand and bent over it.

"Have you been watching the shopping channels again? That is the biggest ring I've ever seen in my life. It *can't* be real. Let me see it." It occurred to Emily to make the point that her sister was already looking at it, but she couldn't muster the strength for snark right now.

"Go ahead." Emily pulled the ring off and held it out to her sister.

"Don't you have something you might want to tell me?"

"What?" Emily stalled. She watched her sister examine the inside of the band through half-opened eyes. She wondered if she should offer Amy twenty bucks to shut off that damn overhead light.

"This is from Tiffany's. Did you find it on the street?"

"Brandon gave it to me."

Amy's sharp intake of breath drained half the oxygen in the room. "Get out," she sputtered. "Why would he give you a ring the size of—of—it's *huge*. Mom said she saw something about your being engaged on the news this morning. How did this happen?"

"Amy, my head's going to explode. Please shut off that light, too."

Amy was never, ever going to buy this. Emily had no other option than to tell her the truth.

"How can you marry someone you don't know?" Amy said.

"Take it easy," Emily said. "If you'll sit down for a minute, I'll tell you what happened."

"Mom and Dad are going to flip out."

"Mom already has. Didn't you say you liked him?"

"I said he was cute. I didn't tell you to marry him," Amy said. She paced from the bedside to the window in the now-dimly lit room. "You can't marry someone you've known for twenty-four hours. How did this happen?"

"Try the ring on," Emily said.

Amy jammed the ring onto her finger. "This is the biggest freaking ring I have ever seen." She moved her hand around in the light from the small lamp at Emily's bedside. The diamonds shot prisms of blue fire onto the walls of the room. "He must have told them he wanted the biggest one they had."

Maybe it was better Amy didn't know that was exactly what Brandon did. Emily pushed herself up on the pillows.

"Did you know that Tiffany's wraps the little box up in wrapping paper, but they don't use tape? When you take the bow off, the paper springs open, and there's a little blue suede ring box," she said dreamily.

Amy gave her a disbelieving look as if she couldn't believe her sister had turned into such a sap. She handed the ring back to Emily, and sat down next to her on the bed. "So, are you going to tell me how this happened?"

"Here's the short version. When I had to go to the hospital yesterday, the nurse was joking around, and called me his fiancée in front of a large group of sports fans."

"And they believed it."

"He thought it was funny. I don't know if he said anything at the time, but then he started getting calls about it early this morning."

Emily crossed her ankles and stuffed another pillow behind her back.

"Why didn't you tell them it wasn't true?" Amy asked.

She fidgeted a little. "I had five booking requests this morning."

A speculative light came into her sister's eyes. "Really? That's great, Em."

"There's one more thing. James called."

Amy reached out for Emily's hand. "That bastard. What did he want?"

Emily felt a lump form in her throat.

"He wanted to congratulate me. He said that he and Heather are happy for me. He wants to let go of the bitterness. After all, we can be friends."

A flush climbed up Amy's neck and spread over her face. Her eyes glittered with anger. "What an asshole." She shook her head.

"I hung up on him. I can't believe he had the gall to call me, Amy. 'Friends'? Not in this lifetime."

"What did Brandon do?"

"He has his own set of reasons why it's good for us to be engaged right now."

A smirk curved her sister's lips. "Let me guess. His ex-girlfriend won't get off his back."

"He also said something about his contract negotiations, and the coach being happy about this." Amy
squeezed Emily's hand as she let go. "So, we agreed that
we'd stay engaged for a month. It tells the ex-girlfriend to
get lost, the team's happy, and James will get the hint that
someone else actually wants me."

Amy squirmed a bit on the bed. "So, Em, I realize
you're not going to know this because you're not here a
lot and you don't watch football, but I guess I'd better tell
you. Brandon's a bit of a handful."

"That's the truth. I can't figure him out. One minute,
he's sweet and funny, the next minute, I'd like to throw
something at him." Emily thought for a moment. "He did
say something about a public relations issue."

"You might say that."

"What happened?"

"You're not going to be happy." Amy studied the ceiling for a moment. "Brandon and a bunch of other players
were at a party last month at a teammate's house and the
cops came."

"Was it drugs? Drinking? *What?*"

"A sixteen-year-old girl who looks twenty-five."

"Oh, God. Oh, no." *His* career. What about *her* career?
She was an idiot.

Amy continued. "There were underage girls at
the party getting body parts signed, and therefore,
Brandon got dragged into it as well. The team has
already traded two guys as a result. The only things
that saved him were his signing closer to her collarbone than her breast, his apology in person to the girl's

father, and his significant donation to the Boys and Girls Club."

"So, he's going to be trolling the high schools," Emily groaned.

"No." Amy shook her head vigorously. "That's not his speed. He likes to have fun, he likes the women, but according to the people I know who know him, he was horrified at what happened. He definitely doesn't want to end up on the online gossip websites again. Plus, they just drafted a new DE, and he's trying to renegotiate his contract right now. He wants to retire with as much of the owners' money as he can over the next couple of years." Amy took a breath. "The other stuff he gets in trouble for is being late for curfew on road trips, that kind of stuff. It's pretty minor."

"You're sure?"

"I wouldn't lie to you about this. Don't kid yourself: That guy is busy, but he's not dangerous. He's just much too charming. There are women all over town that could probably tell you all about it. I *know* there are women who'd like to see him dragged behind the team bus, but they did stick up for him when it happened."

"What are you talking about?" Emily crossed her arms over her chest. This wasn't good news. It sounded like she'd vaulted out of the frying pan and into the fire.

"Everything goes well till he's tired of whoever he's with, and then it's over. It's happened repeatedly. Then again, I can't figure out why he was dating Anastasia Lee. You know, the model. She's a head case."

Amy's supply of local gossip was inexhaustible. "How do you know all this stuff?"

"I'm single and I date. Plus, one of the Sharks' cheerleaders has a yoga studio next door to the shop. I'll ask her if she has any new dirt."

"Has he been engaged before?"

Amy thought for a moment. "Good question. She'll know. She said her cell phone started ringing with this late last night." She flopped down on her back next to Emily. "So, he was nice to you?"

"He stayed with me at the hospital. They wouldn't let me check out unless he promised to watch me, and he did. He slept here last night. He woke me up to make sure I was okay, he fed me, and he tried to make me feel better when James called."

Amy nodded, and her eyebrows lifted. "He might be nice, but he's a player." She propped herself up on one elbow. "This would also mean that I suck. Why didn't you call me? I would have stayed with you."

"You couldn't have left your shop yesterday if you wanted to, and you know it."

Amy twirled a long strand of Emily's hair around her fingertip. "You're my only sister. Plus, you know all my secrets. I would have been here."

"I was okay." Emily stared at the ceiling. "Brandon is also saving my butt as far as the engagement. Overnight, everyone seems to want to book me, even if James told the entire industry I'm 'difficult.'"

An evil smirk turned up the corners of Amy's lips as she considered Emily's comment.

"Oh, I see. You just decided to go along with this."

"What do you mean?" Emily said. Oh, no. Amy was

like a dog with a bone under the best of circumstances, and she smelled steak.

"You hate this, don't you? Don't play dumb. Let's face it, Em, he's gorgeous. I'd hit that. Lots of other women already have." Emily wrapped both arms around herself. She didn't want to think about Brandon "hitting it" with anyone else.

A cross between a laugh and a snort left Amy's lips. "You get to wear a diamond the size of a car headlight; you get to play house with him for a month . . ."

"Ame, come on. I won't be around. I'm working all month, anyway."

Amy tried to control her mirth, and Emily tried to control her annoyance.

"What are we going to tell Mom and Dad?" Amy said. "How are you going to explain getting engaged to someone you've known for twenty-four hours? This isn't going to work."

"Of course it will," Emily assured her. As long as nobody found out the truth, everything was fine.

WORRYING ABOUT WHAT her parents might have to say about all this was actually low on Emily's priority list. She was thinking about her upcoming performances. There were two weeks of rehearsals in Seattle, another two weeks of performances, and she'd be in Chicago for five weeks after that. When Emily wasn't in rehearsals for an upcoming performance, she worked doubly hard with her new voice teacher and her coach to learn more roles.

The more operas she knew, the more roles she was prepared to sing, the more marketable she was.

Sopranos had a limited shelf life in the opera world, and Emily's goal was making it to the Met in the next two years. She could sing the top roles for ten years after that. She'd retire with an incredible body of work. Her goals got her out of bed in the morning. There wasn't time for a relationship, no matter how lonely she sometimes was.

If Emily stuck with the plan, she could have everything she dreamed of and worked toward. This was Job One. She'd find a guy later on.

A few hours after Amy went home, Emily heard a knock at her front door. She peered through the peephole.

"Sugar, it's me," Brandon said. He stood on the doorstep holding what appeared to be an overnight bag. "Maybe you should invite me in."

She pulled the front door open wide enough for Brandon to stroll inside. Pointing at the bag he held, she said, "I'm fine. You have a life! I don't expect you to stay here."

"Of course you should. It's almost dinnertime. You're cooking, aren't you?"

Emily shut the front door behind him. "I don't think so. Which one of us has a concussion?"

He laughed as he dropped the bag next to the little table in the hallway, alongside the two suitcases that were still there from the other day. He took Emily's elbow, and led her into the kitchen. He pulled the refrigerator door open to look inside.

"You don't eat at home, do you?"

"No. No, I don't," she said, somewhat absently.

"Looks like it. Does opera have seasons, like the NFL?"

"It depends on the opera company and when they're mounting productions."

He nodded. He was still studying the inside of the refrigerator, newly full as a result of the grocery run he'd made while Emily slept. She was unused to seeing that much food. Then again, she'd seen Brandon eat. It wasn't going to be enough.

"What do you think we should make?" he asked.

"Let's order something instead."

Emily pulled open the drawer by the kitchen sink, which held every food delivery and takeout menu she collected over the three years she owned her house. She supposed she should have been embarrassed about this, but it wasn't something she spent a lot of time dwelling on. If she was hungry, she ate, and typically it was readymade.

He shut the refrigerator door, and turned to face her. A teasing smile spread over his lips. "You don't know how to cook."

"Well, I can make things in the microwave, and I . . ." Her voice trailed off. She was facing a full-on, naughty grin. The dimple in his left cheek flashed. She resisted the impulse to trace it with her fingertip. What was wrong with her, anyway? This wasn't real. She needed to get a grip on herself and her runaway hormones.

He reached out for her. His voice in her ear was low and seductive.

"I'm a very good cook, and I give lessons. They cost hardly anything."

She tried to break away, but he didn't let go of her. She was torn between nervousness and attraction. Confusion played a role, too. She couldn't imagine what he thought he was doing.

She moved away, and he followed, one inch at a time.

"We have all these menus here." Emily dug around in the pile. "Look. Thai food, British pub food, Mexican, a bistro, pizza, sub sandwiches, there's all kinds. What are you in the mood for?"

She was talking a mile a minute, and he took her chin in his fingertips. Her knees were knocking. She was a little dizzy. She couldn't decide if it was from the concussion or the fact that Brandon had now slipped his hand into her hair, and was slowly drawing her closer. He was touching her again. Wait a minute. This was supposed to be *pretend*.

"A kiss for a lesson," he coaxed.

"I don't know what you want to eat," she protested, but her voice trailed off again. Her eyes were drawn to his lips, to the dimple denting his left cheek, to his half-lidded eyes. His arm slid around her. She took a quick breath.

"Imagine how many lessons you'll need if you've never cooked before, sugar." His lips brushed Emily's forehead. His low voice sent a shiver up her spine. "That might be a lot of kisses. I know I said I'd teach you, but are you up to all that kissing?"

Her knees were doing this odd, melting thing. Her fingertips slid over the warmth of his skin, the silken blond hair on his forearms (and some truly impressive biceps). He pulled her even closer. "I think I'll enjoy it," he assured Emily.

"But we're not supposed to be kissing," she said in a small voice.

"Says who?"

She looked up at him. It seemed urgent that she tell him. "My knees aren't working."

"Oh, they're not? That's terrible. Better hold onto me, then."

He got closer. His mouth was moving toward hers, and her eyelids drifted closed. She'd been here before, but not with him. His arms tightened around her; he was a whisper from her mouth; she licked her lips . . .

Emily's eyes snapped open. What was she doing? She pushed against his chest, shoving herself away. No. *No.* She was not getting in a clinch with this man, even if she wanted to. Even if he was handsome, sexy, and smelled really great. Even if she was dying to kiss him.

Brandon looked a bit startled. "What the hell was that?"

"Self-preservation." One hand shot toward him, traffic cop-style. "Keep your lips to yourself, football boy."

"Really?" He leaned against the kitchen counter, bracing one hand on it: One big, strong, warm, capable-looking hand. His charm was still set on 'stun', too. "Is it me you object to, the kissing, or both?"

There was a Mexican standoff of sorts in Emily's kitchen. She still held one hand out. He looked like it was all he could do to control his laughter. Her arm dropped to her side. "Let's just get some dinner, and we'll talk about it later."

"Promises, promises," Brandon said, but she was shuffling through the menus again. "It's been a long day for you, so we'll stay in tonight. I'll give you a cooking demonstration. Plus, we need to start dating. Maybe we should discuss that."

"You will? We do?"

Emily was attempting to pretend five minutes ago hadn't happened. She was still dazed. Plus, she needed to assert herself a little here. He did not get to make all the decisions. It was time he found out who was in charge here: *Her*. She'd functioned just fine until the day before yesterday, when Hurricane Brandon blew into her life.

"Of course we do. We're engaged. We have to date." He leaned over to sniff her hair. "You smell wonderful."

Abruptly, reason returned. "Oh, I must have misunderstood. Cameras must be rolling. Where's *NFL Today*? Save it for the fans, big guy."

She didn't miss the look of surprise.

"We made a deal. If we stick with the deal, it'll work well for both of us. Let's not screw it up."

She glared at him.

"Fine." He exhaled. "We should be talking, though. We'll get to know each other better so we can pull this off. We both have to eat."

He made it all sound so reasonable. Emily was not one of those stupid women who would let a guy talk her into anything, but for all intents and purposes, Brandon had been talking her into pretty much anything he suggested for the past day and a half. She had to stop this.

"How do you feel about scrambled eggs and toast?" he asked.

"That's breakfast. It's dinnertime."

"You can't tell me you've never had breakfast for dinner before." He shook his head and began opening and closing cabinet drawers. "Where are your pots and pans?"

"I don't have any."

"You have a cookie sheet, but you have no pots and pans?"

"Amy likes to come over and bake cookies sometimes." Okay, she sounded a little defensive, but he didn't have to laugh at her.

"I can't believe you don't cook." His smile broadened. He tucked a loose strand of hair behind Emily's ear. She jumped, and he looked pleased. "What's going to happen if you actually want to cook something one of these days? What will you do then?"

"I can order it from somewhere, or I can buy it ready-made. It's . . ." Her voice trailed off for a minute, then she took a breath and informed him, "It's a waste of my time. I have other things to do."

"I meant what I said about teaching you how to cook."

Emily closed her eyes for a moment. It would be nice if they could get through five minutes without disagreeing about something. But if it was so awful, why was her heart beating so fast? He was going to laugh at her, but he'd find out sooner or later.

"My mom tried to teach me, and it was terrible. I burned everything, and she—"

Her voice trailed off. The faintly mocking expression in his eyes faded. To her surprise, Brandon didn't laugh.

"You'll learn. Cooking's like kissing. It takes practice." He let that sink in for a minute or two. "If we can't have eggs and toast, we'll have to come up with something else. Let's get Chinese."

"That will work." Emily sank into a chair at the kitchen table. He sat down next to her.

"See how easy that was? If you agree with me, things go so much better." He had to be kidding. "Our first fight."

"If that was a fight, we've been fighting since we met."

"Of course it was," he soothed. "Maybe I need to stop at the jeweler's tomorrow and pick something up for you to mark this occasion with."

"Are you serious?" she said. The smile he wore got even bigger.

"Then again, I already bought you something today. What'll I do tomorrow, huh? I like the idea of bringing you something every day." He moved closer to the table, and stretched out one hand to her. His voice dropped to a low rumble. "Maybe I'll get you a nice set of pots and pans."

Cookware never sounded sensual before she met him.

"You can take your pots and pans and—"

"Now, don't get upset. I'll tell you what. Let's call the restaurant and order some food." He spoke with exaggerated patience. Any second now, he'd start spelling the big words. "Do you think we could agree on that?"

She shrugged one shoulder. "I suppose." Despite being half-crazed with frustration, Emily had to laugh. He tried to pretend he was completely disgusted, but his eyes sparkled. They were especially green today. Maybe they changed colors.

"How do you feel about cashew chicken?" He pulled his cell phone from his pocket.

"Brandon," she said.

"You need a pet name for me. Everyone else has one." She couldn't resist teasing him again. "Box of Rocks?"

"That's going to leave a mark." He smiled indulgently. "How about something nice? Pretend you like me." Emily let out a snicker. "I'm expecting some originality here. Everyone is 'baby' or 'honey' or 'sweetie.' You think it over, and we'll discuss it later." His fingers curled around hers. She pulled her now-sweaty hand away.

"You call me sugar," she said.

"That's different. You smell sweet as sugar. I'll bet you taste good, too." He leaned toward her, and his breath brushed her cheek.

"You smell like mint," Emily murmured. She brushed her palms over her jeans-clad thighs. Mint and a delicious, male scent unique to Brandon she knew she'd never forget.

He leaned toward her again. "I know it's a lot to ask"— his lips were a fraction of an inch from her ear—"but someday, you'll kiss me, won't you?" She felt the heat rising in her face. Suddenly she was speechless; all she could do was nod. "That's good."

He rose, rifled through the menus on Emily's counter, and pulled one from the pile. He dropped into the chair next to her again. Even slouched in a kitchen chair, he was graceful.

"We've already agreed on the cashew chicken," he said. "What else might you like to eat?"

It didn't *matter*. Her heart was still ba-ba-bumping around in her chest, her palms were sweaty, she was inappropriately warm, and her toes curled in her shoes. Would she ever kiss him? He might be shocked if she did it now. Maybe she should wait thirty seconds or so. After all, she wouldn't want to seem desperate.

Emily shrugged her shoulders, and attempted to look bored. "Whatever you'd like is fine."

"Fried rice, moo shu pork. How about some soup? I like that egg flower stuff."

"It's all great. Really." She was still trying to regain her composure, and he was acting like nothing had happened.

"So, dinner, maybe we can watch a movie, and then we'll hit the sack."

"You don't need to spend the night. I'm fine." *Inside voice*, she told herself.

"Of course I'm sleeping here."

BRANDON BEAT HER to the door a half hour later. The tabletop was quickly festooned with white cardboard take-out containers, and they sat down to enjoy the feast.

"Would you like more fried rice?" she asked him, wielding the serving spoon.

"Yes. Thank you." Emily spooned more onto his plate,

and he nodded. "Keep going. By the way, you seem to be wearing some hoisin sauce."

She glanced at the front of her sweater and let out a groan.

"Oh, no. I can't eat anything without making a mess."

"It's only me." he said, obviously trying to reassure her she wasn't as clumsy as she thought. "It looks like I spilled some, too. What a shame." He dribbled a bit of sauce on his polo shirt. "See? Not so bad."

"Here. Let me wash it. The stain might not come out." She reached around the table for the hem of his shirt.

"Don't worry about it. Let's finish our dinner," Brandon said. She reached up to brush a few grains of rice off his shirt. "Thanks. So, what's on your mind?"

"How did your meeting go today?"

"They're thinking about making a trade or two before the NFL draft, so there was some discussion about the positions the team might want to strengthen. It wasn't a big deal."

"Do you usually have meetings when you're not playing games?"

"There are a lot of guys who live here year round. We all practice together. The ones that don't are usually talking to the other guys on cell phones or via Twitter, so they can chime in if they'd like." He propped his chin in his hand. "How'd it go with Amy, and when am I going to meet her?"

"Amy's business is a little nuts right now. We might be able to get together when I'm done with my performances in Seattle." By the time her performances were over, the engagement would be over, too. He didn't seem to realize this. Maybe that was best.

"I would like that. My parents would like to meet you, too."

"Do you think that's a good idea? If we're not going to be together that long, it's not really necessary."

His expression was implacable.

"My parents will still want to meet you. I want to meet your folks, and I want to meet Amy. This isn't open for negotiation."

Chapter Eight

AFTER BRANDON INHALED his dinner that evening (and Emily picked at hers) they adjourned to Emily's living room couch. She managed to seize the remote, flipping the television on. Brandon pretended to glare at her. The effect was ruined, however, by a huge grin and the flash of his dimple.

The sports anchorman's voice boomed over the TV's speakers.

"Single women everywhere are inconsolable over the news that the Sharks' Brandon McKenna announced his engagement this morning. The Sharks front office is cautiously optimistic. Will McKenna put up what must be a modern-day version of the 'little black book'—his legendary smart phone 'contacts' list of single females—for auction on eBay as a result?"

"Like I'm that stupid," Brandon muttered.

Emily gave him a combination eye roll and head shake.

The typically unflappable Brandon had been squirming for a few minutes now. "That's really going to put a crimp in your social life, Brandon."

He grunted in response.

The announcer continued. "Our cameras caught up with the wily Mr. McKenna outside of his fiancée Emily Hamilton's home this morning, and he didn't fail to astonish and amuse."

Emily watched them walk down the front stairs on her television screen. One of the reporters asked her if she was surprised at his proposal, and Brandon wrapped his arms around her waist as she responded, "Yes, I was." He gave her an adoring grin. He nuzzled her hair. It looked like he was kissing Emily's ear, but in reality, she had deliberately stepped on his toes. The next piece of tape was of Brandon standing outside of her Escape while she waited inside. Another reporter asked, "Brandon, we understand that Miss Hamilton is a very talented and sought-after young diva. How do you plan to cope with two demanding careers?"

"You know, Emily's talented in *many* areas," he smirked, raised one eyebrow, and gave the camera a look that let all of America know exactly what she was talented at. "Frankly, she wears me out. I'm a lucky man." He shook his head a bit, gave the reporters a dazzling smile, and said, "Thanks, guys," as he pulled the driver's door open and swung into the seat.

Emily let out a gasp of horror. "You—You—What was that?"

Brandon shot her a quick glance. "Take a breath, sugar."

"My *parents* will see that. You just told the entire *country* that I'm some kind of—oh, my God. How could you?" She jumped up from the couch, hurried through the living room, and stormed up the staircase. Her headache was temporarily forgotten. Brandon didn't even have to run to catch up with her.

"Sugar," he cajoled. "It's not a big deal."

"Yes, it is. I can't believe you said that. I am not one of your—" She whipped around to face him; he stopped inches from crashing into her. "Floozies. Trollops. Hos. *Bimbos*. Whatever they're called, I'm not one of them." She poked her finger in the middle of his chest to punctuate. Multiple times.

"Now, you don't need to name call," he said. "They wanted a colorful quote, and I gave it to them."

Emily let out a groan, and turned on her heel. Right now, making a lot of noise was the only option. He caught her elbow. "Don't you have somewhere else to be right now?" she said.

"No. No, I don't." He stroked her arm. "You're not mad about this." He moved closer. Her body double-crossed her, swaying toward him. His arm slid around her waist. "So, I got a little carried away. It's not a problem." He nuzzled the hair at her temple. The temperature in the room shot up twenty degrees in five seconds or so.

She couldn't understand why she wavered between wanting to commit bodily harm on him and wanting to do things to him that would feel really, *really* good. Right now, though, she needed to pull herself together.

Her head jerked up, narrowly missing his nose. "I realize the rest of the world thinks we're engaged right now, but did you need to tell everyone I'm some kind of *insatiable* sex maniac? That stuff is private. It should remain between us. All of America does not need to know what goes on in my bedroom!" She poked him in the chest a few more times for emphasis.

He lifted an eyebrow. "Insatiable sex maniac? Now, that's interesting." The amusement on his face made her realize he wasn't backing off. "I've never met one of those before. Tell me more."

Her mouth dropped open in outrage. At that moment, the phone started to ring. She turned on her heel and stomped away from him only to hear Brandon's laughter again.

EMILY GRABBED THE ringing phone in her room, hitting "speaker" as she sat down on the bed. It was David calling to outline the booking offers he'd fielded that day.

"Your calendar's getting a workout, Emily. So, I'll confirm all three of the productions we talked about, and send the information to your phone's calendar as well."

"Thanks, David. I'm really glad things are picking up."

"I am, too. I just got an email from Seattle Opera's PR group as well. They'd like to do an interview and some pictures with you and Brandon at your earliest convenience. It'll run in the magazine and on their website. If he'd like, we can schedule a date and time with his agent."

She saw Brandon stroll into the room out of the corner of her eye.

"That'll work for me, David. I'll let Josh know to expect your call," Brandon responded, speaking loudly enough for David to hear him over the speaker phone.

"Great. By the way, Brandon, I saw the ESPN interview. You're making my job easy."

"Glad to hear it," Brandon said. "Thanks for taking such good care of my girl."

"Back at you. Talk to you later, Emily." David hung up.

Emily pulled breath into her lungs. Their conversation gave her a few minutes to calm down and think. Three more bookings! She'd never gotten three bookings in a week, let alone one day.

Brandon stretched out on the other side of her bed and picked up the book resting on the nightstand.

"If this keeps up, you're going to have to bring somebody in to feed the cat and water the plants while you're gone. Good job, sugar."

Obviously he was teasing her, but the irritation she'd felt twenty seconds before her phone rang had given way to relief and amusement. Rather than causing some type of irreparable issue, Brandon's outrageous comments in the media led to bookings. How did this happen, anyway?

"Hey, I'm curious." Brandon put the book on the nightstand. "Why did you become an opera singer? I've never met one before."

"Changing the subject, huh?" She propped herself up against the headboard of her bed.

"C'mon, sugar." He stretched out, propped himself up on one elbow, and watched her expectantly.

She thought for a few moments before responding. "I

saw an opera when I was twelve and fell in love with it. From that moment on I always knew what I wanted to do when I was older."

"It's good to have goals. Tell me more."

She pulled a pink cashmere throw over her and wound the fringe around her fingers as she spoke. "Besides Amy and my parents, there is nothing and nobody else in the world I love like I love to sing. Nothing else makes me happier." She looked into his face. "I'm lost in the music, and it's almost like I step outside myself. I can feel the breath in my body. I can hear the notes coming out of me, but I am somewhere else for that time. It's somewhere I can't wait to go back to again."

"So, you've been singing since you were twelve."

"My training didn't really start till I was sixteen."

He propped himself up on the pillows. "How long can you keep doing this? Do you ever wonder what you'll do when you decide to end your career?"

"I will hopefully sing till I die, but professionally? Probably another twenty years or so. I have a plan." He waited, and she took a breath. "I want to sing at the Metropolitan Opera in New York. It's everything I've worked for, because it's the greatest success I could have as a diva in the United States. It's the pinnacle. I'm hoping I'll get there in the next two years. After I get there, I can sing the top roles until retirement."

He reached out to pat her hand. "I think you'll get there."

"Thanks. That's very kind." She sighed. Some days, those goals seemed far away. "I started late. When I got out of the conservatory, I wanted a Master's, and then, to build a repertoire, I spent a lot of time singing roles with smaller opera companies. I'm not sorry, but I wonder if I'm going to pay for not managing my career as well as I should have. That's why I have David. He's really good at it."

Brandon had grown silent.

"You've been playing football for a while, haven't you?" she asked.

"Since I was six." He let out a laugh. "It's a lotta years."

"Have you thought of what you're going to do when you want to retire from football?"

He shrugged, propped himself up on the pillows, and folded his arms across his chest; he was uncomfortable with the subject. "I'll probably end up doing color commentary for NFL broadcasts. I've done it before during the regular season when we had a bye week."

"What's a bye week?"

"We get a week off." He continued. "Right now, broadcasting is my post-football focus. It's fun, I enjoy it, and it pays well." He crossed his feet at the ankles. Despite the fact they really didn't know each other, it was obvious by his body language Brandon didn't want to discuss this, and she wondered why. "Hey." His eyes locked onto hers, and Emily noticed that the typically amused expression in them was gone. "What happens to your ten-year plan if you fall in love? Have you thought about that?"

She hugged herself, and crossed her ankles as well. "I'm not sure."

If there were such a thing as being struck dead for lying, Emily surely would have been a goner at that point. The truth was something she carefully guarded, and she wasn't giving it up to the blond Adonis less than a foot from her. She didn't want to end up like her mom. She didn't want to give up her dreams, no matter how lonely she was. Emily could fall in love and get married later, or not at all. She had known other divas who married and had kids, but she'd already spent enough time screwing around. If she wanted to achieve her goals, she couldn't afford to waste any more time.

"You've thought about everything else. Why wouldn't you think of that?" Brandon probed.

"I just didn't. It didn't seem important." *Sure it wasn't.* She could tell by the look in his eyes he didn't buy her response, either, but she made her best effort. "What about you? Do you think you'll fall in love and have little blond babies?"

His eyes softened, and a smile twitched the corners of his lips. "I sure hope so. I have to find a woman who wants to fall in love for the rest of her life."

"Wouldn't that be most women?" she said.

"I always thought so." His eyes held hers again.

She swallowed hard and quickly changed the subject. "Want to watch a movie?"

"Nope. Not right now. I'd like to spend some more time talking, if you're not too tired."

She wanted to get out of this conversation, and he'd presented her with the best opportunity possible. "I'm pretty wiped out," she said.

He shoved himself off the bed. "Time to get some sleep, then. I'll make a wardrobe change."

"You don't need to stay here. You have your own place. I'm fine. I don't need anyone to watch me. I can sleep on my—"

He laid his fingertips over her mouth. "You're going to wear yourself out with all that arguing. Come on." He reached out for her hand. "Don't you want to put on one of those virginal white nighties?"

She wasn't giving in to his charm again. Even if he'd deliberately dribbled hoisin sauce on his shirt, bought her a ring that must have cost a staggering amount of money, and generally been wonderful, she could resist him. Even if every time he smiled, her heart skipped a beat.

He probably smiled that way at every woman who crossed his path. She wasn't special. The sooner she realized that, the better off she'd be.

"Don't I get an opinion here? It's my house."

"Of course you do. You told me that you're fine by yourself, and I disagree." His eyes twinkled again. "Get changed, and we'll discuss it further."

She heaved a frustrated sigh. "You're—you're just—oooh."

Emily hurried into the bathroom and shut the door only to hear his laughter. She put on another billowing white cotton nightgown, washed her face, brushed her teeth, and thought about what she should do. She could order him to leave. That was best. The scariest thing about Brandon was that he saw behind her defenses. He knew, somehow, she really didn't want him to leave.

This had to stop.

She emerged from the bathroom to find Brandon snuggled into the blankets of her bed. He gave her a sleepy grin.

"If you're staying here, you need to sleep in the living room or in the guest room. This is not working," Emily informed him in her firmest tone. If she averted her eyes from his bare chest, she could do this—as long as she didn't remember how uncomfortable he looked curled up in her bedroom chair, or how he had stayed to make sure she was okay.

"You don't have a bed in your guest room. The living room's cold." On any other man, it would have been whining. In Brandon's accent, it was a crime against humanity.

"What's the matter? The big football player doesn't know how to turn up a thermostat? Too bad." She pointed toward the bedroom door. "Out."

"You don't really mean that, sugar," he said.

"Yes, I do. We still hardly know each other."

He let out a snort. "I know that you snore."

"I do not," Emily said.

"You also make the cutest little whimpering noises in your sleep," he said softly.

She threw the smallest pillow from her bed at him. "Goodnight, Brandon."

The door shut behind him. She breathed a sigh as she crawled into bed, ignoring the twinges of guilt. God's gift to the NFL could take the couch, and she might get some rest.

BRANDON STROLLED INTO Emily's room a few hours later. He'd made a few phone calls, watched all the game film he could stand, and fixed himself a midnight snack. He'd slept in the chair in her room before, but the only way he was going to get any meaningful sleep at all was to stretch out next to her.

She was right; he could have slept at home. But he kept thinking about the expression on her face when she had pushed herself out of his arms earlier. Obviously, that was a physical response to spending the last forty-eight hours or so with someone he found attractive. He wanted to kiss her. Even more, he knew she wanted to kiss him, but she wouldn't. She was stubborn to the tenth power. While he delighted in doing and saying stuff that worked her last nerve, he realized he really enjoyed watching the relaxation that spread through her entire body when she laughed. It would be slow going, but oddly, he wanted to gain Emily's trust.

His long-term plan had been to avoid anything that lasted longer than a New York minute. He didn't want anything permanent, and when things got sticky he made a quick exit. He'd never had any intention of settling down until his football days were at an end, and then he'd take time to find the right woman. These days, though, flavor-of-the month females meant more annoyance and heartache than fun—women like Anastasia, for instance. She was the last straw.

For now, though, Emily the pint-sized ball of fire—with vulnerability she did her very best to hide—intrigued him.

The moonlight draped Emily's bed like netting, and he watched her sleep for a few minutes. He knew she smelled like peaches and freshly cut grass. He wasn't kidding about the little noises she made in her sleep. He heard a soft whimper, even now.

When she wasn't busting his chops, something about her relaxed and soothed him.

He stripped down to his shorts and slid in next to her. Her long hair spread over the pillows like rose petals. He took a few deep breaths of her sweet scent, and then he was asleep.

A few hours later, Emily rolled over and bumped into him. "Mmph," he muttered. The bedroom window indicated dawn was still hours away.

Her voice was sleepy. "Why are you here? We agreed that you're sleeping on the couch."

He popped up out of the blankets. "You're awake," he said. "Let's talk some more."

"What is this? Most guys want to run away from the talking stuff, don't they?"

He stifled a laugh. It seemed he spent a lot of time doing that when she was around. He kept his voice light.

"That's a gross generalization. I'm definitely insulted. I can't believe you would think that."

"You're joking."

"Absolutely not. This isn't funny."

He could see it was all she could do not to scream. He wondered what she'd do if he reached out to tickle her.

"Listen, you big brute, why don't you move over so I can—"

The rest of her comment was muffled by the blankets she dragged over her head. She reconsidered a few moments later, tossed the blankets back, and propped herself up on the pillows. He wasn't so sure about the evil look in her eyes. Unless he was terribly wrong, not only was she irritated, but she'd just figured out her revenge.

"Do you feel better today, sugar?"

"Yeah. My head doesn't hurt as much. I seem to have a little more energy." She took a deep breath. "Thanks for asking."

"You're welcome." Her hand brushed his under the covers, and she jumped. He held on. Her hand was small inside of his. She tried to pull her hand away, and he meshed his fingers through hers. Nice.

"I'm curious, Brandon—"

"I need a nickname. How are you coming on the nickname?"

"Listen, Bruiser."

He laughed. "Good one." He pulled the blankets up to his chest. "And you were saying?"

She glanced away from him. *Here it comes,* he thought. "I'm not even sure how to ask you this."

"Well, that sounds promising." He let out a deep chuckle. "I can hardly wait to find out what you're going to ask me now. Spit it out, okay? We're not getting any younger."

"This is a little embarrassing, but I knew nothing about you. I'd never heard of you before I wiped out in the parking lot."

"Tell me something I don't know." He took a sip of

water from the glass on the nightstand. "I didn't know a lot about you, either."

"That's true." Emily propped herself up on her elbow. Somehow, lying in bed, holding her hand and talking with her in the darkness seemed more intimate than the last time he'd had sex. He knew she would be a man's friend as well as his lover. He'd never experienced that before. He slid further down into the blankets as well, and they faced each other.

"I'm confused," she said. "Cheryl the nurse called you a horn dog. My sister said roughly the same thing. I've spent some time with you now, and you aren't like that at all. How can you have this reputation if you're nothing like that person?"

The room was silent. He thought he'd braced himself, but evidently not. There was *no* correct answer to that question. He'd done some stuff when he was younger to deserve the press he got, but it would be nice if he got some credit for realizing he needed to be a lot more selective in his choice of conquests. Some of his alleged hookups were blown out of proportion by the media, or were flat-out lies by women who thought sleeping with him would enhance their allure to others. Anastasia came to mind. She was the last straw in more ways than one. He really didn't like having his nose rubbed in his mistakes. Those stupid enough to do so got the full force of his anger, every time.

"Sometimes, people say things about us that aren't true," she said. Emily, bless her heart, was trying to give him an out, but it pissed him off. "If you talked to my colleagues, I know that you'd hear embarrassing things about me."

"Really," he bit out. Unless he missed his guess, she was patronizing him. Yup, he was pissed. The more she talked, the angrier he was.

"Of course, I—"

"You know, sugar, we talked about this yesterday. I've done stuff I'm not especially proud of in the past, but I'm normal. In my line of work, there are women who want to brag to their friends that they nailed a pro athlete. At times, I've been happy to oblige them."

"Oh, I see," she said, raising an eyebrow. "You're a real humanitarian, aren't you? I'm amazed nobody's contacted the Nobel committee on your behalf."

That was a low blow, and unfair to him as well. He passed "pissed," and went straight into "fury." This was a sore subject to begin with, and he felt like she was poking him in the gut with a sharp stick. He'd just discovered one of Emily's faults: She didn't know when to back off. "That was pretty harsh."

"Are you listening to yourself?" she said. "How can you believe the stuff you say?"

He dropped her hand, and flipped on his side away from her. It was three AM. The best thing he could do was calm down. If he got in the car now he would get a ticket at best, because he shouldn't be behind the wheel. He also wondered what he did to bring this on.

After a few deep breaths, he spoke. "Whatever I have or have not done, I want you to understand this. I have never cheated on anyone I was with. I've always taken precautions against disease and pregnancy. I don't get involved with women who are involved with other men. I wasn't kidding about the fact my priorities have shifted recently. I'm done running around. I'd like to find a woman I could fall in love with and be faithful to for the rest of my life. If you're under the impression that I'm some kind of man-whore, that's your problem."

An uncomfortable silence fell.

Brandon considered his options one more time. He could get up and go in the other room. He could stay here. He could get in the car, go home, and never see her again. Door number three was sounding increasingly attractive, but mostly he wished he knew why women did the things they did. She'd shoved herself into a six-inch space at the opposite side of her bed.

He had said some stuff he now wished he hadn't. She had said some stuff that hit every hot button he had. Maybe the best thing to do was simmer down, get some sleep, and try to get to the bottom of it in the morning.

He flipped onto his back. A little while later, Emily also rolled onto her back.

He felt her hand slide inside of his. He laced his fingers through hers again and squeezed her hand.

She squeezed back.

EMILY AWOKE THE next morning alone in her bed. The house was quiet. She could hear Brandon's voice as she wandered into the kitchen to find a fresh pot of coffee. He ended the call, and glanced over at her. "Good morning."

"Good morning," she responded. She heaved a sigh, and sat down at the table.

"Did you sleep well?"

He took a sip of coffee. Of course, he looked completely unruffled. She had a bellyful of butterflies. She couldn't believe he was still here. Despite the early-morning cob-webs, she realized she'd started an argument with him last night because he was less than a foot away, wearing nothing but a pair of shorts, and she couldn't seem to uncurl her toes when he was around. She was pretty sure he'd heard the words "I think you're gorgeous and I want to body-slam you" more than once in his life, but she'd prefer to keep a shred of her dignity.

How hypocritical was she, inquiring about the women he'd been with previously while wondering what she'd have to do to achieve the same thing? She owed him an apology, and she'd better make it good. He'd spent the past two days taking care of her. She rewarded that kindness by acting like a piranha with hemorrhoids.

"Brandon, I'm sorry. I said a lot of things to you last night that—" She couldn't even look at him. "I was wrong. I shouldn't have said the stuff I did. Again, I'm sorry." She fidgeted as she made herself shut up.

He was still for a moment. He rose from the table, grabbed the coffee pot and another mug for her, and sat down again. He poured them both a cup of coffee. "I'm sorry too, sugar. My temper ran away with me." He lifted his mug. "Friends?"

Emily touched the rim of her mug to his. "Friends."

She saw the corners of his lips move into a smile. "How do you feel about a bagel and some cream cheese?"

"Great." Before she could get up from the table, he reached out and put one hand over hers. "Listen. I'd like to talk with you some more, but I have an appointment downtown in less than an hour. How about meeting up later?"

Emily nodded. "I'm having dinner with my parents, so I might not be here till after seven or so."

"We can grab dessert or something then."

He got up from the table. Emily quickly smeared cream cheese on a bagel, wrapped a napkin around it, and handed it to him.

"Breakfast to go. Hope it goes well. Bye."

"Thanks. It will."

He bent to kiss her cheek, picked up the bag he'd left in the hallway, and hurried out of the house.

A few minutes later, Emily heard a booming knock at the front door. He must have forgotten something. She was so sure it was Brandon, she didn't even look through the peephole.

IT WASN'T BRANDON. She opened the door to a tall, strikingly beautiful, rail-thin woman she recognized immediately from magazine ads through the years.

According to Amy, Anastasia Lee followed Brandon to Seattle two years ago, after they'd met at a Victoria's Secret runway show in New York. She'd probably been wearing a push-up bra and stiletto heels at the time. She jammed one of those stilettos through his heart by announcing she was dumping him during a live interview with *Entertainment Tonight* about a month ago, also according to Amy. "Brutal" was the word Emily's sister had used. Anastasia also managed to impugn his manhood, his family, and his bank account in less than sixty seconds. Brandon responded with silence.

Now she was standing at the front door, and Emily wasn't sure what to say to her.

Anastasia brushed past Emily and walked into the house without a word. She was dazzling. At the same time, Emily noticed dark violet shadows beneath her eyes. Someone wasn't sleeping.

"Excuse me," Emily said, not using her inside voice. "I didn't invite you in."

"Well, I'm here. Aren't you going to offer me something to drink?"

"You need to leave. *Now.*"

Anastasia cantered away from Emily, and didn't even bother to turn and look at her when she spoke. "I don't think so. We need to have a little chat."

Emily slammed the door shut and followed her into the living room. Not only had Anastasia made herself at home on the couch, she lit a cigarette. She crossed her legs and leaned back against the cushions.

"Nobody smokes in my house. Please put that out," Emily snapped.

Anastasia looked around. "I don't see any ashtrays." She blew out a long, thin stream of smoke.

"Why are you here, and how did you find me?"

"I heard you're engaged." She flipped a perfect, shiny curtain of espresso brown hair over one bony shoulder and gave Emily a look that one could only classify as contemptuous. Her eyes were as blue and cold as an iceberg. They were quite a contrast with her blood-red lips.

"Yes, I am."

"Stay away from Brandon."

Emily stared at her. "You're kidding me, right?" She'd evidently walked into some sort of parallel universe.

"No, I'm not. He loves me. He'll always love me."

"Didn't you dump him? Why do you care at all what he does?" Emily shot back.

She saw Anastasia flinch in response. She crossed her arms across her chest to help her resist the impulse to yank a handful of her unwanted guest's hair out. She also noticed something odd—Anastasia looked like a clothes hanger, but her stomach was slightly rounded. Maybe she was malnourished. In the meantime, her possible vitamin deficiency had certainly not done wonders for her attitude.

"You shouldn't stand like that," Anastasia said. "It's not a good look for you." Her lip curled. "It makes you look—chunky. Then again, you are a little on the chunky side, aren't you?"

"When's the last time you ate something, Anastasia— during the Bush administration?"

"You don't look like you've missed many meals." She sneered. "Brandon must be mercy fucking these days."

"Get out. Get out before I call the cops." Emily pointed toward the front door.

"You let me in."

"Maybe I should call Brandon instead. I'm sure he'd be interested to learn that you're here."

Anastasia's smile was positively feline. "You do that. He'll tell you himself that he wants me." She blew another stream of smoke in Emily's direction. She was obviously out of her mind.

Emily thought about hosing her down with the spray faucet in the kitchen. She'd probably melt.

"You've got ten seconds. I want you out of my house, or the cops are coming."

Anastasia's nastiness had finally registered. Emily was an opera singer, not a rocket scientist. Then again, she'd managed to scoop up a man Anastasia evidently still wanted.

"He still wants you, does he? I'm wearing his ring." Emily held up her hand and watched the diamond sparkle in the sunlight streaming through the living room windows.

The look on Anastasia's face was indescribable, but the words rage, grief, and revenge came to mind. "Bitch," she breathed.

"It took me less than a week." Emily studied her manicure. It was going to be hell to get the smoke smell out of the furniture, but this was worth it. "Maybe you should explain to me how this happened. He loves you, but he asked me to marry him."

"Rebound. He'll be back."

Emily did the best she could to keep the smile off her face. "You keep telling yourself that. I'm sure you'll feel better, eventually."

Anastasia dropped her cigarette into a coffee cup left on the end table. "I'm out of here." She crossed to the front door and yanked it open. She stopped and looked at Emily over her shoulder. For the briefest instant, Emily thought she saw sadness in her eyes. Then they turned hard again and she snarled, "You'll regret this, Emily."

She stomped out, slamming the door so hard Emily heard the pictures on the walls shift.

Emily had never been involved in a scene like this off-stage. For once, she said exactly what she wanted to say, at the time she needed to say it. What a charming woman. She must have been late for that dominatrix outfit alteration or something.

She could tell Brandon about all this later. Amy, of course, must know about it immediately. Emily grabbed her cell phone and hit Amy's number.

Amy was transfixed by Emily's story.

"She came over there? What's wrong with her?"

"She says Brandon's still in love with her." Emily was opening every window in the house while she talked.

"Maybe you should've found out what she's on, and we could get some, too. What the hell's her problem?"

"She's still in love with Brandon. Then again, is it possible for her to feel love? I don't know. I'd never do that. She doesn't know me at all, and she thinks she can stomp into my house and tell me how things are. She was *smoking*, Amy. You know how I feel about that."

"I still can't believe she showed up at your house."

Emily resisted the impulse to gloat. "She looks like hell."

"What?"

"She had these huge violet circles under her eyes. Wait till Victoria's Secret finds out about this."

"They're not going to care. They'll just airbrush it out of the photos. You need to call Brandon," Amy told her. "He needs to know she's resorting to showing up at your house now."

"It's not that big a deal, Amy. It was mostly just annoying. I'll see him later. I'm sure he'll think this is funny."

This was a new experience for Emily. After all, she'd never had anyone's ex show up at her house before. She couldn't understand why Anastasia would act like this, either. She'd said horrible things about Brandon on television, but suddenly she had decided she wanted him back. It was bizarre at best.

"So, where is your fiancé, anyway?" Amy said. "Are you guys sleeping together yet?"

"God, Amy."

"You know you want to tell me," her sister coaxed.

"He had some stuff to take care of today. He said he'd be by later." Emily let out a long breath. At least the smoke smell in her house was dissipating. "Yeah, he's been sleeping here, but nothing's going on."

"That's interesting. What did you say to him?"

Of course Amy was mystified. Emily was a bit confused as well.

"I tried to kick him out, and he won't go. He says he likes the house, the bed's comfortable, I have beer . . ." It sounded lame, even to her.

"That's BS." Amy's voice was brisk. "He's interested."

"This is fake. It's *fake*. Trust me."

Chapter Nine

EVERY SUNDAY EMILY was in town, she had dinner with her parents and Amy at her mom's house. Amy, the Hamilton family's peacemaker, had started it. After their parents' divorce, the task of family healing began around a dining room table while passing bowls and platters of delicious food. Sunday dinners had been awkward at times, but things had been relatively calm for the past few months. She was also a bit surprised that both parents greeted her without a fusillade of questions about Brandon.

She sat down at the dining room table and spread a napkin on her lap. Her dad had been torn away from a basketball game on TV, but he didn't appear to be cranky. Surprisingly enough, he beamed at Emily's mother.

"It all looks delicious."

"Thank you, Mark. Amy, would you like some mashed potatoes?"

"Yes, I would, Mom. Thanks."

They passed the bowls of mashed potatoes, salad, and the platter of roast beef to each other. It was more family bonding time. Emily hadn't been home for Sunday dinner for almost six weeks. She had multiple performances between Seattle Opera productions, and this meant more traveling. She didn't see her mom and dad every day anymore. When she did spend time with them, the changes were pronounced. Her mom's brilliant auburn hair was graying. She'd evidently decided to stop coloring it.

Her dad was not only digging into his plate like he hadn't seen food for a week, he was smiling at her mother like he meant it. Something was going on.

"This is very good, Meg," her father said.

Emily's mother blushed. "I'm glad you like it."

In the past the only way Amy and Emily had managed to get them in the same room for Sunday dinner was to threaten family therapy; something had happened over the past two months. Emily caught Amy's eye and lifted a brow. Amy gave her a quick nod. They'd be discussing this later. In the meantime, Meg Hamilton smiled at her daughters.

"Honey," her mother said to Emily, "How are your rehearsals going, and how are you feeling today?"

"My head hurts a little, but it's much better than it was the other day. The doctor gave me a release, so I'll be back in rehearsals tomorrow. I'm really looking forward to it,"

Mom patted her hand. "It's good to have you home for a little while." Her dad nodded as well.

"It seems like I come home, and then I have to leave again."

"Does Brandon know you'll be leaving again in a few weeks?"

"I'll make sure to talk to him about it."

Emily's dad looked up from his plate. "Speaking of Brandon, we'd like him to come by for dinner at his earliest convenience. Your mother and I want to meet him." He put his fork down and gave her a puzzled look. "Would you mind telling me why you got engaged to a man you've known less than a week?"

Amy covered her mouth with her fingertips. Her mother glanced at him and said softly, "Mark." They looked at each other. "Not at the table, please."

He heaved a heavy sigh. "I want answers, Meg."

"I know. I do, too."

Emily wanted to crawl under the table, but she took another bite of pot roast instead. She had answers, but she was fairly sure her parents wouldn't like them.

"Mom and Dad?" She pulled breath into her lungs. "I ... Well, I ..." She glanced down at her plate for a moment. "It's not that big of a deal."

"You show up wearing the biggest engagement ring I've ever seen, reporters are badgering your mother and me at the office, and 'It's not that big of a deal'?" her father said. "How long have you known this young man?"

"A while."

"How long?"

"Mark," her mother repeated, but she didn't look altogether happy, either. "When will we meet this Brandon? Have you set a date, honey?"

"Everything is fine," Emily said. "Don't get all crazy. We're not planning a wedding."

Emily's mother forgot all about her inside voice. "*Excuse me*? Why not?"

"Meg," her father said. He stared at Emily, and then sat forward a bit in his chair. "Why on earth would you get engaged and not be planning a wedding?"

Emily wasn't a fourteen-year-old anymore, begging her parents to let her move to San Francisco to train with a former diva. She'd been on her own for a long time now. She also knew that her parents were worried something was wrong. At the same time, she should have dragged Brandon over here and let him do the explaining. His parents, at least his mother, hadn't seemed too excited about this, either.

"We're taking our time," she said.

Her dad bent over his plate and said nothing. The color was draining out of her mother's face. Amy's mouth was opening and shutting like a goldfish's.

"It's good for my career. It's good for Brandon's career. It's fine," Emily said. "It works for both of us."

"You think this is going to help your *career*? This is an engagement. It's not a date for coffee." Her mother interrupted him.

"I don't understand this at all." She reached out to grab Emily's forearm. "Emily, don't you love him? There's more to life than your career."

"Mom, Dad, I don't expect you to understand, but I

do expect you to accept my decision. I'm an adult. Whatever agreement Brandon and I have is our business and nobody else's."

Her mother's mouth dropped open. Her father leaned even closer.

"There's something you're not telling us. You got engaged to a man you knew—according to your sister—for less than seventy-two hours. We haven't met him. You have no intention of planning a wedding. What the hell is going on?" he said.

Amy tried to look helpless. Emily knew her sister cratered under the Mark and Meg inquisition, but they'd be talking later. She put her napkin down beside her plate.

"Do you remember what James did to my career? I worked for years. I sacrificed everything in my life for this, and now I'm rebuilding. One man trashed my career, and another man's reconstructing it. Do you know how many booking requests David's had since Brandon and I announced our engagement?"

"Is it that important?" her mother said. "There must be something else that will make you happy."

"Mom, do you know what it's like to work your entire life for something and watch it ruined through no fault of your own?"

Dead silence greeted Emily's comment. Shame engulfed her like a wave. She'd hit below the belt. After all, her mother sacrificed a promising career as a ballerina for Emily's dad. Margaret Hamilton walked away from the thing she loved most to marry the man she loved most.

No matter how tired Emily was of her parents' meddling in her life, she shouldn't have brought it up.

"Emily," her father warned. Amy's eyes got bigger, if that was possible, with shock and horror at Emily's bluntness. Her mother dabbed at her face with a napkin.

"Yes, Emily," her mother said. She looked beaten. "Yes, I do."

"That's enough." Her father shoved his plate away, and rubbed his hands over his face again. "Emily." His voice was hoarse. "It's obvious what's going on here. Your sister told us the engagement is fake, it started due to a misunderstanding, and you agreed to continue it for publicity purposes. What do you think will happen when someone finds out this isn't real? There's no way you can keep this secret. Have either of you even thought of that?"

Yes, she had, but she wasn't going to share that with her father. "It's not going to happen."

He shook his head. "I've been proud of you your whole life. You worked so hard to get the things you wanted. I never dreamed there would be a day when you'd embarrass me."

"Isn't this what you wanted from me—to succeed?"

"Not like this." He tossed his napkin onto his plate. "I am disappointed with you." He got up from the table, and left the room. Emily's mother followed him.

Amy let out a breath, shoved her plate away, and put her face in her hands. "That went well, didn't it?"

"It will be fine. It will work out," Emily said.

She could hardly force the words out over the lump in her throat. Her father's words struck like a lash. She tried to tell herself that she didn't need his approval to survive, but the fact he told her he was disappointed with her was worse than if he'd screamed at her. Maybe she was destined to "disappoint" every man in her life. Maybe she shouldn't care.

No matter how hard she tried not to care, though, she did. It hurt more than he could imagine.

"I'm always with you, Em, but I don't know what you're doing here."

Her voice was wooden. "I have to do this."

Amy reached across the table and took her hand. "Then we'll get through it together, won't we?"

"Thanks, Ame." She looked into her sister's eyes. "What's going on with Mom and Dad?"

Amy shrugged her shoulders. "Damned if I know. They're awfully cuddly."

Emily and Amy didn't spend their whole lives conspiring against their parents, but they kept each other's secrets from babyhood. Amy was also the only other person in the world who knew how hard their parents' divorce had been on Emily.

Their parents had split up when Emily was sixteen, in a firestorm of arguing and bitterness. Now they'd decided they liked each other. It was inexplicable, as far as Emily was concerned.

Their parents argued about everything. Amy and Emily handled conflict differently. When Amy was upset, she couldn't eat. When Emily was upset, she ate everything. As a result, Amy grew into a taller, even more beautiful blonde version of their mother, while Emily stayed on the short, rounder side. The ballet classes helped to keep her weight down.

By the time their mother filed for divorce, Emily was living in San Francisco, and she had hardly noticed when her father moved out.

Well, of course she had noticed. She just tried not to think about it. She wasn't going to get emotionally involved with a man, ever. Romantic love was nothing but pain. Men cheated. They sat in their recliners, watched sports, drank beer, and grunted once in a while in a woman's general direction. They were gruff and uncommunicative. They made your beautiful mother cry and ask what she'd ever done to deserve being treated that way. Emily wasn't going to let her heart be ground into the dirt under some guy's dress shoes. Her career was enough. She could hold out forever. She didn't need a guy to make her life complete.

Her mom's voice brought Emily back to the present. She sat down again at the table. "Emily, you must not be hungry. You've hardly eaten a thing."

"Mom, everything's delicious, but I'm pretty full." Actually, her stomach churned.

Meg reached over to pat Emily's hand. "It probably wasn't fun getting hurt, but it must have been nice to get a few days off."

"Yes, in some ways. I got some rest, and of course, I spent some time with Brandon."

Emily pushed her plate away. Now that dinner was finished, maybe she could escape from her mother's house without answering more of her parents' questions about Brandon. Maybe she could change the subject. Her dad reentered the dining room with mugs and the coffee carafe, and put Amy in the hot seat.

"Amy, tell us what's new with the store," he said, as he sipped coffee.

"It's fine." Amy stirred milk into her cup. "It's a lot of work, but Valentine's Day really helped me."

"What happened with the balloons that got caught in the stadium roof?" Meg asked.

"Well, the removal made the news," Amy explained. "I didn't get fined. The police said that since they'd been delivered, it was out of my hands." They all took another swallow of coffee, and Emily's dad gave her a look. Uh-oh, the subject was back to Emily again.

"Did Brandon just let go of them? How did they get into the stadium's gridwork?" he asked.

"I don't know," she responded patiently. "When he comes over for dinner, you can ask him that."

"Irresponsible. I'm not sure I like him, and I haven't even met him. What would he have done if the police had charged Amy?"

Emily opened her mouth to protest, but he spoke once more. "We're not done with this, Emily, but we'll discuss all of it at another time. Thank you for a delicious dinner, Meg." He rose from the chair and vanished into the family room. He'd take a short nap while he pretended to watch whatever sporting event was on TV.

The dishes were quickly dealt with, and Emily hugged her mother goodbye. It was hard to believe that her mom would be sixty this year. She felt so fragile, thin, and delicate in Emily's embrace. Her dad was only a few years from retirement, too. Maybe the thought of being at a different stage of life had helped them overcome some of their differences. It was hard to say.

Amy and Emily headed into the family room to find their dad fast asleep in his chair. Emily kissed his scratchy cheek and whispered, "Bye, Dad." He stirred, but didn't wake. Amy kissed his other cheek and said softly, "See you soon."

Amy reached out to hug Emily as they walked to their cars. "Well, at least nobody threw food." She looked at Emily for a long moment. "Yet." One corner of Amy's mouth turned up. "They want to meet him."

"I know. We'll deal with it." Emily fumbled for her car keys.

EMILY SPOTTED BRANDON'S Land Rover in her driveway as she pulled in. He was sitting on the couch when she walked through the front door.

"How'd you get in here?" She dropped her keys on the hallway table.

"Greg's at my house with his girlfriend. Plus, you have beer." Brandon pulled a key from his pocket and waved it at her. Emily recognized it as the extra one she hung up in the kitchen.

"Did I tell you you could have that key?"

"I left you one of mine in return," he parried.

"I don't need to get into your house, do I?" Emily tried

to grab the key out of his hand. She wasn't fast enough. "I don't even know where it is."

Brandon got to his feet and held the key over his head. She could probably get it, if she had a ladder. "You might. It's in Kirkland, and I'll write down the address for you. Come over anytime."

Emily shook her head, and immediately regretted the decision. The headache was almost gone, but it still didn't feel great. "I must not be making enough of a point for you."

He jammed the house key deep into his jeans pocket, and reached out to hug her. "Hello, sugar. It's nice to see you." He rested his cheek against her hair.

"It's nice to see you, too. Give me back my key." He just laughed. He finally let her go, and returned to the couch. "I don't know if you've heard of this, but there's a new invention called a grocery store. There are many varieties of beer available, and some of it is even cold," she said. Emily sat down next to him. He was watching something he called "game film" on her DVD player. "I can't figure out why you're still here. I *know* your life is more exciting than mine."

"I told you," he said patiently. "You have beverages, and my roommate Greg's entertaining at home."

"I don't get it." Emily put her feet up on the coffee table.

"How was dinner?"

"It was awkward. My parents kept hounding me about our engagement." She hauled a breath into her lungs. "Did you have anything to eat?"

"Yeah. The guys stopped at the Wingdome. I think they're still there. It was getting pretty crazy, so I left," he said. The Wingdome was located on the main drag in Kirkland, a haven for singles on Lake Washington's waterfront. Even in wintertime, the restaurant was busy. "A couple of the Shark Babes decided to pay a visit." His dimple flashed. "Damian and Zach were having a back flipping contest outside. Tom stopped by. There was wagering involved."

"Damian, Zach, and Tom? On *cement?*" Every time Emily talked to him, she learned something new. Today must have been the "testosterone poisoning" lesson.

"You've met Damian before. He's the one that called you 'pretty lady.' Zach owes you an apology, and you'll be getting that the next time he sees you."

"He's apologizing for what?"

Brandon's eyes narrowed a bit. "He was rude to you. He will be treating you like the lady you are from now on. Tom's our quarterback. He lives up the street from Damian, Zach, and me."

"They were doing back flips outside on the sidewalk," she repeated, mystified. She turned to him in alarm. "Is this a football player thing? What if they get hurt?"

"They won't." He grinned. "It's a defense thing. I once heard someone say that the coach could leave the offensive players in a room with the door shut. He'd come back, and there'd be nothing out of place. Defensive players? Furniture would be flying out of the windows."

"So, you're juvenile delinquents."

"No. We're more physical." He thought for a moment. "What did your parents have to say?"

Emily couldn't imagine why he wanted to know. She knew her parents would not be happy about a fake engagement. Hopefully, they would keep this little fact to themselves. Then again, after her father's reaction, she didn't think he'd be discussing it around the water cooler at the office anytime soon. Brandon's voice sounded like it came from a distance.

"Hey, sugar. I think I lost you." A big, warm hand patted her thigh. "What's on your mind?"

She shrugged her shoulders. "Nothing."

"Maybe you should tell me about it."

Emily wanted to tell him about it like she wanted a sexually transmitted disease. His mom and dad obviously never had a fight, while her parents made an episode of any daytime TV talk show look tame. Actually, she couldn't say that. Her parents were more into the quiet and lethal arguments, the kind of stuff that left her so shaken she still cringed whenever she thought about it. One would think her former ballerina mom would be serene and unflappable. Hardly. Emily's mom was passionate, excitable, wildly affectionate, and there was never a dull moment when she was around. Her father was an engineer. He would have been more comfortable drawing a diagram of his feelings than talking about them.

Emily shifted away from Brandon. "Do I have to?"

"That's up to you." His eyebrow shot up. "It's not a good memory, is it?"

"Maybe you should tell me what you're talking about."

"There are tears in your eyes," he continued. "I'll bet

you think my parents were straight out of a romance novel."

"They were happy." Emily pictured two little boys with unruly blond curls, and the two loving parents that couldn't wait to spend any time at all with their sons.

"It took them a long time. Like I said, my dad traveled a lot, and my mom worried he wasn't being faithful." Brandon leaned toward her. "Let's just say I overheard one too many conversations between my mom and my aunt Pattie."

She turned to face him. "Did he cheat?"

"If there was one thing my dad would never do, it was cheat. There were other women around. Dylan and I went to his games when we were kids, and we saw them. There was always someone who set her cap for my dad."

"He wasn't taking them up on it?" She twisted her hands in her lap.

"There's nobody else for my dad but my mama."

They sat silently for a while. Emily's stomach churned. She really didn't want to talk about this anymore.

"I wish I could say the same," she said.

She got up and walked into the kitchen. There had to be something to eat in there. She pulled the refrigerator door open and was reaching for an apple when she heard Brandon's voice behind her.

"So, let's talk about it."

"How about an apple?" Emily said. "There's several in here. There are oranges in a bowl on the table, too." She straightened, and he pushed the door closed with his palm.

"If we're going to get to know each other, maybe this is something we need to talk about," he said.

Emily took a deep breath. He leaned against the refrigerator, arms folded, waiting for her to speak. She turned to the sink to rinse off the apple. He was still waiting when she tried to leave the kitchen. She couldn't get around him.

"I don't want to talk about it," Emily said in a low voice. After this afternoon's festivities, another confrontation was not in her plans for the evening. At all.

"If even thinking about it makes you look like you're going to cry, maybe we should."

"This is not open for discussion," she said.

He stepped aside so she could pass. He followed her into the living room, tossed himself down on the couch next to her, and took the remote from her hand.

"I need that." Emily's voice shook.

"What are you afraid of?" he asked softly.

"Maybe you should go home now."

"Maybe I shouldn't. I've obviously struck a nerve, sugar. Why are you hiding from me?" He pinned her shoulder to the couch with his big body. She gave him a shove as she tried to push away from him. "Hey, hey, hey. What's going on here?"

"I don't want to talk about this."

"I guess not." He shoved the remote as far down behind the couch cushion as he could. "We'll sit here, then."

"Fine."

All Emily heard was the soft tick-tock of the clock on

the mantel and their breathing. She crossed her arms over her chest, crossed and recrossed her legs, drummed on her thigh, swung her foot back and forth. She wouldn't look at him, even though she knew he was looking at her. The silence and the tension surrounding it grew. She felt like she could reach out and touch it. One big hand came down to cover her kneecap. She still didn't look up.

"I've got all night," he drawled, and Emily rounded on him—well, as much as she could while he pinned her shoulder to the couch cushion.

"You don't want to hear this. Why would you even care?" she cried out. "This is just make-believe. We don't have a relationship, and stop pretending like we do. My parents' divorce was painful. It still hurts me. Why should I talk about it with someone who won't even be here in a month? I can't believe you think that I should tell you everything . . ."

She fought for control of her emotions. Normally, she didn't cry. She'd cried more in the last three days than she had in a year, though, and she wasn't going to cry again right now. She blinked her tears into submission. She pulled the ring off her finger.

"This is not going to work. I'm giving this back to you. You can get a refund or a store credit, and I'll deal with it," she said.

Brandon took her hand in both of his. "I don't want it back."

"I'm not wearing it."

He pushed the ring back down onto her finger. "Are you done yet?" He grew calmer as Emily grew more upset, and this was not acceptable. "You're just pissed off. Better let me know how mad you are."

"No, I'm not going there with you. This is all your fault. If you'd left me alone, this would never have happened, and I—" She was so frustrated that she didn't know what to say, so she blurted out the first thing that might hurt: "I *hate* you."

"Pretty powerful, sugar," he soothed. "You're bringing out the big guns, aren't you? Keep it up. I'm not going anywhere."

"Maybe I want you to."

"What if you do? You don't. You want someone to yell at, really. You could yell at me some more." He tipped her chin up, and looked into her eyes. "I can take it."

Silence fell. They sat for a few minutes. Nobody moved. She studied her lap. Emily heard his voice in her ear one more time. "How did you find out that your dad was cheating on your mom?"

"How did you know that?" She shook all over. The heat of her anger (and embarrassment at her behavior) was fading into a cold she'd never known before. Losing it in front of anyone else wasn't something she indulged in. She prided herself on keeping a tight rein on her emotions. She'd have to work harder on it.

Brandon's response was to slide his arm around her shoulder.

"Did you see him? Did someone else tell you about it?"

"The neighbor," she whispered.

"She or he saw it?"

Emily nodded. She closed her eyes. In a second, she

was back there, and she wrapped her arms around herself again.

"What happened then?"

"I told my mom." Forcing the words out was a Herculean effort for her.

"What did she say?"

Her voice sounded like it was coming from a million miles away. "It was awful. She was so pale, and I felt like I slapped her. She asked me who told me, and then she went upstairs, packed a bag for Amy and me, and we went to stay overnight at our grandma's house. By the time we came home, my dad was staying in the guest room. Mom wouldn't talk about it."

"Did you try talking to your dad?"

"We didn't see him. He worked all the time." She rubbed her nose with one hand. Brandon was stroking her upper arm, slowly. He listened, and he didn't seem to judge. To her surprise, the tension drained out of her as she spoke, and she sagged against him.

"Were you close before?"

"We were closer."

"What do you think would happen if you tried talking to him about it?"

She swallowed hard. "We don't." The unwritten rule of the Hamilton family: Never, *ever* talk about what happened with Mom and Dad. It wasn't open for discussion. She'd tried, more than once over the years. It didn't go well.

"Maybe you should tell me what happened at dinner, then."

Emily took a deep breath. "My parents aren't happy about a fake engagement. They're worried other people will find out." She forced lightness into her voice. "Plus, we're making a mockery of the institution of marriage, according to them."

"Is that so?" Brandon appeared to be stifling a laugh. He patted her knee with his free hand. She felt herself relaxing more and more.

"I'm sorry I yelled at you. I don't hate you." For the second time today, she was apologizing. She evidently enjoyed the taste of shoe leather. Before she could stop herself, she reached up to kiss his cheek. His stubble tickled her nose. She couldn't stop the cross between a snort and a giggle she made.

"I know you don't." He moved closer, turning toward her. "I'm sorry for bringing up something that made you cry." His arm slid to her waist and tightened around her. He took her cheek in his free hand. Electricity sizzled over Emily's skin. He wasn't going to kiss her, was he?

Seconds later, his mouth brushed over hers, the barest contact. "Are we okay?"

Adrenaline arced through her. In an instant, she was breathless, boneless, and nodding at him like one of those bobbing-head dog figurines people used to put on the back window ledge of their cars.

"Um, yeah. Fine."

His voice dropped. He stroked her lower lip with his thumb. "You're sure about that?"

She started nodding again, and his hand slipped to

the back of her neck. He was definitely going to kiss her. Her eyelids fluttered shut.

She felt the tender touch of his lips on hers, the way her mouth molded to his. She couldn't help but smile a little. He kissed her as though he had all the time in the world. He lingered, he teased, and Emily wondered how she managed to get through every other day of her life before experiencing what it was like to kiss him. She felt the tip of his tongue sketch the seam of her lips, and she tasted mint as that tongue slipped into her mouth. Mint, and some indescribable thing that she could never identify to anyone else, but knew she'd never forget. She reached up blindly to slide her fingers into his hair, which curled around them like liquid satin. The melting spread.

She couldn't remember why she originally objected to his kissing her, but she'd officially changed her position on it. He was really, really good at it, she discovered, and she wanted more. She felt the warmth of his breath in her hair as she snuggled against him. She tried to catch her breath.

"It might be tough to be engaged to a woman who hated me," he continued. "I've dated women who've hated me. I've even slept with a few of them. They weren't wearing my ring, though."

Emily had to smile. "There's a first time for everything."

She heard his low chuckle. He hadn't let go of her. She could get used to this.

"Back to the subject." He thought for a moment. "Maybe you should talk with your dad about all this."

Immediately her insides clenched. "I don't think so."

"Hear me out. It's been a lot of years. It still hurts. Maybe you need to hear his side of what happened. Maybe he has something he wants to tell you."

"How could he justify it?"

"Maybe he wouldn't. He might like to say he's sorry."

He propped his feet up on the coffee table, crossing his legs at the ankle. Emily laid her head against his shoulder. They were lost in their own thoughts for a few minutes.

"Didn't you mention dessert earlier? If you'll drive, I'll buy," Emily said. "How about some ice cream?"

Brandon got to his feet and reached out for her hand. "I'm in. Let's go, sugar."

Chapter Ten

BEING ENGAGED REALLY brought the women out of the woodwork. Brandon glanced over at a line of several hundred people snaking around the side of Sharks Stadium, waiting for Sharks players' autographs. One-third of them were females who appeared to be between twenty-two and forty. In other words, he was going to spend the next couple of hours giving the words "No, thank you" a workout.

He sat at a long table with four of his teammates inside the Sharks' pro store. Signing autographs was part of his job description. The team wanted the best PR they could produce. Brandon wanted to remind the team's front office he was someone the Sharks would regret cutting or trading due to community backlash if his contract extension wasn't offered.

Brandon wasn't opposed to female attention. He enjoyed it. He enjoyed the attention he received from a certain diva named Emily who wore his engagement ring the most, however. Unfortunately, Emily was out of town performing. He missed everything about her, up to and including when she got bossy with him. His little diva could be compared to a pampered, purebred Persian. She had no problem tilting her nose in the air, swishing her tail, and walking away when he was pissing her off. She'd throw a sweet smile over her shoulder, though, and he was helpless again.

The perfume she wore drove him crazy, too. He remembered her scent when she was nowhere around: It smelled like peaches and freshly mown grass.

Speaking of helpless, the first woman of marriageable age skipped over his teammates Zach and Tom like they had failed to shower recently. She had long, dark hair. The third finger of her left hand was bare. Her makeup applicator was set on "thick." She wore stilettos, a micro-mini, and a low-cut top showcasing her after-market breasts to their best advantage. She extended a team cap to Brandon, flashing him a huge, whitened smile. "Would you sign this, please?"

"Of course I will." He reached out for the cap. She didn't let go. He gave it an experimental tug.

"You know what I'd like even better than your autograph? How about having a drink with my friends and me later? You'll be thirsty from all this signing." She leaned over the table a bit to give him the maximum amount of cleavage on display.

His buddy Damian sat next to him. Damian let out a snort. Brandon managed to pry the cap out of her hand

and scribbled his name and jersey number with a Sharpie on the back of it.

"Thank you for the invitation, but I'm going to have to say 'no'. My fiancée doesn't like it when I date."

"She doesn't have to know," the woman coaxed.

"Thank you, but no, thank you." He handed the cap back to her.

The guy next to her in line gave her a glare. "Do you actually know anything about football, or are you here because you think he's handsome?"

The woman flounced away. She didn't ask Damian for his signature, either. "I think I'm insulted," Damian said in a low voice, but his broad grin belied his words.

Brandon shook his head. The signing continued. Brandon received many more amorous invitations over the next hour and a half. He did his best to be polite, but he couldn't believe these women thought he would do something as stupid as accepting an invitation to cheat on his fiancée with them. He wasn't interested, and he couldn't imagine where they got the idea he would be. His single teammates were eagerly scooping up a few of the disappointed females, however.

Brandon signed five hundred autographs that evening. He and his four teammates were whisked out of the pro shop and into a waiting SUV for the trip back to their cars by security. Instead of going back to the team facilities, Damian talked the driver into dropping them off at the Sharks' favorite bar.

One of the more frustrating things about being a professional athlete was the fact it was sometimes tough to go out in public. The recognition factor increased along with the number of Sharks involved. Tonight's five meant the group would be besieged anyplace else but the hole-in-the-wall Brandon and Matt Stephens had found during Brandon's rookie season.

The place was older. The décor was early seventies—orange Naugahyde-covered benches, dark wooden tables scarred from years of use, industrial carpet of an indeterminate shade of blue. The place was littered with neon signs advertising various alcohols. At least ten flat-screen televisions were suspended from the ceiling in various places throughout the seating area. The food was plentiful, delicious, and nothing on the menu could be classified as *nouvelle cuisine*. Best of all, it was a fairly open secret among the mid-twenties to fifties clientele that the pro athletes they might see bellying up to the bar (or indulging in an order of chili fries during the off-season,) kept showing up as long as people left them alone.

The BrewPub was comfortable for everyone from Boeing blue-collar workers to thirsty Microsoft billionaires. The athletes fit right in.

After ten PM on a weeknight, there weren't many cars in the parking lot. Brandon's teammates followed him through the front door to the large table against the back wall. A few people glanced up from their beverages or food, noted the arrivals, and went back to discussing the Mariners' latest victory or the upcoming schedule of the University of Washington's football team.

Damian seized a menu as the group arranged themselves around the table. He was deep in consultation while three of his teammates compared notes on how many phone numbers they got slipped during the signing.

"Hey, McKenna, they were all talking about you, too." Tom, the Sharks' quarterback, attempted to imitate one of the women he talked with earlier. "'I can't believe he's getting married. What does he see in that opera chick, anyway? I'm cuter than she is.'"

"If he went out with me, he'd forget all about her," the newest Shark, Chris, chimed in.

"Maybe they'll break up." All five men laughed at Zach's attempt to sound like a female.

Brandon nodded at a passing server. "I need some beer before you ladies start on the post-game wrap-up."

"Your loss is our gain, brother. The dark-haired one with the big rack, short skirt, and spike heels is meeting me tomorrow night at Feedback Lounge. I'm sure she'll forget all about you when she meets my friend," Zach told Brandon. He pointed at his groin for emphasis.

Brandon shook his head. He loved these guys, but he was consistently amazed at how little they knew about him. Ms. Big Jugs wouldn't have been on his to-do list in the first place. There had been too many women over the years with whom there was nothing to talk about five minutes after he pulled his pants back on. That part of his life was over the moment he met Emily, and he was grateful.

The server left with an order that would keep the cook and the bartender busy for a while. Brandon's phone buzzed in his pocket: A text from Emily. She asked him how the signing went. He tapped out, "It was fine. I miss you," and hit "send."

"Let me guess. The other half wants to know what you're doing," Tom teased.

"She's saying goodnight." Brandon took a long swallow of the pint of Mac and Jack's Amber Ale another server had set down in front of him.

"She's checking to see if you're with someone else," Zach said.

"Maybe your woman is jealous and suspicious. Emily's not that type," Damian said. Damian had a bit of a crush on Brandon's fiancée, it seemed.

"Oh, yes, she is. You just haven't seen it yet," Zach informed the entire table.

Brandon responded by draining his pint glass. Maybe it was best if he called a cab and went home. He didn't want to spend the next half hour impressing on Zach why it wasn't a good idea to say anything remotely critical of Emily, or any other young woman of his acquaintance, in his presence. He really wanted some of those chili fries, but Damian would eat his order. He pulled thirty dollars out of his wallet, slipping the bills under the empty pint glass.

He checked his phone to see another "xxx ooo" message from Emily, and hit the "stored contacts" icon to find a number for a cab. A commotion at the front door of the bar made him look up from his phone's screen. His stomach lurched.

Anastasia and two of her model friends were cantering toward their table. She wouldn't be caught dead in this place while they were dating. What the hell was she doing here now? She flipped a curtain of long, straight hair over a bony shoulder. The oversized sweater she wore slid off the opposite shoulder. She wasn't wearing a bra, and the other side of the sweater showed signs of sliding right off, too. Half an inch more, and she'd give a whole new meaning to the words "wardrobe malfunction." The two women she was with wore dresses that left even less to the imagination, and impossibly high heels.

"Well, look who's here," she purred. "Just the man I wanted to talk with." She pulled out the chair on Brandon's right and sank into it. She was glancing around the table already. She clearly wanted a cigarette, and there were no ashtrays available.

"Smoking's not allowed here, Anastasia," he said. "Maybe you should leave."

"They won't care." She pulled out a lighter, laid it on the table in front of her, and reached into her bag once more. Brandon grabbed the lighter off the table.

"Maybe you didn't hear me. You're not doing this," he said.

She tossed her head. "Where's your fiancée?"

"Why should you care? You and I aren't together anymore."

Her smile was feline. It matched the exaggerated cat-eye black eyeliner she wore. She tossed a box of Marlboro Reds onto the table in front of them. "I need my lighter."

He sat forward in his chair. "What is it that you want from me?"

"You must miss me." She shook a cigarette out of the

pack and slid it between her fingers. "I know I miss you. Let's get out of here and go somewhere quieter." He knew what she meant by "somewhere quieter"—her bedroom. He wasn't interested. He wondered why he never noticed how cold her eyes were the entire time they were together. She gave him what he was sure she thought was a sultry glance.

He felt like he was observing the entire scene from somewhere overhead—Anastasia's belief she could seduce him with nothing more than a glance, and his realization that he couldn't believe she'd ever lured him into her spider web in the first place.

The guys pretended not to notice what was going on at their end of the table. Zach and one of Anastasia's model friends went so far as to grab a two-top a short distance away. In other words, they expected trouble.

"Maybe I need to remind you what you said about me on that entertainment TV show." His voice dropped. "I'm not interested. Take your friends and get the hell out."

She let out a sigh of faux distress. "You can't believe I really meant that." She rolled the unlit cigarette between her fingers again. "They wanted a good quote. You know how amazing it was with us." She leaned closer. He almost choked on the wave of stale smoke, too much perfume, and evidence of her preferred method of weight loss—vomiting—hitting his nostrils. "Remember the entire day in bed?"

Oh, he did. He wondered what he could shower with to scrub the images off his brain pan, too. He couldn't believe he spent any time at all with her now. Supermodel or not, she didn't do a thing for him. She reached out and plucked the lighter out of his fist. "You have to know there isn't a guy in this place that would turn me down, Brandon."

The server arrived with a platter of food, noted the cigarette and lighter in Anastasia's hand, and snapped, "There's no smoking here. You'll have to leave."

It happened so fast he had no time to evade her. Anastasia leaned forward, wrapped one arm around his neck, and kissed him. She made it good, too—she writhed against him like a snake, she tried to stick her tongue in his mouth, she did everything but give him a lap dance. He pushed her away.

He sprang to his feet. "Get out," he said in a low voice.

She grabbed her handbag off the table. "You still want me. Your little friend does, that's for sure," she taunted.

Their eyes met. Her smug expression told him she believed she'd won. *Count to ten,* he told himself. *Don't do anything you'll regret later.* He felt the phone in his pocket vibrate again. Emily. He'd never wanted to wipe his mouth off after one of her kisses, or scrub till every trace of her was off his skin and out of his life. But he did now.

"You know where to find me," Anastasia said as she walked away.

Chapter Eleven

A FEW DAYS later Emily was home again in Seattle after five weeks of performing in Chicago, but Brandon was in Los Angeles filming a commercial for Gatorade. He'd be back tomorrow. She missed him like she would an appendage. She was excited to see him again, but apprehensive. Between his absence and her nerves about continuing a fake engagement that was starting to mean a little too much, she wondered how she would broach the fact the thirty days they agreed on had come and gone while she was out of town.

She heard a knock at her front door, threw on a robe, and hurried downstairs to discover a courier waiting on her front porch.

"Good morning, Miss Hamilton. This is for you." The guy handed her a small Tiffany's carrier bag and proffered a clipboard and pen. "Please sign by your name."

"Certainly. Thank you so much."

He reclaimed his clipboard, touched his cap, and got back into his vehicle. She shut her front door, reaching into the little bag. She pulled out a sturdy, cream-colored note card, recognizing Brandon's dark, heavy handwriting.

It read, *They match your ring. Happy engagement, sugar. – B*

She pulled out another small blue box tied with a white satin ribbon and flipped it open to find diamond stud earrings the size of peas. She hugged the little box to herself. If he kept it up she'd need a security guard.

Her phone chirped. A text had arrived. She grabbed the phone out of her robe pocket. Speak of the devil: It was Brandon.

Let's have coffee tomorrow morning at the shop across from Marina Park in Kirkland. We need to talk.

There wasn't an adult on the planet that failed to understand the significance of the phrase, "We need to talk." After all, most adults have used it at one time or another to rid themselves of a relationship that wasn't working out.

He wasn't dumping her, was he? She felt cold shivers race up her spine.

Maybe he wanted to break things off in a public place so she wouldn't cause a scene. He'd shown no indication that he was getting ready to break up with her before now. Hopefully, the diamond earrings weren't a really expensive kiss-off gift.

SHORTLY AFTER NINE AM the next morning Emily walked into the coffee shop and spotted Brandon sitting at a table in the back. He saw her, too, and stood up. As she got closer, she noticed that his curls were still damp from the shower he must have taken after his workout. He wore an LSU t-shirt, Levis, running shoes, and a huge smile.

"Sugar," he breathed into her ear, and kissed her cheek. "I missed you. I like the new earrings."

"I missed you, too." She reached up to touch one earlobe. "I love them. Thank you again. I can't believe you did this."

He stroked her cheek with one big hand. "It's my pleasure."

Emily took a deep breath. If she was confused before, she was now wondering if she needed some type of Brandon translator. He was acting like everything was fine, so why had he used the phrase "we need to talk"? *Relax*, she told herself.

"What would you like to drink?" he asked.

"Tea would be great."

"Coming right up." He moved around her and went to the counter to order.

She had butterflies in her stomach. The blood bubbled through her veins like the finest champagne. She felt lightheaded, excited, beyond happy. She heard Brandon's laughter as he spoke to one of the baristas. He returned to his chair just moments later.

"Look what I have," he said, nodding at the plate he carried. He'd not only brought the tea she asked for, but he'd brought baked goods.

"Chocolate cake and diamonds? A girl could get used to this," she said.

"I have to keep you sweet." He took her hand and kissed the back of it. "Here." He sliced off a bite with his fork and slipped it between her lips. The cake, with the tiniest hint of mint, was delicious. He leaned over the table. "You know I have to kiss you now."

Listening to him speak was causing a fairly embarrassing reaction, along with the barest brush of his lips on the back of her hand. Her poor nipples could've cut glass. She squirmed on the chair, but it had nothing to do with nerves.

"In front of all these people?" she said. Then again, she really didn't care about them right now. She couldn't concentrate on anything or anyone but him.

"Of course, I am." He moved closer. "Would you like me to?"

Someone obviously turned up the heat in the shop. They were lost in their own world.

Emily fed him a forkful of cake. A bit of frosting clung to the corner of his mouth. She wiped it off with her fingertip. He caught her hand in his and licked her finger. His eyes met hers.

"Let's not waste it."

She forgot to breathe.

"Excuse me," Emily heard an excited female voice say. "Aren't you Brandon McKenna?"

Two young women in their twenties stood beside their table. Both were focused on Brandon. They didn't acknowledge her.

"I am," Brandon said.

"Oh, my God," the young woman said. Her pale

blonde hair was pulled into a ponytail. She wore a skin-tight t-shirt and low-slung jeans. "I am such a Sharks fan. It's so exciting to meet you!" She was bouncing on the balls of her feet. She thrust out her hand to him and said breathlessly, "I'm Kris. Could I have your autograph?" She began rooting through her purse for a pen.

"Sure." He smiled. "By the way, this is Emily, my fiancée."

The friend rolled her eyes. Kris handed Brandon a ballpoint pen. To Emily's amazement, she pulled up her t-shirt, leaned over, and grinned.

"Right here."

She wanted him to sign her breast, in a crowded coffee shop, in front of Emily.

Brandon averted his eyes from Kris's perky assets. "I'm happy to sign a piece of paper for you, but I won't sign that." He gave her a look Emily hadn't seen anywhere but in the game film they watched, quickly scribbled his signature on an unused napkin on the table, and said, "It was—nice—to meet you. Thanks for your support."

Kris wasn't getting the hint. She whipped out her cell phone.

"Let's pose for a picture," she said.

She tried to install herself on his lap while pushing her cell phone into her friend's outstretched hand. He managed to shove his chair back before she succeeded. She grabbed the side of the table so she wouldn't fall.

"Sugar, it's time for us to leave." He picked up their coffee cups and moved around the two women to take her arm.

"I'll get more cake to go if you'd like," he said in a low voice.

"You're an asshole," Kris hissed. "You—you screwed my friend, but you won't let me sit on your lap?"

Emily opened her mouth to respond, but he pulled her away. "Keep moving," he said.

She knew from the blank expression in Brandon's eyes (and the flush that was slowly spreading up his neck) that he was much angrier than he appeared on the surface. He stopped at the counter for a moment, said something to the barista, and swept Emily out the front door.

"Let's walk." He handed Emily's cup to her, slid an arm around her waist, and they hurried across the street to Marina Park. "We'll go back for cake later."

"Does that happen a lot?"

"No." He shook his head.

"Do that young woman's parents know she's—Okay. I realize I'm a bit old-fashioned, but ..." Emily's voice trailed off. He was walking so fast Emily ran to keep up with him. She reached out for the waistband of his jeans and panted, "Wait a second."

He tugged her over to a bench. They sat in silence for a while, watching children run and play along the sandy beach.

"So, I hate to even bring it up," she said.

"I wasn't involved with her." His voice was tense. "I prefer women, not little girls." He let out a long, frustrated sigh. "People approach me. Most of the time, they're nice. They want an autograph or they want to talk a little. That stuff?" His eyes hardened again. "That hasn't been happening as much lately, but I'll never get used to it." He thought for a moment. "Do you get people coming up to you?"

"It's usually an arranged thing after a performance or at a benefit. I haven't had anyone who's wanted me to autograph their breast, though."

He gave a low chuckle, and seemed to relax a little. "I'll let you sign mine." His arm slid around Emily's shoulders again. "She was rude to you, too."

"Listen, bruiser, that was the least of it, wasn't it? I'm fine," she said.

"Yes, you are." His fingertips stroked her upper arm.

Emily's face was hot. She knew she was blushing.

"The kids are cute," he mused.

They watched a toddler in a hot pink cotton romper and pink Nikes lurch through the sand. Her blonde pigtails bounced with every step, and her eyes were cobalt blue marbles in a rounded baby face. She chanted, "Mama Mama," as she moved.

"She's sweet, isn't she?" Emily commented.

A woman Emily believed was the little girl's mother hurried after her with a jacket, a bucket, and a small shovel. Princess must have been digging in the sand.

"You want one of those?" Brandon asked, inclining his head toward the little girl.

"Maybe. Someday."

The little girl plopped down on a well-padded rump. She couldn't decide whether to laugh or cry, and her mother swept her up in her arms. "We have to go, Kate," she said.

Kate's response was to screw up her little face. A couple of fat tears rolled down her cheeks. Kate's mama put her down on the path in front of them, and Kate lurched toward Brandon at surprising speed.

She hurled herself onto his thigh, regarded him with wide eyes, and said, "Da."

He laughed, and gently stroked her cheek. "Hello, Kate. I'm Brandon."

She scrambled into his lap, sat up, and grinned.

"Katie, that's not okay. We need to go."

Two more big tears rolled down Kate's cheeks. "Da," she insisted.

"No, honey, Dada's at work. We'll see him later." The woman hurried toward Brandon with outstretched hands and an apologetic smile.

"I should be so lucky," he told Kate's mama. "She's beautiful."

"How old is she?" Emily asked Kate's mother. Kate crawled into Emily's lap.

"She's fourteen months old," her mother said. "She's fast."

"I've heard about that," Emily said. Emily gestured toward Kate, who leaned back against her chest. "Is this okay?"

"Sure," her mother said.

Kate smelled like baby shampoo and laundry soap, overlaid with a sweet, clean scent. Her cotton romper was soft against Emily's fingertips. Kate reached out for Brandon again. Emily relished the sweet weight for a moment, and then handed Kate to him.

"She's in love with you already," Emily said.

"I have that effect on women," he deadpanned. "Katie, you've stolen my heart. What will I do?" He pressed a kiss onto her cheek. Kate let out a baby laugh and captured his face in her hands. She put her little mouth on his chin. To her surprise, Emily choked up.

"She's giving kisses," Emily managed to say.

"You'll have one of your own someday," Kate's mother assured her.

Emily had heard that many times before, but she always dismissed it as something that happened to other people, not her. Today, Kate's mother's words pierced her heart.

"I have to get Kate to a doctor's appointment," Kate's mother said, "or we'd love to stay."

Brandon carefully transferred Kate back to her mother. "Bye, sweetheart. Maybe we can play at the park another day," he said.

"Are you here often?" Kate's mother asked.

He glanced over at Emily. "Not usually, but I see that's going to change."

Emily held out her hand. "I'm Emily. This is Brandon."

"I'm Brianna. Maybe we'll see you around."

With a wave, Brianna and Kate hurried up the path to the parking lot. Brandon pulled Emily a little closer as they continued watching other children play in the sand.

"What do you think our baby would look like?"

"Hmm? What are you talking about?"

Emily was a million miles away. Actually, she imagined a small, soft bundle in her arms and the look on

Brandon's face when he saw her for the first time. Amy was always the one who longed for a home and a family. Suddenly, Emily knew why. She couldn't rock a career to sleep at night, or watch it play in the sand.

He waved one big hand in front of Emily's eyes. "You're daydreaming."

"Our baby? Are you on crack?" she said. He let out a laugh. Emily smiled in response. "Probably lots of blond curls, like you."

"Maybe I want her to be a redhead, like you."

"She'd probably be a spitfire, then." She patted him on the thigh. "It could be a boy."

"Maybe. I think I'd like a daughter," he mused. Brandon stared out at the lake in front of them. "She sure was cute."

Something new and sweet unfurled inside Emily. In only a few minutes' time, the biological clock she believed was broken beyond all repair started ticking. Surprisingly, she knew the only man she wanted to remedy the problem sat next to her.

He hadn't said a word about the time ticking away on their engagement. Then again, she hadn't brought it up, either. Obviously, bookings had never been better. The arrangement worked well for both of them. At the same time, she enjoyed his company. She looked forward to seeing him. She realized that after all the hours of talking there was still more to talk about. She confided things to Brandon she never told anyone else before, and he seemed equally comfortable with her.

The silence stretched on as Brandon and Emily

watched people strolling through the park. She tugged the ring off her finger. After all, he'd said thirty days.

"You probably want this back," she said.

He turned toward her, and she put the ring in his palm. "What are you talking about, sugar?"

"The thirty days is up," Emily said. It was hard to force the words out past the lump in her throat. It was best to keep this businesslike. "We agreed."

She saw momentary confusion in his eyes, but as she watched, amusement took over. He raised one eyebrow. "So, you think you'll get rid of me that easily."

The tiniest flicker of hope came to life.

"Let's see how it goes," he said.

He took her hand in his, and put the ring back on her finger. Emily didn't realize she was holding her breath till that moment. Their fingers tangled, he slid his arm around her shoulders again, and she moved closer. She saw the dimple in his cheek deepen as he smiled.

Two weeks later, Emily was scheduled to take part in Seattle Opera's annual fundraising auction. It was a great chance for those who loved opera to meet performers and bid on items such as dinner with major opera stars that typically performed at The Met, Covent Garden, or La Scala. It was formal, so she spent most of the afternoon getting ready to go.

She glanced out the upstairs window in time to see Brandon pulling into the driveway. He got out of the Land Rover, and her mouth went dry. He wore a tailored black tuxedo. For a guy who spent most of his time in threadbare Levis and rugby shirts, formalwear suited him. All that black, combined with his angelic blond curls and perpetually innocent expression, was scalding hot. He dazzled.

Emily's biggest job at the moment was getting down the stairs without tripping over her dress. She could drool over him later.

She wore a royal blue silk, sleeveless gown that ruched from the deep V-neck down over her abdomen, pulling the fabric against her hips. The dress flowed into a full skirt with a short train. It fit her like it loved her. She left her stilettos in the closet; low-heeled sandals worked better, since she'd be on her feet all evening. The only jewelry she wore were Brandon's engagement ring and the diamond studs he gave her.

She managed to sweep to the front door without sustaining a sports injury, and she pulled it open for him.

"You changed your mind about the powder blue tux," she said. Her fingertips strayed down his sleeve.

"The designer in question was fresh out of that color."

"Must have been last season, huh?"

"Sugar," he reproved. "My mama would have my—my hide, and so would you." He kissed her cheek. She closed her eyes for a moment, breathing him in.

"You look beautiful," he said; around his fingertip he wound a tendril of hair that had escaped the French twist she spent two hours in a stylist's chair over that afternoon

"Oh, this old thing? I wear it to wash the floor in. You look great."

"I'm glad you like it." He picked her evening purse up

from the hallway table and handed it to her. "You'll need a wrap. It's chilly out."

She turned her back to retrieve it and heard him attempt to stifle a snort. He draped the black cashmere shawl she handed him around her shoulders.

"I hate covering all that up," he said.

"You are such a flirt—"

"Shall we?" He offered his arm.

They walked out the front door of Emily's house, and he opened the passenger door to his Land Rover. Emily looked up at the seat and wondered how she would get herself and her voluminous dress into it. She reached down to gather up the skirt of her dress in her hands.

Brandon noticed her difficulty. "I've got you." He swept her up in his arms. "Are you sure you want to go to this thing?"

She wrapped her arms around his neck. "Right now, no." Her fingers tangled in his curls. He chuckled, and she felt spreading heat low in her abdomen. God, he was sexy. Her wrap slipped off her shoulders.

"Nice view," he said.

"You're looking down my dress." She tried for outrage, but the effect was lost when she let out a laugh.

"Of course I am. Damn, sugar, you have some great lingerie."

"I had to wear a push-up bra to make—why am I telling you this?"

"You can't resist me." He sniffed the air. "You smell great, too. What *is* that stuff?"

"It's called Petite Cherie," she said.

"Mmm. I can't decide if I want to kiss it, or eat it." He nuzzled her hairline. She was fairly sure the neighbors were getting quite a show. At the same time, right now she didn't care. Darkness and silence covered the street she lived on, and they were hidden in shadow.

"We'll be late."

"You say that like it's a bad thing." He held her even closer. The warmth of his breath teased her ear. "Think how much more fun we'd have if we stayed home, and I peeled this dress right off you."

Emily stifled a gasp, but it wasn't like the idea hadn't already occurred to her, too.

"You know, you drive a pretty hard bargain," she said.

"You have no idea."

Well, yes, she did. She could feel a fairly impressive erection against her hip.

His tongue trailed around the shell of her ear. "You're going to have to take this earring off. I can't nibble your earlobe with all of that hardware on." Emily shifted restlessly in his arms. "Got ants in your pants?"

By now, her entire body was throbbing. She could fight fire with fire, though. She traced the muscle in the side of his neck with her tongue. She felt him tremble in response. She kissed the skin behind his earlobe, letting her mouth linger.

"Two can play at this game," she said. She heard a choked laugh.

"Well, then, my evil plan's working," he said. He set her down on the car seat, made sure the train to her dress was inside, and shut the passenger door behind him. A few seconds later, he hurled himself into the driver's seat and pulled her into his arms with one fluid motion. "I'm going to kiss you until you change your mind."

His mouth came down on hers, firm but tender. She speared her fingers through his curls. His tongue slid into her mouth, stroking hers, teasing and igniting. She grabbed at him with greedy hands, pulling him closer. He was a starving man, and she was a four-course feast. The lipstick she'd applied earlier was long gone. Minutes later, she was flushed, sweaty, and more turned on than she could remember being since the last time they went at each other in a semi-public place. She would have to do some thinking later about why they were making out in his car when she had a perfectly good bed behind a locked door, less than a hundred feet away.

"More?" he asked.

"God, yes," she groaned.

He slid one hand under the fabric of her dress, slowly scraping her hardened nipple with his thumb as he kissed his way down her neck. The rough calluses on his fingers from lifting weights almost drove her out of her mind when he cupped and caressed the delicate skin. She let out a moan. She heard his soft laugh.

In the midst of a drugging stew of hormones, adrenaline, and lust it occurred to Emily that she was going to have one hell of a beard burn later. It didn't stop her from grabbing his face and pulling his mouth onto hers again. Second base wasn't enough right now. She reached out to drag her fingers over the bulge in his pants, too.

She heard something that sounded like tapping on the

driver's side window. They both ignored it. The tapping got more insistent.

Brandon pulled his mouth off hers, and jerked his hand out of the V-neck of her dress. He was breathing hard. His blue-green irises were almost black with arousal. He turned in his seat to wipe enough of the condensation off the car's window to see out of it.

Emily yanked up the top of her dress, and ran one finger over her lips to salvage whatever lipstick she could.

One of Emily's neighbors, a previously harmless older woman, was standing outside the car when Brandon lowered his window.

"Emily, I got some of your mail by mistake. I thought you might need it." She smiled innocently as she handed two sales flyers, an envelope full of coupons to local businesses, and the garbage bill to Brandon. "Have a nice evening, you two."

The neighbor scuttled inside her house after Brandon showed his teeth.

IN THE END, reason prevailed. Well, she also knew it would not be a great idea to blow off Seattle Opera's management and the company's most ardent financial supporters. It took a Herculean amount of self-control to resist dragging him to her bedroom and finishing what they'd started. Putting herself back together without benefit of hair stylist or makeup artist was quite a challenge as well. Tendrils of hair dangled from her formerly perfect French twist. Her skin was rosy from Brandon's kisses and the amateur dermabrasion of beard burn. Her dress was surprisingly intact.

"If we stayed home, I'd turn you inside out," he assured her.

"I still have to go to the benefit. I have to . . . Well, I promised I would be there."

His mouth curved into a smile. He looked rumpled and even more adorable as a result. She was afraid she just looked like a mess.

"You've talked me into it. I'm going to need more than appetizers, though. We're stopping at Burgermaster on the way home."

They could both afford the finest restaurants. At the same time, the thought of going to a drive-in with a man in a tuxedo made her smile again. It wouldn't be an NFL star and an opera diva, for once. It would be two people who enjoyed each other's company, no matter where they found themselves.

They arrived at McCaw Hall a few minutes before starting time. Brandon surrendered the keys to the valet, but he insisted on helping Emily out himself.

"Maybe I should carry you again."

"I'd make quite an entrance."

He set her on her feet, draped the wrap around her shoulders, and offered his arm again. "Shall we, my lady?"

"Please tell me I do not look like a gigantic mess," she said.

"Every guy here will take one look at you and know I am the luckiest man in America," he said.

They walked through a gauntlet of video cameras and press photographers shouting their names.

"Sugar, if we pose for them, they may leave us alone," he said into her ear.

"That's what you think."

He turned toward the cameras, sliding a protective arm around her waist. She rested her forehead against his chest for a moment. The flashes were blinding. "Emily, smile for us," one of the photographers shouted. "Let's see that ring."

She laid her left hand on Brandon's arm. More flashes erupted as a result.

Brandon thanked them, and then ushered her inside the hall.

"That went well," he said.

She snagged two glasses of champagne from a passing waiter. Brandon was pretty much a beer guy, but he sipped champagne and stuck by her side while she greeted a stream of Seattle Opera supporters.

"You're a star, sugar," he said. "They love my girl."

She had to chuckle a little after overhearing, "Who's the guy with Miss Hamilton?"

"Some of these people have had season tickets to the opera for thirty years," she told him. "They may not be NFL fans."

"Hopefully, that means you're giving me the quick and dirty tutorial." He glanced around at the framed posters advertising upcoming productions.

"What would you like to learn first—roles sung predominantly by full lyric sopranos, or the operas of Verdi?"

"This is going to be tougher than Sharks defensive sets," he murmured.

A few people turned around, smiled at Emily's obvious amusement, and went back to discussing productions and singers they'd seen, what would be on the schedule for next year, and the auction. The auction, and passed appetizers, would start in a few minutes.

One of the items being auctioned off was post-performance drinks with Emily after next season's *Cosi fan tutte*. The other addition to the catalog had just been confirmed yesterday. Some lucky woman (or women) would be in charge of spray-tanning a group of Sharks players before their performance as spear-carrying barbarians in *Norma*. The players in question were supposed to be here tonight.

"Do you see any of the guys yet, sugar?" Brandon said, echoing her thoughts. "They should be around here somewhere. I told them they needed to wear black tie."

"I'm sure they'll turn up soon," Emily said. She extended her hand to a corporate supporter, who brought her knuckles to his lips.

"It's lovely to meet you, Miss Hamilton," the debonair older gentleman said and extended his hand to Brandon. "This must be your young man."

Emily was drawing a blank on the gentleman's name. "This is my fiancé, Brandon McKenna."

"It's a pleasure to meet you, too, Brandon. I'm Adam Schaeffer, Seattle Opera's board chairman. When I'm not there, I'm with Schaeffer, Schaeffer and Schaeffer." He and Brandon shook hands.

"Mr. Schaeffer, it's an honor. I play football for the Sharks." Brandon smiled and said, "I'm a bit curious. Perhaps you could fill me in on what a board member for Seattle Opera does."

"I'd love to. Call me Adam, Brandon."

To Emily's surprise, the two men walked away, deep in conversation. It was the oddest couple she could remember, but Brandon seemed comfortable.

A beautiful older woman in vintage Dior took Emily's hand.

"I'm Lillian Tollifson. This is my grandson, Jake."

She tipped her head toward the man standing beside her. Jake Tollifson appeared to be in his late thirties. Emily wasn't familiar with Jake, but her sister was. Amy saw his name in one of the programs she got at a performance last year and filled Emily in. Single, handsome Jake had done very, very well in the software industry.

Emily spotted Mrs. Tollifson, who looked like a stiff wind would blow her away, at the auctions in previous years; but last year, she sang. She was unavailable to mix until after her performance. Most of the crowd was gone by the time Emily emerged from the dressing room.

"It's great to meet you both," Emily said. Brandon's hand touched the small of her back once more. "This is my fiancé, Brandon McKenna."

Brandon kissed the back of Mrs. Tollifson's hand. She winked at him. There didn't appear to be a woman alive he could not charm.

"Grandmother loved your Sophie," Jake said to Emily. "Will you be singing it again?"

"I know Santa Fe Opera's mounting the production next year, and I'm already signed to sing the role. I'm sorry it won't be here."

Mrs. Tollifson poked her grandson with an elbow. "We can fly there."

"Of course, Grandmother." Jake smiled sheepishly at Emily. "She loves you."

Emily reached out to give Mrs. Tollifson a gentle hug.

"I told Jake that he waited too long," she said into Emily's ear. "If that young man of yours doesn't treat you right, you let me know."

"Of course. It was so nice to meet you. I'll look forward to seeing you in Santa Fe."

As they strolled away, Greg, Zach, Damian, and Derrick made a beeline for Brandon and Emily. To say that everything in the lobby came to a screeching halt when they walked through was an understatement. There typically weren't many defensive linemen taking in the opera. Emily grinned, remembering Brandon's request the day before.

"Sugar, are there some opera CDs that might be user-friendly? The guys want to listen to some before they go to the auction," he'd asked. And so Emily had sent Brandon to his workout at the Sharks headquarters that morning with a compilation called "Operatically Incorrect," a recording of Seattle Opera's *La Boheme*, and the arias CD she had recently finished recording.

Brandon had called a couple of hours later. "They loved yours. They'll listen to *La Boheme* tomorrow."

Looking at them now, it was clear to Emily that the guys had listened to Brandon's warning that they must wear black tie, but they put their own spin on it. Damian wore a modern-cut tuxedo with a black shirt and a long silk tie. Derrick wore a retro-looking black suit with a white shirt, a skinny tie, and boots. Greg had on a long black jacket with a mandarin collar. Zach wore a cowboy hat with his traditional tuxedo, which he whipped off his head after a hard look from Brandon.

"Gentlemen," Brandon said, "we'll need to go backstage and get ready to walk on while our auction is being held."

Damian kissed Emily's cheek. His comment, "You look stunning, love," earned him a death glare from Brandon. "Would you like another glass of champagne?" Damian asked, as he glanced around for a server.

"Not right now, but thank you. I think I'll go sit down so I can watch you all."

Five men immediately offered their arms. She took Brandon's. Damian was still chatting with her.

"We listened to your CD today."

"Did you like it?"

"I did. Do you think you might sing that 'O Mio Baby' song for me sometime?"

"*O mio babbino caro?*"

"Yeah." The other guys smirked at him. He looked a little embarrassed, but continued. "I liked it." He raised an eyebrow at Zach, who attempted to stifle a laugh.

"The most famous version of that song is sung by Luciano Pavarotti. Have you ever heard of him?" He shook his head. "You might like his CD's, too."

"I liked *Phantom of the Opera*. Do you know Sarah Brightman?"

"No. I don't know her. I enjoyed her CD, though." Emily thought for a moment. "I'm singing in a recital next week at Benaroya. I could get you some tickets."

"Yeah. I'd like that. McKenna, you're fine if I tag along?" Damian said.

"You're bringing your own date," Brandon said.

Greg interrupted him. "Now you're an opera fan? Don't get me wrong. I liked Emily's CD. It's pretty good. Some of that other one, though, sounded like—shit, it was like cats being run over or something."

"There was no Mandarin Chinese opera in those CD's," she whispered frantically into Brandon's ear. He let out a chuckle.

"Hey. Rappers are doing standards these days. We might as well branch out," Damian informed Greg, who was attempting to contain his laughter and failing miserably.

Emily kissed Brandon's cheek when they reached the seating area.

"See you guys in a little while."

Everything was going well, maybe a little too well. Emily knew that her relationship with Brandon was outwardly accepted because of the publicity it brought to any production she performed in. Obviously, ticket sales were a good thing. At the same time, she heard the gossip. According to some of her colleagues, she had shamed the opera world and sullied her career. She wasn't stupid. She knew there must have been endless rehashing of her breakup with James, too.

"Hello, Emily," said a deep, all-too-familiar voice.

Her stomach lurched. *Oh, no, please, don't let it be him,* she thought. She turned her head and looked up into the face of her ex, James Peterson.

Chapter Twelve

JAMES SAT DOWN next to Emily without asking permission. He motioned to a server for a glass of champagne and then turned to face her.

"Good to see you. How are you doing?" he said.

She fidgeted with the evening bag in her lap. "Fine."

Nothing could be further from the truth, at least right then. In a world full of people, James was the last person she wanted to see. She wanted to vomit. She wanted to run. Even more, she wanted to disappear.

"Where's Heather?" Emily said.

He lifted an eyebrow. "I'm doing well. Heather's at home. She's . . . She's feeling a little under the weather."

"I'm sorry to hear she's ill." Emily's voice sounded like it was coming from far away. Truthfully, she wanted him to go elsewhere. "I hope she'll feel better soon."

He took a long sip of champagne, and flashed his perfect, insincere smile. Too bad that she seemed to be the only one who knew what was behind the seemingly flawless display. "She'll be fine. We're having a baby."

Obviously Emily was hearing things.

"I could have sworn you just told me Heather's pregnant."

"Yes. Yes, we are. It's a girl. Heather's in her second trimester."

"You said you didn't want children," she blurted.

"I changed my mind." He motioned to the server for another glass of champagne. "Where's your fiancé?"

"He'll be onstage in a minute."

James licked his lips as his gaze traveled slowly over her. "You look lovely, Emily. Engagement obviously agrees with you."

She swallowed hard, resisting the impulse to slap him into the middle of next week.

"So, when's the wedding?" he asked. "We'll look forward to receiving the invitation."

Emily leaned forward. There was no way she wanted those seated around them to hear her comments. News traveled fast, but bad (or scandalous) news traveled even faster.

"You must be out of your mind. Leave me alone."

James assumed the pouty, supercilious expression he'd always worn whenever he wanted to let her know she didn't measure up to his expectations. In anything.

"I'd like to think we could be friends, Emily," he said. "You insist on holding so much envy and bitterness toward us. Why can't you be happy? We are."

People in surrounding rows were swiveling around to hear what was being said. James was really putting on a show.

To Emily's surprise, a big, warm hand took her arm and propelled her to her feet. "Sugar," Brandon said. "I've got this."

"I thought you were backstage," she muttered.

Instead of responding, he faced James and said, "I'm Brandon McKenna. And you are?"

"James Peterson." James stretched out his hand.

Brandon ignored James's gesture. "Hey, Peterson, my fiancée asked you to leave her alone. Wouldn't it be the gentlemanly thing to find another place to sit?"

"I wanted to catch up," James whined. Emily watched his Adam's apple bob as he tried to swallow. There was fear in his eyes. Brandon was at least half a foot taller than James, and outweighed him as well.

Brandon's eyes narrowed to slits as he moved closer.

"No, you didn't. You wanted to cause a scene." His voice dropped. "If you don't leave Emily alone and stay away from her, I will remove you from this event. And not gently."

"You can't tell me what to do," James sputtered.

Brandon smiled, but his eyes bored a hole through James' chest. "Want to bet?" He waited a beat. "Leave, Peterson. Leave *now*." He took a step toward James, who jumped up from his seat like it was electrified. It was all Emily could do not to laugh at the panic on James' face.

James half-ran from the seating area.

Brandon turned to Emily. "Sugar. Shall we?" He picked up her evening purse and her wrap, cupped her elbow in his other hand, and walked her from the auditorium.

"You okay?" he asked as they hurried down a corridor.

"You scared the crap out of *me*, bruiser."

"I don't think he'll be bothering you again," he said, steering her backstage. "We'll be done with our auction in a minute. Let's get out of here afterward."

"That'll be fine. I greeted people, so I can go."

"Good. I'm going to have to hurt him if he comes near you again."

He draped Emily's wrap around her shoulders, gave her a reassuring squeeze, and walked onto the opera house's stage with his four teammates when their names were called to thunderous applause.

The spray-tanning auction went for ten thousand dollars.

Ten minutes later, Emily swept onstage to applause. The bidding was spirited and fierce, but Mrs. Tollifson prevailed. The fifteen thousand dollars bid on post-performance drinks with her was probably the equivalent of a parking ticket for her grandson.

One hour later, Emily and Brandon sat in his Land Rover at Burgermaster. He draped her in a combination of napkins and his tuxedo jacket while she ate. He had a patty melt with extra tomato, and managed to keep his evening clothes immaculate.

"I never knew I'd be visiting a drive-in wearing an evening dress," Emily said.

"Stick with me, and you're going to do a lot of things you've never done before."

BRANDON TRIED TO concentrate on the road in front of him, but the distraction currently sitting in the passenger seat of his Land Rover was presenting a significant challenge. Considering the fact they'd barely made it out of her driveway due to mutual lust earlier this evening, maybe it was time to take things to the next level. *Maybe?* Hell. If he didn't kiss her again in the next few minutes, he was going to spontaneously combust.

He let go of her hand for a moment to make the turn onto her street. He tried to keep his voice casual.

"So, are you inviting me in for a nightcap, sugar?"

Emily leaned forward in the seat, peering through the windshield. "Amy's van's in my driveway."

"Maybe she's dropping by for a visit." He wanted to meet Amy, but he wondered what he could bribe her with to visit Emily at a later date. He pulled into Emily's driveway next to the brightly painted van.

"No, something's wrong." He shut off the ignition. Emily already had her seat belt off.

"I'll walk you to the door," he said, but she was out of the car and hurrying toward her front door. Luckily for him, he could keep up with her shorter steps. He reached out for her hand. It seemed his plans for the rest of the evening had just cratered in a spectacular fashion.

Emily was tugging on his hand. "Come in with me," she said. "I don't know what's going on with her right now, but I want you to meet Amy. Plus, I've got beer." She paused in front of the door. "Thank you for such a wonderful evening, Brandon." She stood on her tiptoes to wrap her arms around his neck.

"I'm not saying goodnight to you yet, sugar," he said.

She was warm and soft against him. She slid her fingers into his hair, touching his mouth with hers.

"Good," she said. She took his hand again, and opened her front door.

BRANDON SPOTTED A tall blonde with a tear-streaked face; she was wrapped in a blanket on Emily's couch. She must have stopped at the grocery store on the way over. Various types of junk food were sitting untouched on Emily's coffee table, including three different flavors of Ben & Jerry's. He liked her style.

She got to her feet. "I—I didn't realize you guys had a date. I'm so sorry—"

Emily crossed the room at the speed of light and threw her arms around her sister. "What happened, Ame?"

For a few minutes, the only sounds in the room were Amy's sobs as she held onto her sister. The smartest thing he could do right now was excuse himself and leave, but Amy seemed to remember they weren't alone. She mopped up a little, and glanced over at him. "You must be Brandon."

"Yes, I am," he said. He crossed the room. "I think you need a hug," he told Amy.

EMILY EXCUSED HERSELF a few minutes later to change her clothes, and Brandon sat down on the couch next to Amy. "So, squirt, how can I help?"

A few more tears escaped. He handed her another tissue.

"I broke up with my boyfriend."

"I'm sorry to hear it," he said. She wasn't meeting his eyes. He'd bet his next contract bonus that the guy dumped her. Women didn't cry like this over telling a guy to hit the road. They put on some spike heels, called their girlfriends, and hit the club instead. In the meantime, the guy in question was an idiot.

"It wasn't working, but I can't figure out why I'm crying like this." Amy sniffled a few more times, and reached out to pat him on the knee. "I'll get myself together and clear out. You'd like to be alone with my sis." She started to get up from the couch, and Brandon reached out for her elbow.

"No. You need some girl time right now. That Ben & Jerry's isn't going to eat itself, you know."

Amy gave him a watery smile. "Want to split it with me?"

A FEW DAYS after the opera benefit, Emily was on a plane again. Her performances with San Diego Opera went well. She stretched to do *Turandot*, and the outcome was worth it. These were the greatest performances of her career so far, in a venue that would get international notice in the opera world. To say she was happy about this was an understatement. There weren't words to describe how it felt. It also didn't hurt that she had a wonderful and tragic death scene, too. She didn't want to leave the stage afterward, and she didn't come down from the adrenaline high of having an audience fall in love with her and her voice for hours afterward.

She scheduled additional practices and worked with others in the production to make sure everything was seamless. She got wonderful reviews, and David was fielding even more calls from opera companies hoping for holes in her schedule. The media was also interested in the diva with the NFL-playing fiancé. She spent every post-performance evening on the phone with Brandon. He wasn't able to be there. He was ramping up his lifting and required practices before training camp.

"So, you miss me?" he asked every night, with laughter in his voice.

"Yes, I miss you. Do you miss me?"

"Hurry home, sugar."

No matter how long they talked, there was always more to talk about. He never said a word about ending their engagement, and she wasn't going to bring it up. She was having too much fun with him. Obviously, it was really helping her career . . . or so she kept telling herself.

EMILY ARRIVED BACK in Seattle just before Memorial Day weekend. She missed the routines of home, but mostly, she missed Brandon. The slow progression of their relationship was about to undergo its first big test. Brandon was coming to Sunday dinner to meet her parents. When the day arrived she broached the subject at the breakfast table.

"Good job, sugar." Brandon pushed his empty plate away and patted his stomach.

"All it took was a phone call." Restaurant takeout was

a modern miracle. Emily was still attempting to master the basics of cooking without supervision. She took a deep breath. "Baby."

"Hey, where's my latest nickname?"

"For today, you're Godzilla."

He laughed, and squeezed her hand. "You look a little apprehensive."

"It's my parents. I don't even know how to explain them."

"Try me."

"They're still really mad about the engagement." She gripped her hands together. "They accepted James because they thought he understood my schedule and my goals. I've told them they need to meet you before they make up their minds about who you are and why I'm with you."

He let out a chuckle. "I wish I cared about James, but truthfully, sugar, I don't. Right now, though, what you're trying to tell me is that I may not get an especially warm reception from your parents."

"I—I've talked to them about you. They're freaking out."

"I spend all day Sunday from September to February dealing with people who don't necessarily like me." Emily felt herself relax at his amusement. "Listen. I'm going to dinner. I'll do my best to show them I'm not a jerk."

"Everyone else loves you."

"You're good for my ego."

"It's true," she said. Everywhere they went, women were helpless in the face of his charm. Emily should know. She was one of them.

The ride to Emily's mother's house was quiet until Brandon murmured, "Penny for your thoughts."

"I'm nervous."

"I'm the one who's supposed to be nervous," he said, but his lips curved into a teasing smile. "It's going to go perfectly."

Emily's nerves increased as she reflected on the fact Amy wouldn't be at dinner today. She was delivering and setting up wedding flowers. She might stop by later.

Brandon pulled into a parking space in front of her mom's house. As Emily reached down to pick her handbag up off the floorboard, he slipped his arms around her.

"Everything will be fine. I'm right here."

"I know you are." She rested her head against his shoulder, and pulled in a long breath. "I'm right here, too."

He chuckled. "Protecting me from the big, mean parents, are you?" Emily concentrated on the warm, solid man in her embrace. "You'll kiss it and make it better."

She couldn't stop the snort she made. He grinned again. "I know you want to see your mama and daddy. Now, give me a kiss."

She reached up to kiss him. His mouth was gentle on hers. He kissed the corner of her lips, and she smiled against his mouth. "Now, that's what I want to see. Let's go."

It occurred to her that they were co-conspirators, instead of two people tied together by fine jewelry and career aspirations. The feeling of being a team happened slowly over the time they were together. She couldn't imagine facing most things now without him.

He reached into the backseat, grabbing the bouquet of flowers and a bottle of wine he'd stopped on the way for. He took her hand as they walked up the steps to the front door.

"Mom?" Emily called out as she crossed the threshold.

"Smells good." Brandon said.

Emily's mother emerged from the kitchen with a smile that didn't meet her eyes.

"You must be Mrs. Hamilton," Brandon said, and extended his hand. "I'm Brandon McKenna. It's great to meet you. Emily's told me so much about you."

"Hello, Brandon. It's nice to meet you, too," her mother told him. Brandon presented her with the bouquet of flowers. "Thank you. They're lovely. I'd better get these in water." She turned to vanish into the kitchen again.

"My dad will be in the family room," Emily said.

Her father was half-asleep in his chair. He didn't live in her house anymore, but her mother made sure there was a recliner for him in the family room. He used it when he came for Sunday dinners. The Mariners game was on TV.

"Dad?"

He sat up with a "Hmph." He didn't look especially happy, either.

"This is Brandon. Brandon, this is my dad, Mark Hamilton." Her father got to his feet and shook Brandon's hand.

Emily kissed her dad. His returned kiss was less than attentive. He glared at Brandon, who handed him the bottle of wine.

"Mr. Hamilton, I brought this along. I thought maybe you and Mrs. Hamilton would like some wine with dinner."

"I'll ask her." Mark's voice was gruff. "Sit down."

Brandon and Emily moved to the love seat across from his recliner. Her father set the bottle on the coffee table, and sat back in the chair.

"So, Brandon, Emily tells us that you play for the Sharks."

"Yes, sir, I do."

"How long have you been in the NFL?"

"This will be my thirteenth season."

"You've always played with the Sharks?" As a sports fan, Mark Hamilton would know the answer to his questions. Emily wished she knew why he was asking them.

"Yes. Yes, I have."

"Do you have plans for what you'll do when you decide to retire from professional football?"

Brandon sat forward, and rested his forearms on his thighs. "I've spent a lot of time over the past three off-seasons working on my future. I initially thought I'd like to go into coaching, but I am interested in having a wife and a family. The work hours of most coaches aren't compatible with family life."

Mark's eyebrows shot up.

Brandon continued. "I did some color and game analysis during the preseason last year, and according to my agent, the network's interested. I'm pursuing this, and we've had preliminary contract talks. I've been working with other announcers to prepare as well. It's what I plan on doing."

Emily's father nodded. "Where'd you go to college again?"

"I went to LSU, majoring in mathematics. I graduated with my class." This was impressive. Brandon explained to Emily previously that many football players either didn't graduate from college, or graduated years after their class was gone. "I also hold a Master's in math from the University of Washington."

Emily broke in. "You didn't want to teach?"

"I enjoyed the studying, sugar."

Her father leaned forward in his chair as well, but his wasn't the relaxed, easy pose Brandon exhibited. He braced himself as if he would spring from the chair at any moment.

"Brandon, I'm not going to play games with you. Mrs. Hamilton and I aren't happy with how this engagement came about, and I notice that my daughter is still wearing your ring. Would you mind sharing with me what it is you thought was going to happen here?"

"Dad—"

"Emily, maybe it would be best if you went to help your mother in the kitchen for a few minutes," her father said.

"I'm not a child."

"You're still my daughter, and I need to talk with Brandon privately. He'll see you in a few minutes." Her father's voice was stern. He wasn't relenting.

Emily got to her feet, leaving the room. She heard her father's voice rising and falling as she walked through the house, but she couldn't make out what was being said.

Her mother glanced up in surprise as she entered the kitchen.

"What are you doing here, honey? I thought you were visiting with Daddy. Where's Brandon?"

"Dad's raking him over the coals. He said I had to leave."

"He just wants to get to know him."

"That's not what's happening right now. He made that clear enough." Emily paused by the kitchen table. "Would you like some help?"

"Everything's almost done. Maybe you could put the garlic bread in the breadbasket and take it out to the table." Her mother bustled around the kitchen. She didn't meet Emily's eyes. Emily reached out and caught her hand.

"Mom, are you still mad?" Emily felt her chin wobble. "I'm sorry about what I said. It was—it was awful. I know you and Dad are disappointed."

Her mother reached out to stroke Emily's cheek. "Honey, I can't stay mad at you." She took a deep breath. "Your friend seems nice. Frankly, I wasn't sure what to expect."

"Why?" The timer on the stove went off.

"We can talk about it later. Let's carry the rest of the food into the dining room." Her mother poked her head into the family room. "Dinner's ready."

Emily's father still looked like a thundercloud. Brandon squeezed her hand and said in a low voice, "Things are fine, sugar."

"I'm worried."

"Smile for me." His palm was warm and comforting on the small of her back.

At the table, Brandon pulled the chair out for her, settled her into it, and held the chair for Emily's mother as she sat down. This earned him another less-than-happy look from Emily's father. Meg smiled at him and said, "Thank you, Brandon."

"You're welcome, ma'am. Dinner smells delicious."

"I hope it'll taste delicious, too. Would you like some lasagna?"

"Yes, please."

Her mother appeared somewhat bewildered by Brandon's impeccable table manners. Her father must have thought it was some kind of act. Emily wondered if they thought he would throw food or something.

Her dad got up from his chair and left the room. He returned with Brandon's bottle of wine, still frowning.

"I almost forgot about this. Meg, would you like some of this with dinner?"

"Yes," Emily's mother said. "It was thoughtful of Brandon to bring such a nice gift."

She was flirting with him now. The friendlier Emily's mother got, the more her father's expression soured.

"It was my pleasure, Mrs. Hamilton. I'm glad you like it." Brandon gave Emily an almost imperceptible wink. He was workin' it.

"So, honey, you and Brandon are staying engaged?" her mother asked.

Emily had a mouthful of lasagna. She glanced across the table at Brandon and nodded in response.

"Brandon, if you don't mind my asking, how do your mom and dad feel about this?" Meg Hamilton sipped her wine. Her ex-husband's lips formed a thin line of disapproval.

"They were unhappy with me." The twinkle in Brandon's eyes was gone. "I'd also like to say that, while this did not start well, it has been my pleasure to spend time with Emily, and I'd like to keep doing so if she'll have me." He and Emily's eyes met across the table.

"I'm not happy with your beginning any relationship with a lie, and frankly, Brandon, this reinforces what I've heard and read about you," her father told him.

"Dad," Emily pleaded.

Brandon gave her a slight head shake. He sat up in his chair and squared his shoulders. "Sir, I'll have to prove I'm not that person." The men sized each other up. It was like two bulls pawing and snorting before the inevitable clash.

"Mark," Meg interrupted, but Mark was on a roll.

"Our family sacrificed so Emily could have the success she enjoys. Once she was out of the conservatory and performing with opera companies, she made her own luck, but at the same time, the cost was enormous, not just financially, and not just on Emily, but on everyone in the family."

Emily's bite of lasagna turned to sawdust in her mouth. Her dad's insistence on bringing up their family problems in front of Brandon was humiliating.

Her father continued. "I worked two jobs for years. My wife worked. When we weren't working, we were taking Emily to voice lessons and dance lessons till she was old enough to get herself there." His eyes narrowed. "Our daughter's not throwing her career away because you think it'll be fun to play house with her, or because you'd like the publicity. There was no other way you could possibly get yourself in the paper?"

Emily's mouth dropped open in horror. "I'm as responsible for this as Brandon is. My name was in the paper, too," she blurted out. Brandon shook his head at her again, but she couldn't remain quiet. "And I am not 'throwing away' my career. Maybe we should talk about how much my bookings have taken off since this all happened."

"Mark, we're at the table. This isn't the time," her mother said.

"Yes, it is. This needs to stop, right now. You're not continuing a sham engagement for Brandon's convenience," Emily's father told her. "I won't stand by and watch your career blow up in a huge scandal."

"It wasn't all his idea. It's helping me, too," Emily said. "I just said my bookings are up."

Meg Hamilton was white-faced and silent.

"For the record, I've offered to repay you and Mom over and over for the lessons and my schooling. You keep saying no. We've both told you that this was our decision, and Brandon apologized. What more do you want?" Emily said.

"It's not the money," her father ground out.

"Then why bring it up?" Emily asked.

"Sir, this seems to be a painful subject. Maybe we could talk some more about it later," Brandon said.

"There won't be any more discussion. My mind is made

up." Mark glanced over at his daughter. "As an adult, you are free to make your own decisions, but I want you to know I don't agree, and I won't support this choice."

Emily sat silently for a few minutes. She knew all families fought, but their arguments never seemed to have a resolution. She loved her dad, but he never tried to understand how she felt about a situation or see her point of view. She'd had a fairly shocking revelation between bites of her mother's lasagna: She didn't want their "engagement" to end, no matter what her father thought about the subject. She and Brandon's slowly growing relationship deserved a chance to thrive.

Emily tossed her napkin on the table, pushed her chair back, and got to her feet.

"Mom, thank you for the delicious dinner," she said, despite eating only a few bites. "Dad, excuse us."

"Sit down and finish your dinner," her father said.

Brandon got up from his chair, rounded the table, and took her arm. "Are you sure you want to do this?" he asked in a low voice.

"Yes. Mom, I'll talk with you later."

"Honey, please stay."

"No, thank you." She hauled breath into her lungs. Showing her anger, frustration and embarrassment was out of the question right now. "No matter how you feel about my choices, you're right. I'm an adult. I'm capable of making my own way, and I have been for a long time now." She looked into her father's eyes. "Thank you for supporting me for so long. I love you both very much, but I can take it from here. Brandon's my guest. Even more, he's—he's my friend. I'm choosing to be with him, and I don't understand why you're treating him so rudely."

"Maybe we should talk about this some more," Meg said.

"No, Mom. Dad's done talking right now, and so am I."

Emily hurried out of the dining room without waiting for an answer. She snatched up her handbag from the hall table, flung open the front door, and stumbled down the porch stairs. Brandon was right behind her.

"Emily," her mother called out.

Emily heard the *chirp* of the locks as Brandon's car doors disengaged. She wrenched the passenger door open and turned to look back at her mother.

"Don't leave like this," Meg pleaded. She stood on the sidewalk only feet away from them. She clasped her hands in front of her.

"Mom, I love you a lot, but we need to go."

Meg extended her hand to Brandon. "It was nice to meet you."

"It was nice to meet you, too, ma'am. I apologize for leaving such a delicious dinner." He thought for a moment. "I hope we'll meet again under better circumstances."

A surprised expression crossed her mother's face, but she said, "Yes, that would be nice." She turned and went back into the house.

BRANDON FOUND A parking spot a couple of blocks away and pulled into it. He turned toward Emily. She wrapped her arms around herself like she was attempting to keep her organs inside. She felt terrible, but she felt even worse for Brandon. He didn't ask for this.

"I'm so sorry," Emily gasped. "I can't believe my dad acted like that. Does he think I'm not old enough to make my own decisions? Why does he . . . I'm sorry."

"Come here. We'll be fine." His arms slid around Emily. She felt him, warm and solid against her. "You have nothing to apologize for."

"It was awful. I am so embarrassed."

"Shh," he comforted.

"Aren't you mad?"

"I don't like the fact your dad upset you like this." He kissed her forehead. "We will work this out. I want to keep seeing you, so I need to make peace with him."

"I am as responsible as you are. Why can't he see this? I . . ." Her voice trailed off as he cupped her face in one hand, stroking her cheek with his thumb. She remembered she had pulled him away from an entire plate of food, too. "You're probably still hungry."

He looked somewhat amused. "Let's go grab a bite. We'll go for a walk at Marina Park later."

"Baby, I still—"

"No more apologizing. Everything's going to be fine." His dimple flashed as his lips curved into a dazzling smile. "So, I'm your pal." He sat back in his seat, but he didn't let go of her hand.

She lifted a brow. "Maybe."

"Maybe Katie's at the park today, too."

He shifted the car into gear and drove away, but not before Emily saw gratitude in his eyes.

Chapter Thirteen

HUNDREDS OF PEOPLE enjoyed the sunny spring afternoon in Kirkland's Marina Park. Boats zipped by on the lake; kids ran and played on the beach while their parents relaxed on blankets spread over the grass. Brandon and Emily were shown to a table at The Slip, a small restaurant overlooking the park. Brandon reached across the table for her hand after drinks and food were ordered.

"Listen," he said. "We need to talk about something."

"You keep using that phrase," she said. "Doesn't 'we need to talk' usually mean bad news?"

She saw him hide a smile while pretending to rub his nose. "Gotcha." He took a deep breath. "I'm not mad at your dad, because he's telling the truth. I'd be the same way if it was my daughter."

Emily shook her head vigorously. "You would not."

"Oh, yes, I would. My little girl isn't dating till she's thirty." Emily rolled her eyes. Brandon grinned back at her. "No matter how old you are, you're still his little girl, too. He remembers you with pigtails and no front teeth, sugar. He doesn't want anyone to hurt you, and he certainly isn't sure about some guy who ended up engaged to his daughter less than twenty-four hours after they met." He took a swallow of his pint of beer. "I'll invite him out to lunch."

"He'll tell you no."

"I think you'll be surprised." He pulled the smart phone from his pocket. "May I have your dad's phone number?"

"I don't think this is a good idea—"

"I need the number," he said.

Emily reached out for his phone, keyed the number in, and handed it back to him. "All you have to do is hit 'Send.'"

Brandon held the phone to his ear.

"Mr. Hamilton, it's Brandon McKenna. I would like to have lunch with you this week. How does Tuesday sound?" Emily couldn't hear her dad's response, but Brandon said, "I'll meet you at a restaurant by your office. How about the Metropolitan Grill at noon?" After a bit more conversation, Brandon said, "Great. I'll look forward to it. See you at noon on Tuesday." He punched a button to end the call.

Emily regarded him in shock. "How did you manage that?"

Brandon raised an eyebrow. "Your dad doesn't want to lose his daughter. He also wants to know that I'm a man, not a boy."

"Maybe you could explain that, too."

"If I don't have the balls to face him, you shouldn't be with me. Eat up, sugar, or you won't get any dessert."

It sounded like Attack of the Alpha Males. Brandon convinced her father to have lunch with him. Then again, Emily's dad wouldn't stage a DEFCON-1 freak-out in one of Seattle's most exclusive restaurants.

AFTER THEIR MEAL, they walked hand-in-hand to the same bench they always sat on during visits to the park.

"I don't see Katie today," Brandon said.

"Maybe her mom and dad took her somewhere else."

"Could be. But, hey, we need to discuss something else your dad mentioned. My mama wants to know when the wedding is. She says her friends are driving her nuts about it."

Emily swiveled to look at him in disbelief. "We can't pick a date." It was one thing to have a fake engagement. A fake wedding date? Now, that was taking things a bit too far.

"It's obviously a problem for your dad. Plus, I think we should set a date," he persisted.

"I thought we said we'd see how things went. I don't understand why you're changing the rules."

"Listen," he said patiently, "Engaged people typically pick a wedding date. There's only so long we can avoid it." He wrapped his arm around the back of the bench and stretched his legs out in front of him. He seemed perfectly relaxed. She was a bundle of emotions: surprised, shocked, and more than a bit scared.

"This is crazy." Emily said.

"We need a date. Pick one."

"You've decided this is real now."

His eyes sparkled with amusement. "Maybe."

The ring on the third finger of Emily's left hand felt like the weight of the world. Most women waited their whole lives for this moment. Obviously, there was something wrong with her.

Her feelings for him grew every day. He was the first person she ran to now when she wanted to talk or she needed encouragement. Even when they sat on the couch and said nothing to each other, his presence was enough. He made her laugh. She missed him desperately when they were away from each other. Maybe it was shallow, but if they weren't in public, she'd want to push him down and jump on him. Then again, she wanted to push him down and jump on him anyway.

She wondered how shocked he'd be if she actually did it. James made it clear so many times he didn't welcome Emily's displays of affection toward him, and she worried Brandon would think she was aggressive, too. Then again, he never shrank from her touch.

Maybe she should start off small.

Brandon squeezed her shoulder with one big hand. "Hey, where'd my fiancée go? I could have sworn I was just talking to her."

"I'm still here."

She reached out impulsively, pulled his face down to hers, and kissed the corner of his mouth. His mouth twitched into a smile, and she traced his dimple with one fingertip. He nuzzled her hair. She snuggled against him. She wanted to kiss the hollow between his shoulder and his neck for so long, so she did.

"Trying to distract me? You're doing a fine job, sugar." His mouth touched hers, the most fleeting of kisses. He wrapped his arms around her. She felt the laughter in his chest before she heard it, and her heart soared. "June works for me."

"I'm not sure about June. I have bookings. July's better, but you'll be in training camp."

He glanced away from her for a moment. "Maybe it's time for me to retire. I can do the broadcasting thing, and I can spend more time with you."

"You love playing football, though." Emily said. "You—you'd miss the guys. You'd miss the games. Why do you want to give it up?"

"I've been thinking about it for a while now. I'm lucky to still be able to play, but as I get older, that luck may run out. Plus, I saw what my dad went through. I don't want to play till I can barely limp off the field. I'd like to get out while I'm still feeling good." He shook his head. "You don't want to be dragging some broken-down guy around."

"I want whatever makes you happy," she said.

"That's good. Let's pick a date for the wedding, then. That will make me very happy."

Emily twisted her hands in her lap. "February second."

"You like February, huh?"

"It was my parents' anniversary."

He gave her a quizzical look. "You're trying to tell them something."

"I—I don't know. They're spending a lot of time to-gether these days. I wonder what's going on."

He rubbed his chin. "I know that I asked you to come up with a date, but now I'm asking you to change it."

"Why?"

"It's Super Bowl weekend. It's a long shot that we'll go, but, somehow, I'm thinking you won't want to wear a wedding gown at Miami Stadium."

"Maybe not. The train and my veil would get beer spilled all over it." The thought made her smile. "How about next January?"

"Too long." he complained. His fingers curled around hers, and her heart did a funny little "ba-bump." "I know," he said, and pulled her closer. "We'll get married February fifteenth. Everyone gets married on Valentine's Day. Let's be different. Plus, you'll get two dinners out every year instead of only one." He leaned back again, a smug grin on his lips. "Just think. If you play your cards right, you'll also get to go to the Pro Bowl with me. That's in Hawaii, you know."

"You want to get married on February fifteenth so you won't forget our anniversary," she teased.

He brought her hand to his lips and pressed a kiss into her palm. Warmth spread low in her abdomen. She squirmed a little.

"That's not true." He wiggled an eyebrow. "We're cel-ebrating your engagement ring's first anniversary." He spoke into her ear. "We could always have a very private party."

"Is that so?"

"Oh, yeah. You and me. You won't even need a dress."

Emily's face burned. She knew she was blushing. She was more than a little breathless. Unless she was really wrong, he wanted her, too. "We're not getting married naked."

"The preacher can marry us, and then we can get naked."

"Try explaining to your mom that we didn't invite her. What about my mom? They'll freak out. It—"

He laid his fingertips over her lips. "The wedding can be as big or as small as you'd like. It doesn't matter. I want it to happen. You and me."

Emily dragged breath into her lungs. "Yes. This is real."

"Wait till you find out where we're going on our honeymoon."

Her hands shook. Her mouth went dry. She shifted on the bench. "The NFL Hall of Fame?"

His chuckle was low and sexy. He pulled her earlobe into his mouth, nibbled it, and said, "Nope. I'm not taking you anywhere anyone will recognize either of us. I want you all to myself."

"I might be able to arrange that."

"Good," he purred.

Being close to him was like sticking a wet finger into an electrical outlet. She kept telling herself to breathe. She couldn't imagine there would be a day she didn't feel like this.

"So, we have a deal." he said. "February fifteenth."

"Maybe we should discuss where we're getting married."

"That's your job. You get to have whatever you'd like, and I will be happy with it."

"It's the First Church of Elvis for you, bruiser."

"Great. I'll wear blue suede shoes." His brow furrowed. "You're not serious."

"Maybe. You'll be so cute in that big black pompadour."

"You'll be sporting the long, teased black hair, won't you?"

She had to laugh. "We can't get married there. I love your hair the way it is too much." She reached up to brush the curls off his forehead.

"Sugar, aren't you sweet?" He thought for a moment. "You'll let my mama help you, won't you? She loves that stuff."

"I will," Emily promised. She ran her fingers through his curls again. The sun shone down on them. Hundreds of people enjoyed the Sunday afternoon all around them. It was just another day with one large exception: They'd set a wedding date. But Brandon never actually asked her to marry him. They had never talked about being in love, either.

Chapter Fourteen

THE HOUSE WAS painted a bluish gray with immaculate white trim. The older architecture was dwarfed by the large homes surrounding it, but Emily loved the old-fashioned overgrown gardens and the stone path from the sidewalk. Several steps led down the walk to the front door. The front porch needed a glider. If she lived here she'd pick some of the wild roses that grew over the railing.

"Home sweet home," Brandon said with a grin. "Nordquist's allegedly in Hawaii with his girlfriend for a few days, so we have the place to ourselves."

"Who's Nordquist?" Emily took a deep breath of wild rose-scented air.

"You've met Greg. He's on the practice squad. He lives in the basement when he's in town."

The front door of Brandon's house was inset with leaded glass: an old-fashioned, intricate design. She wasn't sure what to expect, but it didn't look like him. He opened the front door, and ushered her into the cool dimness of an entry hall with wide plank flooring. She set her handbag down on a large maple storage bench with hooks for coats.

"How about a drink?" Brandon called as he went into the kitchen, which was to the right of the front door.

She followed him. A maple kitchen table and cream-painted chairs sat in front of a sunny bay window. The cabinets matched the table and chairs. The countertops were neutral granite. Another window over the kitchen sink offered a view of the postage stamp-sized front yard. The appliances were stainless steel, and appeared new. There were even sunflowers in a sage-colored pottery vase on the kitchen table.

He opened the refrigerator door. "I've got Coke, bottled water, beer, juice, and sweet tea. I can also make some coffee, if you'd like."

"I'll take a Coke."

"No ice," he mumbled to himself. He'd seen her order enough drinks without ice to know she stayed away from it.

Emily wandered over to a bulletin board hanging above a maple-and-cream writing desk. Even a bachelor needed somewhere to put the grocery list, the team schedule, and the folder of bills to be paid. The rest of the board was covered with snapshots of what she imagined were family and friends at various vacation spots. She noticed a photo of Brandon with a dark-haired guy about the same age and with the same eyes and facial structure, along with an older couple. They were standing on what appeared to be the same deck she saw through the arched entry into the dining room.

"Are these your parents?"

He glanced over. "Yeah. It was taken a few months ago."

Brandon had his mom's blonde curls and her eyes, but the rest of him was his father. The four of them had their arms around each other, with his petite mom standing in the protective embrace of her husband. Brandon and his dad were laughing. Dylan kissed his mother's cheek. She was beaming.

"Your mom is tiny." Her head barely came up to Brandon's dad's shoulder.

"Imagine how much fun it was for her to have two ten-pound sons, eleven months apart."

Emily did her best not to flinch in sympathy.

Brandon handed her the drink. He poured himself some iced tea. "Let's go out on the deck for a minute."

Besides wondering if Brandon had stock in some type of maple furniture factory, Emily had a better idea why he bought the house. It was bigger than it looked from the street. The view from his dining and living room was breathtaking. The rooms overlooked Lake Washington, stretching all the way to the 520 floating bridge and the Space Needle and Columbia Center over the hill on the opposite side.

"This must be great in the summertime," she said as they passed through the French doors onto his deck.

"It's great even when it's freezing out here. I love the view."

Emily enjoyed watching the boats move across the water until the breeze kicked up. She shivered.

"You're chilly, sugar," Brandon said. "Let's go back inside. Plus, you haven't had the grand tour yet." He took her elbow.

"I thought we were going to Damian's for dinner."

"There's time. Come on."

The dining room featured an expandable maple table and hardwood chairs with padding in a hunter green fabric. "I don't eat in here unless my mama makes dinner for everyone," he explained. "She kept telling me, though, that I needed a nice table and chairs, so I bought them."

They moved into the living room, which had overstuffed furniture in dark green patterned upholstery. A heavy-looking wood-and-glass coffee table sat in front of a gas fireplace. More framed family photos leaned against the opposite wall. A folk-art painting of what looked like Tuscany leaned against the wall over the mantelpiece. It all looked comfortable, but there was an air of the unfinished. Brandon either didn't spend a lot of time at home, or he wasn't big on hanging pictures.

"I love that," Emily said. She nodded at the painting.

"I was told I needed something bright for when it's gray outside."

He led her down the hallway to a door he opened with a flourish. "This is my room."

This, too, was nothing like she had expected. The king size bed was of more maple, a simple design with a Mission-style headboard and no footboard. She imagined his feet hanging over this bed the way they hung over the edge of hers. The sheets and pillowcases were navy blue. The whole thing was covered with a quilt in varying prints, but predominantly in shades of blue. Another quilt was folded lengthwise and spread across the foot of the bed.

It looked cozy and comfortable. Emily resisted the impulse to crawl inside.

The nightstand had a stack of books, a cordless telephone in a base, and a clock radio. Her roaming gaze caught a professionally framed photo of Brandon on the wall. He stood in what appeared to be an end zone, his arms over his head, holding a football.

She pointed at it. "You have the ball."

"I picked off Denver's quarterback on a tip drill and ran it into the end zone last year."

"Good job, bruiser. That's a touchdown, right?" He grinned at her as he nodded. "It's nice in here," she said.

"There's nothing pink or ruffly," he said.

"I could fix that for you." Emily touched the quilt at the foot of his bed. "This is gorgeous."

"My grandma McKenna made it for me." He indicated an open door on the other side of his room. "I had a jetted tub put in the bathroom last year."

The upstairs of Brandon's house boasted two large skylights and the steepest staircase she'd ever encountered.

"I sleep up here when my parents come to town. It's easier for me to get up and down the stairs than it is for them. Dylan stays here, too."

There was more of the simple overstuffed furniture

Brandon seemed to like, along with a window seat that showed off the gorgeous lake view. Emily spied an office and another half bath at the other side of what must have been a former attic.

Emily heard a faint "Meow," and a very large brown tabby cat jumped off the window seat to wind around Brandon's ankles.

"Hey, buddy." He reached down and gave the cat a pat on the head. "Decided you'd wake up and join us. This is Deacon," he explained. "He's part of the reason Greg hangs around here. When I'm on the road, I don't worry that he's going to starve or run away."

"Interesting name for a cat."

"His name is really Deacon White, but we call him Deacon for short. Deacon White was the best defensive end to ever play the game, sugar."

Emily tapped one finger on her chin. "So, he played the same position you do."

"You get a gold star for that football knowledge. I'm proud of you." He leaned forward and kissed the tip of her nose. She reached out for his hand, while inching her other hand toward the cat.

"Maybe he'll let me pet him."

"You might want to rethink that. He's ferocious." Nothing could have been further from the truth. Deacon stood on his hind legs and pawed at her. He wanted to be picked up.

"I want to have a pet, but I'm gone so much, it would never work," she said. Deacon cuddled against her, and with a soft "Mew" he laid his head on Emily's cheek.

"Hey, Deacon, back off. Get your own woman."

"Does he sleep in your room?"

"Of course not," he smirked. Emily remembered the plush cat bed in one corner of Brandon's bedroom.

Deacon rubbed his face against Emily's.

"I get a woman in my house, and the first thing she does is go for the cat," Brandon said.

Emily set the cat down on the floor, and Deacon regarded her with an injured expression in his amber eyes. "I know. I'll be back another time," she told him. She glanced up at his owner. "We probably need to leave for Damian's." They descended the stairs, and she picked up her handbag. "Maybe I should drive."

"We don't need the car."

"He must be close," Emily said as they walked outside.

"You could say that. He's right across the street."

Emily glanced up, spotting Damian standing on a deck that overlooked Brandon's house.

"Hey, dawg," Damian shouted. "Get your ass over here or the steak's going to burn. Hey, pretty lady."

Emily waved at him in response.

He continued talking as they made their way across the street. "I got some tickets to go see you in that—what the hell is it—Der, die, something."

"*Die Fledermaus*," she explained. "You're going to Cincinnati? That's wonderful." Emily clapped her hands.

Damian pulled the front door open as Emily and Brandon reached the doorstep and threw his arms around her. "There she is."

She hugged him back. "It's good to see you, too. I can't believe you'll be at the performances in Cincinnati!"

"It's really hard to get tickets to see you perform around here now," Damian complained.

"I'm not singing here till later in the season, but I could get you some tickets to one of Seattle Opera's upcoming performances. It's not *Die Fledermaus*, but you might like it."

"I want to go if you're singing," Damian assured her.

"I'm standing here. Stop trying to pick up on my fiancée," Brandon told him.

"He sounds jealous," she murmured to Damian.

"Damn straight, love." Damian did an elaborate handshake with Brandon. He turned to Emily again, and slid his arm around her shoulders. "Maybe you should go out with me instead. I'll hook you up. Cornerbacks and safeties are the real men of any football team. He must have told you this."

"He's getting mad," Emily said.

"He knows I speak the truth, baby."

Brandon rolled his eyes. "I hope you invited the young lady you were flirting with yesterday at lunch," he said.

"Of course I did. She should be here soon. In the meantime I have to chat with my pretty lady. Listen, girl, I bought some of those opera beats you told me about. They're sick."

Brandon took Emily's hand, tugged her over to the couch, and pulled her onto his lap. Damian laughed, and went out onto the deck to check the food on the grill.

Emily looped one arm around his neck. "Should I ask him if I can help with anything?"

"No."

Damian's house made Brandon's look tiny. The front door led into a soaring entryway with a large crystal chandelier. The living room was up a flight of stairs, and opened onto the deck, which had the same view Brandon's did. Damian's living room appeared big enough to park a Humvee in. The décor was formal, and appeared to be done by a professional. It was beautiful, but Emily preferred the simplicity and coziness of Brandon's house.

Two men and two women in server garb emerged from the kitchen with trays of food, arranging the platters on a long table set up against the far wall. One of the women approached Brandon and Emily for a drink order.

"Hey, Damian," Brandon called out. "You said this was just us."

"Gotta' feed everyone."

"He caters a backyard barbecue," Brandon muttered. "Now everyone will expect me to do it, too."

"What does he mean by 'everyone'?" she said into Brandon's ear.

"Let's find out. Drake," Brandon called out, "How many is 'everyone'?"

"Dawg, everyone."

Brandon let out a groan. "He invited the team, along with whoever it is they're married to or going out with. You'll probably see an awful lot of single women."

"You probably have parties as well."

"Mine are smaller," Brandon said. "Plus, the police don't typically make an appearance."

Two hours later, Damian's house was so crowded that it was impossible to move across the room. Emily gave up counting the people she saw after a hundred. Brandon introduced her to his teammates and others he knew, but it was overwhelming. They couldn't get near the food. The alcohol was flowing, though, and they both had a few drinks. Emily decided to visit the bathroom, and came back a few minutes later to find Brandon missing.

Brandon was completely at home here. She wasn't. She had a much better idea how he must have felt at the opera benefit, especially when she noticed two women on Damian's deck staging an impromptu Shark Babes tryout. They wore nothing but thongs with Sharks logos on them. She liked to have fun, but she preferred something quieter with the possibility for conversation.

Emily needed some fresh air. Mostly, she wanted to get away from crowds of people and the blasting sound system. Maybe Brandon had wandered outside, too. She found herself in the backyard; it was a beautiful June evening. As she rounded the side of the house, she saw Brandon on one knee next to a little dark-haired boy. She heard sobs. Brandon laid a hand on the boy's shoulder. She stepped behind a lilac bush, not wanting to startle the little boy more.

"I might not find him," the boy said. "He'll be hungry. He doesn't know where his mom is."

"Another mama frog will help him, buddy."

"All I did was let him out of the 'tainer for a few minutes. He must be in the grass."

"They're pretty good at hiding."

"They can hop pretty fast, too." Emily heard the boy hiccup, another little-boy sob, and he rubbed his eyes with what looked like grimy fists. Brandon patted him on the back.

"Simon, your mama and dad are going to wonder where you went. I'm going to take you back to your house, and I'll keep looking for Froggy."

"My mom and dad went out to dinner. Madison's babysitting me."

"I'll bet she's scared, too, because she doesn't know where you are. We'll take you home, and I'll find your frog. I'll make sure he gets back to you."

"But he doesn't know you."

"That's true. He might come to me, though, because he'll know I want to bring him back. I think it'll work."

Simon let out a long sigh. "Maybe." He glanced up into Brandon's face. "Do you know how to take care of frogs?"

Emily heard Brandon's low chuckle. "My brother and I spent a lot of time catching frogs when I was your age." Emily saw him looking under the plants in the garden as he spoke. He appeared to be searching for the frog. "We used to bring snakes in the house and put them in the clean laundry basket. My mama screamed."

"You caught a snake! Did they bite?"

"Aww, not these ones. We weren't supposed to be in the swamp, but we went there anyway. You probably do some stuff you're not supposed to do, too."

"I snuck out of the house," Simon informed him proudly.

"Let's make a deal." Brandon patted him on the back, and waited till Simon looked into his eyes again. "It's really fun to do stuff you're not supposed to, but sometimes it's not a great idea. I know you came over because you wanted to talk to Damian. You need to tell an adult where you're going. It's not safe for you to be out here in the dark by yourself." Brandon was still looking around the plants in the garden, but he turned back to ruffle Simon's hair. "If you'll agree to do this, we can look for some frogs. Or, we can play catch."

Simon thought for a moment. He shifted his weight onto one foot, then the other.

"Can you play football with me?"

Emily heard Brandon's laugh. "Sure. I'll play football with you. Maybe Damian will want to play, too."

"Yeah!" Simon punched the air with a small fist. "That'll be fun."

"Let's get you back home, then. My fiancée's probably wondering where I am."

"What's a fiancée?"

Brandon got to his feet and took Simon's hand. "That means we're getting married."

"Oh." Simon thought about this for a moment. "Is she pretty?"

"She is. She's nice, too. I bet you'd like her."

"I like girls who like frogs."

"I don't know. We'll have to ask her." Brandon and Simon moved off toward the sidewalk in front of Damian's house. Maybe it was best if Brandon showed up at the neighbor's house with her, too. It was time for Emily to make an appearance.

"Hey, guys," Emily said, as casually as possible.

"There she is." Brandon held out his other hand. "Sugar, this is Simon. We're looking for his lost frog. Simon, this is Miss Emily."

Emily shook Simon's hand. He gave her a gap-toothed grin and her heart melted. The three of them walked down the sidewalk. "Sugar, do you like frogs?" Simon said.

There was laughter in Brandon's voice. "You're flirting with my girl."

Simon looked up at her expectantly.

"Well, I haven't seen that many frogs in my life. Maybe you could show me one," Emily told him.

"If Brandon finds my frog, you can play with him."

"I'll do my best, buddy." Brandon was leading them up the walk to another impressive home a few houses down from Damian's. "Let me do the talking," he told Simon.

BRANDON SHOOK HIS head and glanced back at Simon's house with a fond smile.

"I looked all over Drake's backyard. He'll be disappointed if I don't find another one." Brandon unlocked the front door of his house, tugging Emily inside. "Let's get a jar or something, and we're set." He pulled open the refrigerator door in his kitchen, dumped the contents of a jar of pickles into the sink, rinsed it, and jabbed several holes in the lid with a fork. "C'mon," he said as he stuck his keys into his pocket. "I'll bet you've never had a guy take you to a swamp before."

"You're really doing this," she said. He reached into a kitchen drawer for a flashlight.

"Are you sure you're okay to drive?"

"I haven't had a drink in two hours now. I also wouldn't get behind the wheel if I wasn't." He reached out for her hand again. "Ready to go?"

Brandon parked his Land Rover a short distance from a swamp a couple of miles from his house. He handed her the flashlight.

"This is how it's going to go. Tilt this up so I can see, but not so much that it scares them off."

"Aren't there frogs at the pet store?"

"Naww. This'll be easy." He kissed her forehead. "You stay up here, or you're going to get really dirty."

Emily watched him move away from her. The sky was brilliant with stars. The silence was broken by tall grass brushed by a soft breeze and what must have been a huge bullfrog looking for his girlfriend. Brandon was rustling around. She heard a *plop*, a muttered, "Shi— Shoot," and Brandon spoke up. "Hey, sugar, tilt that flashlight in this direction."

She turned the flashlight toward his voice and let out a gasp. "What happened to you?"

"It's a little mud. Nothing to worry about." He crouched down at the shoreline, looking intently into the water. "They're here. Just gotta get one. You should see how many tadpoles there are." He dipped his jar into the pond. "The frog'll think he's right at home."

Emily inched her way down the bank. The tall grass brushed her calves as she moved along. It wasn't muddy up here at all. As long as she stayed away from the swamp, everything was fine. Lost in thought, she walked along, eyes focused on him.

Brandon had left a party most fun-loving adult males would give an appendage to attend to help a little boy find his frog. He made it clear that he'd enjoy spending more time with that little boy. There were no cameras, no press, nobody that would see him and think he was a great guy. She now knew what it was about him she couldn't resist, besides the way he looked.

This was who he was, instead of what he thought people wanted him to be. He wasn't the shallow, stereotypical NFL star. Despite the show he put on for everyone else, she'd seen his gooey marshmallow center.

The things that meant the most to him were not found on a football field: his family, his friends. He didn't care about the party his teammates were still at. He spent an hour wandering around in the mud to make a little boy happy. Suddenly, she was breathless.

Most of all, she wanted to be the person that made Brandon happy.

She skidded on a previously invisible patch of mud. Both feet slid out from under her, and she sat down hard. "Ow!"

It didn't really hurt. Her pride was dented, though. The flashlight flew into a nearby tuft of grass. She felt the cold, squishy, wet ground seeping through her cotton pants. The hands she tried to brace herself with were covered in mud, too. She shook off as much muck as possible. She *hated* getting dirty. She wasn't a big fan of wardrobe destruction, either.

Brandon hurried toward her. "You okay, sugar?"

"I'm fine. I feel a little stupid." She reached out for the flashlight.

"I got it," he told her, and he pulled her onto her feet. She saw his smile in the darkness. "I got you, too. You're going to need a shower." He walked her a few steps over to a dry patch of grass, and put the now-filthy flashlight back into her hand. "You're sure you didn't hurt yourself?"

"Of course not."

He strode down the bank, approached the water's edge, and dipped the jar into the water. She heard his triumphant, "Gotcha."

He showed her the glass jar, which held an inch or so of dirty pond water, a rock, and a small green frog. "Let's go home."

She wasn't the only one who needed a long, hot shower. Brandon was covered in mud from the waist down. His hands were filthy; he had mud in his hair. He was ecstatic.

"I haven't had this much fun since college," he told her. He glanced at his (evidently waterproof) watch. "His parents will be back by now. We'll drop it off."

Brandon stripped off his muddy jeans, shoes, and socks, tossing them into the backseat. She was horrified to note her beautiful ring had mud caked in it, too. When he saw her wiping her hands on the grass to clean them off a bit, he took off his t-shirt and handed it to her. "Use this."

"So gross," she muttered.

He fixed her with a flirtatious grin and said, "All that nasty mud must be really uncomfortable for you. Maybe you should take your pants off, too."

She let out a gasp. "I don't think so."

"It's important that you're comfy," he assured her, and she burst into laughter. He threw himself behind the wheel in nothing but a pair of black boxer briefs. He was a mess, and he was still gorgeous. He handed her the jar. "Take care of him, sugar."

"Do you often drive half-naked?"

"Nobody's going to see," he said. They were driving on a heavily traveled street in a highly populated area. Maybe Brandon thought they were invisible.

A few minutes after Emily dropped the frog in his jar off on Simon's front porch, they pulled up in front of Brandon's house. She kicked off her muddy shoes and left them under the bench in the hallway. Brandon tugged her down the hallway to his room.

"I need to find something I can wear home. My pants—" she tried to tell him.

He pulled her into his arms. "Right now, getting cleaned up is Job One." His voice dropped. "There's plenty of room in the shower for both of us."

"Your car needs a bath, too."

"I'm not so worried about that at the moment."

He shut the bedroom door behind them and made no move to flip on a light. The dimness wrapped around them like a blanket, dense and soft. She played in his chest hair. She laid her cheek against his scratchier one as she closed her eyes and clasped her arms around his waist. Her clothes were trashed, she smelled like a swamp, and he didn't seem to care. He drew her closer.

He started slowly—the slightest brush of his lips on hers. His mouth was warm and tender on hers. He did it again. She slid one hand into his hair, tangling her fingertips in his curls. He kissed the corners of her mouth. His stubble scraped her, and she let out a moan. She stood on her tiptoes, and sealed her mouth over his.

Brandon kissed her till she was breathless, till her knees threatened to buckle, till she fumbled at the button and zipper of her pants. He moved her hands away, and took over.

Desire surged through her, an unstoppable force. At that moment, it didn't matter to her that he'd gotten busy with innumerable women before, or that she was about to get smashed like a bug on the windshield of Brandon's love life.

They were still engaged. They were dating. Hell, they had a wedding date. They kissed—a lot. They touched each other. Things would get hot and heavy between them, and then, one or both of them would run away. Maybe he was waiting for her. It was possible.

She'd tasted his kisses and felt his arms around her when he was hundreds of miles away. She'd heard his quiet voice in her ear when she couldn't sleep, and lay wondering if he was thinking about her, too. His scent was imprinted on her memory: Clean skin, and a hint of his aftershave. She saw his smile even when he was no-where around, and she saw a dimple she could lose her car keys in when he laughed. She felt safe with him.

Tonight, right now, she wasn't running away. She wanted him. She knew he wanted her. His voice dropped to a murmur.

"You're not afraid of the dark, are you?"

He pushed her pants down. She stepped on the toes of her trouser socks, attempting to pull them off.

"There might be monsters under your bed."

He nibbled at the base of her neck. "I'll make sure they're all gone," he said.

He stepped on the bunched-up clothing at her ankles, pulled her out of the tangled pants and socks, and led her into his bathroom.

She tugged her sweater off over her head and dropped it onto the bathroom floor. She tried to wrestle the clasp of her bra around to her front to unhook it. Damn thing. She wasn't letting a lingerie salesperson talk her out of those front clasp bras again.

She felt Brandon's big hands over hers, brushing skin ultra-sensitive with arousal.

He reached into the shower, flipped on the taps, and undid her bra clasp with one smooth motion.

"How did you learn to do that? I can't get that thing off myself."

"Of course you can't," he said into her ear. "I'm a profes-sional." His hands moved over her, sliding down her back, pulling her into him. Two thin layers of cotton and elastic separated them. She'd have to do something about this.

"You must have taken some kind of class," she teased.

"I was a very good student," he said. "Wait till you see what else I learned."

Imagining what that might be made her toes curl.

She managed to shove his underwear off and tried pulling at her own. It was still wet from landing on her butt in a mud puddle, and peeling it off took some effort. Finally, though, they tugged each other into the shower enclosure.

A rain bath shower nozzle directed a steady stream of soothing, warm water over their heads. Numerous recessed body sprays on the walls massaged their tired muscles. Brandon's mouth came down on hers again as he backed her against one of the walls. Their tongues tangled as he pressed his hips into hers. He was hard and hot against her belly. She reached out to cup his butt in her fingers, pulling him closer, and ground her pelvis against his erection.

He hauled his mouth off hers long enough to say, "Uh-uh. Ladies first."

"We don't have a condom," she gasped out.

"I can think of lots of things to do without one, sugar."

He licked down the side of her neck, nibbling at her collarbone. His hand slid over her belly and onward. He tangled his fingers in the curls between her legs, slipping through the wetness there. He sucked one of her nipples into his mouth, teasing the hardened flesh with his tongue as he rubbed between her legs. Her breathing accelerated.

"I'm going to come," she murmured.

His voice was low and dark. "Not quite yet." He dropped to his knees, his hands moving her legs apart slowly.

Her universe shrank to the size of Brandon's double shower, his hands holding her hips, his mouth on her, his tongue moving slowly over her clit. She couldn't be quiet if her life depended on it. She pulled one hand out of his hair, and clapped it over her mouth. James didn't like it when she made noise. Maybe Brandon wouldn't, either.

He took his mouth off her for a moment. "What's wrong?"

"The—the noise," she said through her hand.

"You get as noisy as you want. Don't hold back."

"You like it?"

"Hell, yeah. I love it," he said.

Emily braced a hand against his shoulder; her knees weren't doing a great job of holding her up right now. His tongue darted and slipped over the small button between her legs that sent shockwaves of arousal skittering over her skin. He pulled one of her legs over his shoulder to offer better access, and slid two fingers inside her, mimicking the movement of his tongue.

"Oh, God. Oh, please. Don't stop," she said.

She felt the familiar sensations of an oncoming orgasm—the feeling of being flung outside of herself, the shocks that started at her fingertips and toes and raced through her body, the noises she made in time with the thrusting of his fingers inside of her. He braced her with one hand on her hip and did something with his tongue she couldn't describe to anyone else, and it sent her over the edge. She let out a scream.

The orgasm went on and on, racing through her like an electrical current, leaving her gasping for breath and trembling. Fireworks went off behind her eyelids. She sagged against the shower wall.

He rested his cheek against her belly for a moment. He licked drops of water out of her belly button. Finally, he got to his feet and pulled her into his arms again.

She tried to catch her breath. "That was amazing."

"I got you clean, sugar. Now I'm going to get you nice and dirty," he said into her ear.

His voice sizzled against every nerve ending in her body. She loved his hands, his mouth, his body, but his voice almost sent her over the edge by itself.

He reached behind him and shut off the shower. Steam warmed them while they nestled in each other's arms.

"You okay?" he said.

She let out a contented sigh. "I feel incredible." She kissed one of his flat nipples. "It's your turn."

Seconds later, the sweet intimacy of their naked embrace was broken by what sounded like a herd of elephants stampeding up the front walk of Brandon's house. The front door opened with a bang.

"McKenna?" a male voice yelled out. "Honey, I'm home."

"Get your ass out here. Where the hell did you go?" another guy shouted.

"Don't tell me he's already asleep for the night. What a pussy." This comment brought laughter she could hear from behind the closed bedroom door.

"I'm going to kill those ass— dirtbags." Brandon

pulled Emily out of the shower. He grabbed a towel off the rack, wrapped her in it, and snatched one off for himself. "I'll be back." He strode out of the bathroom, securing the towel around his waist.

Emily dried herself while she heard him shouting above what sounded like a houseful of men talking and laughing.

"What. The. Fuck. Don't you ladies have a party across the street? This isn't the Holiday Inn. Why are you here?"

His comments were greeted by a chorus of responses.

"Cops came. We had to leave."

"That's all the beer you've got? We'd better send a rook to get some more. Hey, Matthews, hope you've got your wallet."

"Nice outfit, sexy. You know I love your legs."

Emily could hear more commotion in the hallway outside of Brandon's bedroom door. She tiptoed over and locked it. She tried to comb her wet hair with her fingers, which was always a good look. She had no clean clothes. Maybe it would be a good time to raid Brandon's dresser for something to put on. Plus, her underwear was trashed. She'd have to go commando. She pulled on a pair of his shorts and a t-shirt that fell almost to her knees.

"Hey, McKenna, we heard some screaming. You sure there's not a dead body somewhere?"

An indeterminate number of men fell silent. She couldn't see what was happening, but she heard Brandon again.

"Nice to know you've never made a woman scream before." She heard his chuckle. "That's too bad. Maybe you need to put a little more effort into it."

She didn't hear anything for a few more seconds, and then she heard them interrupting each other.

"Emily's here? Shit."

"We'd better leave."

"We fucked up. Later, guy."

Emily heard the front door slam and Brandon's voice again.

"You're not driving anywhere. I'm calling you ladies some cabs. Grab a seat." She heard the footfalls of overly large men moving into the living room. A few seconds later, someone tapped on his bedroom door.

"Who is it?"

"Sugar, I need my phone."

She opened the door enough to admit him. He shut it behind himself. "Don't you look cute in my clothes?"

"It was that or go naked."

She saw his mouth curve into a smile. "You know which I'd prefer."

He reached into his dresser to grab some underwear and clothing for himself, pulling them on as he spoke. She got a great look at his gorgeous butt as he pulled up his boxer briefs.

"Do you need my help at all?" she said. "What happened?"

"They got out of Damian's before they got arrested." He nodded toward the window. There were ten squad cars parked around Damian's house, red and blue lights still swirling. The sound system was off, or significantly turned down. Things appeared quiet. "You're sweet to offer, but things are under control. They shouldn't be driving. I'll make sure they're on their way home safely, and we can spend some more time together afterward." He reached out to stroke her cheek. "I'll be changing the locks in the morning. Make yourself comfortable, and I'll bring you something to eat or drink if you'd like."

"Thank you, but I'm fine. Thanks for checking on me."

"Anytime." His lips twitched into a smile. He reached out to grab his wallet and smart phone off the bedside table, shoving both into his pocket. "Maybe you should rest up. I intend to make sure you're exhausted later."

"I'll look forward to that," she managed to say. That voice. It should be illegal.

She wrapped her arms around his waist. He kissed the side of her neck and the sensitive spot behind her earlobe, then let himself out of the room again.

She heard conversation from the living room, a few bursts of laughter, and Brandon giving the address and cross-street to his house. Emily pulled the blankets on his bed back, and wiggled between the sheets. A little nap wouldn't hurt. The bed smelled like him, too.

She glimpsed a flotilla of cabs arriving in front of his house through Brandon's bedroom window. Several of the neighbors came out of their houses and stood on the sidewalk, watching men they saw sixteen Sundays each year stuff themselves into the cabs. A few minutes later, the cops joined in on the impromptu block party.

Chapter Fifteen

EMILY HEARD BRANDON's voice in her ear much too early the next morning. "Sugar. Wake up. It's gorgeous outside. Let's go to Icicle Creek today."

She let out a groan. "No. I wanna sleep." She pulled the pillow over her head. He took it away from her.

"If we go now, we'll have the place to ourselves."

"AaaaaAAAAGH." This time, Emily pulled the blankets over her head. Her chances were better of escaping detection this way. Actually, it would be moments before Brandon tore off the blankets, too, but a girl could dream.

He let out a laugh. "We're playing the pillow game today."

"Why do you have to be so cheerful when you wake up?" she complained.

"Because you're not."

"Please tell me you have a hangover," she moaned. His

typically sunny outlook was adorable. Well, it was sweet after ten AM. The rest of the time, it was annoying.

"Hell, no. Don't make me haul your pretty little ass out of bed."

"Let's snuggle for a while instead."

He pushed her hair aside, and kissed the back of her neck. His lips lingered on one of the more sensitive spots of Emily's body. "We can stay in bed all day if you'd like."

"Mmm," Emily purred. He pulled her closer. Finally they were alone, and they were about to get naked.

The bedroom door flew open, hitting the wall with a bang.

"Hey, McKenna. Top Pot says 'hi.'" Greg shoved a paper tray with two cups of coffee and a box of doughnuts onto Brandon's dresser. "Breakfast in bed, guy." He nodded at Emily. "Hey, Em."

"Hey," she said weakly, and pulled the blankets up over her head again.

ICICLE CREEK WAS located ninety minutes east of Seattle, and just outside of Leavenworth, WA, a small town with Tyrolean flair. Brandon had promised Emily an "easy hike," but his idea of an easy hike would probably incapacitate the average woman. They'd walked for a couple of hours already. Despite working out five days a week, Emily was getting tired. Her steps slowed. She pulled the water bottle off her belt, and took a swallow.

As they hiked, Brandon was still musing over the beatdown he was going to give Greg at his earliest convenience. He couldn't actually hit him. Maybe he'd just get Greg in a headlock, or tell his girlfriend about last year's road trip to Tampa Bay. Greg seemed unfamiliar with basic Man Code: Stay out of another guy's room without knocking first.

Above all, his house wasn't a frat.

If that wasn't bad enough, Brandon was currently feeling the most intense sexual frustration he could remember since he was sixteen and got caught messing around with his junior prom date in the guys' locker room. If he'd waited till later in the evening, things might have gone better for everyone concerned. Then again, he'd seen Missy at a few school reunions since. She didn't seem mad about it.

The whole pretend engagement thing had him thinking; only an asshole would seduce a woman he didn't really have a relationship with. When he and Emily first met, it was a business thing. Somewhere along the way, they'd abandoned "pretend" and went straight for "let's give it a try." Their relationship—and they sure as hell had one now—started slowly. The physical side took time, too. Emily's ex had done such a number on her that at first she had jumped every time he touched her. In other words, he was all for casual sex, but this was something more. Plus, he really liked Emily. Nailing a woman for the sheer enjoyment of it was poor form. Well, unless she wanted him to. He was fairly positive she wanted him to, after last night's fun in the shower.

If Greg hadn't come busting into his bedroom right about the time Brandon felt Emily rubbing up against his junk this morning, it wouldn't be an issue. They would have spent the day in bed, and his frustration would be gone.

He hadn't spent time with anyone he was more interested in. If he was really honest with himself, he didn't think he'd meet anyone he'd be more interested in again.

"Asshole," he muttered to himself.

"What did you say?"

"Nothing." He spotted a clearing off the path. "Hey, let's rest for a minute." He pulled a blanket from his backpack, spread it out, and dropped onto it. He pulled his smart phone out of his shorts pocket, noted he had coverage, and dashed off a text to Greg: YOU'RE AT YOUR GIRLFRIEND'S TONIGHT.

"Please tell me you're tired."

"Hell, no. I could go another five miles. It's a gorgeous day and we're out here all alone . . ." His voice trailed off. It was one of those rarities in Washington—several days of over-seventy degree weather in May, and he could take advantage of the situation.

He turned to Emily, quirking a brow. "Ever been skinny dipping?" She looked alarmed, and he tried to smother his laughter.

She scooted away from him. "No. No, no, no. We have no towels," she argued. "The water's cold. I don't think this is a good idea . . ."

He reached over and untied her hiking boots. She half-heartedly pushed his hands away, which made him laugh even more. Emily pretended to be upset, but he saw the flush slowly climbing her cheeks. She was more shy than fearful.

"Are you scared, little diva?"

"Of course not."

He half-rolled toward her, stretching across the blanket and moving closer. Initially she scuttled away, but she stopped at the edge of the blanket. She wasn't frightened of the water. From the way her arms wrapped around her midsection, trying to fold herself in half, she was a lot more afraid of being seen naked in the great outdoors than anything else.

A naked Emily was now number one on his "to-do" list, and he was going to talk her into it. All she needed was some gentle persuasion. Luckily, he excelled at talking shy women out of their clothing.

"Let's go wading," he coaxed.

"I don't trust you." She wrapped her arms around her knees.

"Oh, you shouldn't," he agreed, and reached out to pull off her boots and her socks. "You're alone with me, and it's the middle of the week. There's nobody else for miles, and I have an agenda."

She tried to brush his hands away, but he tickled the bottom of her foot. She mumbled, "I don't know about this."

He stripped off his own hiking boots, socks, t-shirt and shorts. They landed in a pile. The sun felt great on his skin, and he crawled over, sprawling out next to her.

Her voice trembled. "What are you doing?"

She was looking everywhere else but at him, and she

blushed even harder, if it was possible. He'd never seen this side of Emily before. He couldn't believe his bossy little diva was so shy about the whole thing.

"No one's going to see us," he reassured. He stroked her cheek with one fingertip. She opened her mouth, shut it, and opened it again.

"We don't need to take our clothes off to go wading—"

"Oh, come on. Where's your sense of adventure?"

Her voice dropped to almost a whisper. "This is not a great idea." Her voice was muffled as he tugged her t-shirt over her head, and unzipped her shorts. "We're in public. You're taking my clothes off. Maybe this is an experience I don't need to have."

"It'll be fun. Getting naked is always fun."

She let out a groan, which made him laugh again. He unhooked her bra, slid it off, and pulled her panties down her legs. She looked like she wanted to argue with him some more, but she shut her mouth just as quickly. She lay on her side facing him, crossed her arms over her abdomen and her legs at the ankle, and reluctantly met his eyes.

"It's warmer out here than I thought." She sounded surprised. Her face was still flushed, but the rest of her— God, the rest of her . . .

He looked at her, and then he stared. He hadn't seen much last night, but right now he was seeing it all. His eyes traveled over her with glacial slowness, from toenails painted candy-apple red, up pale thighs she probably thought were too large, and over parts of her that never saw the sun. He reached out to brush her arms away.

"Let me see," he breathed. She lowered her eyelids under his scrutiny, and he saw her eyes fix on the bulge in his shorts.

She was going to short out if this kept up. She colored. She stammered. She couldn't take her eyes off of him.

He looped a lock of hair behind her ear.

"You look like one of those paintings I saw in Art History class," he said. Emily was Christmas morning, and the presents were all for him. "You're beautiful, sugar. You're all lushness and curves. I can't wait to touch you." He watched her lips move into a smile, and reached out to tickle her.

BRANDON LOOKED LIKE a sun-kissed version of Michelangelo's David, with better abs. Even though her fiancé still wore his boxer briefs, David suffered in comparison. Emily reached out to lay her palm on the mother of all six-packs. His skin was warm and his abdomen rockhard; the hair curled around her fingers as she slowly drew them over the rippling muscles.

She was rapidly losing whatever resistance she'd mustered up.

"Come on, sugar." He pulled off his boxer briefs, dropped them on the pile of clothing, and held out his hand. "Try it," he coaxed. She struggled to her feet. He scooped her up in his arms and waded out into the water. Emily crossed her legs and pulled herself up against him, hoping to stay dry. "Aren't you cold?"

"Of course not," he said, but his teeth were chattering. "It'll be okay in a minute."

He waded out until the water was above his waist and glanced down at Emily. She grabbed for herself. "You're looking at my boobs. Quit it."

"Make me." He pulled Emily closer and kissed her.

One of her feet slipped and dangled in the freezing water, but she didn't care. She forgot she was naked. She forgot she was in a public place. She forgot everything but his lips and his tongue and the way he tasted.

Then Brandon tossed Emily through the air and into the water.

She came up sputtering. It was freezing. She'd never experienced anything so cold. She got to her feet and yelled, "What the hell was *that*?"

Brandon waved a wet finger at her. She splashed him. Emily's hair dripped liquid icicles down her back. The water was up to her ribcage as she moved slowly toward him.

"You're gorgeous when you're mad," he said.

"You are *so* getting dunked, NFL Boy." She hurled herself at him. He didn't move.

"Now you're talking trash. Bring it." He shook the water out of his curls like an overgrown golden retriever. His teeth weren't chattering anymore. He was too busy laughing at her. She didn't miss the gentle amusement in his eyes.

She hooked her foot around his ankle, managing to pull his leg out from under him. They both fell into the water again.

He came up laughing. "That'll teach me." He pulled Emily closer. She felt something against her leg that wasn't either one of them.

"Ewww. What was that? I don't like it!" she shouted.

"It's a fish saying hello, sugar." He rubbed his ear. So, she was a little loud when startled. "Take it easy."

Emily was getting used to the freezing cold. They were in one of the most beautiful places she'd ever seen. The mountains rose around them; the sky was a brilliant azure blue. The water flowed white over various boulders.

Suddenly aware of the water's currents, Emily said, "We're floating."

"I've got you. Look over there." He nodded toward the shore.

Two young deer stood in the clearing where they left their things. The doe regarded them with liquid brown eyes. The young buck bowed his fur-covered antlers toward them as if he were tipping his hat. He ambled to the blanket and nudged Brandon's backpack with his nose. His lady friend followed him. They delicately picked their way to the water's edge, and dipped their muzzles into the rushing water.

"Maybe they'll steal your shorts," Emily murmured.

"That's not going to happen. Even if it did, you like me naked anyway."

Emily could feel her face flaming again. Another look at that package wasn't unwelcome.

"It's so cold," she said, "but I wouldn't miss this for anything."

The deer continued to drink from the river. Butterflies danced around the clearing in the sunshine. The gentle breeze ruffled the grass and the wildflowers. It was a Disney movie come to life, except for the whole "nude in the great outdoors" angle.

Slowly but surely, wherever Emily's flesh touched his, she was warm. She rested her cheek against his chest, and the wiry blond curls there tickled her nose. Brandon bent his head and captured her mouth in another long, slow, sensual kiss. She brought her hips against his and wrapped her arms around his neck. His tongue moved against Emily's, darting and slipping. Of course, her knees weren't working.

"I've got you," Brandon said. "But you're cold. Let's go lie down."

He led Emily out of the water and up the bank. They slipped on the wet rocks a bit, but made it back to the blanket. The deer had wandered away. The only sounds besides their breathing were the rushing water, trees rustling in the breeze, and birds chirping in the distance. She lay down in the sunshine, rolled onto her back, and held her arms out to him. Even if they were both still dripping wet, Emily wanted him as close as she could get him.

"Still mad at me?" he asked.

Her fingers tangled in his chest hair. "I don't know what you're talking about."

His head rested on her shoulder. She dropped a kiss on his forehead. He circled one of her nipples with a fingertip. "They look like little raspberries."

Brandon and Emily lay quietly for a few moments,

drying in the sun, and then he shoved himself up on his elbow. "Where were we?" he murmured as he took her face in his hand. His leg slipped against hers, and he covered her with his body. He was hard against Emily's belly, and she realized she'd been waiting for this since the moment they met.

"You were kissing me, and then you dumped me into the water."

"It was an accident. I'll make it up to you," he said.

"I'm not sure that's possible," Emily said.

"You don't say." He covered her breast with one hand, and teased the nipple with his thumb. Shocks of sensation rolled through her body. "There's no Tiffany's out here. I'm fresh out of the usual offerings. Will you take a rain check? I'd hate to think you were so mad at me that we couldn't continue enjoying ourselves . . ."

He pulled his hand away from her.

"It wasn't . . . It wasn't that bad," she burst out.

"Maybe we should go swimming again, then."

"Oh, no. I want to!"

His hand resumed its previous position, and he nibbled at her collarbone. His voice dropped to a sexy rumble. "Tell me what you want." He watched her through half-lidded eyes. "Don't leave anything out."

She tried to draw air into her lungs. "You," she said. Her arms slid around him, and she pulled him even closer. "I want you."

He took the nipple he'd been idly stroking into his mouth. His tongue swirled around it, and she wrapped one of her legs around his. She relaxed into his arms.

Everything was great, until an awful thought crossed her mind.

"Wait. Wait a minute." Emily pushed him off enough to sit up, and scrabbled around for her clothes. "I have to get dressed. We don't have any condoms. We can't do this without a condom."

"We're fine, sugar." He reached over, rooting through the pile of clothes, pulling something from his shorts pocket. He pushed the small foil packet into Emily's hand as he eased her back down onto the blanket again. "All set."

Obviously Emily wasn't a virgin. He wasn't, either. Even if she wanted this, she was nervous, and it was now a lot more than a no-strings encounter. This would change everything. "It's broad daylight, we're outside, and—"

She didn't finish her sentence. His mouth came down on hers. She was too busy kissing him to think of anything else. His lips tasted like water. His tongue stroked in and out, lingering and exploring. He moved against her with exquisite slowness, his hand straying down her belly. His fingers mimicked what his tongue was doing, slowly, so slowly.

Emily felt the scratchy foil edge of the condom wrapper in her palm as she stroked his back with her fingertips. His fingers were making her tremble and shudder, and she arched frantically against him.

"Easy," he said, his voice soft in her ear.

"I want—I want—"

"I know you do. You're going to get there."

He suckled and played with her breasts until Emily's

nipples were hard and aching. He stroked up and down, his fingers moving in and out of her. She let out a moan. He wasn't done. He kissed his way over her belly, down, down, until she felt him spread her legs. He tasted her where his fingers had been.

"Oh. Oh. Oh, God." He was making more of those little circles with his tongue and then his fingertips, and she gasped. She moaned. She begged him. "Please, Brandon, please."

His voice was dark, rough, and it came from somewhere she'd never heard before. "Do you want me, sugar?"

"Yes. Oh, yes, oh, God, please."

More licks, more stroking, more rubbing. Emily felt the waves start at her fingertips, the skittering rush of sensation over her skin, and the flashes of heat in her blood. "Come for me." He pulled her into his mouth, suckled her, flicked his tongue over that small nub of flesh, and gently bit.

Emily came so hard she saw stars. She cried out and heard his soft chuckle. He rolled onto his side, gathering her into his arms. She let out a contented sigh. A few minutes passed. She was sated, drowsy, and warm, and all she wanted was to fall asleep.

He had other plans. "We're not done yet."

"Thank *God*," she said with feeling.

Brandon kissed her through his laughter.

His hands roamed over her body once more. He took the foil packet from her hand, tore it open with his teeth, and unrolled the latex disc onto himself. Moments later, he moved over her again. She felt the prodding at her entrance, and heard him say, "Ready?"

Emily's eyelids fluttered closed. The sun beat down, the water rushed, the breeze blew over them. Brandon's breath was warm on her cheek, and she felt the thin sheen of sweat on his skin. She wrapped her legs around his waist. She reached down to cup his butt in both hands and froze.

Maybe she was hearing things, but it sure sounded like voices coming from the path nearby. She let out a gasp. They weren't done yet, she thought wildly. They hadn't even started!

Emily heard him whisper, "Sugar. Don't move."

Chapter Sixteen

BRANDON PULLED AWAY, grabbing the edge of the blanket and flinging it over them. "Shhh. They'll be gone in a minute."

Emily heard footsteps and voices. A group of people walked on the path, which was probably twenty-five feet away. Brandon did his best to conceal her, but he was almost completely exposed.

"We need to do something," she whispered.

"Stay still."

It was all Emily could do to remain immobile. She wanted to move. She could lose herself in him. But first, they needed to lose the intruders.

Emily heard a young boy shouting, "Hey. What are those people doing over there?" She heard running footsteps and even more voices, which were a little too close for comfort. "They're naked. Dad, look."

"Boys, you shouldn't see this." The more the man must

have tried to herd his kids away, the closer they came. Emily looked up into Brandon's face in a panic. She saw a flush high on his cheekbones. She knew he was probably as embarrassed as she was, but he was doing his best to remain calm.

An older male's voice rang out. "Hey. Aren't you Brandon McKenna?"

If Brandon moved, he'd expose Emily. If he didn't move, one of them was going to ask him for an autograph.

"Get out of here," Brandon ground out.

"You're fornicating in a public place," the adult male informed Brandon.

Brandon's voice dripped with sarcasm. "Thanks for letting me know. Take your kids and leave."

"Do you know what effect this will have on young, impressionable boys?"

Brandon laid a hand over the side of Emily's face so the guy couldn't see it. "The longer you stand here, the more they're going to see. Get out. Now. Just go."

Emily heard a chorus of young voices:

"What are they doing, Dad? Why don't they have any clothes on?"

"My parents do that, too. They told me they were wrestling."

"I can see his butt."

"What's 'fornicating'?"

"Oh, my God," she whispered to Brandon. Her heart was pounding. Her cheeks were burning with embarrassment. She could feel Brandon's body tensing against hers as he tried to pull more of the blanket over them with his free hand.

Finally the group's footsteps moved off down the path. Brandon waited until all was silent again, and rolled off of her.

"I'm so sorry," he said.

"For what? It's not like we invited them."

"I don't think they saw you. Well, I hope not."

Emily stroked his face. "You were so sweet to protect me."

"Naked wrestling," he mused.

She couldn't help it; she laughed. At first, Brandon looked a bit annoyed, and then he threw his head back and roared right along with her.

"So much for the big romantic moment," Emily said.

"That's me, Mr. Romance. I finally get a beautiful naked woman all to myself, and the Cub Scouts come calling."

They laughed until they cried, and then Brandon and Emily dressed each other. It took a little longer to zip and snap and button than it did to get the clothes off in the first place. They lay back on the blanket again.

Brandon grinned at her. "We'll never forget our first time."

"It's a good thing to have sex without an audience."

"We'll probably have to leave the country to do it, but it'll happen." He raised an eyebrow. "You know, I'd like to try this again without the scouting troop."

"Doing the wild thing outside?"

"It sounds great, but I have a better idea. There's a

really nice bed at my house, and a bottle of champagne in the fridge. Greg's probably cleared out by now."

"Race you to the car."

BRANDON FROWNED AS he concentrated on the treacherous road over the mountain pass that led back to his house. Emily knew she wasn't helping. At the same time, she couldn't take her hands off him.

"So, what are you going to do to me when we get there?" Emily said, laying a hand on his thigh.

"Sugar, if you don't keep those hands to yourself, we're gonna slide right off the edge here. It's a pretty steep drop."

She moved her hand a fraction of an inch higher. "I can think of some things I'd like to do to you. First, I'll take your clothes off very slowly. I'll work my way up from your feet, up over your ankles, up your calves and thighs. I'll lick my way to your—"

"Maybe we should talk about something else," he interrupted.

Emily slid her hand another fraction of an inch up his thigh in response.

"We'll never make it home. Jesus, sugar, have mercy." His lips curved into a smile, though. "Then again, we have a backseat." He wriggled his eyebrows at her.

"Maybe we'll meet the police this time instead of the Cub Scouts," Emily said. "My parents will be so proud."

"We'll show them how it's done."

Finally, the Kirkland exit came into view, and Brandon's Land Rover came to a screeching halt in front of his house. They raced up the walk and piled into the front door as he tried to get the key to work.

Emily panted, "What if we can't open the door?"

"We're breaking a window, sugar. There's no way in hell I'm not getting in here."

Finally, the lock opened.

"Greg," he shouted as he burst through the doorway. "Nordquist." There was blessed silence. He shut the door behind him with one foot as he reached for her. Emily's back thudded against the foyer wall as they slammed against it.

"Champagne," Emily gasped out between hot and hungry kisses. Half her clothes were off before she heard Brandon relock the front door. She was pulling his t-shirt over his head and trying to unzip his shorts at the same time.

"Bed first, and then I'll drink it out of your belly button," he promised. They dragged each other down the hallway.

Brandon tossed her onto his bed, pulled off her boots and socks one more time, and threw himself down next to Emily. He stretched one arm over her head, pulled open the drawer of the bedside table, and emptied a warehouse-store sized box of condoms onto her bare belly.

"I know you worry about these things. We have plenty."

They crawled between the bed sheets. Emily tangled her fingers in his hair and kissed him. She heard his low, sexy laugh as she came up for air.

"I thought I was supposed to be in charge," she said.

"Next time, sugar."

He took her mouth with long, slow, plundering kisses, and then, he took *her*. She couldn't resist him. He owned her. He conquered her. Emily reveled in the touch of strong, sure, gentle hands, his quiet murmurs, and the desire she saw in his eyes.

Brandon, she discovered, was more than generous with his attentions. She also enjoyed the resulting (and explosive) orgasms.

She lay against him as they both tried to catch their breath. Everything was quiet for a few moments. Emily traced his dimple with her fingertip.

"Is it always that good?"

A grin stole over his face, and his arms tightened around her once again. "We'd better do it again, just to make sure."

It was so successful that Brandon and Emily couldn't resist doing it once more before they fell asleep from sheer exhaustion. They finally managed to make love without roommates, teammates, Cub Scout troops, cell phones, or interruptions of any kind.

Sometime later, Brandon's stirring awakened Emily. She watched him sleep in the darkened room. His lips curved into a faint smile. She wanted to kiss him again. Actually, she never wanted to stop kissing him. She never wanted the hot, breathless, heart pounding excitement she got every time he pulled her into his arms to end, either. Even though Emily wasn't sure she wanted to be owned or conquered, she realized that she was done, in more ways than the obvious. Slowly but surely, she'd fallen in love with him.

THE NEXT MORNING, Emily awoke to the aroma of freshly brewed coffee drifting in from the kitchen, but that wasn't the only thing tickling her nose. His chest hair rubbed against her face. She breathed in a lungful of his clean skin and the familiar wisp of his aftershave. She snuggled against his warmth. He still wore that faint smile as he slept, and he kicked off the blankets sometime during the night. The tan lines on his thighs and at his waist made her smile. Maybe she should just stay put and enjoy the view.

In the end, though, the coffee won out. Emily slid out from under the arm he flung around her during the night and slithered off the bed. After putting on one of his robes, she padded into the kitchen. She poured two mugs out of the programmable coffee pot, picked the newspaper off the front porch, and carted it all back to bed.

He'd claimed last night she'd worn him out. She wasn't moving especially fast this morning, either.

Emily sat up against the headboard of Brandon's bed, skimming the front page stories.

"Oh, no. Oh, my God." She nudged him. "Wake up."

Brandon rolled onto his back. "What's the matter, sugar?" he said sleepily.

"The Scout leader gave an interview to *The Seattle Times.*"

It took him a few seconds to rub his eyes and stretch.

"You're shi— you're kidding me." Brandon pulled himself up against the pillows. He kissed Emily's cheek and wrapped one arm around her.

"He's talking about going to the police and having you arrested for indecent exposure and lewd behavior. Plus, he claims to have cell phone photos of us."

Brandon grabbed the paper, read the short article, and then threw it on the floor. He rubbed his face with one hand, but Emily saw the sadness in his eyes before he turned his face away from her.

"At least they didn't recognize you," he said, referring to the article's "unidentified redhead." It also said that Emily Hamilton "could not be reached for comment."

He took a deep breath. "Coffee must be ready."

She handed him a mug from the nightstand.

"You'll need to stay overnight more often," he said.

"This is the closest you're getting to breakfast in bed, bruiser."

He chuckled. "More cooking lessons? You know I'm up for it." His lips grazed the back of her neck. God. She wanted him again.

The telephone rang. He grabbed it. "McKenna." He listened for a moment and then said, "Hey, talk to my agent." He hung up.

"Who was that?"

"ESPN. They know what's going on in my life before I do." He rolled his eyes. The phone rang again. Brandon picked up the receiver, said, "McKenna," listened for a while, and frowned. "Listen, Coach, I apologize. I didn't mean to embarrass the team. I'm surprised the commissioner's up that early on a Sunday." He was quiet for a few more minutes. He was making light of this, but it sounded like he was in trouble, and her stomach twisted in sympathy. "Okay. I'll pay the fine. I understand why you're doing it." Emily heard the coach's voice, some laughter, and Brandon said, "Thanks for being so understanding. I'm available whenever you'd like to set it up. Thanks again." He hung up.

"They gave you a fine." If that guy really had photos, both she and Brandon were in a lot more trouble than they knew how to get out of.

"It's not a big deal. The commissioner's having a shi— He's a little upset."

Emily slumped down in the bed. She tried to pull the blankets up over her face, but Brandon wouldn't let her.

"I'll bet you twenty dollars that guy is on the morning news today," she said.

"I'm not taking that bet, sugar. Let's have a look." He clicked the television on with the remote.

They didn't have to wait long before a news program came on. When it was time for the sports report, yesterday's little escapade was first up.

"The Seattle Sharks are a bit red-faced this morning over the off-the-field antics of their Pro Bowl defensive end, Brandon McKenna," the male sportscaster began. "It seems that McKenna was spotted yesterday by a group of Cub Scouts just off a hiking trail outside of Leavenworth with an unidentified redhead. The couple was involved in what a team spokesperson calls 'a compromising situation.' McKenna is engaged to opera diva Emily Hamilton. We couldn't reach Miss Hamilton for comment. ESPN is reporting that McKenna has been fined $25,000 by the NFL commissioner for 'conduct unbecoming a professional athlete.'"

The female anchorperson gave the sportscaster a smirk. "Isn't Emily Hamilton also a redhead?"

"No comment," he said smoothly. "The Seattle Mariners are celebrating a nine-game winning streak with the latest victory by their red-hot closer . . ."

Brandon shut off the television. "Best twenty-five thousand dollars I've ever spent."

Her stomach churned. So far, he was taking the brunt of this, and it wasn't fair.

"Brandon, we're in a bunch of trouble, and that's a lot of money. I feel really badly about this."

He put the coffee mug down on the nightstand with a thud, and gathered Emily into his arms. "Listen. Am I sorry that we did it? No. Am I sorry we got caught? Only because it might affect you." He pulled her closer. "One thing's for sure, it was pretty damn memorable."

Emily laid her cheek against his. "I'm worried about the photos that guy says he has—"

"He doesn't have any damn photos. He's a liar."

"I'm sorry about the money."

"Don't be sorry. I talked you into it."

"Your fingers talked me into it," Emily said. She felt heat rising in her face.

He tipped her chin up and waggled one hand in front of her face. "They're still here." The phone rang again. He ignored it. His fingers were already a bit busy. "I should shut that damn thing off."

"Oh, yes," was all she could say.

He reached over and pulled the cord right out of the wall. "Kiss me, sugar."

Emily was only too happy to comply.

They didn't get out of bed for the rest of the day. The next morning, though, Emily found several messages from Amy on her cell phone. "David's looking for you. What happened yesterday, anyway? If he was with another woman—call me. Call me *now.*"

David also left a message. "Sweetie, you've gone from famous to red-hot. You've had three more booking requests already this morning."

The sheer irony that getting caught naked in public with her fiancé would bring additional bookings wasn't lost on Emily.

THE NEXT MORNING, Brandon and Emily made a quick trip to her house on their way to Sharks headquarters. She insisted she needed a change of clothes. After a day and a night together he didn't want to get out of bed, but they had to face the world at some point.

"I'm writing a check, sugar, not accepting the Nobel Peace Prize," Brandon called out from the kitchen, and poured himself a fresh cup of coffee. Emily had already discarded three different outfits on the living room sofa.

"I need an outfit that works for meeting your coach *and* my voice lesson this afternoon."

"This isn't that big of a deal. I believe business casual will suffice," he teased.

Emily bolted from the room. He could only imagine the carnage she wreaked on her bedroom closet. Every time he went somewhere with his little diva, she required at least two costume changes before making up her mind about what she was going to wear. Maybe it was best to keep the truth about today's appointment to himself, or they'd never make it out of the house.

He should feign annoyance. It wouldn't do to let her believe that he would happily wait all day for her. A man had to draw the line somewhere.

"Let's go, Miss Hamilton," he shouted up the stairs.

A few minutes later, Emily reappeared in the first outfit she tried on, a long sleeved, V-necked, floral print knee-length dress that showed off her curves to perfection. "Here I am," she said, pulling on a pair of bright red high heels. She spun around in front of him. "How do I look?"

He reached out for her hand, and twirled her into his arms. "Like my every fantasy. Where'd you find that dress?"

"It's a Ralph Lauren." She glanced up at him under her lashes. "You don't really care about designers."

"You got me. It's a nice dress, but I'll like it even more when you take it off again, sugar."

She wrapped her arms around his neck. He took a deep breath of the scent that always reminded him of warm peaches and freshly mowed grass. "I can't go naked all the time."

He let out a laugh. "Naked always works for me."

Half an hour later he pulled into a parking space at the

Sharks' headquarters. The visitors' parking lot was full, which wasn't a good sign. Even worse, he saw news trucks lined up outside the building. Emily glanced around at hundreds of parked cars and turned to him.

"There are an awful lot of people here today," she said. "Maybe you should tell me what's going on."

"I'm appearing at a press conference with the coach and the team's general manager in a few minutes."

She clasped her hands in her lap, crossed her ankles and leaned back in the passenger seat. He saw the two little worry lines that bracketed her nose whenever she frowned make an appearance. In other words, she was mad at him.

"I should have told you what was really going on, but I didn't want you to worry. All you have to do is sit there and look gorgeous," he reassured. "We'll be out of there before you know it."

She shook her head.

"Don't be mad at me, sugar," he cajoled. He reached out to lay one hand over hers.

She was silent for a minute or two. She turned to face him. "It hurts my feelings when you aren't truthful with me about what's really happening. I feel like you don't trust me when you do it."

He thought she might be a bit irritated with him. He couldn't have been more shocked if she doubled up a fist and drove it into his gut.

She pulled in another lungful of air. "If we're going to stay together, if we're going to move forward, I need to feel like you trust me enough to tell me what's going on."

All he heard was "*if.*" Fear skittered up and down his spine, a cold, slimy presence. Her quiet anger shook him more than if she'd screamed at him. Even more, she didn't wrap her fingers around his hand like she usually would. She turned to look out the window again.

He swallowed hard. "You're right. I should have talked to you about this. I'm sorry. I will do my best to make sure it doesn't happen anymore."

She scooped her handbag off the floorboard. "We're going to be late."

He hurried around the front of his car to loop an arm around her shoulders. A few seconds later, he felt her arm slide around his waist. He let out the breath he'd been holding.

A SHORT TIME later, Brandon, the Sharks' coach, and the team's general manager sat before a packed room. Emily was sitting in a chair he found for her in the back of the room. He winked at her. He saw her lips twitch into a smile.

"Mr. McKenna has a prepared statement, and then we'll take questions," the general manager said.

Brandon cleared his throat, took a sip of water, and said, "I'd like to apologize to the young men who observed my conduct yesterday. It was regrettable, and I apologize to them and to their parents. The group will be my guests at an upcoming Sharks game as well. I have paid the fine I was assessed by the league. I hope that we can put this incident behind us and move on."

The first reporter didn't even wait until the echo from the microphone was over. "Were you with Emily Hamilton?"

"My mama always told me that gentlemen don't kiss and tell."

"Has Miss Hamilton apologized as well?"

"She has nothing to apologize for." Brandon's hands curled into fists. Wait till that guy was looking for "an exclusive" next season.

The general manager held up a hand. "Let's leave Miss Hamilton out of this."

"She was with you, wasn't she?" The press smelled blood in the water. He wasn't going to give them what they wanted.

"No comment," Brandon said.

"If you weren't with her, who were you with?"

"No comment," Brandon said, but with a bit more emphasis.

"Are you and Miss Hamilton still engaged, and does she know you were with someone else yesterday?"

He really didn't care what they said about him, but trashing Emily was out of the question. *Don't flip out*, he told himself. *It's what they want. Stay calm.* As much as he wanted to punch that asshole from the second-place sports radio station, it wasn't going to help her. For the first time, the downside of being engaged to a man whose every public activity had the potential for media coverage was making itself known to Emily. More than his own embarrassment, he felt badly for her.

Brandon scanned the crowd till he found Emily again.

Their eyes met, and held. He saw color rising in her face, but she touched her fingertips to her lips, and lightly blew. At that moment, he knew he would walk through a wall for her.

One of the female reporters spoke up. "What were you thinking, Brandon?"

"What's any man thinking when he's alone with the woman he loves?"

A wave of laughter cascaded through the room.

"How'd you feel about the fine?" another reporter asked.

"It's the best twenty-five thousand dollars I've ever spent." He grinned at the guy. "I think we're done here. Thanks, everyone."

People yelled out questions about Brandon's contract and would he be signing for another year with the team. He saw Emily surrounded by reporters. He hoped she knew the two magic words: "No comment."

He threw himself into the crowd. At last, he grabbed her hand. "Let's go, sugar." He swept her out of the room.

More reporters and at least one news crew ran after them. Brandon hustled Emily through a door marked "Staff and Players," shutting it behind them, and pulled her through another doorway and out into the parking lot.

"If we run fast, we might make it," he said.

DESPITE TRYING TO blush herself into a coma, Emily was proud of how Brandon handled a roomful of reporters.

They threw themselves into the Land Rover and drove away just as the reporters arrived in the parking lot.

Brandon glanced over at Emily. "We'll have to decide what we'd like for lunch."

"I'm fine with almost anything."

He played with her hand. She laced her fingers through his. Her voice was soft. "Those questions were pretty harsh."

He brought her hand to his lips and kissed the back of it. "Just a day's work. Not a big deal."

Emily realized she was mad at him earlier for not being truthful with her, but this whole conversation proved what a hypocrite she was.

She was too chicken to ask him if he meant it when he told the reporter he loved her; she didn't have the guts to bring it up.

"Somebody's pretty quiet. Is something wrong?" Brandon said.

"No. Everything's fine."

"Now, I realize I'm a man and that makes me pretty much oblivious to this kind of thing, but I've had experience with that 'everything's fine' stuff. Usually, it means something's wrong."

"I'm still thinking about the press conference," Emily said. She was lying to him, after she let him have it for lying to her. God, she sucked.

"They wanted the details because it sells newspapers. I don't like what they said about you. I know we both wanted publicity, but not this kind of publicity." He shook his head. "I promise I'll take care of this."

"You don't have to do that—"

"Trust me. I'll handle it." Brandon turned his attention to the road.

"Maybe I can help," Emily said. "It's not fair that you should take the heat by yourself. I was there, too."

"Aren't you sweet." He flashed her a quick smile. "I know the press can be tough on women in these types of stories. They're not so anxious to take me on, though." He reached out for her hand again. "I hope you're hungry. I'm starving. Let's go get some pancakes, and then I'll drop you off at your lesson. We'll make some dinner later. I'll teach you to make lasagna."

"Will there be more kissing?" Emily asked.

"Absolutely." He braked for a red light, and gazed into her eyes. "You're my dessert. I do amazing things with chocolate sauce."

Emily's toes curled.

Chapter Seventeen

EMILY BREEZED THROUGH the front door of Amy's flower shop five minutes after she opened for the day, carrying two nonfat lattes and a box of baked goods. Amy narrowed her eyes at her sister.

"Nice to see you stopped by the bakery. I told you I was gaining weight."

Emily set the box and the coffee tray on Amy's worktable. "It's a pretty big occasion," she said.

"Better be." Amy pulled a chocolate iced doughnut from the box and took a bite. "God, this is good. I can only imagine what you might be celebrating." She leaned closer to Emily. "Let's see here. Flushed, smiling, eyes sparkling, hair's got that tousled look." Her sister pointed at her with the doughnut. "You just boinked Brandon."

Emily bit into a lemon tart, and tried not to look so damn obvious.

"Oh, I need *all* the details." Amy grabbed her coffee cup and another doughnut. "Spit it out."

"Have you talked to Mom?"

"Quit it. I need to know." The phone rang. "This will not get you out of some answers. Hello, Crazy Daisy." Amy listened for a moment, and Emily saw an evil smile steal over her lips. "Brandon, it's so nice of you to call." Emily choked on her coffee. "No, no, things are fine. I'd love to help you with that. Is there anything specific you'd like to send?" She listened for a few more minutes and said, "I'll get right on it. What would you like on the card?" She scribbled on the notepad next to the phone. "I'll make sure she gets them this afternoon. Thanks for thinking of me." She laughed. "I'll be sure to do that. You, too. Bye."

She hung up the phone and said, "If you don't marry him, I will. He said he wanted to send something as lush and as beautiful as you are."

"He makes me sound like the Amazon rainforest."

"You're getting Ariana roses and freesia," Amy said. "Maybe some white lilies and greens. I got some this morning. They're gorgeous."

"Maybe it's bad that he's not sending red roses."

"Everyone else does. They're boring." Amy grinned at her sister. "He said that I was the professional and I knew what would make you happy. He also said that he wants a bunch of my business cards to give out to guys on the team who are always looking to send flowers, so I scored. Maybe he'd like a case of microbrew as a thank-you gift." She plunked down on the stool by the worktable. "Out with it. What happened yesterday?"

Emily was ebullient, but also a little scared. She'd spent the previous night having sheet-scorching sex with a man she adored. A box of baked goods sat open in front of her, Brandon was sending flowers, and the day was shaping up to be spectacular. At the same time, she had a big confession to make.

"I don't know what to do," Emily said.

"Take him back to bed later. Doesn't that sound like a plan? It does to me." Amy bit off another huge chunk of chocolate-frosted doughnut.

"I'm in love with him."

Amy flew around the table to throw her arms around Emily. "Finally. I have been waiting to hear you say that." She returned to her chair, sat down, put her chin in her hand, and said, "You're shaking. You're scared shitless, you big chicken."

"I thought I was in love before," Emily said.

"You are the only woman on the planet that could have an evening with a man most women would do just about anything to body slam, and not be quivering with happiness afterward," Amy said. "Buck up, little camper."

"It's not that I'm not happy—"

"I can't believe you. You're not doing this, Em. I *know* you. What happened?"

Emily let out a sigh. "Well, you know about what happened at Icicle Creek."

Amy's grin was positively saucy. "Everyone knows by now. Where'd you go after you guys gave the Cub Scouts an eyeful?"

"His house. We didn't get out of bed all day yesterday."

"Details."

"I don't think so," Emily said.

Amy took a sip of her coffee. "Was it good? And how many times?" Her sister was teasing her, but Emily saw the happiness in her face.

"I'm not going to t—"

"You tell me everything else."

Emily closed her eyes for a moment.

"It was incredible. He's—Amy, he's beautiful. All of him. His chest is just—I couldn't stop touching him. He smells so good, he tastes so good, and he's an amazing kisser. He's funny and wonderful, and he's really good at taking my clothes off. He made me forget my own name." Emily grinned. "Lots of orgasms. *Lots of them.*"

Her sister's mouth dropped open. "And you're not home in bed with him now?"

"He had to go to his workout, and meet with his trainer. I missed my lesson today." Emily wrapped her arms around her midsection. "It's going to cost me."

"Who gives a shit? I wouldn't." Amy shrugged. "Maybe I should date his brother."

"Dylan isn't an athlete. He's a doctor."

"I'm still not getting what the problem is here," Amy said.

"Maybe he doesn't love me back," Emily said.

"If he's not already in love, he's been on his way for a long time now. Why do you think every guy you meet is another James?" Emily flinched, and Amy reached across the table to squeeze her hand. "I'm sorry. That was an awful thing to say, but Em, it's true. You meet the greatest guy ever, and—well, that's ridiculous."

"The whole time I was with James, I kept thinking things were moving along. We were dating, we were sleeping together, Mom and Dad loved him, things seemed like they were falling into place. I thought he was the best I could do." Emily fiddled with the paper sleeve on her coffee cup.

"You never felt about him the way you feel about Brandon."

Emily shrugged.

"You've obviously forgotten whom you're talking to," Amy said. "I saw you post-James. I never saw you like this. Plus, I seem to remember that James had a few—shall we say, *problems* in the bedroom."

James had a low sex drive. He shrank from Emily when she tried to hold his hand. He wanted to be in control. He dictated every instance of physical affection between them. It was "inappropriate" to kiss him in public. A hand on the thigh when they sat together was deemed "too aggressive." Emily spent the entire year she and James were together in a state of utter frustration. She loved touching and being touched in return. She longed for passion. She wanted to be with someone who valued what she wanted to share with him. Even Amy had no idea how extensive James' problems were.

The few times James and Emily entered his bedroom, things went downhill fast. According to him, Emily was too noisy. She was too fat. Her boobs were not as "perky" as they should have been, and she shivered at the memory. She couldn't imagine why she stayed with him, and even more, why she was still letting him inside her head. Somehow James had managed to penetrate into areas of her psyche nobody else had, and Emily's job was to oust him. Permanently. She deserved better.

"Brandon's the exact opposite," Emily said. Just thinking about last night made her smile again. He had celebrated and cherished every inch of her—several times. "I understand why Anastasia went so sideways after they broke up. I'd miss it, too."

"She said on that entertainment show his nickname should be 'Tiny.'"

"Amy, she's nuts. He's definitely proportional."

Her sister's eyes lit up with glee again. Time for a subject change.

"Mom and Dad are still a little cautious around him," Emily said.

"There's nothing you can do. Just wait them out," her sister advised. "They'll get over it."

"I don't understand why they liked James and Dad is hesitant about Brandon. They had lunch, and Brandon said it went well. I thought Dad would warm up to him as a result, but it seems to be taking a little time." Emily took a sip of her soda. "Brandon's the better guy here. He makes me happy."

"I think you're worrying about this too much. Maybe you should talk to them."

"I did. It was the same arguments. 'He'll ruin your career. Can't you find someone at Seattle Opera to date? At least then he'd understand your schedule.'"

Emily rubbed her temples as Amy got to her feet. She knew her parents loved her, and they worried. She wondered how long it would take them to realize she'd made a good choice in Brandon.

"I have to do some stuff. You can help me," Amy said. "Come on. You know you want to," she teased. Amy dragged Emily into the refrigerated unit. A few minutes later, they were cleaning and preparing roses.

"Tell me what's new with—Steve, isn't it?"

"I dumped him. He was too clingy." Amy pretended fascination with a thorn caught in her shears.

"There must be someone else you'd like to date."

"Hell, no." Amy brushed the debris into the garbage can below her worktable. "There was a guy at the Chamber of Commerce meeting. He's a stockbroker. I don't know what he was doing there." She ran water in the sink to fill a bucket for the newly cleaned roses. "I heard he's thinking about running for the City Council."

"Eww, Amy. Not a politician."

"You dated one," Amy said.

"That was the mayor of Bellevue, and it lasted about twenty minutes. He considered lying to be a recreational sport. Tell me about the stockbroker."

"Tall, dark-haired, looks like he works out. He was talking to some guy about playing basketball in a league. He's not bad. Maybe a little buttoned-down for me."

Amy needed a guy who liked to play as hard as he worked. Steve, the ex, owned a restaurant group with his twin brother. At the same time, he sported an earring and rode a Harley on the weekends. He might have been clingy, but he also had Amy's number. Emily wondered what happened, but Amy wouldn't answer her questions on the subject.

Amy grabbed half a dozen roses out of the newly cleaned bucketful. She pulled another handful of flowers out of her walk-in to make an arrangement.

"You're going to have to tell Brandon how you feel."

"Oh, no. I'm not going there. Not for a while."

"You're wearing his ring. I'm thinking it's the perfect time."

"No. Not doing it. I'll sound like every woman on one of those cheesy reality dating shows that can't have sex without confessing true wuvvv."

Amy glanced up from her work to catch Emily's eye. "You have a ring. You guys did the horizontal mambo and, evidently, things went well. Life's short. Chop, chop."

"I'm not ready."

"I think you're crazy." Amy's hands flew as she worked. The arrangement took rapid shape inside a square glass cube vase.

"Maybe you should tell me what's on the card."

Amy let out a low laugh. "You'll be finding that out for yourself."

She stepped away from the worktable, plucking an enclosure card from the assortment on the front counter. She spent a few minutes writing whatever Brandon had dictated to her, returned to the workroom, and secured the card in the arrangement with a plastic holder. She put the arrangement into Emily's arms.

"From Brandon. Enjoy it."

Emily smelled the flowers, admiring her sister's skill. "You do excellent work."

"I know. Be sure and thank him for this."

"There's a very good chance he's about to get lucky again." Emily kissed her sister goodbye. "I'm going home before the traffic's insane."

"See ya. Take your damn doughnuts out of here, too."

Emily managed to make it back to her car before tearing the little white envelope open to read the message Brandon sent with the flowers.

Sugar, I long for you. – B

She closed her eyes and hugged the notecard to herself. He could have written hundreds of words, but he'd packed a world of emotion into four. She slipped the message into her handbag so she wouldn't lose it.

EMILY SPENT THE drive to her townhouse musing over Amy's comments. As much as she hated to admit it, Amy was right. She needed to tell Brandon how she felt about him. Truthfully, she hoped Brandon would say those three little words before she did.

Her cell phone rang, and she hit the speaker function.

"Hey, sugar, how are you?"

Brandon's voice made her heart rate pick up. She flashed on a great mental picture of a rumpled bed and a blond, naked, sleepy-eyed man highlighted with morning sunshine.

"Fine. How are you?"

"Never better. I hope you're free a little later."

Emily's voice dropped to a purr. "That depends. Maybe you should tell me what you have in mind."

"Let's have some dinner and see what develops."

"Where are you now?"

"One lane over, and a car back from you." Emily glanced into her mirror, recognizing Brandon's black Land Rover. "Maybe I should follow you home."

"Maybe you should," Emily said. "Don't tell my fiancé, though."

"Really?" He was the only man on earth that could make one word sound unbelievably sexy. "Will he be jealous?"

Emily took the exit to her house. "I think so," she said.

"We'll have to make sure we don't get caught."

"Maybe you'd better tell me what we're doing when we get there."

"I'll think of something. Right now, though, I think I should turn you over my knee and spank you."

"What? Me?"

"That's right. Flirting with other men. I'm shocked, Emily Anne."

Emily was never into that before, but right about now, it sounded tempting. She hit the remote control buttons, and pulled into her garage. She grabbed her handbag as Brandon came around to the driver's side of her car. He reached in for the flowers, put them on the hood of the Escape, and pulled her into his arms.

"Somebody sent me flowers today," she breathed against his mouth.

"Some other guy's trying to pick up my girl. I'll have to deal with him."

"His name's Brandon." She shivered. "He's amazing."

"Not as amazing as you are. I missed you today."

"You must have made it to your appointments." She reached up to run her fingers through his still-damp curls.

"I was late. I got a lot of sh— crap from the guys." She saw a faint wash of color over the top of his cheekbones. "Let's just say that I don't typically use the lavender and vanilla fabric softener, and that's what I smelled like when I got there."

"I'll need to use something more—manly—on your sheets."

Emily heard a low chuckle in her ear, and he traced the shell of her ear with his tongue.

"Sugar, the only thing I care about is that you're lying on them, and that you're naked while you're doing it. Let's go."

Two DAYS AFTER Emily and Brandon finally pried themselves out of her bed, she left for performances in Washington, DC. The diva scheduled to sing Gilda in *Rigoletto* had just come off a series of successful performances at Mexico's national opera house. She'd also evidently eaten tomato *Provencale* with her breakfast one morning, and had contracted the worst case of Montezuma's Revenge known to mankind. Emily sang the role after the cover came down with a bad cold as well. She was very happy with her performances and the reviews. Of course, the press was more interested in her fiancé and their engagement.

The daily grind of voice lessons, rehearsals for upcoming productions, occasional interviews, and photo shoots flew by as she counted the hours till she raced home to be with Brandon.

Emily arrived back in Seattle on a sunny, late afternoon in July. Brandon was due at the Sharks' training camp the next morning. He'd be there for three weeks. He also had an appearance he couldn't get out of that evening. Her job required travel, too, but Emily was sad about not seeing him before he left. Showing up at the team's facilities was out of the question. At least they could text and talk on the phone.

A little after ten o' clock that night, she heard a knock at the front door of her house.

"Sugar, it's me," Brandon said as she peered through the peephole. Her heart leapt. She pulled the door open.

He wore dark dress slacks, a heathery-brown, long-sleeved, cashmere V-neck sweater with a t-shirt beneath, and a huge grin.

"Aren't you going to get in trouble for this? What time do you have to be there tomorrow morning?"

"I don't care. I have to see you."

He strode inside, shut the door, and kissed her. She wrapped her arms around his neck. He pulled her off her feet and swung her around the front hallway of the house.

"Tired?" he asked several minutes later.

"A little," she admitted. "I missed you, though."

"I want to take you somewhere. Throw some clothes on."

"I don't have any makeup on," Emily argued.

"You look great. Let's go, sugar."

Emily ran upstairs to her room. She pulled on jeans, a knit top, socks, shoes, and a hooded sweatshirt in record time.

Five minutes later, they were on the freeway.

"Please tell me we're not going somewhere that requires dress clothes."

"Persistent little thing." His voice was affectionate. "I'm taking you out for fish and chips."

Emily tore her eyes away from the moonlight rippling over Lake Washington on either side of the 520 Bridge to turn and look at Brandon again. Even an hour with him was a thrill for her. If he got another fine from his coach over this, she might have to split it with him. He was worth it.

"When I first came to Seattle, one of the other guys dragged me all over town. We ended up at Ivar's Fish Bar on the waterfront." Brandon said. "I've been back many times since. I especially like coming down here late at night. It's not crowded, and it's quiet. We can get a bite and visit with each other."

"I haven't been there for a long time."

He reached over and took her hand. "Happy?"

"Yes." Emily clutched his hand in both of hers. She couldn't wipe the smile off her face. Then again, he was beaming, too.

They pulled up in front of the outdoor restaurant. People were strolling along the sidewalk, but no one

seemed to notice them. They must have been as transfixed as Emily was with the beautiful summer night and
the full moon. Brandon ordered food and drinks to go,
and hurried back to the car.

"I have somewhere special I want to show you," he
said, pulling away from the curb.

A few minutes later, Brandon and Emily arrived at
Sharks Stadium. He pulled into a space marked "Re-
served." He grabbed the food, took Emily's hand, and
hurried her inside a door to the stadium.

"Hey, Stan," he greeted the security guard.

Stan tipped his baseball cap. "Brandon. This must be
your young lady."

"Yes, she is. This is Emily. Sugar, this is Stan. He runs
the place." Stan let out a low laugh. "I'd like to go upstairs, if that'll work for you," Brandon said.

"Yeah. Have fun."

Brandon dragged her onto an elevator. Well, maybe
not quite "dragged," but he was definitely on a mission.
They exited a few floors up and walked through a concourse until they reached a group of picnic tables. Emily
sat down on the bench as Brandon unpacked their feast,
and she gazed at the perfect view of Elliott Bay from the
top level of the stadium.

"What do you think?" he asked.

"It's gorgeous."

"The view from the baseball stadium is pretty good,
too, but they don't know me over there." He pointed at
the sky, where the stars were thrown like diamonds over
black velvet. "Did you make a wish yet?"

"It's not the first star," Emily said.

"Make a wish anyway."

"No harm in trying." Emily closed her eyes and wished. Little did Brandon know, but all her dreams were already coming true. "What did you wish for?" she asked.

"You know I can't tell you that."

He fed her a piece of fish instead. It was delicious.

"I never knew you were a fish and chips guy," she teased.

"I had to get you up here. I have something for you." He dug into his pocket.

"You already bought me a really nice ring, and I love the earrings. I enjoyed the flowers, too," she said.

"But that was all a few months ago. I . . . Well, this is almost as good." He put an envelope with a Sharks logo into Emily's hand. "I'd really like it if you would come to my first preseason game. The view isn't quite this breathtaking from the other side of the stadium, but you'll be under the roof if it rains." He waited expectantly. To Emily's surprise, his hands trembled as their fingertips brushed. He licked his lips and wouldn't meet her eyes. She peeked at the date printed on the tickets. Luckily, it was the only week she wasn't booked in August.

"I'll be there. Thank you for asking me."

He reached out to embrace her, miraculously missing the food and drinks spread out in front of them. At the same time, the food was pretty secondary at this point. She relished the scratchiness of his cheek against hers and the warmth of his embrace.

"You must think I wouldn't want to go," Emily said.

He studied his food for a moment. The self-assured, funny, masterful guy Emily believed she knew suddenly turned into a shy, hesitant high schooler.

He shrugged. "You might have a scheduling conflict."

She wiped her fingertips on a napkin, and took his chin in her hand to look into his eyes. "I can't wait to watch you play again," Emily said. She held up the tickets. "I'll bring Amy. I know she'll want to be there, too."

"Sure. If you need more tickets for your mom and dad, let me know."

"I'll do that. Thank you." She kissed his cheek. "Did you really think I wouldn't be interested?" She stuck the tickets and envelope into her handbag.

He shrugged, took a sip of his iced tea, and ate another bite of fish. As usual, he'd devoured a double portion of fish and chips and was now working on hers, too. Finally, he spoke.

"Anastasia never wanted to see one of my games."

"I'm not Anastasia."

"No," he agreed, "you're not."

"I'm a little curious . . ."

"Hit me." He slid his arm around Emily's shoulders and let out a sigh.

She took a deep breath. "I'd love to know exactly what it was about Anastasia that appealed to you. Why did you ask her out?"

"Sugar, you're going for the gusto."

"You don't have to answer if you don't want to. I just wondered."

"I'd love to tell you it was her brains and personality, but, mostly, it was what she looked like. And I kept asking her out. Sometimes she'd say "no," and sometimes, she'd say "yes." I had to chase her. It became a challenge." He shook his head. "Would it make you feel better if I tell you it's probably one of the more stupid things I've ever done in my life?"

"Wanting to ask someone out isn't necessarily stupid—"

He shook his head. "I knew the first time we went out that it wasn't good. I kept at it, though, because she was a model, and, to be truthful, I got to show her off." He rubbed his chin with his free hand. "Yeah, she was a challenge, but she had no interest in anything I find valuable. She doesn't like football. She couldn't understand why I work out through the off-season, or why it's important to me to see my parents and my brother as often as I can. Not surprisingly, my parents weren't that crazy about her when they finally met. I didn't want to go to New York and hang out with her model friends. The guys thought I was godda— a little crazy to break it off with her when it finally happened. All professional athletes want to date women the normal guy can't get."

Now it was Emily's turn to feel awkward and insecure. She wasn't sure what to say, but Brandon, as usual, sensed she wasn't overly thrilled.

"Sugar, I'm an ass," he said as his hand closed around hers. "What I should've said is that I'm damn lucky to be here with you tonight. I can't believe you're wearing my ring. Out of all the parking lots in the entire world, you wiped out in mine."

Emily had to laugh when she saw his slightly crooked smile. "I just didn't understand how you could . . . Well, Anastasia and I don't have much in common."

"Thank God."

Emily laid her head against his shoulder and looked up at the endless, starry sky. "You're not an ass."

"I really messed up just now."

She slid her arm around his waist. "No. You were being truthful. Every guy in America wants to go out with a Victoria's Secret model."

"Not this one," he said firmly. "I like opera singers."

"You are such a liar."

"Listen. I have a fiancée that can bitch me out in five languages. Plus, I'd be nuts to go out with someone who's elevated getting rid of the dinner I just bought her to an art form."

"So bulimia doesn't make you hot."

"I love watching you eat," he assured Emily. "You enjoy it. You enjoy everything, though."

"Are you looking forward to this season?"

"I'm always looking forward to the season. I want to play forever, but I can't." He looked out over the bay. "I might have another couple of years. Maybe."

"What's it like to be out there?"

"Playing in a game?"

Emily nodded. He thought for a moment. "You perform for an audience, too. What's it like for you when you're standing onstage? You've just sung. The crowd's applauding. What happens?"

"I love the feeling. There's nothing like it. There's

energy, and adrenaline, and the fact people love what I just did. I can't wait to do it again."

"Okay. That's usually a couple thousand people."

"Yes, it is."

"Well, I'm listening to fifty thousand people screaming my name. There's nothing else I could ever describe that matches it. I'm doing something I love, and I want to keep doing it forever. When I get home after a game, I can't sleep because I'm still so wound up from the energy in the stadium."

"I'm looking forward to seeing it."

"You will. When guys retire, they don't know what to do with themselves. There isn't a stadium full of people cheering for them when they mow the lawn and drive the carpool. They're guys that used to be somebody, and now they're not."

Emily bit her lip. "They're always somebody. They still mean a lot to their families and friends."

"Of course they do," he said gently, "but it's not the same. It's never going to be the same. That's what I'll be facing. I'll have to find something to do with the rest of my life that won't be anywhere near as exciting as what I've been doing since the first day I ran out on a football field and played in a game. I love the sport. I always will."

He folded his lips. A shadow passed over his features, and Emily felt her stomach clench in empathy. She didn't know what to say. Mostly, she knew that whatever she did say would probably be wrong. She would have to try till she got it right, though, because she wondered how she would feel if she woke up one morning and could never sing again.

"Maybe there's a new adventure for you," Emily said.

"I'd like to think so. I'll still be there if I'm doing the announcing thing."

She squeezed his hand. "I'll be there, too. We'll get through this." Emily watched Brandon's eyes widen in surprise.

They sat quietly for a few more minutes, and then he murmured to her, "You aren't getting rid of me. You know that, don't you?" He buried his face in her hair.

Emily reached out to kiss him. She tasted the malt vinegar they splashed on the fish and chips, a little salt, and what she would always know as Brandon—the taste she still couldn't identify, but craved more than anything else she ever wanted.

Of course, one kiss turned into many. Brandon finally pulled away. "We'd better stop this, or our PG rated date's going straight to triple X."

Chapter Eighteen

EMILY'S WALK-IN CLOSET remained the coolest place in her townhouse during August's heat in Seattle. She stripped to her bra and underwear while pawing frantically through a selection of clothes that would make a buyer for Nordstrom green with envy. No matter how many clothes she might own, however, she had nothing that was right for this evening's event: Brandon's first preseason game.

Only a builder would think an exterior window in a walk-in closet was a good idea. The late-afternoon sun shining through it, though, gilded the small mountain of clothing she tried and discarded onto the closet floor. Nobody wore a little black dress and spike heels to a football game, as far as she knew. Jeans and a t-shirt were so *ordinary*, not to mention unbearably warm in the heat. She grabbed a scoop-necked, cap-sleeved cotton sundress off a hanger. Too garden party-ish.

Emily's rapid perusal—and incipient panic—gave way to full-on terror when she heard a key in the front door lock.

Amy called out, "Hey, Em, we gotta go. Where are you?"

Emily heard Amy's footfalls on the stairs, and she appeared in the bedroom doorway.

"You're not dressed yet. We're going to be late." Amy said.

"No shit."

They stared at each other. Amy looked like the Sharks' team store threw up on her. She wore a Sharks hat, a Sharks t-shirt, and a Sharks patterned knit scrunchie on her ponytail. Shiny plastic beads shaped like footballs and painted in the team colors hung around her neck, while little football earrings dangled from her earlobes. Her Keds had Sharks shoelaces. She even sported a temporary tattoo of the team logo on her cheek. The only thing on her body not branded with "Sharks" or "football" was the denim shorts she wore.

"Did you buy it all?" Emily asked. "No wonder I can't find anything to wear, if that's what everyone else will have on. This can't be typical."

"You need to wear Brandon's jersey. I know he gave you one," Amy said.

"It's enough that I'm wearing his gigantic ring. I am not dressing up like it's Halloween."

"Everyone else wears them. Go put it on. He will love it." Amy pulled Emily out of her closet, grabbed the jersey off a hanger, pushed it against her sister's chest, and started yanking items out of a plastic shopping bag looped over her wrist. "You can wear that cute denim mini-skirt you have with these. I have beads, earrings, and a hat. I even have a scrunchie thing for your pony-tail."

Emily snatched the denim skirt from halfway down the pile in her closet. "I'm leaving my hair the way it is." She stepped into a pair of cobalt-blue flats with gunmetal-gray buckles on the toes.

Amy frowned. "Camisole." She extracted one from Emily's dresser drawer and handed it to her. "The jersey's a bit see-through," she said. It wouldn't do to flash an entire stadium full of people.

When Emily was finally dressed to Amy's satisfaction, Amy looped beads over her head, put the scrunchie on her wrist, handed her a hat, and said, "You need to put on the football earrings."

"No. Absolutely not." Emily pointed at the pea-sized diamond studs in her ears. "Brandon gave these to me. He wants me to wear them. The other girlfriends and wives don't dress themselves up like this."

"Wait till you see them," Amy said. "I have one word for you: Bedazzler."

Emily tossed the scrunchie, hat, and the earrings on her bed. "I'll wear the jersey and the beads. That's it."

"Come *on*," Amy pleaded. "You have to look like a *fan*."

"This is what I'm wearing. If you keep bugging me about it, I'll wear a bandage dress and my new pair of five-inch heels."

Amy heaved a heavy sigh. "You'll wish you'd worn it all when you get there," she warned.

"I guess I'll have to live with that."

Emily made a knot in the side of the jersey as Amy dragged her down the staircase, and managed to hook her handbag with one hand on the way out the door.

Amy drove like a madwoman on a good day. Today, she was even more determined to get where she was going before she and Emily missed a second of the action. She swerved around slower vehicles; she switched lanes, jabbering the whole time. Shortly after Amy skidded into a parking space, they joined the thousands of people making their way through the parking lot into the stadium.

Emily glanced around at a huge crowd of Sharks fans attired in jerseys, team t-shirts, and even a few people dressed up in old-fashioned zoot suits in the team colors. The area around the trash cans was littered with what looked like thousands of red plastic cups already.

Amy was so excited she was practically levitating as they moved along a huge concrete concourse. "We'll go to our seats, but first, you have to see Brandon." She pointed to the sidelines. "If we walk down the aisle closest to the field, he can see us when we get to the bottom."

"Where is he now?" Emily scanned the guys on the field. None of them wore Sharks blue, and none of them wore Brandon's number 99 jersey.

"They'll be out in a minute to stretch. He'll see you."

They made their way down what seemed like a thousand steps to the railing only feet from the team's bench area on the field. Emily gripped the railing and looked around. The afternoon's heat was dissipating as the sun sank lower in the sky. A soft breeze ruffled her hair. Even an hour before the game, there was already what looked like thousands of people sitting in their seats and waiting for it all to start. The cheerleaders were already on the sidelines as well.

"Shark Babes," Amy explained, and waved at a dark-haired woman who waved back. "That's McKenzie. She owns the yoga studio next door to my shop."

McKenzie not only had a gorgeous face, she also had a perfect body. Emily ignored the momentary twinge of jealousy over McKenzie's figure as she heard a huge roar from the crowd. The Sharks ran onto the field, and Amy was jumping up and down.

Brandon spotted them almost immediately. He dropped his helmet onto the team bench, ran to the wall, leaped up, and sat on the railing in front of Amy and Emily. "How're my two girls?" He patted Emily's cheek. She took his hand to look at the glove, and the tape around his wrist.

"We're great," Amy told him.

"Looking forward to the game?" he asked Emily.

All Emily could manage was a nod. She was momentarily speechless, and she couldn't seem to stop touching the pads and other paraphernalia he wore to do his job. She couldn't imagine why seeing him in his uniform affected her like it did. He was the same guy who lounged on her couch, slept in her bed, tormented, teased, and kissed her. She spent most of her free time with him now. *Don't freak out*, she told herself.

He leaned forward and said into her ear, "It's me, sugar."

By now, though, other fans advanced on Brandon, and he said to Amy, "Gimme a kiss for luck."

She kissed his cheek and said, "Win."

"I'll do that. I need a kiss from you, too," he told Emily. His mouth touched hers. She felt the familiar rush in her blood as his arm wrapped around her. Her knees went weak. She leaned into him. He laughed softly as he leaned his forehead against hers. "Save some for later."

A fan thrust a pen and a piece of paper at him. He took a quick moment to sign his name, jumped down from the wall, then waved at them and ran back onto the field.

Brandon told Emily a few days ago he probably wouldn't be playing in this game. After all, it was a pre-season game, and the coach wanted to make sure he'd have the starters when the season began. This was actually a good thing, according to him.

"If Jon's playing, I'm not starting, sugar. That's what I wanted."

"I won't get to see you, though."

"You'll see me plenty during the regular season," he said. "Really. I'll be all over the place."

"But I won't *be* there. I have to go to—"

At that point, Brandon kissed her breathless, and she forgot that she wouldn't be able to watch him play in person when she was performing elsewhere. Maybe it didn't matter.

Amy had rented a tablet-sized satellite television receiver for the season, which she'd taken from her purse and set up on her lap. "That's odd. Didn't you say Brandon wasn't playing today?"

"He said he wasn't."

Amy made a sound like a grunt, stared into the tiny screen, and listened intently to the headphones.

The team ran off the field. They evidently finished their warm-up and were going to the locker room. Emily couldn't believe the amount of noise in the stadium. Finding anyone who could out-yell or out-sing her was quite an achievement, but there seemed to be an entire stadium full. She could feel the stadium shaking when the team made their entrance and the game started.

The Sharks won the coin toss and elected to defer. When the defense lined up for their first series, Brandon ran out onto the field. "Amy." Emily grabbed Amy's arm. "There he is!"

"I can see, I can see," Amy told her, but she was laughing. "The coach must have put him in for a series so you could watch. The TV guys are talking about it right now. They said the coach will play him for a few downs, and then he's sitting for the rest of the game."

Emily still clutched Amy's arm.

"I love you, Em, but you need to lay off the weight-lifting. Damn, you're breaking my arm," Amy said. She reached out to give her sister a half-hug, though.

The ball was snapped. Players crashed into each other, and Brandon managed to wrap his arm around the quarterback and drop him to the turf. "Look," Emily called out.

"I needed that eardrum." Amy was grinning at Emily's excitement. "Yes, yes, he did well. Look at Damian. He got pig piled."

"Isn't he supposed to be sitting, too?"

"Next series," Amy said.

The players on the field formed their lines again. The ball was snapped, and Brandon took off after the runner carrying the ball. He wrapped his arms around the guy and pulled him down to the turf. The crowd went wild. Obviously Brandon tackled him, but Emily was a bit confused at the reaction around her.

"What happened?"

"He dropped the guy behind the line of scrimmage. The other team lost yards," Amy said. Evidently, this was good. She'd have to remember to ask Brandon about it later.

She glanced up at the scoreboard. Third and fifteen. Brandon told her before that when the other team had "third and long," it was the defense's job to make sure they couldn't get enough yardage to get a first down.

Brandon lined up a short distance away from the other guys on the line, the ball was snapped, and he ran toward the other team's quarterback. He leaped on the guy, but something must have happened during the tackle. A few seconds later, Brandon lay on the turf in obvious pain. He pushed his helmet off and was writhing, flipping from side to side. Emily looked on in horror. He couldn't be hurt. He never got hurt, according to him. What on earth could be wrong?

"Oh, God, Amy, he's not getting up. What happened?" The crowd was silent.

"He's fine," Amy soothed. "Maybe he just got the wind knocked out of him."

The trainer, the team doctor, and the defensive coaches ran out to Brandon. Emily couldn't believe what she was seeing. She jumped up out of her seat. She had to get to him.

Amy grabbed her arm. "Stay here."

"He needs me."

"No. Em, he'll be fine. He's just—let's see what happened." Brandon was still rolling around on the turf. Someone had picked up his helmet, and it looked like he was clutching his thigh. Amy consulted her TV receiver. "They turned down the sideline microphone. They're bleeping every other word. It's picking up Brandon. I think he's in pain." Amy smiled wryly. "He likes the 'F' word, that's for sure."

Finally, the three men clustered around Brandon helped him up. He leaned on them as they made their way back to the sidelines. There was a short discussion with the team's doctor. Moments later, the same men walked Brandon to the tunnel that led into the locker room. People clapped. Emily watched with one hand over her mouth.

"Where are they going?" Emily said.

"He'll have an exam and a couple of X-rays," Amy said. "He'll probably be back in a few minutes."

She'd evidently attracted the attention of the people sitting around them as well. Even in a noisy stadium, she could hear people murmuring, "McKenna's fiancée," and "Why is *she* sitting in the stands?" Emily wasn't sure where they all thought she should be sitting, but they seemed angry somehow. She pasted on a smile she didn't feel, and Emily and Amy alternated between watching the tiny television screen and waiting for Brandon to re-emerge from the tunnel.

Amy wrapped her arm around Emily's shoulders. "Listen. The sports guys are all saying that the preliminary injury report looks compatible with a thigh bruise. It's not his knee, it's not a broken bone, it's just painful as hell and he won't be playing for a couple of weeks. But he'll be okay."

"How do you know?"

"Now, buck up, little camper. If the camera guys figure out where we're sitting and he sees you crying on the video screen, Brandon's going to be upset. He said to the reporter that he's hurting, but he's going to be fine."

"You're *sure*."

Amy nodded. "In the meantime, we're going to beat the Mustangs. Their quarterback got sacked and their running back got dropped for a significant loss in the first series of the game. They're toast."

A few minutes later, Brandon walked back onto the sidelines to applause from the crowd. He'd changed into Sharks logo warm-ups, and leaned on crutches. Someone had wrapped his leg in ice packs. His teammates were either heckling Brandon or cheering on Jon, the second-team guy behind Brandon, who was putting on quite a show for the Denver offense. Amy was still listening to her television receiver, and Emily was staring off into space.

Amy reached out for her sister's chin, scanned Emily's face, and said, "Okay. You look fine. They're talking about you, so you're probably going to be on TV fairly soon. Smile and wave," Amy prompted. They both did. The people around them patted Emily on the back and waved at the cameras. "They're talking about the fact that Brandon must have asked the coach to put him in for a series, and now he's going to regret it."

"So, this is my fault."

"Of course not. He knew you were excited about being here, and he wanted you to see him play. They can get injured at any time. It's not like this is something new."

"Goddamn it," the guy behind Emily complained. "McKenna's going to be out for at least four weeks. The preliminary report is a deep thigh bruise."

"Shit. What the hell was he thinking? He should have been riding the bench with the rest of the starters," someone else chimed in.

Amy turned in her seat. "He's not injury prone, and he's motivated to play this year. He'll work with the trainer till he's one hundred percent again. It'll be fine."

"Did *she* tell him to play today?" an angry-looking woman demanded, pointing at Emily.

"No, she didn't." Amy's voice was authoritative.

"Can't she speak for herself?"

Emily was now irritated along with being afraid for Brandon, but she forced herself to take a deep breath. Getting into a screaming match with a complete stranger wasn't going to help matters. Maybe the best thing to do was to ignore her. Amy stuck one of the ear pods into

Emily's ear so she could hear Brandon's interview with the network's sidelines reporter.

"Brandon, what happened?" the woman asked.

"I tackled Mr. Davis in the open field, and his cleats got tangled up with my thigh. The team doctor and trainer think I have a thigh bruise. One thing's for sure, it hurts."

"You weren't expected to play today. Why did you change your mind?"

"I wanted to see how the rookies handled a game situation. Obviously, it wasn't the greatest decision I could have made." Emily saw his slow grin. "This'll give me a chance to catch up on my knitting or something."

"This is your fiancée Emily's first NFL game. Sources are telling us that you asked the coach to play as a result."

The smile didn't leave Brandon's lips, but his eyes hardened. Emily wondered if anyone but her would notice the change in his expression. Brandon spoke before she'd even put the microphone back up to his mouth. "Not true," he snapped, and the reporter looked surprised.

"Back to you, guys," she said quickly.

The picture switched to several sportscasters sitting in a studio. "Thanks, Courtney," one of them said. "Let's face it, this wouldn't be the first time a player has asked to play a few downs because a loved one was in the stadium watching, but this could be disastrous for the Sharks' defense."

"McKenna's played thirteen years without significant injury," a second man said, "which is almost unheard of in the NFL. Our sources state he's worked hard in the weight room and with the trainers as the years have passed, and it shows on the field. He's had the usual twisted ankles, bumps and bruises, but for the most part, he's the workhorse in a punishing defense. It's early. It's hard to say what effect this will have on the team. One thing's for sure, it's had a fairly immediate effect on McKenna."

"Yeah," the third announcer sighed. "Thigh bruises are a bitch."

The Sharks ended up winning the game. Emily wanted to call Brandon's cell phone, but she didn't want to bother him. It turned out she didn't have long to wait. Her phone rang as they walked through the stadium on their way to Amy's minivan.

"Hey, sugar." Brandon's voice was a bit slurred.

"Hi, baby. How are you feeling?"

"Youreallywannaknow." He was either drunk, or partaking of significant pharmaceuticals. "Can't drive. Need a ride home."

"Tell me where to meet you."

"Lockerroom. AskAmy."

"I'll be right there. Just—just sit tight." She hung up the phone. "I hope you know where the locker room is," Emily said to Amy.

AFTER A QUICK conference Amy and Emily decided it would be easier to get Brandon into the minivan. To say that he was high on painkillers was an understatement. "Sugar," he shouted triumphantly when he saw them. "We won."

"Yes. I saw that. You sacked the quarterback, too."

"I did. Where's my kiss? I deserve one." He gave her a loopy grin.

Damian poked his head out of the locker room door. "Have fun with him, darlin'." He rolled his eyes.

"What if he wipes out on the way into his house? What will I do?"

Emily tried to hang onto her calm, but it wasn't working. Brandon's leg was wrapped in Ace bandages and ice packs from hip to knee. She couldn't imagine how she'd be able to maneuver him around.

"He's a bit looped, but he's not incapacitated," Damian said. "You'll need to keep the ice packs on him. When you get him home, put him to bed. Don't let him get up and roam around the house."

She couldn't imagine how she could stop a man who was a foot taller and outweighed her by at least a hundred pounds from doing anything at all.

The trainer and the team's doctor came to the rescue, pouring Brandon into the passenger seat of Amy's van. "McKenna, you'll need to stay low and ice this for a couple of days," the doctor said. "I'll give your medication to Emily. Don't be a martyr. If you keep up on the pain meds, it'll actually help you heal faster."

"Hokay. Sugarwill take care of it."

Emily took the prescription bottle the doctor handed her, and slipped it into her handbag. Brandon launched into a disjointed story about a game he'd played in college in which a live alligator somehow got onto the playing field. Then he forgot what he was talking about and started complaining about the cleating he'd received. If she didn't feel like she wanted to cry, it would've been funny.

"Jesus, Doc, that hurt like a mother— Sorry, sugar. I shouldn't talk this way in front of a lady."

"I'm sure she understands," the doctor assured him. "He should be out like a light before you even get him home," he said to Emily. "See if you can get him to lie down on his bed, or into an easy chair. Keep up on the ice. If you can't get ice into a gallon Ziploc, bags of frozen peas work well."

The team trainer stuck his card in her hand. "My cell phone's on there. If you need anything, call me."

Amy handed Emily her car keys, and reached out for Brandon's shorts pocket. "I'll drive your rig home for you, big guy."

He roused for a moment, looked down at the hand fiddling in his pocket, and fixed Amy with a pointed look. His hand shot out to grab her wrist. "Don't touch my junk."

Amy laughed. "You wish."

"Just rest." Emily soothed him as she pulled onto the freeway, heading toward Brandon's house. "We'll be home in a few minutes, and you can lie down in your bed."

"You, too," he muttered. A few minutes later, his even breathing told Emily he was fast asleep.

On the ride home, Emily listened to the post-game commentary. There was still speculation as to why Brandon decided to play one down in a game he'd been told he wasn't playing in. The commentators weren't the ones she was worried about. The fans calling in were acting like she was Yoko Ono.

"You know she told him to play," one caller complained. "Why would he give in to her? Now we're screwed for at least the next three preseason games, and if his injury lingers into the regular season, we're fu-"

The audio cut out and the announcer said, "Well, someone's mommy needs to hot sauce his tongue. We're sure that everything will be fine in Sharks Land. In the meantime, let's hope that Brandon McKenna's fiancée doesn't decide to talk him into taking up hang gliding or something."

"Women can talk us into almost anything," the caller said.

"Shut up," Emily said to the radio in response.

Brandon stirred. "Whazzamattersugar?"

"Don't worry about it," Emily said.

"Don't listen to those jerks. They don't know what they're talking about." He drifted off again.

It took both Emily and Amy to get Brandon into the house and onto his bed. Emily propped pillows up behind him, pulled his shoes off, and left him in his t-shirt and shorts while she rifled through her handbag for the pain meds. Two pills and a glass of water later, his eyelids fluttered closed, and she kissed him.

"Sweet dreams, baby."

"Thanks, sugar." He let out a huge sigh and snuggled into his blankets.

Emily turned away to wrap another ice pack in a kitchen towel when she heard an "I love you" so soft she wondered if she had imagined it. Brandon's chest rose and fell. He was asleep, she told herself. He was talking in his sleep. He didn't really mean it.

She leaned down to brush her lips across his brow. "Sleep."

The corner of his mouth twitched a little, and his hand curled around hers.

Chapter Nineteen

A COUPLE OF days after Brandon's injury, Emily opened her eyes to the soft golden-pink light of an early, summertime morning. Somebody was knocking insistently at Brandon's front door. She reached out to shake his shoulder.

"Someone's here."

"They'll go away," he muttered. He pulled Emily closer. She let out a contented sigh, and snuggled against him.

More knocking ensued. The doorbell rang. Three times.

"If this is Damian's idea of a practical joke, I'm going to kill him," Brandon said as he shoved himself out of bed. "Stay here, sugar. This could get ugly." He hobbled down the hallway in nothing but a pair of boxer briefs.

Emily scrambled out of bed, grabbing Brandon's terrycloth robe off the chair in the corner. She stuck both arms into it as she heard him tell whoever was on the other side of the door, "This better be good."

"Oh, it's good, Mister. Open the door," a feminine voice assured him.

"Mama?" Emily heard him pull the door open. "What are you doing here?"

Oh, no. Emily padded into the hallway against her better judgment.

"How many times are you going to kiss Emily on live television before we even meet her? I've been asking for six months now." Emily watched Suzanne McKenna dragged over the threshold by her half-naked son. "I also can't believe you answered the door in your shorts! Brandon James McKenna, I bought you a robe last year. Why aren't you wearing it?"

In that split second, it didn't matter that Emily was an adult, with her own life, responsibilities, and moral decisions. Getting busted by one's potential mother-in-law sporting bedhead and wearing her son's bathrobe was enough to make any female cringe inside. Emily pulled the robe tightly around herself, and attempted to blend in with the furnishings.

The replica of Brandon's dimple flashed in Suzanne's left cheek as she noticed Emily standing just feet from her. "Oh. I see." Suzanne let go of her son and held out her arms to Emily. "Come here, sweetie. It's so good to finally meet you!"

Despite being almost a foot shorter than her son, Suzanne could crack a rib or two with her embrace. Her hair was perfect. Her clothes were perfect. She looked like she'd strolled over from across the street, instead of spending several hours sitting on a flight. The most secure woman in the world would wish for a full-length mirror, a mani-pedi, and a lipstick touch-up after spending only a few moments in Suzanne's presence.

"I'm thrilled to meet you, too," Emily managed to gasp.

"I realize we're a little early. One of Jack's buddies offered us a ride in his jet. He's playing golf this weekend with Seattle's pro basketball team's owner, and those guys start before dawn. On the bright side, this gives us some extra time together." Suzanne gave her one last squeeze. "We can do some wedding planning. Won't that be fun?"

Emily nodded, and attempted to look delirious with excitement. She saw the same wicked twinkle in Suzanne's eyes that her son employed to devastating effect on the female population. Suzanne, however, wasn't angling for a date. She made it clear (in the nicest possible way, of course) that Emily was spending the day knee-deep in wedding details, and she was going to like it, too.

Suzanne turned her attentions toward her son.

"You'd better get in the shower, young man. Emily's mama and I had such a nice chat on the phone yesterday, and she'll be here shortly with Emily's dad and Amy. We girls will be doing a little shopping. I'm sure you men will manage to find some kind of trouble to get yourselves into while we're gone." She gave him a gentle push toward his room.

Suzanne talked with Emily's mom? Emily's mom's phone number wasn't a state secret, but it would have been nice if she'd had some advance warning.

"Where's Dad?" Brandon said. He looked dazed.

"He'll be right in. He's bringing the bags." Brandon reached out for the doorknob. She put one hand out to stop him. "Oh, no, you don't. You need to put some clothes on before you go out there." Her lips curved into a smile as she glanced over at Emily.

"Excuse me." Emily pivoted on one heel. "Nice to meet you," she called out as she ran for the safety of Brandon's room. She tossed the robe onto the end of Brandon's bed and sealed herself in his bathroom. It might be good to make sure she was fully dressed before any additional encounters with Brandon's parents. She flipped on the shower and waited for the water to warm.

"Hey, sugar, let me in there," Brandon called out.

Seconds later, she heard him jimmying the bathroom door lock. Within seconds, the door swung open. Emily felt the rush of cool air on her skin as he shut it behind him. He stepped out of his boxer briefs.

"Let's conserve water," he coaxed.

Despite the fact she'd welcome his company in the shower any other time, she flung out an arm and pointed in the general direction of Brandon's hallway. "Your mom is here. With *your dad*! I'll be out in a minute."

He grinned like she'd said the most hilarious thing he'd ever heard. Before she had a chance to duck under his arm, he reached out to pull her against him. He kissed her, sweet and slow. She wound her arms around his neck. He didn't seem to need the encouragement. He was already hard against her.

"Stop it," she said, but there was no heat behind her words.

"What's the problem? We're adults."

"I don't want your parents to think I'm some kind of ho."

It was a bit late to be fretting about what Jack and Suzanne McKenna thought of her. She was torn between embarrassment over the fact that an awful lot of people knew they'd been caught in the act in public, and the fact that there weren't many women who wouldn't have done the same damn thing.

"You worry too much." He pulled her hips against his. "Let's see how quiet we can be."

"We're *never* quiet. You know this."

"I'm willing to give it a try, sugar, if you are." He zeroed in on the spot behind her earlobe that always left her a quivering wreck. "C'mon."

She summoned whatever resistance she could, reached out, and shut off the shower with one hand.

"Playtime's over," he said. He shook his head. "I'm in trouble now."

She took a few deep breaths and willed her racing heart (and hormones) to slow down.

"Speaking of worrying, Bruiser, we need to have a little chit-chat before we make an appearance at the breakfast table." She took his face in her hands. "Our mothers are expecting us to take some role in planning our wedding, but there's just one problem."

He raised one eyebrow. His arms tightened around her. He rocked against her, barely moving. "What might that be?"

"You never actually proposed to me."

She wanted answers, but she was starting to wonder why this conversation was quite so important at the moment. He was moving against other parts of her body that left her more flustered than kisses on the spot behind her ear. Her breathing quickened.

His face was a mask of outraged innocence. "I most certainly did. I seem to remember a conversation about getting married in the First Church of Elvis, and I also seem to remember we're getting married February fifteenth. You're wearing my five-carat diamond ring. Pretty damn official, sugar." He was backing her up against the shower door, still rocking, slowly, so slowly. "I don't see a problem at all."

"But you never—"

His drawl passed warm honey and went straight to sultry nights and tangled sheets. "I told you. Let me know where and when, and I'll be there. You'll know me. I'll be the one in the tux."

"But—but—but—"

"Let our mamas plan whatever they want. It's less of a headache for both of us. There's going to be a wedding, sugar." He twirled her away from the shower door, reached in, flipped the water back on, and patted her on the butt. His voice dropped. "Imagine how lonely you'll be in the shower without me."

He grabbed a bath sheet and strode out of the bathroom, closing the door behind him. She resisted the impulse to run after him.

BRANDON SHOWERED AND dressed in the downstairs bathroom. He loved his parents, but right now, he'd really enjoy some privacy to spend more time in bed with his little diva. Instead he was doomed to a day in the company of two determined females. His mama was planning a wedding, come hell or high water, and his fiancée was trying to get him to say those three little words before she did.

He knew he hadn't actually proposed to her. He'd suggested. It wasn't the same thing. He hadn't gotten down on one knee in front of her, either. She deserved it. She was the only woman he could imagine marrying. His feelings for her weren't just infatuation or lust. Lust was always good, but it wasn't the real thing.

He shook his curls dry, brushed his teeth, and stepped into a pair of shoes. They'd make some plans, and he'd propose . . . for real. He'd have to think of something amazing, though. He was sure this was the only time in his life he'd ask.

A FULLY DRESSED Emily walked into the controlled chaos that was Brandon's kitchen. Suzanne and Emily's mom were performing the complicated dance of assembling breakfast for seven people. Her dad and an older version of Brandon with graying, closely cropped curls sat at the small kitchen table, drinking coffee. Amy whizzed by with a load of plates, silverware and napkins destined for the dining room table.

"Nice to see you could join us," her sister said, but she grinned. Emily kissed her mom's cheek as Meg hurried past.

Brandon's dad unfolded himself from the chair and held out his arms. "I'm Jack," he said, beaming, "and you must be Emily."

Emily heard Brandon's voice from the other room. "Dad. She's mine."

"He gets all the pretty girls," Jack confided as he wrapped his arms around her. "You'll sit with me at dinner later, won't you?"

"Don't you want to sit with Mrs. McKenna?" Emily teased.

"I've been sitting with her for a few years now, and I'll be sitting with her for as long as she'll have me," Jack said. He had the same roguish manner as his son. Emily lost her heart on the spot. "She won't mind. She'll be too busy with our boy."

"I heard that," Suzanne said with a smile. "We're taking Emily with us before you scare her half to death, Casanova."

Jack released Emily and extended his hand to Mark. "You're a lucky man, Hamilton. Two lovely daughters and a beautiful wife. Life doesn't get any better, does it?"

Emily's mom smiled and blushed as Mark said, "No, it doesn't." She couldn't help but notice that neither parent corrected Jack's belief that they were still married.

EMILY TOOK ONE last swallow of coffee as her mother said, "Ladies, we'd better get moving, or we're going to be late. Our appointment is at ten."

"What appointment?" Emily said.

"You need a wedding gown, silly. Suzanne and I thought this would be a great day to shop. We're all together."

"Oh, yes." Suzanne got up from the table, too. "Let's get Emily in the car. Her gown should have been ordered three months ago, and it's already nine-thirty."

"I'll drive," Amy said.

"We still have six months," Emily said. "We'll be fine. There are women on those bridal shows that buy a dress two weeks beforehand, and—"

Emily heard Brandon chuckling under his breath as she was pulled from her chair by her mother and her future mother-in-law.

"Come on, sweetie. You won't want to wear something you bought two weeks before. Plus, your mama has been looking forward to this your entire life," Suzanne said. She snagged both her and Emily's handbags off the hall tree as she went.

A few minutes later, Emily found herself standing on the sidewalk next to Amy's mini-van. The moms were already ensconced in the back seat. Brandon followed them out to the car.

"You must have called shotgun," Brandon teased Emily. "Have a great time."

"I know nothing about wedding stuff," she whispered to him. "What do I do now?"

"Let them handle it," he reassured her. "I'll see you later." He kissed her, made sure she was belted into the passenger seat, and waved goodbye as Amy burned rubber down the quiet residential street.

Meg and Suzanne didn't seem to care that Amy was exceeding every posted speed limit in the state as she took the freeway entrance to Seattle.

"Hey, weirdo, slow down, will you?" Emily said.

"You have to be there on time. This bridal salon takes appointments six months in advance. If you're even ten minutes late, they'll turn you away, and you'll end up buying a gown at the thrift shop."

Amy reached out to pat her sister's hand. Emily's other hand was clutching the armrest. Suzanne and Meg were chatting away like they'd known each other since childhood. They'd been discussing the plans for Brandon and Emily's wedding for the past twenty minutes, with no signs of letting up anytime soon.

"Suzanne, wait till you see the church. It's about a mile and a half away from Brandon's house. The view of Lake Washington from the sanctuary is stunning. They also have a choir loft, which would be great for a string quartet."

"Oh, I agree. I booked the reception space two weeks ago, so that's all set. They're doing a tasting later this afternoon for us. They don't bake cakes on premises, but they have a list of bakeries they recommend. I was surprised there don't seem to be a lot of groom's cakes served here. They're a must-have in New Orleans . . ."

Amy glanced over at Emily while swerving around a

Jaguar driven by someone who had the temerity to obey the posted speed limit on the 520 bridge to Seattle. "If there's something you especially want at your own wedding, you might speak up now."

AMY PULLED UP in front of Emerald City Bridal eleven minutes later with a Washington State Trooper on her tail.

"Mom, Suzanne, go ahead and go inside so Emily doesn't lose her appointment," she said.

A tall police officer in reflective aviator sunglasses was making his way to Amy's window. "Are you nuts?" Emily said. "Stay in the car, or he'll shoot us! Amy, I can't believe you—"

"Amy Margaret Hamilton, how many times have you been pulled over this year?" Meg said.

"He'll just give me a ticket. It's not that big of a deal."

"License and registration, please," the officer said.

"Will you please let my sister go inside the salon while I talk with you? She's about to lose her appointment."

The officer pulled off his sunglasses and regarded Amy with disbelief. "How fast were you going when you took the exit, Miss Hamilton?"

"It's not good when they already know your name," Suzanne said in a low voice.

"I'm not sure. I just know we're about to be late. I'm really sorry, officer. If I promise not to do it again and sign the ticket, will you let them go inside?"

He took the license and registration out of Amy's

hand. "I ran your plate. You've been pulled over four times already this year. You managed to charm your way out of a ticket all four times."

"Well—uh—"

"Do you know how dangerous speeding is? What about your passengers? How is your sister going to keep her appointment when she's dead?" The officer propped both hands on his hips. "Fine. You ladies can go inside. Miss Hamilton, you and I need to have a talk about your behavior behind the wheel, and this time, you're getting a ticket. Plus traffic school."

Meg and Suzanne hopped out of the van. Emily turned to her sister, who was receiving a blistering lecture on how many accident scenes Officer Hottie had witnessed in his fifteen-year career as a trooper.

"Do you need me to stay?"

"No. I'll be in in a few minutes," Amy said. "Go."

Emily grabbed her handbag, hurried into the store, and almost bumped into Meg and Suzanne. They were still staring at the opulence. All four walls were covered with racks of plastic-covered bridal gowns. A raised dais in the middle of the store was surrounded by 180 degrees of mirrors. A sumptuously upholstered couch sat a few feet from the dais for observation. The lighting was indirect, the classical music was soft, and all sounds were muffled by pale carpeting with the thickest pad known to mankind.

Emily spotted an ice bucket with an unopened bottle of champagne and four glasses on the low glass table in front of the couch. She could use a glass right now.

"So many beautiful dresses," Meg said.

"I'm enjoying this already," Suzanne responded.

A young woman in head-to-toe black and pearls approached them. "Ladies. It's wonderful to have you here. I'm Nicole. Who's our beautiful bride?"

Emily extended her hand to shake Nicole's. "That's me."

"Why don't we have a seat, and we can discuss what kind of dress you're looking for. Also, do you have a budget in mind?"

Emily had no idea what kind of dress she was looking for besides a) white, and b) not too expensive. She knew her parents would offer to pay, but she'd like to buy the dress herself.

Amy was the one who played "wedding" over and over when they were little girls. Emily's dreams consisted of her standing alone on the great opera stages of the world, a bouquet of red roses in her arms, listening to an enraptured audience applauding her and shouting, "*Brava!*" as she took yet another curtain call. Lately, though, she found herself daydreaming about seeing Brandon at the end of a church aisle.

Amy would know what to try on. If she could escape the clutches of an enraged police officer, she could advise Emily. A few seconds later, however, Emily realized she had the best advisor of all: Suzanne, former beauty queen and bridal show junkie. Meg and Suzanne whispered back and forth for a minute or so.

"Nicole, why don't you bring a ball gown to try first? Emily wears elaborate costumes as part of her job, so we'll need to come up with something more fabulous than anything she's worn on stage before," Suzanne said. Meg was nodding. "Let's skip the mermaid. They're getting married in a church, so a corset style needs to be somewhat modest. She might like a fit and flare, or maybe an A-line. We can add bling later with accessories if she likes it. The ball gown, though, should be first."

Amy skidded into the salon and sat down next to Emily on the couch. "We made it. Phew."

"How much was the ticket?" Emily asked.

"I have to go to traffic school. No ticket."

"How do you *do* this?"

"I might have cried. Let's find you a dress," Amy said.

Five minutes later, the champagne had been opened, full glasses handed around, and Emily was sitting in a dressing room bigger than her bedroom at home. Nicole would be "right back" with a selection of dresses, but first up would be the ball gown Suzanne had recommended. Emily knew she should feel some sense of outrage that her mother (and potential mother-in-law) weren't asking what she wanted. Meg and Suzanne had evidently made up their minds she and Brandon were getting married, no matter what. Obviously, they'd managed to overcome their initial misgivings about Brandon and Emily's engagement. This probably had something to do with the fact they both had their eyes on the prize: potential grandchildren. She wondered what the term would be to describe a wedding their moms planned without consulting either of them first. Arranged marriages weren't typical in the Hamilton family, to her knowledge. She wondered if Brandon would be required to give her dad a few goats (or tech stocks) in exchange for her hand.

Truthfully she was more worried about Brandon not really answering her question earlier in his bathroom.

He never actually used the words "Will you marry me?" when they talked about getting married. His insistence that it already happened was a bit odd. She was still wearing a big-ass engagement ring. Everyone else seemed to think this was a done deal. Plus, she had to admit in her heart of hearts that she could think of a lot worse things in life than being Emily Hamilton McKenna for the rest of her life. When she wasn't musing on Brandon's behavior (or lack of it), she also wondered if it made her a Bridezilla to want him to get down on one knee and actually pop the question. Other guys did it. Maybe she worried too much, as he said. She twirled the engagement ring on the third finger of her left hand. Was it really so unreasonable for her to want something other women would expect as well?

Her mind was whirling. Nicole seemed to be taking her sweet time, too.

Emily got up from the sumptuously upholstered chair she sat in and wandered out into the store in her dressing gown. Nicole was a few feet from her, rifling through dresses at a high rate of speed.

"Hi," Emily said.

"Oh! You're here. I didn't mean to take so long. I'm still thinking about a couple of these."

Emily walked over to the rack. Finding a wedding gown couldn't be that much different than shoe shopping, and she should have some type of professional certification for *that*. She flipped as rapidly as possible through the dresses.

"No. No. No. No. God, no."

To Emily's surprise, she realized she had more ideas than she thought about how she'd like to look on her wedding day. She didn't want strapless, she didn't want crystals, and she didn't want something that made her look like she'd gone after the skirt with the kitchen shears. She wanted lace. She wanted something that would make Brandon gasp when he saw her in it.

"This one." She reached up to pull the gown off the rack.

Nicole looked amused. "How about looking through some of the other dresses?"

"Not right now. Let's try this one on."

BACK IN THE dressing room, Nicole unzipped the protective plastic slowly.

"We just got this gown in from New York. It's formal without being stuffy. This is a diva's dress. I hope you'll love it." She demonstrated how Emily should hold her arms in front of her face so she wouldn't get makeup on the delicate fabric and slid the gown over Emily's head.

Emily heard the rustle of a silk taffeta ballroom skirt. The bodice was a corset, covered with soft lace, embroidered with pearls. It had cap sleeves and a high neck, a slightly dropped waist, and buttoned up the back. It reminded Emily of the photos she'd seen as a teenager of

Princess Grace's wedding gown, with a modern twist. The skirt had a pickup of fabric on one side. A small train swept the floor behind her. It was dramatic without being over the top, young without being childish.

In the past Emily had heard her various co-workers talking about putting on a wedding gown for the first time. Their descriptions paled in comparison with the reality. She trembled as she regarded the curvy redhead reflected in the mirror. She felt overwhelmed, surprised, a little disbelieving. Her fingertips trailed over the soft lace and the silk taffeta. She couldn't stop touching it. Even if the sample wasn't an exact fit, she loved it.

The realization smacked her in the face so hard tears rose in her eyes. She was going to marry Brandon, and she was going to wear this dress when she did.

"We can get your size when we order it," Nicole reassured. She pulled a small golden headpiece off the table behind her, formed of flat leaves, and extracted a long piece of tulle from another zippered plastic bag. Nicole pinned Emily's ponytail into a bun, and fastened the headpiece and tulle in her hair.

Emily couldn't resist twirling around in front of Nicole. "How do I look?"

A broad smile spread over Nicole's face. "I'm so glad I didn't bring you a room full of bling and ruffles. This dress was made for you." She adjusted the headpiece once more and said, "Let's go show you off."

Emily stepped into her own high heels so the dress wouldn't drag on the floor and rounded the corner to show them.

"What do you think? Mom, Suzanne, Amy?"

Emily's mother let out a gasp, and grabbed for Suzanne's hand. Her cool, collected, elegant potential mother-in-law burst into tears.

"That's the dress," Amy said, with tears in her eyes, too. "Buy that one."

Chapter Twenty

BRANDON GLANCED AROUND the Sharks' workout facility a few weeks after his parents' unexpected visit, mopping the sweat off his face with a well-used hand towel. He had the place to himself. Early morning sunshine through floor-to-ceiling windows bounced off a fortune in exercise machines, free weights, and other paraphernalia. He glanced up at the ceiling-sized panoramic photo of Sharks fans that the team photographer took during a game last year. Every crunch, every butterfly, every rotation of the elliptical meant he improved his game for those fans and for himself.

The other guys didn't usually show up here till later in the morning. He stuck the *iPod* earbuds in, turned the beats up as loud as they would go, and draped the towel over his head. It was time to work his neck.

Forty-five minutes later, the smart phone in his shorts pocket was on perma-vibrate. Five calls from his agent in an hour. The Sharks must have agreed to their latest contract extension offer. He clicked over to an incoming text: CALL MY OFFICE. ASAP.

The team's front office probably wanted him to sign before the first home game. They'd make a big production out of it, too. He grinned, imagining how long it would take his little diva to choose an outfit before the press conference. Maybe he should buy her a new dress for the occasion. He'd make sure it was scheduled on a day she could attend.

His phone vibrated again. A text from Emily: PLEASE CALL YOUR AGENT. HE'S LOOKING FOR YOU.

"What the hell's the fire drill?" he muttered to himself. He got up from the weight bench, loped into the locker room, stripped, and stepped into the shower.

BRANDON THREW HIMSELF into his Land Rover twenty-five minutes later, and hit "Josh" on his contacts list. Most guys saw their agent as a necessary evil—someone who handled the business end of football. They didn't want to think about contracts and endorsements. The year he was drafted Brandon came home from the Senior Bowl with a fistful of business cards from potential agents. He hired Josh when Josh answered his own telephone and didn't hide behind bullshit when Brandon asked him tough questions. Their relationship over the years was business-like but cordial.

Josh's contract negotiations with the Sharks were a work of art. He managed to stay on good terms with the team, while getting Brandon every dollar and perk one of the best pass-rushing defensive ends in the NFL deserved. He put multiple lucrative endorsement deals together for Brandon, endorsements that would live on long after his football career was over. Brandon was a very wealthy man as a result, and Josh hadn't done badly for himself, either.

Today, Josh didn't even say "hello."

"McKenna, where the hell have you been?"

"Lifting. Shower. You must have prevailed in the negotiations."

Josh waited a few beats. "I'm at Sea-Tac Airport. My flight just landed. We need to meet."

BRANDON NOSED HIS vehicle into the curb by the Alaska Airlines baggage claim area. Josh moved through the crowd of passengers waiting to be picked up by loved ones, tossed a laptop backpack onto the back seat of the car, and hopped into the passenger seat.

"What's up?" Brandon asked.

"Let's get a beer. It's on me," Josh told him. He stared out the windshield of Brandon's SUV.

Brandon felt the first icy fingers of dread slithering up his spine.

TEN MINUTES LATER, they sat down at the bar in a restaurant across the street from the airport. Josh ordered two microbrews. Brandon ordered a glass of ice water.

"Out with it," Brandon said. "I'm guessing you're not here because you missed me."

Josh took a sip of his beer. "I'm not quite sure how to tell you this, so here it is. The Sharks declined your contract extension. This is your last season with them."

Brandon didn't drink during football season. He took his training regimen seriously, not to mention his commitment to staying out of trouble. He'd been quizzed on this fact many times by sports reporters over the years. Good thing it was still pre-season. He wrapped one hand around the second beer on the bar, lifted it to his lips, and chugged it. He nodded at the bartender for a second.

"Did they give you a reason?" Brandon said.

"The team wanted a significant pay cut for an extension. They also wanted a waiver from the injury guarantee portion of the contract." Josh put his empty glass back down on the bar. "I reminded them you restructured two years ago to help them land McCoy when the Vikings cut him loose due to the salary cap, and restructured again when they went after Tampa Bay's backup QB last season. I reminded them you live here in the offseason. You encourage most of the defense to live here as well, so the group hits the ground running in July. I reminded them you had twelve sacks last season."

Brandon drained his refilled pint glass in three long swallows. He nodded at the bartender once more and said, "A shot of Jameson's, too."

"Please tell me you're not driving," Josh said.

"I'll have my rig towed home." Brandon dropped the

full shot glass into his third beer. "How long until this hits the national news?"

"Not sure. I got on a plane three hours ago."

"You must have other meetings here today."

"I didn't want to tell you over the phone."

"Thanks." Brandon stared at the boilermaker in front of him. "I think."

"You'll be highly sought after in free agency."

"*Fuck* free agency." Brandon drained his glass again. He had no interest in getting shipped off to whatever team could write him the biggest check.

The bartender dropped off some bar snacks.

"Where's Emily today?" Josh asked.

Brandon pulled out his smart phone. "She's on her way to Atlanta by now. She's doing promotion or some damn thing for upcoming performances."

She'd be gone for three days, which meant he'd spend the next seventy-two hours doing whatever he needed to do to keep from picking up a telephone and begging her to come back.

EMILY CIRCLED THE park-and-fly lot just outside of the airport. She wanted to park anywhere there was a chance someone wasn't going to open their car door into hers. She hated leaving Seattle when the sun was out. Atlanta would be a huge, sticky, humid mess.

She reached out to flip on the car stereo. Maybe some music would help. The last time Brandon was in her car, though, he tuned it to the sports station. She reached out again to change the channel, and her hand froze in mid-air.

"Twitter is on fire with the news that the Sharks declined the contract extension Brandon McKenna was looking for. We're trying to get some official confirmation. Our phone lines are burning up right now, but if you'd like to weigh in on what might be the biggest story of the Sharks' preseason, give us a call. Will McKenna demand a trade as a result? He always said he wanted to retire a Shark, but this might be enough to make him think the grass is greener in Dallas or Green Bay. Call us."

Emily steered into a parking place that materialized from nowhere, stepped on the brake, and pulled her phone out of her bag. Brandon didn't answer. She scrolled through "calls received," and hit "dial" on Josh's phone number.

"Josh Williams."

"Hi Josh, this is Emily Hamilton. Where is Brandon right now? He's not answering his phone."

EMILY WALKED INTO the dim, old-fashioned bar area of a restaurant she hadn't been to in at least ten years. Josh was gone. He was already on a plane, flying back to Los Angeles; one of his kids had a soccer tournament.

Brandon was hunched over the bar with a string of empty pint glasses lined up in front of him. He didn't glance up when she slid onto the barstool next to him. "Hey, bruiser," she said softly.

"They cut me off," he said.

She counted four pint glasses and three shot glasses. Brandon's eyes were red-rimmed, but he wasn't slurring his words. Yet. The bowl of peanuts in front of him was untouched.

"Want to go home?"

"Hell, no. I want to drink." He shook his head like he'd been caught in a rain shower. "I thought you were going to Atlanta."

"I thought I was, too. Damn mechanical problems." She set her handbag down on the bar.

He turned to look at her. "There was nothing wrong with that plane."

"You'll have to update the pilot. He was pretty convinced." Emily nodded at the bartender. "I'd like a club soda with a twist of lime, please. Also, I'd like an appetizer or two, if there's a menu available."

"Coming right up." The bartender moved away from them. She reached out and laid one hand over Brandon's bigger, warmer one. He narrowed his eyes.

"Don't give me any of that 'It's going to be okay' shit."

She swallowed hard. "Of course not."

"I don't want anything to eat. I want to get so drunk I don't sober up for a week."

"I guess I'm driving, then," she said.

Emily's club soda with a twist of lime appeared, and the bartender brought one for Brandon, too. Brandon studiously ignored it. He asked for another Guinness with a shot of Jameson's.

"You know I can't serve you if you're drunk," the bartender said.

Brandon fixed laser eyes on him. "I'm not drunk."

"Trust me. You're drunk." The guy moved the second glass of club soda in Brandon's direction. "Maybe you should talk about it. The booze won't fix it."

The look on Brandon's face was murderous. Emily slipped both hands through his arm.

"Take it easy," she said into his ear.

"Maybe we should leave this dump. I can drink as much as I want at my house."

A platter of meatball sliders landed on the bar in front of them, along with saucers, silverware, and napkins. The bartender moved away. Emily arranged two sliders on a saucer, grabbed a napkin, and put them down in front of Brandon.

"Eat."

"Not hungry."

"If you don't eat, I'll check you into a hotel without an honor bar. You are not throwing up all over my house, Brandon McKenna."

"Who said I was going to your house?" He took a bite of one of the sliders.

"I'm driving." She helped herself to a slider. Brandon's phone vibrated so hard with incoming calls it slid across the bar. He grabbed it, switched it off, and put it back in his pocket.

"You should have gone to Atlanta," he said. The expression in his eyes was bleak as a bitter-cold morning in January. "I can grab a cab home."

She raised one eyebrow.

"I can take care of myself," he said.

She picked up a fork and took a bite.

"You're using a goddamn fork to eat a goddamn burger—"

She spoke into his ear again. "I realize you're having the worst day of your life, but this does not mean you get to act like an ass toward me."

"You can leave at any time." He looked down his nose at her.

She sat up straighter on the bar stool that must have been pressed into service for the first time during the Cold War. The bar was still deserted, but she spoke loudly enough to be heard over the omnipresent soundtrack of rock n' roll oldies from the sixties and seventies playing from tinny-sounding speakers.

"No, actually, I can't leave. I have other commitments and responsibilities right now, but you are more important. I would spend the rest of the night worrying that you didn't make it home, you fell down the stairs, or you gave an interview that made Charlie Sheen look like a Rhodes Scholar." She looped her handbag over one arm. "We're packing up the rest of the food I ordered, and we're going to my house. You're going to sober up. We are going to talk about what to do next."

"There's nothing to do next."

She captured his chin in her fingertips. They stared into each other's eyes. Her voice dropped. "That's bullshit, and you know it."

Neither of them moved for a few moments. The world shrank to the circle of space around them. His eyes dropped.

"Bossy little thing, aren't you?" he said.

Emily took a deep breath. "I'll tell you what you're going to do. You're going to put up stats this season that will make the Sharks GM and front office the laughing stock of the league. You're going to go into free agency with more buzz than Peyton Manning did. You're going to get the biggest contract offers Josh can field, and *you* will decide when it's time to walk away. Not them." She let go of his chin, picked up the slider on her plate in two fingers, and consumed it.

"More buzz than Manning." His voice was dry.

After listening to Brandon's football tutorials, she knew her example was over the top and more than a little ridiculous, but Brandon's agent's phone was probably already ringing.

"It's your choice. Let them beat you, or beat them at their own game."

She sipped her club soda. She knew her words were like waving a red flag in front of a six-foot-four, two-hundred-seventy pound bull who didn't consider losing an option.

He met her eyes again. He reached out for her hand, and squeezed it. Despite having drunk enough alcohol to anesthetize an elephant, one side of his mouth twitched as the supremely self-confident, ultra-competitive Brandon McKenna roared back to life.

Chapter Twenty-One

EMILY AND BRANDON met at baggage claim. She was back from her previously delayed trip to Atlanta. He was home after his last pre-season game. Sea-Tac Airport wasn't the most romantic place in town to schedule a meeting, but it didn't stop Brandon from pulling her into his arms and making sure they'd be trending on Twitter within the hour. Emily could hear the *click* and see the flashes of cell phone cameras going off.

One of Brandon's teammates gave him a nudge. "Hey. Get a room."

"Fu— Go to hell," he said, but there wasn't any heat in Brandon's voice. "Maybe you could get a girl, if you weren't so ugly," he told the guy, who laughed out loud.

Brandon teased Emily the whole way home about a "surprise." As they walked through the garage door into her house, he pulled his tie off, making a blindfold out of it for her.

"I can't see—"

"I've got you," he drawled. He slid his arm around her waist, and held her other hand to steady her footsteps. "One at a time. We'll get there."

Emily smelled roses as they moved into her house. The door shut behind them.

"What are you up to, Brandon McKenna?"

"This is taking too damn long." Brandon swept her up in his arms. "You'll see."

She looped her arm around his neck. "I can't see anything through this."

She heard his low laughter. "So, take it off."

She reached up and pulled the makeshift blindfold off as he carried her. It took a moment for her eyes to adjust to the darkness, but she glanced around.

A trail of rose petals covered the floor from the front door, down the hallway, and into Emily's bedroom. More rose petals were heaped on the turned-down bed, and flickering candles lit the room. A bottle of champagne chilling in an ice bucket and two glasses waited for them on the dresser. Another bowl of fresh strawberries with a dipping bowl of thick, dark chocolate sauce sat next to it.

"This is incredible," Emily said. "Did you do this?"

"I might have had some help."

Amy was the only other person besides Brandon that had a key to Emily's house. Even without the rose petals, it wasn't tough to figure out who his helper was. Emily reached out to pick up one of the candles, flipping it over to examine the base.

"This must be one of those LED candles. They look real, don't they?" she said.

"If that's all you can think of at a time like this, sugar, I'm falling down on the job."

He set her down on her feet. She set the candle on the closest flat surface and wrapped both arms around him.

"I always wanted to make love on a bed of roses," she said.

He pulled her closer. "I think you're going to get your wish." His mouth took hers. "I missed you so damn much."

Emily pushed his suit jacket off his shoulders, fumbling with the buttons down the front of his dress shirt. He responded by unzipping the pencil skirt she wore. A few minutes later, the only trace of two fully dressed people was a pile of clothes on the carpet.

"Leave your shoes on, sugar." He picked her up again, setting her down in the bed.

"Lucky me," was all she could say.

Emily lay in an unbelievably soft and fragrant pile of rose petals. Brandon heaped them over her breasts and abdomen, too. She marveled at how soft they felt against her skin, but she found herself a lot more interested in the six feet four inches of naked distraction lying next to her. Plus, he'd just licked the spot behind her earlobe that made her weak with desire.

"I miss you so much when I'm gone now," she gasped out. "It's awful." She traced the shell of his ear with her tongue. "Maybe we should move somewhere there are no schedules, no agents, nothing else but you and me and—"

His voice was low but amused. "We can't."

"Why not? We're adults. We can do anything we want."

"You might get bored," he teased. "No schedule, no agents, nothing else to do? We'd be forced to make love all day every day, and gather enough food to keep us going. Sounds rugged. I don't know if you could keep up the pace."

She pushed him onto his back, and rolled atop him. "Shut up and kiss me, bruiser."

DAWN'S SOFT LIGHT illuminated Emily's room as she awoke. Brandon slept on, the sheet twisted around his hips, one hand tucked under his pillow. He'd flung his other arm around her. Blond stubble covered his chin and a slight flush colored his cheekbones. His long lashes looked oddly delicate on him. His skin was golden in the morning light. The scent of roses was almost overpowering. Emily knew she would never smell roses again without remembering last night.

She disengaged herself carefully from under his arm and swung her legs over the side of the bed. She smiled as the rose petals fell off her and onto the floor. He stirred, but didn't open his eyes. She stood up, leaned over the bed, and carefully brushed the errant curl on his forehead back with her fingertips.

"Sleep, baby," she whispered.

"Mmph." He rolled onto his stomach. His butt was as gorgeous as the rest of him. She couldn't resist patting it before she padded into the bathroom.

After taking care of the morning business, she was reaching in to flip the shower on when the telephone rang. Fearing it would wake Brandon, she hurried back into the bedroom to answer it. The caller ID revealed it was Amy.

"Kinda early for a social call," she stage-whispered into the receiver.

"Is Brandon still there?" Amy asked.

"He's sleeping. Thanks for the rose petals, you weirdo."

Amy's laugh sounded more like a choke.

Brandon's arm snaked around Emily's waist, and she heard his sleepy whisper: "Come back to bed, sugar."

"Just a sec," Emily murmured to him. "What's up?"

"Anastasia's on ESPN. She's pregnant."

"Well, that was fast. Good for her."

"No, Em. She says she's seven months pregnant. She says Brandon is the father."

Brandon wrapped his arms around Emily's waist, and kissed the small of her back. She stood up and moved away from him.

"Excuse me?"

"Turn on the TV."

"This can't be true," Emily said.

"Call me back."

Emily hung up the phone in a daze. She went into the bathroom and shut the door. Brandon opened it, sticking his head in.

"What happened?" he said.

She sat on the toilet lid, turning her face away from him. In two steps he was in the bathroom, on his knees in front of her.

"Sugar, talk to me."

"Did you call her 'sugar,' too?"

"I don't know what you're talking about," he said.

"Anastasia. She's pregnant." Emily tried to do math in her head. They met in February. It was now almost September. Anastasia could not be seven months pregnant unless she and Brandon—it was too awful to think about. They would have slept together after he and Emily announced their engagement. In other words, he cheated.

"Listen to me. Anastasia doesn't matter to me. We broke up." Brandon wrapped his arms around her. She pushed him away. "I don't understand why you're doing this. Talk to me."

"She's been on ESPN all morning. She says it's your baby."

Emily stared into his eyes. The color drained from his cheeks. "That can't be true."

"When was the last time you were with her?"

She shook all over. Even worse, she was freezing cold. Brandon drew her to his chest. This time, she didn't resist him. His voice was low and barely audible.

"I used a condom every time. Every time."

"When was the last time you were with her?"

"Before I met you."

Emily's brain whirled. *Eight months ago*, he said. Either he was lying, or Anastasia was. She wanted to believe Brandon, so badly. She wanted to believe Anastasia was lying. In that moment, though, she realized she knew better than to trust a man not to cheat. She'd learned that lesson before.

Her voice shook with anger and repressed hurt. "When was the last time you saw her?"

"Shortly after we met. I told her it was over. She didn't want to take no for an answer." He stroked Emily's hair. "I never called her 'sugar.' There's only one, and that's you."

"Maybe you should have told me."

"It didn't seem important."

She cut him off. "What if the baby's yours?" She had to ask.

"It isn't. She showed up at the bar I go to with the guys, and she made it clear what she wanted . . . I left her at the bar. Sugar, there's been nobody else but you since that day in the parking lot."

She dropped her head into her hands. "I keep coming up with the same number of months."

Brandon's mouth fell open. "You can't believe she's telling the truth about this?"

Emily wrapped her arms around herself. "There's ways to prove paternity. If she lied about it, she'll get caught. Why would she risk it?"

He let out a snort. "Sugar, you don't know Anastasia."

Emily's throat felt like it was closing up. She concentrated on pulling breath into her lungs. It was her worst nightmare, come true. There had to be an explanation, but no matter how many times she counted on her fingers, it still didn't look good.

"You saw her. You never told me. Now she says she's pregnant with your baby, and you're wondering why I don't believe you."

"Sugar, I should have told you. I'm sorry," he said.

"Her baby's not mine." He took Emily's face in his hands. "Not mine," he repeated.

But then a photo of Anastasia passionately kissing Brandon time-stamped in late March was all over Twitter and entertainment news within twenty-four hours of her announcement. That wasn't all. Anastasia's friends were also coming forward and insisting he'd been seeing her the entire time he was with Emily.

ANASTASIA'S DAUGHTER WAS born three weeks later. The baby, supposedly premature, weighed almost ten pounds. Brandon's lawyers buried Anastasia's lawyer in a blizzard of paperwork. Brandon submitted to paternity testing the day after the baby was born. Emily spent an additional three weeks at performances in Boston. She'd never been so happy to leave town. She needed some time to think.

Brandon and Emily were still talking, but barely.

Brandon was in Chicago now, preparing for a Monday night game with the Bears. He asked Emily to visit him on her way home to Seattle.

"We need to talk, sugar. Please."

"I can't. I have rehearsals in Seattle this week, and I need to get back."

He was silent for a moment on the other end of the telephone. "Can't, or won't?"

She let out a sigh. "I will see you when you're back from the road trip."

Amy arrived at Emily's house a few minutes before

Brandon's game started that Monday night. She stopped in the entryway, reaching out for Emily's upper arm.

"Have you slept or eaten at all since you left Seattle? Your clothes are hanging on you. There are dark purple circles under your eyes."

Emily pulled away from her sister's probing eyes. "I'm fine." She moved into the kitchen. "How are you doing?"

"Better than you are, I think," Amy muttered.

They sipped beer and talked a little while they waited for the broadcast to start. Of course, there was only one topic.

"Emily, he's not that guy. He wants to be with you. He's not going anywhere." Amy shook her head. "I've never heard of a preemie weighing almost ten pounds, either. That's weird."

"Brandon said both he and Dylan weighed ten pounds when they were born," Emily said. "Maybe he lied. Maybe he's been lying for a long time now."

She couldn't forget the fact she'd risked her heart, again. It hadn't gone well before. She didn't think she could recover from another guy who cheated, lied about it, and then asked her who she believed—him, or her lying eyes.

"You know that condoms fail. Birth control fails. Accidents happen." Amy shook her head. "Em, he would never do this to you on purpose."

"Here's a question." Emily turned to face her sister. "How do we know that?"

"You're kidding. You must have me confused with someone who didn't have a ringside seat for this whole thing. He's told you he doesn't cheat. I was a little worried when you guys first started going out, but he's shown you over and over that he chose you. Brandon's a freaking prince, and you can't believe him?" Amy wrapped her arms around herself. "When are you going to finally evict James from your head?"

"This has nothing to do with him."

Amy cut her off. "Oh, yes it does." They glared at each other.

"You don't understand."

"No, Em. *You* don't understand." Silence fell. Amy took a long swig of beer. Emily stared mutely at the television.

She and Brandon's entire relationship started on a lie. She wondered when—and if—she could learn to trust.

The color commentators were talking about different players before the game started, and of course they talked about Brandon.

"You know, guys, Brandon McKenna may be a bit distracted this evening," one of them said. "Anastasia Lee announced a few minutes ago through her publicist that DNA tests prove McKenna fathered her newborn daughter."

Amy grabbed Emily's hand. Emily's stomach churned. She felt like she wanted to vomit. She couldn't stop shaking. She'd been right to accuse him.

Oh, how she'd wanted to be wrong.

The commentator continued. "Those who've followed this saga know that McKenna's been dating opera diva Emily Hamilton. Let's hope his romantic misadventures won't hurt the Sharks' defense tonight."

"He lied," was all Emily could say.

Despite being so mad ten minutes ago she couldn't look at Emily, Amy wrapped her arms around her sister. "We'll get through this." The phone rang. Amy answered it, and said briskly, "No comment." She hung up. The phone rang again. "Should I answer it?"

"Please unplug it," Emily told her. "I'm going to go lie down."

Emily got up off the couch and hurried into her bedroom. She threw herself onto the bed, burying her face in a pillow. The phone kept ringing. The pillowcase still smelled like Brandon.

A few minutes later there was a soft tap on the doorframe, and Amy said, "There's someone who'd like to talk with you."

"Not right now," she choked out.

Amy crossed the room and put the phone up to Emily's ear. Emily could barely hear him over the racket in the locker room.

"Sugar," he said, "God, I'm so sorry. I—we'll talk about this later. I want to see you later."

"Why?"

"I'll come over when we get back to Seattle. I just—I want to see you."

She was numb. She was torn between screaming in pain and wanting to kill him with a dull fork. She felt like a block of ice: freezing cold, nobody could touch her.

Emily walked back into the living room with Amy's cell in her hand. Amy shut the TV off.

"Watch the game," Emily said. "I know you want to see it."

"To hell with the game." Amy patted the place next to her on the couch. "Let's have some food, Em."

"Not hungry."

Amy ate pizza, drank beer, and the sisters talked about anything else but Brandon, Anastasia, and their daughter. Emily couldn't bring herself to take a bite.

"I can stay," Amy said. Emily handed her a foil-wrapped package of leftover pizza to take home.

"I'll be fine. Don't worry about it."

"Just don't answer the phone."

Emily's home phone and her cell rang almost continuously throughout the evening. She unplugged the cordless in the living room, but it still rang in her room. "I won't."

Amy threw her arms around Emily. "Call me if you need me."

"I will."

"Liar." She grinned. "I love you."

"Love you, too. Thanks for coming over."

Amy put her hand on the doorknob and then turned to Emily once more. "Give him a chance. There has to be another explanation. You met Anastasia. She's awful."

"He still wanted to sleep with her, didn't he?"

Then he had slept with Emily. She swallowed hard. Maybe she wasn't his type after all and he still preferred rail-thin supermodels. He said he loved her, but maybe she never was what he really wanted in the first place.

Maybe they were all wrong for each other.

"He's not James." Her sister grabbed Emily's chin in her hand. "You never loved James, Em."

She pulled away from Amy. "I'll—I'll be fine."

EMILY CHANGED INTO an old, comfortable flannel nightgown and lay in bed, reading. Allegedly. She was too distracted to concentrate, or see the words on the page. She dropped the book on the nightstand and shut off the lamp. She tossed and turned for hours as she planned and plotted what to say to Brandon.

She would be strong. She was not letting this happen to her again. She would come out of this wiser and more resilient. The team's plane wouldn't arrive until very late and she expected Brandon to call and say he wasn't coming over.

Instead she awoke in the dark to his murmured, "I'm home." She'd forgotten he still had a key.

Brandon got into her bed fully dressed and tugged her into his arms. She jerked away from him.

"Come here." He reached out for her.

"No. No, I don't want to."

Emily got out of bed and stood, trembling, next to it. The helpless, numb feeling she had earlier that evening was now white-hot fury. Against every outward indication, she had trusted him. She had believed in him. He had used it against her. How many times would she have to learn that maybe things *were* exactly as they seemed? To quote an old cliché, tigers didn't change their stripes. And ladies' men didn't become one-woman guys, either.

She was an idiot. She wanted to hurt him as deeply as he'd hurt her, but there was nothing she could say or do that would accomplish this. She wrapped her arms around herself.

He took a deep breath.

"Sugar, I know you probably think I'm nuts, but I don't understand how this happened."

"It happens the way women have been getting pregnant for thousands of years. They have sex—"

"No, I never got the results. It was my understanding they wouldn't be back for at least several more days."

"It doesn't matter." Emily's voice shook. The trembling increased. She wanted to scream at him, but somehow she kept her voice low. She was cold again. She knew the cold wasn't ever going to thaw. "You lied to me."

He cut her off. "I didn't sleep with her. Not since I met you. I swear on everything that's holy. Do we have to go over this again? I made it clear I wasn't interested, we were done, and she needed to leave. She attacked me that night at the bar." He jabbed the air in front of him with one finger.

"It still means that you lied to me about seeing her," Emily insisted. "Why should I believe you now?"

"I didn't lie to you!" he shouted. "It's just a picture! Why are you inventing things in your head that never happened?"

Emily didn't listen. "Stop it, Brandon. I trusted you. I believed you. I defended you, and you did this. How could you?"

"What exactly did I *do*? I went out for a beer, and my

ex showed up. I wasn't responsible for her pregnancy. What are you driving at, anyway?"

He was around the room in a flash, pulling her into his arms. She tried to wrench away, but she was no match for his strength. Emily forced herself to look into his eyes. Even in the middle of her hurt and anger, she loved him. The pain she felt over what happened with James was nothing compared to this. Her chest squeezed. She had a lump in the pit of her stomach that wouldn't go away. She wondered if it were possible to die of a broken heart, because right now she felt worse than she had in her life. She took a gasping breath.

"This isn't going to work," she repeated. "I—you have to go."

"*What?* You're just mad. Let's talk about this."

"I can't do this. I can't be with someone who—I can't wonder when it's going to happen again."

"It never happened in the first place. I don't know how she claims that baby's mine, because I haven't seen the results of the tests I took yet."

"Brandon, it's not just the test. This isn't working."

He took Emily's face in his hands. "I'm telling you the truth."

"Why would she get on national television and lie?"

In the faint light from the hallway, she saw his eyes narrowing. "Why are you defending Anastasia over me?" His voice dropped to almost a whisper. "Haven't I proven you can trust me?"

"What do you expect me to think? Do I believe you, or do I believe my eyes?"

"It's not what it looks like." He flung the words at her. "I'm not James, and I'm not your dad."

"Brandon. Stop talking now. Stop talking and get out." This time she succeeded in wrenching the ring off her finger. It felt like she peeled the skin back from the bone. She put the ring into his hand.

"No." He grabbed her hand and shoved the ring into it. "Put this back on."

"No, I can't," she said.

"Why?"

"It's over."

"It's over." His voice tightened. The ring fell to the floor with a soft thump. "You're dumping me? How can I convince you I'm telling you the truth?"

"You can't," she whispered.

"You go right ahead. I shouldn't expect any different from you. I know you've done this before. After all, you don't want anyone getting too close." They were almost nose-to-nose. Emily stood up straight and squared her shoulders. If she let him see weakness at all, she was through. "If you really play your cards right, you can spin this as the poor little diva getting dragged through the mud by the big, mean football player. Imagine the press." Brandon spread his arms wide as he gestured. "If being with me was great for your career, imagine what the breakup will do. You'll end up singing at La Scala." Now it was her turn to gasp. His voice was hard; his mouth was a thin, angry line, but she saw agony in his eyes.

"I would never do that!"

"Well, gosh," he sarcastically noted, "I sure as hell

wouldn't, either, but you don't seem to believe it." His hands came down on her shoulders. "You know what? I think you're possibly the most impossible woman I've ever known." He blew out an angry breath. "Here's the thing, though. I love you, sugar. I'm always going to love you, and I'm never, ever giving up on us. Until you can manage to figure things out, though, you get what you want."

He gave Emily a hard peck on the mouth and strode from her room. His footsteps echoed down the hallway and the staircase. The front door opened. She heard it shut behind him, and then there was silence.

She slid to the floor. The engagement ring twinkled up at her from the carpeting.

Chapter Twenty-Two

EMILY COULD NEVER tell another person how she got through the rest of that night. She finally slept, due to sheer exhaustion. Amy arrived before nine AM. the next morning with a huge bouquet of red roses and fast-food breakfast in a bag.

"You'll need to take these. Brandon sent me a text message really late last night and told me he didn't care what it cost, just keep them coming. There's a card."

Emily tried to push the card back into Amy's hand. Amy wouldn't take it.

"Read it," her sister ordered.

Emily's hands shook as she pulled the card from the envelope. She recognized Brandon's handwriting: *Sugar, I will never, ever give up on us.* Her eyes flooded with tears again. At least she didn't have a rehearsal today.

"You're getting a bouquet every day this week," her

traitorous sister said. "Wait till you see what's coming to-morrow."

"I thought you were supposed to be on my side."

Amy threw herself into one of Emily's kitchen chairs, and dropped the fast-food bag on the table. "I am on your side," she explained patiently. "I'm always on your side. The problem is, I don't understand what you're doing. Why are you so mad at Brandon?"

"He cheated on me."

"Bullshit," Amy said. "I'll bet the results aren't even back yet. He would have been notified the same as Anastasia was. She's got to be lying. There's no way in hell a ten pound baby is a preemie, either. I can't understand why you're taking her word over his."

"You're defending him. What about *me*?"

"So, it's all about you." Amy opened the bag and shoved an egg sandwich across the table to Emily. "You got hurt by James, the cheating ass. You're projecting his issues onto Brandon. Plus, you're being completely unreasonable." Amy heaved a sigh. "If I thought Brandon cheated on you for real, Em, I'd rip his face off. He told me that he didn't do this, and I believe him. I think, deep down, you believe him, too. You're running away before he can hurt you."

"You must have gotten your psych degree from watching TV."

"You know I'm right. Plus, Anastasia's a nut. Why would you believe anything she says is true?"

The sisters glared at each other for a few moments. Finally Amy reached one hand across the table.

"Em, you know that I love you, no matter what, don't you?"

"Yes. I love you, too," Emily responded in a shaky voice, "But please don't yell at me anymore right now."

"I want you to be happy. I want you to have something more than practices and hard work and sitting in a hotel room somewhere waiting to sing. I know you want something more, too. I—shit. I always wanted to be like you. But I don't want to be alone, and I don't think you want to, either. Listen to him. He's telling you the truth."

It was nine o' clock in the morning, and Emily was so exhausted already she could barely keep her eyes open. "I want someone I can trust."

"You already have that."

"I don't. I can't trust him."

Every man in Emily's life she ever trusted had hurt her. It was what they did. She wondered how she could make anyone else understand the constant refrain inside her head.

The scent of the roses reminded her of the night she and Brandon spent together, how soft and velvety the rose petals scattered over the sheets were against her skin, and how they woke each other up again and again to make love.

Obviously, she'd had sex before. Even with an insane schedule, Emily met guys, she dated, and there were follow-up dates and resulting relationships. At the same time, those relationships felt like something expected, not like something she'd waited for.

Ever since she opened her eyes in the Sharks parking lot that icy afternoon, it felt as though Brandon had led her by the hand through somewhere she'd never been before. Her heart opened to him slowly, but surely. He let her set the pace, and he wooed her. She didn't know men had that kind of patience. Just the thought that the feelings she believed matched her own might be a lie encased Emily in ice. People could see through it, but nobody could touch her, and nobody could hurt her.

"You realize, don't you," Amy said quietly, "that you're never going to fall in love until you will risk letting someone in?"

"I know that. I *know* that," Emily said. "I want someone who . . . Oh, forget it. I can't explain it. I—Thank you for coming over."

"You're welcome." There was a smile in Amy's voice. "So, listen. When was the last time you skipped out for the day? Spend a little time with me."

Emily's voice teacher was on vacation. The only appointment she had today was with a treadmill. Maybe she should take a day off. She'd have to deal with more of Amy's nagging, but she'd also get some time with her sister, always a treasured commodity.

"You know what? You're on. Let me get my stuff."

Emily hurried into her room to put on a pair of shoes and grab a jacket. She picked up Brandon's engagement ring off the carpeting. She stared at it for a moment. She could have put the ring in a drawer or her jewelry box for safekeeping, but she didn't. For some insane reason, she slid it into the front pocket of her jeans.

A FEW DAYS later, Emily went to her parents' house for Sunday dinner as usual. The Seattle skies were as gray and leaden as her mood.

She opened the front door, called out, "Mom, I'm home," and walked inside. She smelled a roast cooking in the oven. Her dad wasn't in his usual spot: the recliner in the family room. She hurried into the kitchen to find her mom polishing wine glasses with a soft towel.

"Hi, honey," her mother said. "How are you doing?"

Emily kissed her cheek. "Dad must be running a little late."

Her mother didn't meet her eyes. She turned away from Emily instead. "Want a soda or some water?"

Her mother was hiding something. She and Amy had speculated on what was going on between their parents for a while now. Neither was brave enough to come right out and ask, however. Maybe Emily should bring up the subject before her dad arrived. If she grilled her mother about her love life, hopefully, it would distract her mom from doing the same to her.

"I'll have one if you're having one. Mom, what's going on with you and Dad?"

Emily's mother pulled two cold cans of Diet Coke from the fridge, grabbed glasses, and filled hers with ice from the ice maker. They sat down at the kitchen table. She still wouldn't look at her daughter as she concentrated on pouring the soda into a glass. With knit brows and pursed lips, anyone would think she was performing a surgical procedure of some sort.

"Mom."

Meg still didn't look up.

Emily let out a gusty sigh and rolled her eyes. She was going to have to spell it out, it seemed. "He's spending more time here. Amy said she saw some of his things in the bathroom when she went in there the other day," she said.

"Last time he was here, he was tired, and he didn't want to drive back home." Margaret stared at the tabletop. A flush spread up her neck, staining her normally pale skin.

"Mom."

Meg finally met Emily's eyes.

"If you and Dad are trying to get back together, Amy and I—We just want you to be happy."

"We probably shouldn't discuss this . . ."

Emily laid her hand on her mother's forearm. "I'm not asking for details. I just want you to know that we're both happy about this."

Margaret Hamilton rubbed her face with housework-reddened hands. The long French braid she'd worn ever since her daughter could remember slipped over her shoulder. Margaret's hair was gray now instead of the rich auburn it used to be. She moved a little more slowly than the woman who twirled her eldest daughter around the kitchen floor when Emily was younger, but she still had the graceful movements of a former ballerina. There were lines in her face, but her eyes were still a youthful cerulean blue.

Right now, those eyes were full of unshed tears.

"I didn't want to say anything," Margaret said. "I was afraid the two of you wouldn't understand." She let out a sigh. "You'll both marry someday and have families. I didn't want to be alone, and I'm not good at dating. I thought your father would remarry. I know he dated a little right after we split up, but for some reason, it didn't work."

"He was still in love with you."

"I don't know. I was still in love with him. I thought I'd die when the neighbor saw him out to dinner with your classmate Christy's mother. He met her at a PTA meeting. Maybe she had fewer bills than I did."

Emily shook her head. Her parents couldn't help bringing up the huge financial and emotional cost of her career preparation, and she couldn't help the guilt she felt when she reflected how their lives would be different if she'd chosen another path instead.

"Honey," her mother said, "I didn't mean it that way. You know we would do it all again."

"I feel badly that you both spent so much time focusing on what I needed. I worried about Amy."

Margaret's lips softened into a smile. "I think the fact that we didn't fuss over her made her more independent. She wanted to succeed on her own terms, and she has." She took a sip of her soda. "I worried about you girls when you were younger. Amy's so assertive. I know you had to be as well, and I was afraid you'd end up hating each other."

"You taught us to stand up for ourselves."

Margaret shook her head again. "There are so many

things I wish I could do over. You're both strong women. I'm not sure how much I had to do with that."

"Mom. We wouldn't have known how to be strong if it wasn't for you."

She took Emily's hand in both of hers. "How are you doing with the rehearsals for *Die Fledermaus*?"

"It's fine. The role is tough, but I've been doing some extra practicing that's paying off." Emily had all kinds of time to practice, it seemed, since she was minus one fiancé. Her mother's fingers lingered on Brandon's ring, which sparkled in the sunlight coming through the kitchen window. After carrying the ring around in her pocket for a few days, she had worried it might fall out and jammed it back on her finger. She couldn't bring herself to take it off again.

"Amy told me you were still wearing this." Margaret raised one eyebrow. "Maybe you should tell me what happened, sweetheart."

"I—I can't talk about it." Emily swiped at her eyes. Her misery threatened to engulf the earth, or at least her tiny part of it.

"The ex-girlfriend turned up pregnant, and you broke up with him." Margaret took another sip of soda, regarding Emily over the rim of her glass. "Maybe you should give him another chance."

"No. No, I can't."

"You're being a little melodramatic. Emily Anne, you're in love with that man, and he's still in love with you."

"Mom, can't we talk about something else?"

"Do not tell me that you're doing this because of what happened between your father and me," her mother said. "What happened with us—you girls—I was stupid. We fought so much when we should have been pulling together. It's mostly my fault."

"How can you say that?"

"It's the truth. When I was young, I thought marriage was one long candlelit dinner. Moonlight and roses, romance. I was spoiled and immature, and I never gave him a chance. Your dad's not Mr. Warm and Fuzzy. Instead of realizing that the way he showed love was to provide, I thought he didn't love us because he spent so much time at work. He wanted to make sure we had everything we needed. When your music teacher sent a note home about how talented you are, his response was to get another job. He knew we'd need the money for voice lessons. I thought he was rejecting us because he was gone fifteen hours a day."

"He seemed mad all the time."

"Honey, he was exhausted. It wasn't just the work. We weren't being kind to each other. He felt misunderstood, and I felt ignored. If we'd talked about it . . ." Her voice trailed off. "You need to talk to Brandon about this."

"I did."

"Breaking off an engagement isn't talking," her mother said. "Would you rather have him, or would you rather end up alone and bitter? We wasted so many years, your dad and I. I was so angry for so long. If I would have talked to him about how I felt, instead of assuming what he thought and trying to hurt him the way I thought he was hurting me, we would have stayed with each other."

"He cheated. End of story."

Margaret rolled her eyes. "Amy says he didn't."

"But the paternity test—" Was she the only one who thought the test mattered?

"I've seen the way he looks at you. There is nobody else for him. He met with your dad when he had every indication that your dad didn't like him. Brandon wanted him to know how serious he is about you." She poured the rest of her can of soda into the glass. "He loves you. Sweetheart, love hurts. I'm not going to lie. At the same time, if you walk away from him, you will regret it for the rest of your life."

The front door opened and shut, and Emily heard her father's footsteps in the entryway. "Honey?" he called out. That was new, too. Even when they were married, her father called her mother "Meg."

"We're in here," Margaret responded. Emily heard the joy in her voice and saw the love in her mother's eyes. No matter how gruff her father could be, in that moment, she knew how much her mom still loved him.

He walked into the kitchen and laid a bouquet of mixed flowers in Margaret's arms, wrapped in clear cellophane and tied with a springtime green ribbon. "Amy talked me into these," he told her. Margaret inhaled their scent deeply, clasping them against her chest as if they were the most precious things she'd ever seen.

"Thank you, baby." She got up from her chair, embraced him, and kissed his cheek. Emily saw his shy smile. "Why don't you sit with Emily while I give these some water? How about a beer?"

"That would be great." He sat down heavily in the chair, tugged his tie off, dropped it on the kitchen table, and regarded his daughter. "Someone's been crying. Want to tell me about it?"

"I'm okay."

Emily saw a quick flash of hurt in his eyes, and she realized something in a split-second that took her most of her life to come up with. They all tuned him out. Her mom, Amy and Emily banded together, and at some point maybe he gave up trying. Just once, she could give him the benefit of the doubt.

"Dad." Emily's voice quavered. "I need you," came out before she could stop it. She pressed her hand against her mouth.

He held out his arms. "Come here."

She got up from the table, and wrapped her arms around his neck. "I still love him," she whispered.

"Maybe you should tell me something I don't know."

Her father's voice was warm as his arms surrounded her. He had the comforting father smells she remembered—coffee, starch in his shirt, and aftershave. He laid his scratchy cheek against the top of her head. Her position was a little awkward as she stooped, but his embrace was soothing.

"I hate the thought of his ever being with anyone else," she said.

"That's not fair. You're both adults. Of course you'd have relationships before you met each other."

"I miss him."

"Maybe you should tell him that," her dad said. "You know, he probably feels worse about this than you do."

"What do I do if he—"

"What happens if you do something he's going to have to forgive *you* for?"

Emily stood up. She had to be hearing things.

"You're defending him."

"He's all right. We've talked a couple of times."

She looked into her father's face. "You didn't like him," she insisted.

"No, that's not it. I wanted to make sure he wasn't playing around." He shook his head a bit. "I don't want my little girl marrying just anyone. I don't care if he's in the NFL. He doesn't scare me."

Emily heard her mother bustling around the kitchen, the reassuring sounds of her footsteps, the oven door opening, and the delicious scents of a meal cooking. She sank into the chair next to her dad again. They sat at the same kitchen table they had owned since she was a child. She was doing things she'd done hundreds of times in her life before, but things were new and different today. Her dad took her hand.

"You need to make this right. Tell him you love him, and you're sorry you fought. He'll take care of the rest."

She took another sip of her soda. "I hope so."

"He will," her father insisted. He squeezed her hand.

"Do you have a few minutes right now?" Emily asked.

He stroked her cheek. "Dinner's not ready yet."

Emily's insides were knotting, but if she was going to

find out once and for all what happened to their family, there was no time like the present. She led him into the family room. They sat down on the couch. She stared at her shoes for a moment. Suddenly, she was a confused fifteen-year old who wanted to hold her parents together with whatever means she had. Fear rose inside her like the waves battering the shore after a storm, but she had to know.

"Dad, when you and Mom called it quits, what happened?"

"Punkin, are you sure you want to discuss this?"

Emily nodded.

He rubbed his chin with a free hand, and slid his arm around the back of the couch. "I wasn't home much. As a result, your mom and I fought a lot. Instead of talking about it, it was easier to leave. I thought she'd be happier with someone else." His voice dropped. "It was my fault."

"I don't understand how it could get to that point. You still loved each other. You never talked?" Emily said.

They sat silently for a while. The anniversary clock on the mantel ticked. Finally, she gathered every bit of courage it took to ask. "Was there someone else?"

"For your mom, no. For me, never."

"You never cheated." She picked at a loose thread in the couch cushion. She concentrated on pulling breath into her lungs. He gave her a squeeze.

"There's never been anyone else for me but your mom, and there never will be."

"But you left because she said you cheated."

"No. I left because I realized I asked her to give up

everything she ever wanted, and maybe she'd be happier with someone else." She glanced over at him in utter astonishment. The ex-neighbor who spitefully told Emily that her father cheated on her mother was the liar, then. How could anyone tell a lie so monstrous?

"Honey," Margaret called from the kitchen. "Dinner's ready. Come and eat while it's hot."

"We'll be right there," Mark responded. Emily got up from the couch, and he held out his arms to her again.

"Let's not go this long before we have another conversation." Her father held her. She felt his tears on her cheek. "Maybe we could talk some more after dinner." His arms tightened around her. "Buddies?"

"Buddies." Emily gave him another squeeze. "Do you still love Mom?"

"I never stopped."

In one afternoon, her world had shifted on its axis. Brandon was right. It was too bad Emily wouldn't get the chance to tell him that.

Chapter Twenty-Three

THREE DAYS AFTER Emily's conversation with her parents about Brandon she was in San Francisco, preparing for performances of *Rigoletto*. Rehearsals were finished for the day. She had an hour to herself before a reporter from one of the local TV stations arrived for an interview that would run tomorrow on the news. She decided to treat herself to a pedicure in the hotel's spa.

She melted into the soft leather of a pedicure chair. The warm water, infused with essential oils and slices of fresh lemon, felt like heaven on her feet. She reached out for a copy of *People* magazine to flip through while she de-stressed. She almost dropped it on the floor when she saw an all-too-familiar face.

Anastasia Lee posed with her infant daughter, Delilah, in a highly stylized black-and-white photo shoot scheduled to appear in *Vogue*. Anastasia's expression was remote as she sat in a high-backed chair. Her hair was pulled back in a severe bun. She wore a black silk chiffon knee-length dress with décolletage that was only possible with aggressive use of duct tape, and impossibly high heels. The baby was a replica of her mother, dressed in a white couture gown with a black sash. Delilah had her mother's bee-stung lips and miniature high heels of her own. The caption under the picture read: "Anastasia Lee shows off her first-born, Delilah Marie, with Seattle Sharks' Brandon McKenna."

It was the oddest baby photo Emily had ever seen. At the same time, she didn't want to see more. She dropped the magazine onto the floor next to her chair, turning away from it.

THE REPORTER SUBMITTED questions prior to the interview. It should have been twenty minutes of the usual—talking about the role, how much she loved working with the opera company and seeing San Francisco again, and urging people who had never been to the opera to give it a try. She could do these interviews in her sleep, which is why she told David she could handle it on her own for once.

The reporter was young. He was handsome. He veered off the script almost immediately.

"Miss Hamilton, I'm quite a sports fan, as well as an opera buff. You must be thrilled about the Seattle Sharks' three-game winning streak."

"It's terrific. Congratulations to them." She felt an invisible, icy fist grip her stomach. She smiled brightly.

"Let's talk a little more about *Rigoletto*, and why I'm looking forward to singing this role so much."

His smile was dazzling in response. "You know, Miss Hamilton, I've gotta ask." He almost looked apologetic. "What's the status of your engagement to Brandon McKenna? You've been very quiet about your wedding plans. Our viewers would love to know what's in your future."

Emily recrossed her legs, and resisted the impulse to cross her arms over her chest. She forced herself to sound casual. "We appreciate your interest, but we're not ready to announce our plans as of yet."

"Are you and Brandon still engaged?"

"I'd prefer we didn't discuss my private life." She smiled at him again. "Do you have any remaining questions about the performances?"

He tried again, a couple of times. Finally, Emily pulled off the lavalier microphone pinned to the neckline of the cobalt-blue silk blouse she wore, extracted the battery pack from the back waistband of her skirt, and got to her feet. She extended her hand. "Thank you so much for stopping by."

"I'm not finished yet."

"I have another appointment. Let me show you out." She walked to the door, pulled it open, and waited for the camera person and his assistant to gather their equipment. The camera person and assistant shook her hand on the way out. "Thanks again for the interview."

Emily extended her hand to the reporter. He didn't shake it. "Are you often this difficult?" he said.

"I'm here to answer questions about my performances

and about the opera, not my private life. All questions were agreed upon in advance." She gave him a nod. "Thanks again."

The suite door shut behind him. David was right: Meeting the guy without his presence was just plain stupid. She could only imagine what was going to end up on the newscast. At the same time, she didn't raise her voice, she was courteous, and she didn't bite on the guy's insult. She sent David a text to call her. He would be upset, but she'd deal with it when she talked with him.

She sat down on the couch in the living room of her suite, grabbing the smallish tote bag holding her knitting. The interview was the least of her problems right now. She couldn't get the photo of Anastasia and her daughter off her mind. She couldn't imagine the Anastasia she'd met as a parent. Was she affectionate and loving toward her little girl, or was Delilah an expensive prop? As she sat knitting, she wondered if Brandon had seen the photos. The last place he would want to see his infant daughter was at a high-fashion photo shoot.

Brandon would take his daughter to the park. He'd put her in a jogging stroller, making sure a blanket was tucked close around her so she didn't get a chill. He would take un-posed, casual photos of her on his smart phone, and he'd e-mail them to everyone he knew. She'd wear soft cotton, age-appropriate outfits, mostly pink. Definitely no heels. When they got home, he'd tell her a story as he rocked her to sleep. He would think baby spit-up on his shoulder was a fashion statement.

Hurt and jealousy swamped her. She never thought she wanted a baby, but she wanted his.

She'd been pulling the yarn so tightly on the needles she couldn't get her needle back into the work. She tossed the knitting onto the couch cushion, picked up the remote, and flipped on the TV.

She needed noise. Any distraction from her thoughts would do. She flipped channels until she landed on ESPN. After all, they might have something about Brandon. She grabbed up the knitting again, watching *SportsCenter* from the corner of her eye. She ripped out the row she had ruined.

Emily's head snapped up from her work when she heard the announcer say, "We have a breaking story tonight in the Brandon McKenna saga. For those who've been breathlessly monitoring the situation, this story has taken an unbelievable twist. Brandon McKenna, all-planet defensive end for the Seattle Sharks, discovered his ex-girlfriend, model Anastasia Lee, was pregnant with what he was told was his daughter, Delilah. By the time the baby was born, McKenna was engaged to opera diva Emily Hamilton. That engagement evidently ended. We're not sure, because neither McKenna nor Miss Hamilton will answer questions about it. Despite the fact McKenna took another DNA test recently, he's been showing off photos of the tyke to anyone and everyone in the Sharks locker room. Happily ever after, right? Let's go to the tape."

The tape showed Brandon emerging from the team headquarters and making his way through a knot of reporters to his car. Her heart beat faster to see the man she still loved. The camera flashes were blinding, and one reporter stuck a microphone in his face.

"Brandon, is it true that paternity tests show that Delilah is not your daughter?"

"No comment."

"We have unconfirmed reports that Miss Lee lied that you were the baby's father."

"No comment."

Brandon's face looked cold and unyielding, as though it were carved out of granite. His lips were pressed together so hard they were white. Nobody else, though, seemed to glimpse the anguish Emily saw in his eyes.

"How do you feel about this?" another reporter asked.

Brandon whirled on the guy. "How would you feel about it?" He finished pushing his way through the crowd and climbed in his Land Rover. He pulled away without another word.

The guys on *SportsCenter* were still talking, but Emily wasn't listening. Her stomach had dropped away. Cold chills swept over her. "Oh, no," she gasped out.

She was wrong. He'd tried to tell her. Tell her? Hell, he begged, and she didn't listen. She threw his words back in his face. She called him a liar, and told him she could never trust him. She'd made the worst mistake of her life.

The memories of the last few minutes she spent with Brandon came back with sickening clarity. Brandon pleaded with her to listen, and Emily ignored him. Even worse, everyone told Emily she was making a mistake, and she ignored them all, too. Her fear of being hurt overshadowed her willingness to take a risk. She was going to spend the rest of her life knowing she tossed away the best thing that had ever happened to her out of fear and insecurity.

She ripped out another row of her knitting, but dropped it on the coffee table when she realized she couldn't concentrate. She walked to the window that looked out over San Francisco and gazed at the falling dusk. She could go to the coffee shop downstairs and get a bite to eat. Who was she kidding? She had lost her appetite, maybe permanently. She reached out to pick up her handbag, accidentally dumped it over, and her smart phone shot out onto the carpet.

She still had his number. She wondered if she had the guts to use it. She hit the "Brandon-cell" stored contact, and waited. It rang, and rang. Finally, his voicemail picked up. "Hey. It's McKenna. You know what to do."

There was so much to say, and Emily couldn't speak. She finally hit the "end call" button. The silence of the room enveloped her.

EMILY RETURNED HOME on an early-morning flight from San Francisco two weeks later. Nobody she loved waited for her at baggage claim, and right now, she wondered if anyone would again. She wanted to talk with Brandon. A hundred times she'd reached for her phone, pulled up his number in her contacts list, and chickened out.

She ventured out into a cold, drizzly Seattle morning. She was meeting Amy for coffee and a chat before Amy's store opened for the day. Emily's schedule was insane right now: A voice lesson, a costume fitting for an upcoming production, an afternoon rehearsal with Seattle Symphony. She was singing in their holiday performance of *The Messiah*.

Emily stepped inside the Starbucks across from Amy's shop. She'd been to their stores around the world, but she had to smile when she noted the lone, still-dripping umbrella propped against the front door frame. The only people in Seattle that used them with any regularity were tourists. She breathed in the tangy scent of ground coffee. The slight humidity of heat and multiple other customers wearing damp clothing brushed her skin. Yes, she was home again.

Amy seemed uninterested in Emily's recitation of the appointments that crammed the calendar on her smart phone. She sipped her coffee and raised an eyebrow.

"You still haven't called Brandon."

Emily fiddled with the cardboard sleeve on her coffee cup. She didn't meet Amy's eyes.

"If we weren't in public, you'd be getting the chicken arm motions and the bok-bok-bok," Amy told her. "You can do this. Call him."

"It's the holidays. It's football season. He's probably busier than I am."

"You're miserable," her double-crossing sister pointed out. "Put yourself out of your misery. Make a move."

Jake Tollifson, the grandson of the nice woman Emily had met at the opera benefit, called several times while Emily was in San Francisco to ask her out. She kept telling him "no." He kept asking. Dating wasn't even a consideration, at least for her. All she could think of was Brandon, and how stupid and stubborn she'd been.

Amy broke off a piece of doughnut and popped it in her mouth, giving Emily a tiny headshake as well.

"We are going to have quite an argument if you keep this up," Emily warned. "I told you, Brandon and I are over."

"He still loves you," she argued.

"It's not an option. It's not enough." Emily got to her feet. She knew she was in the wrong, but admitting it to another person was a completely different story.

"You're leaving?"

Grabbing her handbag, her car keys, and the cup of coffee, Emily hurried out of Starbucks. She didn't want to talk about Brandon right then, especially since any thought on what an idiot she'd been brought inappropriate-in-public emotions.

The rain picked up just in time for her to get drenched while she walked to her car.

Amy emerged from the coffee shop and headed toward Emily's Escape. She tapped on the driver's side window. "What if you're making the worst mistake of your life, Em?"

It would come as a real news flash to her sister, but Emily already knew that. She hit the button to lower the car window.

"Everything's going great with my career. That's what I care about. Everything's fine."

"I suppose that career keeps you warm when you wake up alone at three AM, right?"

Emily must have looked shocked, because Amy smirked.

"We're not discussing this," she sputtered.

"Brandon still loves you, and I know you love him."

"I have to go. I'm going to be late."

"Give me a hug," Amy said. Emily reached through the car window to fling her arms around her sister. Amy drove her crazy, but there wasn't a minute of Emily's life she could imagine without her. Emily backed out of the parking space, waving to her once more.

"Think about it," she mouthed.

It became the "think of anything but a pink elephant" game. The harder Emily tried to distract herself with other things, the more she attempted to think about anything other than Brandon, the more he was all she could think about.

The voice teacher was pissed she wasn't paying attention. Emily apologized to her, resolved to work harder, and escaped to her car as quickly as possible when the lesson was over. Luckily she managed to pull it together for the rehearsal that afternoon.

Amy was right. Even more than Emily's list of appointments and things to do, she needed to gather her courage and call Brandon. There was nobody else she dreamed of and longed for.

She arrived home, threw her stuff onto the table in the hallway, and picked up the cordless. It was only a phone call. Emily had made many in her lifetime. There wouldn't be another as important as this, though.

Cold sweat trickled down her back. Her hands shook. Her heart pounded. Stage fright was nothing compared to this. She missed him, she wanted him back, and she had to find the words to persuade him. She made a horrible mistake, and she needed to beg his forgiveness. If there was ever a time in her life when she needed to admit that she really, *really* screwed up, this was it. She scrolled through the caller ID and hit his number.

The phone rang four times. She waited to leave a message. She heard Brandon's voice instead. "Emily?"

The rush of emotion stunned her. She swallowed hard. "It's me. How are you?"

"Fine. How are you doing?"

Where was the smile in his voice she loved so much? A knot formed in the pit of her stomach, right on top of the butterflies that were already there. She took a breath.

"I'm fine. I was wondering if we could get together for a cup of coffee."

He was silent for so long she thought the phone had disconnected. "Brandon?" she said.

"I'm still here. Sugar, that's not a good idea." His voice was empty, defeated. The air instantly sucked out of her lungs.

"Why not?" she forced out.

"I'm pretty busy. Maybe another time." She heard him let out a breath. "I've got to go. Thanks for calling—"

"Please," was all she said.

More silence ensued. She waited.

"Why do you want to see me?" he asked quietly.

"I made a mistake," she choked out. "I want to apologize."

"You want to apologize."

"Yes." She bit her lip hard. She couldn't bear his silence. Finally, the floodgates opened. "I was wrong. I should have listened to you about Anastasia and the baby. I didn't. I thought you cheated, and I couldn't stand the thought that you slept with someone else when you were with me. I miss you. I wonder if there's any chance we could—"

It was his turn to interrupt her.

"Are you sorry because you didn't trust me, or are you sorry because you had to admit that you were wrong?" His voice was raw. She couldn't breathe. His words were like a folding chair to the gut: The pain was instant and overwhelming. "Sugar, I told you that I'd never give up on us, and I don't think I ever could, but you gave up on me a long time ago. I can't be with someone who doesn't take me at my word and doesn't trust me. Even more, I want someone who loves me the way I love her, and you don't."

Now it was Emily's turn to be silent. More than her own pain, she felt his. She heard the strain in his voice. He thought she didn't love him? She loved him like her next breath.

She leaned against the kitchen counter for support.

"You still there?" Maybe it was her imagination, but his voice was a little warmer.

"Yes. I'm still here."

"Are you cryin'?"

"Of course I'm not." She swiped at the tears with her free hand. She took the deepest breath she could with the weight of grief and regret that crushed her. "I fell in love with you. I'm in love with you."

"That's nice, sugar, but you're going to have to do better than that."

This was not a great time for her fiery redhead's temper to ignite. Of course, it happened anyway.

"But I apologized. I'm sorry. I was wrong. I said I love you! What else can I say?" she cried out. "Don't you believe me?"

"I'm big on action, not words. If you love me, I need to see it. I need to feel it."

"I don't know what you're talking about."

"I want the sweet, funny Emily I met while she was flat on her back in a parking lot. I want the woman I made every excuse I could think of to stay with. The minute I looked into her eyes for the first time, I knew I could never let her walk out of my life. I want the only woman I've ever said 'I love you' to and meant it." He took a breath. "I need someone who can put her pride aside and tell me she loves me before her back's against the wall. I need someone who will stand with me, no matter what. Someone who trusts me and wants me, no matter what. The day I see that, I'll know you love me. When you're ready to show me, I'll meet you anywhere, anytime." His final words were barely above a whisper. He waited a few seconds for her to answer and quietly added, "It's up to you."

She heard a click on the other end of the phone, and

the sudden silence that followed a call ending. He wasn't
waiting any longer for her response.

CHRISTMAS CAME. AMY was dating a guy she met at the
shop named Brian. David was brokenhearted over this
development, but he managed to recover quickly after he
met a beautiful young diva from Chicago Lyric Opera who
asked him out. Listening to Amy and Brian spar was ex-
hausting, but Emily had to smile at what seemed to be his
blossoming love for her sister. Wait till Amy figured it out.
She was so happy, and the twinges of jealousy Emily felt
over their sweet romance were quickly swallowed up in the
joy she felt for them. Her parents were still spending every
available minute together. Emily wondered if her father
was contemplating popping the question, or if he would.

"Honey, give him a chance," her mother said for the
thousandth time since Emily finally confessed to calling
Brandon. "He's hurt. You're hurt. It's just going to take
some time."

The Hamilton women met in Meg's kitchen for a
time-honored family tradition: Turkey and cranberry
sandwiches late on Christmas night. Margaret passed the
cranberry sauce out of the refrigerator to Emily.

"It's not going to happen," Emily told her mother, and
turned away so Meg couldn't see her quivering chin. She
never used to cry, and now it seemed like she'd never
stop. Amy caught her sister red-handed.

"Buck up," Amy said to Emily in a low voice. "You can
do this."

"I don't need him. I—I'll be fine," Emily insisted. "My career is going really well, and I—"

"I'll tell you what you're going to do." Amy pulled Emily in for a side hug. "You're going to put one foot in front of the other, and you're going to keep trying until he accepts your apology."

Emily knew she was just trying to help. Brandon wasn't relenting. She also knew there would be nobody else but Brandon for her. Ever.

Chapter Twenty-Four

AT EIGHT-FIFTEEN AM on New Year's Day, Emily was
already late for a meeting with her agent, David. She
attempted to breeze through the front doors of Seattle's Grand Hyatt hotel. The non-fat latte clutched in
one hand had other ideas. The lid popped off her coffee
cup as she pried the door open, splashing foam and
coffee over one leg of her pale-oyster colored wool trousers.

In the good old days of opera, something like this
would call for a full-on diva meltdown. She allowed herself one angry "damn it," and surveyed the damage with
a sinking heart: A gigantic stain. The detergent pen in her
handbag wouldn't fix it. She hated looking like a mess. If
she wasn't nervous enough about this meeting already,
walking in looking like she'd spent the night camping
underneath the Alaskan Way Viaduct wasn't helpful,
either. She'd like a do-over.

If the rest of the year turned out like the first eight hours of it, she was *not* going to be happy.

The concierge flew across the lobby with a handful of tissues. "Let me help." She wiped at Emily's dripping hand. "I'm not sure what we can do about your pants."

"It's not like we have a lot of options there. I was due at a meeting fifteen minutes ago in your restaurant." Emily reached out for the tissues, dabbed unsuccessfully at the coffee stain, and handed them back to the concierge. "If you could point me in the right direction, I'd appreciate it."

"Follow me," the concierge said.

David was the only customer in the restaurant. He got to his feet as Emily approached, looking impeccable as usual, and holding out his arms for a hug. She resisted the impulse to spill what was left in the cup on him. He wore dark dress slacks, a maroon lightweight knit sweater, and an air of invincibility. It would be nice if he had the decency to look somewhat disheveled on a holiday known primarily for football games and hangovers.

"What happened there?" he said, indicating the stain on Emily's outfit.

"I had a dispute with a door, and the door won. How are you, David? Happy New Year." She handed the offending paper cup to a server as she sat down at the table. "May I please have another non-fat latte? If there's any of the non-spill type left, I'll take one of those. Thank you so much." She gave him a dazzling smile. He grinned at her in response.

"Right away, miss." He indicated the two menus lying on the table. "I'll be back to take your breakfast order."

David sipped his coffee and reached out to pat Emily's hand across the table. "I'm fine. Late night?"

"Hardly." Emily's New Year's Eve date had been a handsome, funny, charming, and very successful local businessman she'd met after a recent performance. She did her best to join in the fun at the high-profile party on the top deck of the Space Needle, but her heart wasn't in it. She couldn't stop thinking about Brandon, or how badly she'd wanted him to be the man she kissed at midnight. She'd pleaded a terrible headache. The pain was actually eighteen inches lower. She was home in bed alone by 12:30. "Did you go out for the evening?" she said.

"I watched the fireworks, and I had some champagne. My girlfriend is in Chicago for the holidays." David picked up his menu. "I have some news."

She told herself to take deep breaths. Her career was booming. Her schedule was nearly booked for the next three years. He wouldn't fly to Seattle to tell her about a cancellation. She draped a napkin over her stained pants and took a sip of water.

"I was wondering why you asked me for a meeting on a national holiday."

David reached out, took the water glass from her hand, and put it back down on the table.

"The Met called me late yesterday afternoon. They're presenting La Boheme early next month. The woman scheduled to sing Musette is struggling with some health issues. They need a cover who's highly experienced with the role and can step in to sing it at a moment's notice. Are you interested?"

She opened her mouth, shut it again, and opened it. She looked at him in shock. Heat rolled over her body like a wave. Maybe she was dreaming. Maybe she hadn't heard him correctly. It was understandable. She'd worked for years to hear those words. It couldn't be possible that attaining her biggest goal would be this easy.

A latte with a heart drawn into the foam was set down in front of her. She knew the server was talking to her, but she couldn't respond. She heard David say, "Give us a minute." David reached across the table and passed his hand in front of her face as his lips curved into a smile. "Emily. Talk to me."

"Please tell me you told them yes."

"Of course I did. Let's have a toast." He picked up his coffee cup. "Cheers. Happy New Year."

THE INITIAL EXCITEMENT Emily felt at the achievement of her biggest goal was swallowed up in the numbness that was her constant companion without Brandon. She wondered if he thought about her at all, if he missed her, too. Two weeks after her meeting with David, Emily found herself driving to Amy's shop at lunchtime on a dreary January day, a take-out bag next to her on the car seat. Maybe a heart-to-heart with her sister might banish the blues.

Amy greeted her with a hug. "What's in the bag?"

"Lunch," Emily said. "I hope you still like turkey and Swiss on whole wheat."

"Yeah. It's good to see you." Amy peered into her sister's face. "Something's wrong."

Emily dropped the bag on the chest-high table in Amy's work area and pulled up a stool. "Hopefully you have sodas. I forgot them."

Amy was tapping away at the screen of her smart phone. "Pop. I'll get some," she said distractedly.

"Quit texting and get over here."

"Hang on a minute. I have to answer this. It's Brandon."

The hair stood up on the back of Emily's neck. Amy must have been sending him another message. She hadn't looked up from the screen since Emily arrived. "Since when do you text with Brandon?" she asked, doing her best to sound uninterested. She was anything but. The green-eyed monster was clawing at her guts.

"He's checked in a few times," her sister said. "It's friendly." She glanced at the screen again. "He has tickets for this weekend's game, but I already told him I can't go."

Amy stuck her phone back in her work apron pocket. It was all Emily could do to resist grabbing it away from her. If she gave any indicator of her fear, jealousy, and hurt, she was lost. She concentrated on pulling sandwiches, salad, and cookies out of the bag with trembling hands.

Amy grabbed three Diet Cokes out of her walk-in cooler and settled onto a stool across from Emily. "You're jealous."

Emily closed her eyes for a moment, fighting for composure. "That's ridiculous. I'm fine. I'm too busy getting ready for New York to worry about what he's doing."

"He asks me what you're up to," Amy said. "He knows

you'll be singing at the Met on Super Bowl weekend. He's happy for you."

"That's nice."

"He says he'll retire if the team goes to the Super Bowl. The NFC Championship Game is this Saturday. If they win, they'll go. You'll want to see it, Em." Amy's voice was soft. "Are you sure you won't reconsider? I know you've worked so hard for this performance, but Brandon's last game will happen once in a lifetime. Don't you want to be there?"

"I have to be on the plane to New York on Saturday afternoon. I can't cancel." Her words sounded hollow to her own ears. It was eerie—a windup doll in designer clothes and French perfume kept parroting what she thought everyone else wanted to hear, but the words didn't come from her heart. She remembered with a pang how many times she and Brandon discussed his retiring from the NFL. She said she'd be there, and he wouldn't have to go through it alone. He must hate her.

"He won't even know I'm there."

Amy grabbed her sister's forearm. "Yes, he will. Think it over."

Emily shook her head, and broke off another piece of cookie. She could eat a thousand of them. It wouldn't make her feel better.

ONE WEEK LATER, Emily felt her phone vibrate in her pocket as she walked into her hotel room for the evening. She clicked on a newly arrived text from Amy: *Sharks are going to the Super Bowl. Are you sure?*

EMILY GOT OUT of a cab at Lincoln Center, home of the Metropolitan Opera, in a driving rain. Standing outside the building was still a thrill. The dress rehearsal was tonight, and she would take the stage as Musette. The diva originally scheduled for the role was resting on doctor's orders, in hopes she would be able to perform on opening night.

Dress rehearsal day was always a little stressful. She was early. The other principals had sung here before. To them, it was another work day. They went about their preparations in their dressing rooms. She could hear snatches of vocal warm-ups, the sound of a piano playing, and laughter emerging from someone's dressing room further down the hall. She paused in front of the computer-generated nameplate outside of her own dressing room. Taking a picture of it with her phone was a little weird, but she did it anyway.

The guy playing Marcello stepped out of his dressing room and grinned at her. "I thought the paparazzi were out here again."

A flush crawled up her neck. "Mom wanted a picture," she quipped.

"Of course she does."

He went back inside his dressing room, shut the door, and she walked into her own. Most of the colleagues she'd spent the past several days with were known to her from other productions over the years. She'd asked them about their families, caught up with industry gossip and their schedules, but she'd spent most of her time outside of rehearsals on her own. It offered time to think.

Maybe she needed a little less time to think, especially today. Even the sanctuary of music didn't make her happy. The euphoria of performing before a live audience, feeling the music as well as singing it, wasn't there. Maybe it was because she hadn't actually stepped onto that stage in front of an audience yet. It would come.

EMILY STOOD IN the wings a few short hours later. Her pre-performance butterflies were worse than ever. She wondered if she'd lose her lunch. She glanced into the audience and noted a full house, most likely full of media and major Metropolitan Opera supporters. "You've done this a million times before," she told herself. "Buck up."

The diva singing Mimi reached out to squeeze Emily's hand and smile. The conductor raised his baton to begin. On cue, she sailed onto the stage.

Emily was already sweating through her costume. The heavy stage makeup felt like a mask. The pins fastening the wig onto her head were stabbing into her skull. She knew from experience that all she had to do was step out there, open her mouth and sing the first note. The worst would be over. She closed her eyes and concentrated on taking deep breaths. Her self-soothing was so effective she almost missed her cue.

She'd flounced onto so many stages in her career as Musette, sung "*Quando me'n vo*" more times than she cared to count, and she reached inside herself for that little bit extra tonight. Her voice soared over the audience. She charmed and coaxed, flirted and played with her co-stars. As the most user-friendly and oft-performed opera, those in the audience had probably seen *La Boheme* scores of times before. She was determined they would remember her Musette.

The dress rehearsal went flawlessly. The ovations were deafening. She waited for the explosion of joy at that realization, but it didn't come.

Emily walked out of the opera house when rehearsal was over, hailed a cab, and threw herself onto the seat. The sights of New York City whizzed past her window as she headed for her hotel room. She craned her neck to see while pulling her smart phone out of her handbag, and hit Amy's number.

"Hey, weirdo." Emily heard the smile in her sister's voice. "Been mugged yet?"

"No." She had to smile, too. "What's happening?"

"Same shit, different day," Amy assured her. "Just remember. Small business is the backbone of the American economy." Emily let out a snort. "Oh, laugh all you want. Someone has to do this."

"I'd like to send some flowers."

"That depends. Are you paying for them?" Amy said. "Who's getting them?"

"I'm wondering who might know where Brandon's staying in Miami."

Amy was silent for a few moments. "I could find out. What are we sending?"

Emily closed her eyes. "I have no idea. Maybe you could suggest something."

"Screw the flowers." Her sister's voice was fierce. "What are you writing on the card?"

"How about 'Good luck on Sunday'?"

Amy let out a long sigh. "How about, 'I'm sorry. I still love you. I'm so proud of you. I will never doubt you again.'?"

The cab pulled up in front of the hotel Emily was staying at. She handed the fare over the seat, grabbed her bag, and stepped out onto the sidewalk.

"Amy, let's just go with 'Good luck on Sunday.'"

"Fine." Amy's tone made it obvious her sister's suggestion was anything but. "You're making a huge mistake."

Emily stepped into the revolving door at the hotel's entrance. "I make lots of them, all the time. Let's do this." She thought for a moment. "I know he really likes wildflowers. Please charge my card."

"I'll make sure he gets them," Amy said. "Are you excited to sing tomorrow?"

Emily was at the elevator banks. She knew she'd lose Amy if she stepped on, so she leaned against the surrounding wall. She swallowed hard. "No. I wish I was." She rubbed her free hand over her face. "I have to go, Ame. Thank you so much. I'll talk to you later." She hung up the phone.

BRANDON PUNCHED THE hotel pillow again and flipped onto his back. The digital clock radio at his bedside read 2:17 AM. He'd been glancing at it for the past three hours and seventeen minutes. He wondered if he'd be looking at it for the next four hours or so. His wake-up call was at seven AM. It was Super Bowl Sunday, otherwise known as the biggest day of his life.

He'd spent some time tonight reliving a kaleidoscope of images in his mind—his Pee Wee/middle school/high school/college football coaches' motivational speeches. The day he got a recruitment visit from the only college he wanted to play for. The tears his mama cried when he packed his bags and went off to school. What it felt like to run out onto the field for the first time at LSU. More tears from his mama as he stood on-stage at Radio City Music Hall with the NFL commissioner as a first-round draft pick. Signing his first pro football contract, and signing a new one two years later. Of all his memories, though, the ones he replayed most in his whirling thoughts involved a curvy redhead he called Sugar.

He remembered the first time he saw her sweet, sleepy smile from the pillow next to him. The first time he held her hand. The first time he kissed her. She tasted so good, he went back for more. The first time he coaxed her out of her clothes. The first time he saw love for him in her eyes. He knew how much her career and her goals meant to her. When he'd needed her, though—and was too pigheaded to admit it—she was there. She'd dropped everything for him, and she'd done it more than once. He glanced over at the computer desk in the dimness of his hotel room. She sent flowers yesterday. He'd read the note a hundred times already.

Brandon, I'm so sorry. I love you. I'm so proud of you. I will never give up on us. XO

Amy didn't answer his text asking for Emily's information. If it wasn't 2:17 AM in New York City, he would call every hotel in Manhattan till he found her. It was the most important day of his life, and the emptiest. She wasn't here to share it with him.

EMILY'S STOMACH WAS in knots as she awoke Sunday morning. She lay in bed and wondered if Brandon was lying awake in his hotel room, too. This was the most important day of his life. Amy was right, and the realization was bitter: She should be there for him, watching him achieve his biggest dream. Flowers weren't enough for something like this.

She forced herself out of bed, showered, and dressed in casual clothing. She threw herself into the backseat of another cab less than an hour later. She needed the quiet of her dressing room, the routine she'd been through so many times before.

The security guard on duty at the artists' entrance grinned as she approached. "Miss Hamilton. Your performance isn't for hours."

She nodded. "I couldn't wait."

He pulled the door open for her. "Let me show you to your dressing room." They walked down the silent, darkened hallway. He unlocked her dressing room door. "Break a leg, miss."

Emily extended her hand to shake his. "Thank you so much."

"The building is secured, but lock the door behind me," he said. She heard his footsteps receding down the hallway.

She warmed up her voice. She pulled the makeup she needed out of her bag. She checked to make sure Musette's full-skirted costume was complete. The wig Emily would wear sat on a form on another table. Her thoughts, though, were twelve hundred miles away. Those damn flowers, and that damn card. She had Amy write 'Best of luck on Sunday'? "Lame," she said to herself. "Totally lame."

Maybe she should have told him how she really felt, but there wasn't a flower enclosure card big enough for that. She remembered the sweet cards Brandon had written that came with all the flowers he'd ever sent her, and that was the best she could do?

Emily sank onto the couch against one wall, and wondered what she was doing there. For the first time in her life, she didn't want to be where she was. She was alone on the biggest day of her career so far. She would spend the future alone, too, unless she took her courage in her hands and told Brandon what she'd known for months now: She loved him, and she always would.

Even if he didn't love her, even if he sent her away, she would say what was in her heart. She'd screwed up horribly. She had to apologize, and this time she had to put the diva—and her temper—aside for a little while. The dream she'd been working toward for so many years didn't matter anymore. What mattered was the rest of her life. If Brandon wasn't in it, no matter what she attained in her career, she'd never be truly happy again.

She pulled the cell phone from her bag and hit David's number.

"Hey, Emily." She heard the smile in his voice. "Big day for you." She could hear people chattering all around him in the background.

"David, I have to go to Miami. I'm going to Brandon's game." There was silence for a moment. "You're still there, aren't you?"

She heard David's sigh. "Do you have a flight yet?"

"No. I thought I should call you first."

"You don't have a ticket for the game, either."

"I'll see if I can buy one from someone there. I'm sorry. I know this is completely unprofessional and I am really screwing—"

He interrupted her.

"Emily, I have been hoping you'd do something like this since I've known you. You need a life, not just a career." He let that sink in for a moment. "I wish it hadn't been the Met, but Alicia will go on. Will you come back for the performances later in the week?"

"If they'll have me." She took a shuddering breath. "Am I doing the right thing? What if I get there and I can't get in? What if he doesn't want to see me?"

"Get yourself to the airport, get on a flight, and go talk to him. I think he'll want to see you. I will take care of things in New York. Call me when you get there."

Emily reached out to grab her handbag. She had a change of clothes and everything else she needed after her performance in her backpack, so she didn't need to go back to the hotel. She needed to get to Miami. She needed to see Brandon.

The cab ride took forever. She tipped the driver, she

prayed, she did everything she could, but it still took forever. Finally she got to the airport. She bought a full-price ticket on a flight that was leaving in half an hour and ran to the security checkpoint. She ran through the concourse, backpack banging against her shoulder, and hurried to the gate. The waiting area was empty except for the gate agent, who was shutting the door to the Jetway.

"Please wait!" Emily cried out.

"I'm sorry, Miss, but the flight's already late."

"I have a ticket."

"I can't let you on. I'm so sorry. There's another flight to Miami in four hours."

"I have to be on this flight. *Please.*"

"I'm sorry." He locked the door.

Emily tried to catch her breath. She'd missed the only chance she had to make it there before the game started.

She was dry-eyed, but shaking all over. Her heart pounded, her stomach rolled, and she broke out in a cold sweat. She barely resisted the impulse to fall to her knees and beg in front of someone who was, evidently, just doing his job. She had to get to Brandon. She couldn't afford to rent a plane. Buying another last-minute, full-price ticket wasn't an option. She couldn't drive there in time.

She sank into one of the waiting area chairs and dropped her backpack onto the carpeting. She put her face in her hands and tried to think, tried to still the shaking that she couldn't seem to control. On some level, she was amazed that, in an airport containing thousands of people, she was completely alone. She took deep breaths. She had to calm down, or she'd never figure out what to do.

The later flight wasn't going to work. Brandon would be gone by the time she got to the stadium. He'd be somewhere with the rest of the team, celebrating or commiserating, and then he'd be out of reach. Emily wouldn't see him. It was too late, and her heart was breaking.

She heard footsteps close by, and the rustle of clothing. Someone sat down in the chair next to her. A woman's voice broke into Emily's frantic, panicked thoughts.

"Ms. Hamilton?"

Emily looked up to see a dark-haired woman with kind eyes. She was wearing the airline's uniform. "Yes?"

The plane hadn't left yet. She could see it through the window. It was taunting her. It was something else she wanted desperately, but couldn't have.

"Are you all right?" the woman asked.

Emily chewed on a lower lip as dry as the Sahara and tried to swallow. "I—I'll be fine." Sure she would. She wanted to scream in agony. She wanted to cry and beg. Anything. Most of all, she wished she hadn't been so stubborn with Brandon.

"There's a minor mechanical problem with the plane, so we have a short delay. I understand you were told you couldn't board earlier."

"Yes. Yes, I was."

"Please come with me," the woman said. She got to her feet. "May I see your boarding pass?"

Emily's hands were shaking so hard from panic and

adrenaline it was hard to unzip her backpack. She dug the boarding pass out and handed it to the woman.

The woman crossed the waiting area, unlocked the Jetway door, and beckoned to Emily. "Go ahead. They're expecting you," she said. It was like a mirage. Emily wondered if she'd vanish, but she walked to the doorway.

She gave Emily a comforting pat on the back. "I hope someone you love is on the other end."

A few minutes later, Emily was in her seat. The flight attendant slipped her a few tissues before Emily belted herself in for takeoff. Emily didn't know how she would get in to see Brandon. He'd be getting ready for the game. He'd be whisked out of there when it was over. It wasn't like he had office hours. He probably wasn't answering his phone. She could find out where the team was staying, but then she'd have to find his room. NFL teams locked down entire floors. It wasn't like she could stroll up to the front desk to ask.

Emily settled back to wait some more. The pilot announced that due to the mechanical problem and resulting delay, those connecting to other flights would be delayed. She'd have to rent a car and drive like a bat out of hell to have any chance at all to be at the stadium before kickoff. Oddly enough, though, she was relaxed. It was out of her hands. She did her best, and the rest was not in her control. If this kept up, she'd join hands with the others in first class and recite the Serenity Prayer or something.

The people seated around her went back to working on their laptops, watching a movie on the individual

DVD players the flight attendant handed out, or staring out the window. It was another Sunday afternoon flight for them. The minutes dragged by for her.

After what seemed like an eternity, the plane landed in Miami, taxiing to the gate. The best part of Emily's planning was to bring her backpack. If she ran, maybe she would make it to the rental car desk before the stampede and get on the road.

The plane's door opened, and she broke into a sprint as she rushed through the Jetway. She turned into the concourse leading to baggage claim and the car rental desk. She dodged people and their bags as she went. Running through any airport isn't exactly effective, but she had ninety minutes to get to Miami Stadium and get a ticket before kickoff.

She was so absorbed in avoiding toddlers with pink rolling luggage and entire families of people who insisted on walking together that she didn't pay much attention to anyone or anything around her. A hundred feet or so ahead, though, she glimpsed a tall, muscular man in dress clothes with a wild mop of blond curls, and her heart pounded.

It *couldn't* be him. It also couldn't be anyone else on the planet.

"Brandon!" Emily cried out, and a huge grin spread over his face. She darted around a woman with a double stroller and a businessman talking on his smart phone, and tried to speed up. It was like running through quicksand.

He pushed through the crowd of people surrounding him and broke into a run, too.

"Sugar," he called out. He threw open his arms, and Emily ran into them. It was just like the movies, except it wasn't perfect. It was all arms and legs. Her backpack went flying. She kissed his ear instead of his mouth, but finally, they made it work.

He pulled her up off the floor, swinging her around and around, and she wrapped her arms around his neck. She threaded her fingers into his hair. He was saying something in her ear, but she blurted out, "Baby, I'm so sorry. I wrote something so stupid on your card. I should have written something better. It was terrible. I—"

"What are you talking about?"

Emily wanted to pull him around her. She wanted to crawl inside of him. She had spent hours planning what she would say when she finally saw him, but now she forgot it all.

"I said 'Best of luck.' Best of luck. What the hell was that? I should have said I'm sorry. I should have said I love you. I should have said that I'm so proud of you, and that I wished I could be at your game, and that I'd never give up on us. I—oh, baby, I messed it all up. I—"

He cut her off. "So, you flew here from New York to tell me this." He looked amused.

"I came here . . . I came here to tell you that I love you, and I'm sorry. I wanted to tell you—"

"You did." He lowered her to the floor, but didn't let go. His fingers tangled in Emily's hair. "I love you, too."

She wrapped her arms even tighter around him— anything to get him closer. For the first time in months, she could breathe. She was warm. Joy bubbled through her veins like the finest champagne. "I should have trusted you. How could I do that to you?" Emily fisted her hand in his dress shirt. "Why are you *here*? I was—"

He laid a finger over her mouth. "Amy texted me with your flight information. I said I'd meet you anytime, anyplace, and I'd accept your apology." He cupped her cheek in one hand. Brushing her lips with his, he murmured, "God, I want more," and sealed his mouth over hers. She pushed herself even closer to him, and she heard applause. He lifted his head.

They were surrounded by a semi-circle of passersby, who were smiling and clapping. She glanced around in surprise. All these people must have something else to do.

They heard a voice from the crowd. "Aren't you Brandon McKenna of the Sharks? What are you doing here?"

"Damn Gatorade commercial. I can't go anywhere," Brandon murmured to Emily, and then said more loudly, "Had to pick up my girl."

"You're supposed to be at the stadium right now," someone else called out.

Emily saw Brandon smile. "What do you think, sugar?" He picked up her backpack, looped it over his shoulder, and kept one arm around her. The knot of people still hadn't dispersed, and most of them appeared to be listening intently to them. "Should we take in a football game?" His voice dropped a bit. "You blew off The Met for me?"

"I didn't exactly *blow them off*," she said. "I—I needed

to be here for you. Maybe I'll get another chance, some other time."

"What if there's not another chance?" he asked.

Emily bit her lower lip. She had walked out on them. She'd gained the success she'd worked so hard for, but it was empty without Brandon there to see it, too. She turned her back on the growing crowd of bystanders and looked into his eyes.

"I was in New York on that stage. It meant nothing without you. That's why I came here," she said. "Let me do this for you."

For the first time since they met, Brandon was speechless. He kissed her. Hard.

She reached up to stroke his scratchy cheek. "Let's get the hell out of here." A group of police officers had arrived and were trying to break up the crowd blocking the concourse around them. In the midst of hundreds of people, the only person she saw was Brandon.

Brandon rested his forehead against hers. "On one condition."

"What might that be? We have to go."

"We're leaving right after the game's over. We're going to New York. I'm going to do whatever I can to make sure you'll have that chance." He rubbed his nose against hers. "Deal?"

She opened her mouth to argue with him. She told David she'd be back for the performances the rest of the week, but she was fairly sure those in charge would have made arrangements for another diva to sing the role instead. Walking out on a performance guaranteed it.

Brandon had no idea about how operas were cast, how careers were built, how competitive roles were, but the fact he wanted to help . . . Her heart melted.

"Deal."

"I mean it, sugar."

The police were still trying to get people moving through the concourse. Emily heard murmurs of "Sharks" and "Super Bowl" and "What's he doing here, anyway?"

"Okay. Show's over. Break it up. Let's go." The officers made shooing motions. One of them glanced over at Brandon and said, "I know you. Why are you here?"

Emily knew all these people were most likely in shock at seeing Brandon, but she wondered if they could have something read out over the public address system. She reached out and tugged on one of the officers' sleeves. "We need some help."

"I'm a little busy right now," the officer said. He smiled at her, though.

"We have to get him to his game. He's late. What can we do?"

Another police officer took Emily's elbow.

"You can't drive fast enough to get him there before it starts, but we can. Follow us."

Chapter Twenty-Five

THE POLICE OFFICERS were only too happy to show Brandon and Emily to the back seat of an unmarked vehicle parked outside the terminal.

"Good thing it's a slow work day," one of them joked. "I never thought I'd be a escorting a player to the Super Bowl. You're about to see a miracle. Watch this." He grabbed the car's radio microphone while they maneuvered out of Miami International Airport.

The officer behind the wheel turned to wink at Emily. "The other guys will be jealous. Buckle up, miss."

Emily felt the click of her seatbelt and hissed, "You, too, bruiser." Brandon was already fumbling with his own seat belt.

They pulled onto the freeway, flanked by multiple cop cars with lights flashing and sirens screaming. The traffic was bumper-to-bumper across all lanes. The police car maneuvered into traffic and picked up speed. Cars all around them parted like the Red Sea as a result. Emily sat up a little and peered through the clear Plexiglas separating the two seats. The speedometer read eighty miles an hour already. She reached out to grab the arm rest in alarm.

Brandon snatched her other hand.

"Sugar. We're going to be fine. They do this all the time."

She peeked over the seat, saw the car's digital speedometer pass eighty-five, and turned her face away. Maybe it was better for everyone if she didn't look.

The cop riding in the front seat turned around to them. "How do you feel about the Sharks' chances this afternoon, Mr. McKenna?"

"We're going to win," Brandon assured them.

"You seem pretty positive."

"I am."

Brandon and Emily rode along in silence for a few minutes. The exit signs were passing in a blur, but the last sign she could make out said they were still ten miles from Miami.

"We'll take you to the players' entrance, Mr. McKenna. Your guest will be shown to her seat," the officer driving called out to Brandon.

"Thank you, and thanks for the ride."

"It's our pleasure," the officer in the passenger seat assured him.

"I don't have a game ticket," she murmured into Brandon's ear.

"You'll go to the owner's suite, and the team will take

care of it." He reached out to stroke her cheek. "You and I aren't done yet, though."

"I can't believe you left. The coach must be freaking out."

He extracted a small white florist's card out of his pocket. "Remember that card you said you wrote? This is why I left." He put it into Emily's hand. "Amy texted me. She said you'd left New York, and you were on your way. Let's just say there was some arguing with Coach on my way out the door. I told him I'd be back before kickoff." He let out a breath. "There may not be a game for me, either. We might be watching from the stands, but at least we'll be together." He snorted. "The stuffed frog was a nice touch."

Emily stared at the card, reading the sweet message she was too scared and full of pride to write. Her sister engineered their reunion. A wave of emotion washed over her. Amy wanted Emily's happiness badly enough to take the risk her sister was afraid of.

"Hey. If you cry all over that, I can't frame it." Brandon put the card back into his wallet as the police car bounced over a speed bump at the entrance to the stadium twenty minutes later. It screeched to a halt in front of a doorway that read "Players' Entrance." The police officers escorted them into the building.

Brandon reached out to shake both their hands. "Thank you so much. I'd like to send you some autographed Sharks merchandise as a thank-you as well."

The officers interrupted each other.

"We can't accept that."

"Thank you for the offer, but no."

Brandon gave them a nod. "I'll see what else I can come up with that won't get you in trouble with the chief. It was great to meet you. Please tell your colleagues thank you from me, too. C'mon, sugar. We gotta go." He picked up his suitcase and Emily's backpack in one big hand and wrapped an arm around her waist.

"I'm not supposed to be here," Emily protested to Brandon, but he wouldn't let go of her. He pulled her down the hallway.

"Just let me find someone."

He held the door open for Emily, and she walked into the locker room. She expected piles of dirty laundry, awful smells and half-naked guys wandering around. It was surprisingly luxurious, and at least everyone was dressed. It took a couple of minutes, but sixty pairs of eyes focused on Brandon. They didn't look happy. In fact, "angry" was the word she'd use.

Damian stood. "I was about to put your ass on the back of a milk carton, dawg." He crossed the room with a hand extended to Brandon. They shook hands, hugged each other, and Damian kissed her cheek. "Hello, love." He frowned. "Why are you here?"

"Take your lips off my woman," Brandon growled, but he didn't object when Damian gave her a hug, too.

The coach called out, "Nice to see you could make it, McKenna. Hope you brought your goddamn checkbook." He smiled at Emily. "Hello, Miss Hamilton. I'm fining McKenna an additional ten thousand dollars for bringing you into the locker room before a game. Of course, it's a pleasure to see you." He crossed the room to them, and Emily reached up to kiss his cheek.

"A kiss for luck," she explained.

"We'll catch up after the game," he assured her. "You're going to have to leave."

"Bye, Coach. I know you'll win."

"I've always liked you," the coach said.

She tugged on the coach's jacket. "Maybe the fine could go to Lake Washington High School's music program."

He laughed in response.

A team employee stepped out of the crowd and took her arm. "Please come with me."

"Hang on," Brandon said to Emily. He hurried to his locker. He returned with a game jersey in his hands, which he draped over Emily's head. "Perfect."

"You might need this later."

"Forget it. You gotta go, sugar."

He turned back to the team, but not before she got a quick kiss and an, "I'll see you later." The kiss brought on a cacophony of whistles and applause.

Emily heard Greg shout, "Get a room!" He was suited up for the game. The team must have put him on the roster today.

"Win," she told Brandon.

"You bet your ass." He clapped his hands loudly. "So, ladies, I understand there's a game this afternoon. Who's going to help me tape up?"

Emily could still hear the whistles, shouts, and stomping feet from inside the locker room as she and the Sharks employee hurried through the hallway outside.

She walked into the Sharks' owner's suite a few minutes later. There weren't many women present. The other wives and girlfriends must have been scattered all over the stadium. The media lurking around the Rose Bowl snapped photos of her in Brandon's jersey. His ring was still in her jeans pocket. She rubbed her fingers over it as she paced in front of the suite's windows, waiting for the kickoff.

For someone who appeared in front of a couple thousand quiet, formally dressed people to do her job, it was shocking to experience 100,000 people screaming their heads off at Brandon's workplace. There seemed to be some kind of elaborate pre-game procedure, too. The teams were introduced as a unit, and emerged from the tunnel. Kelly Clarkson sang "America the Beautiful." The team captains walked to midfield holding hands, introductions of players and dignitaries present at midfield were made, and a coin toss determined who would defend each goal. Seconds afterward, Aretha Franklin's voice filled the stadium as she sang the national anthem. Fighter jets roared overhead only moments after the last note.

The Sharks' owner, John Campbell, milled around the suite with his guests. After a recent split with his much-younger second wife, he was considered one of Seattle's most eligible bachelors. He was entertaining what appeared to be a couple of lingerie models today. Maybe they knew Anastasia. He also hosted some former Sharks players. Brandon could have told her who they were, but he was a little busy at the moment.

John broke away from his guests long enough to greet her.

"Emily, it's good to see you. Weren't you supposed to be singing at the Met today?"

"Well, I *was*." She smiled up at him. "I had to see this."

"Help yourself to something to eat or drink." He nodded in the direction of the huge buffet.

"Thank you so much for offering, but I think I'll wait awhile."

He squeezed her shoulder, and said, "If you need anything, let me know. Excuse me for a moment."

Emily grabbed a soda and sat down. She waited nervously for the game to finally start. She'd never felt this way before, either. A perma-knot formed in the pit of her stomach, and she wanted to jump out of her own skin. She hoped he would play well. Even more, she wished the experience would be everything he'd dreamed of over the years. Her nerves were probably nothing compared to his.

Brandon ran up and down the sidelines before the first play with the Sharks defense. He raised his arms up in the air, asking the fans for noise. She saw his huge smile on the video screen, and he pointed toward the suite. She knew he couldn't see her, but she got to her feet and blew him a kiss anyway.

The fans cooperated, roaring loud enough to make the ground shake. The Sharks faithful were here today, too. The game began, with an even louder roar from the crowd. Oddly enough, Brandon was on the sidelines. The coach must have still been mad.

"Why are you benching him?" she muttered to herself. "Are you nuts?"

Emily got up out of her chair, found a quiet corner, and paced as she watched the game. The first quarter passed rapidly. After all, New England's offense spent most of it on the field.

The second quarter came, and Brandon still wasn't in the game. The sports commentators on the televisions all over the suite seemed horrified that Brandon wasn't playing.

"We're a little surprised to note that the Sharks' All-Universe defensive end and the centerpiece of their defensive line, Brandon McKenna, is still riding the pine in the second quarter," one announcer said. "His team's getting beat, and we have no information about a possible injury that would prevent him from playing."

"He's worked his entire career for this," said another. "I understand that the Sharks wanted to teach him a lesson, but is it worth a potential Super Bowl loss to do it?"

The first one took up the story again. "We have an unconfirmed report that McKenna told Coach Olsen he wanted to skip the game to attend his ex-fiancée Emily Hamilton's debut with the Metropolitan Opera this afternoon. According to the same source, Miss Hamilton is at today's game, so something happened. We're working on getting more information."

A former player on the announcing team piped up. "Hey, I've played with McKenna, and that's a damn lie. There is nothing more important to him than football.

He's not going to do stupid shit like that on the eve of the Super Bowl."

Despite her worry and nervousness, Emily had to laugh. The "bleep" came about five seconds too late. Little did the guy know that Brandon had done "stupid shit like that" only hours ago.

"We'll get more of the story as it's available," said the first announcer. "In the meantime, McKenna's on the sidelines, he hasn't played a down yet, and the Sharks are being badly beaten at the line. Their pass rush is non-existent as well."

Emily saw Brandon look up toward the suite again. All around him was the controlled chaos that was the Super Bowl, and she wondered what he might be thinking. She got to her feet and moved to the window. She blew him another kiss. To her surprise, he pantomimed catching the kiss in his fingers. She saw a video camera out of the corner of her eye, but she couldn't take her eyes off of him. Despite a getting-crowded suite, nobody else was there. She folded her hands under her chin.

"God, please let him play," she murmured. "Please."

Emily turned to see John Campbell standing next to her. "He's going to play, isn't he?" she asked him.

"It's up to the coach, Miss Hamilton."

She let out a heavy sigh. "It's not going well."

"You're right. It's not."

John picked up the telephone next to the seating area and asked to be connected with the coaches' booth above the field. He must have been patched into the coach's headset on the field.

"We're not going to lose this goddamn game," John said. "They're driving on our 20, and you're punishing the entire team over something one guy did? Put McKenna in." He listened for a few moments. "Just do it. I'll handle it later." He hung up, turned to face Emily, and said, "You're about to get your wish. In the meantime, let's have a drink. What would you like?"

"I'll have what you're having." Hopefully he wasn't drinking Jagermeister.

He beckoned the server. "Two scotch and waters, please."

Their drinks arrived unbelievably fast, along with a variety of snacks—one more perk of owning a pro football team. John gestured to the seats. "After you, Miss Hamilton."

Down on the field, the coach made his way over to Brandon. Moments later, Brandon put on his helmet and ran onto the field. The ovation was deafening.

Emily threw her arms around John. "Thank you." To her surprise, he looked a bit embarrassed and gave her a shy grin.

"Oh, no, thank *you*. He's going to win me a Super Bowl."

John laughed, and clinked glasses with Emily. She wasn't typically a Scotch drinker, but she sipped. It wasn't bad. Then again, they weren't drinking the cheap stuff, either.

Brandon played like a man possessed. He'd once told Emily that if he was ever actually in the Super Bowl, he feared he'd freeze. It had been his goal for so long. He visualized running onto that field so many times that it must have been like home to him. He had two sacks before halftime. He was menacing, and he was all over the Minutemen's quarterback. If he didn't make the sack himself, he helped his teammates by knocking offensive linemen out of the way, or getting his arms up to deflect New England's passes. He rallied a team that had spent most of the first half letting New England run all over them. The offense was still having some trouble, but the defense was making opportunities.

They'd destroyed New England's ability to run the ball. The Sharks secondary managed to intercept the New England quarterback's passes three times, too. The TV commentators were predicting this could end up being Brandon's greatest game as a pro. The others in the owner's suite were cautiously optimistic, wondering if the Sharks could win their first Super Bowl.

Just before the halftime show came on the field, the network commentators broadcast the footage taken by the camera guy Emily saw earlier from the corner of her eye—a few seconds of her blowing Brandon a kiss. Another photographer had filmed Brandon pretending to catch it, and winking as he did so.

"Brandon McKenna's catching everything that's coming his way today," the commentator said.

Shane Falcon, former Super Bowl–winning quarterback of the Pittsburgh Steelers and part of the announcing team, responded, "Hey, guys, there isn't a man alive who doesn't understand what's happening here. He's trying to impress the lady in his life, and he's doing a damn fine job."

One of Seattle's former running backs was providing color commentary this afternoon.

"Maybe she should always be on the sidelines."

"Hell, yeah. Let's hope there's more where that came from, Seattle fans."

At halftime, while Beyonce and Jay-Z's music echoed through the stadium, Emily got up to stretch her legs. Maybe she should go out and walk in the corridor. A little exercise might settle her world-class case of nerves.

The moment she ventured out of the suite, she was surrounded by cameras and reporters. Don, a reporter Emily recognized from *The Seattle Times*, led the group.

"Don, do we have to do this now?" she pleaded. "I'm a mess."

He grinned at her. "A couple of questions, okay?"

She heard another producer count "three, two, one," the bright lights of television cameras shone in her face, and a female reporter Emily hadn't met before said, "Surprisingly enough, there are some things more important than the Super Bowl. The Sharks' Brandon McKenna announced three weeks ago that he would retire from the NFL after today's game. He's been working toward this goal over his thirteen-year career. McKenna was reportedly so unhappy about missing his ex-fiancée Emily Hamilton's debut at the Metropolitan Opera today he considered leaving the team and flying to New York to see it. Emily was scheduled to sing the role of Musette in *La Boheme* this afternoon. Instead, she's here in Miami. Emily, what made you decide to come to the game?"

"I had to be here. It's the biggest game of Brandon's life."

"Are you worried about the effect on your own career?"

"Yes. I am." The realization sat in her stomach like a lump of lead, cold and heavy. She'd tossed away years of hard work today. Emily chewed on her lower lip. "I . . . I just had to come, though."

"Does this mean you're back together?" another reporter asked.

"No comment." She fingered the ring in her pocket.

Don's smile got even broader. "Is there anything you'd like to say to Brandon, Emily?"

Emily looked into the camera. She wanted to tell him again that she loved him. She wanted to tell him she couldn't live without him. She wanted to wake up every morning and go to sleep every night in his arms. She wanted his babies. Even more than that, she wanted his heart.

That wasn't what she said, though.

"I'm so proud of you, baby," she said. "Win."

"Back to you, guys," the female reporter said, and then to her: "Thanks, Emily. Catch you on the field after the game."

The media hurried away, and Emily walked back into the suite.

The second half started with a vengeance. The Sharks would make a good run or get better field position, then the Minutemen's defense would force a fumble, or Seattle couldn't convert third down. The defense did their part. Damian picked off a pass and ran it into the end zone to score. The Minutemen's quarterback spent a lot of time sitting on the turf as Brandon and his teammates sacked him repeatedly. The Sharks fans were doing their best to pump the team up, but as the minutes ticked on, hope was fading fast. Seattle was still down by six, and Emily folded her hands under her chin. They couldn't get this far to lose the game.

Emily rubbed her fingers over her lips. Thirty seconds left on the clock. The Sharks were driving on their forty-five when disaster struck. The Minutemen's cornerback intercepted a pass from Tom, the Sharks' quarterback. She heard the cries of disbelief in the suite; she went cold inside. He continued to run, only to be shoved out of bounds by Tom. Tears blurred her eyes.

After listening to Brandon's football tutorials, she knew what was going to happen. The Minutemen would line up for a play in what he called the "V" formation, protecting the ball at all costs. They would run out the thirty seconds left on the clock by snapping the ball from center twice. The game would be over, without any chance for the Sharks to recover the ball in time. The Sharks would lose, and Brandon had played his entire career to lose the biggest game of it.

All the Minutemen's quarterback had to do was take a knee when the ball was snapped from center. The teams trotted back onto the field. Emily couldn't see exactly what happened on the snap, but she saw what happened next. The ball bounced off the quarterback's foot, and flew into the air. Time stood still as bodies crashed into each other, but the ball landed in a pair of hands wearing electric blue gloves.

Brandon tucked the ball into his arm, and took off for the end zone.

"Go!" Emily called out, jumping up and down. "Go, baby!"

The crowd was on its feet, cheering him on. The suite was a cacophony of shouting. All she could see was Brandon, and he was still running. He'd made it past the secondary, he was feet from the end zone, and she was still shouting, "Run!"

He couldn't hear her over the noise of 100,000 people. Maybe he'd feel it. One of New England's players threw himself toward Brandon. He grasped Brandon's ankle, and Brandon stumbled. He took a few more steps. The guy hung on. It seemed like it took forever, but it was only seconds in reality. Brandon fell, but he landed in the end zone. The official held his arms straight up in the air—touchdown.

The crowd went wild. Emily put both palms on the windows of the suite. The noise from the stadium concussed against them like a cannon firing. As quickly as the noise started, though, it stopped.

"Oh, sweet Jesus," she heard John say.

Nobody moved. A flutter of yellow fabric hit the turf. Flag. The crowd was silent. All Emily could hear was the television commentators.

"Wait. Let's see what it is. There's no preliminary indication of a penalty, and there'll be a booth review . . ."

John stood up from his seat, walked over to the phone, and punched in a few numbers. He listened intently to whoever was on the other end.

Brandon was on his feet. He still held the ball. The coach signaled for a time out; the defensive players clustered around him in a knot. Everyone waited. Emily buried her face in her hands. If the waiting was awful, this was worse. She had no idea what she would say to him if the penalty meant the score was disallowed.

"Here we go," John called out. The official emerged from beneath the replay camera hood, and made his way onto the field. He switched on his microphone, and stuffed the flag back into the waistband of his pants.

"After a booth review, the clipping penalty against the Minutemen has been reversed. No penalty. Touchdown, Sharks." He held both arms straight up in the air.

The crowd's roar started slowly. It bounced off the windows of the suite. The suite was full of people who patted each other on the back and smiled, but the game wasn't won yet. They all held their breath and waited for the same thing: the point after. If the kicker made the extra point, the Sharks would win the game.

The kicking team trotted out. Tom ran out on the field to hold the ball. Ryan the kicker lined himself up, took three steps to one side, two strides forward, and kicked. The ball rose. The noise rose as well. Emily's heart was in her throat as she watched the ball soar perilously close to the crossbar. Time stood still while a football passed through thin air.

The ball headed toward the left column of the uprights. Ryan shook his head. Tom threw both arms into the air. At the last possible second, the ball made a slight correction, it soared through the uprights, hit the net, and Emily let out a cry. They won.

The final whistle blew. Confetti rained down on the spectators. Emily followed the people racing down the hallway to get to the underground tunnel, and onto the field. It took a few minutes, but the noise in the stadium was still deafening.

The players drenched the coach with the Gatorade bucket. The guys pulled him up onto their shoulders, threw new "Super Bowl Champions" hats into the crowd, and all she could hear was the roar of almost 100,000 people in the stands. There were hundreds of celebrating people around her, and the confetti was so thick it was hard to see.

The rolling stage was making its way across the turf. New England's players headed back to their locker room after shaking hands and exchanging a few words with Sharks players. She looked for Brandon, but she couldn't find him.

Damian emerged from the confetti. He picked Emily up, twirled her around, and said, "He went into the locker room for a few moments, love. He'll be back for the trophy presentation."

"Damian, you had such a great game. You got an interception!"

"Just another day's work," he teased.

"How's your girlfriend?"

"She's here somewhere. I'll find her. I'll see you soon." He moved away.

In only moments, a stage was set up. A few stairs were pulled up in front of it, and microphones waited for the team owners, coaches, and captains. The Seattle fans were clustered in the stands nearby. Tom's wife, Lauren, walked over to Emily. She was heavily pregnant, and she had another month to go.

"Emily, it's so good to see you."

Emily hugged her. "Tom was wonderful today."

Lauren laid a hand on her belly. "I wish Justin could have seen it. We can make a DVD for him to watch when he's older."

On the stage, Shane Falcon and the FOX Sports announcers interrupted their conversation. "Welcome, ladies and gentlemen, to the victory celebration of Super Bowl Forty-Two. The Seattle Sharks defeated the New England Minutemen, 27-26, to win their very first Super Bowl championship. Let's hear it for Seattle." More deafening applause, and, to Emily's amazement, Lauren put two fingers in her mouth and whistled.

"I taught Tom how to do it," she explained.

"Maybe you could teach me, too."

"Later," Lauren assured her.

Shane continued. "The commissioner of the NFL would like to present the Lombardi Trophy to the owner of the Seattle Sharks. Commissioner?"

Emily resisted the impulse to shout, "Hurry up!"

Brandon and the other team captains were heading toward the stage. The owner's speech was brief. He thanked everyone. He lifted the trophy. Brandon, Tom and Damian climbed onto the stage, and the place went wild. Tom was first.

"I'd like to thank my teammates. I knew this day would come. My bride is somewhere on the field. She's having our son next month. This is for the two of them, because I can't imagine this celebration without them. I love you, sweetheart."

"I love you, too," Lauren shouted.

Tom handed the trophy to Brandon. Brandon scanned the crowd until he found Emily. He gestured for her to come to the stage, and she shook her head no. This was his day.

"Sugar, nothing's happening till you're up here with me," he said, and held out his hand.

"Go, go," Lauren urged.

Brandon was still beckoning her, and Emily finally moved through the crowd toward him. Harry McCord, former tight end of the Miami Kingfish, was speaking.

"Brandon, how does it feel to play the greatest game of your career? Three sacks. Nine tackles. An interception and a resulting touchdown. Amazing."

The crowd cheered, and a grin spread across Brandon's face.

"It's about to get better," Brandon said to Harry, and reached down to help Emily up the stairs. The look in his eyes made her knees weak.

Champagne dripped from his tangled curls. The eye black he wore at every game was smeared all over his cheeks. He was covered in sweat, mud, grass, and bloodstains. He'd pulled off the gloves he wore to play. Even with grimy tape covering it, his hand was big, warm, and comforting, as always.

"I couldn't have done this without you," he said to her. She heard his voice echoing around the stadium, and she shook her head again.

"No, baby. This was all you. I'm so proud of you." She tried to smooth the hair off his face.

"I got you something." He laid the trophy in Emily's arms. It was surprisingly heavy. She pretended to examine it.

"Thank you. It's really nice."

The others assembled on the stage laughed. Emily glanced down to see that their families had materialized on the field only a few feet away. Her mom and Suzanne McKenna stood arm-in-arm. Behind them were Brandon's dad, and Dylan. Amy held their dad's hand. She couldn't believe her agent David was there. He *hated* football.

"Baby, look, there's your mom and dad," she told him.

"Your folks are here, too." The crowd was cheering again. Brandon waited until it was somewhat quiet, and said, "You gave up an opportunity you've been working toward most of your life to be here to watch me play. If I didn't know you love me before this morning, I sure as hell know now."

He dropped to one knee, looked into her eyes, and squeezed her hand again. She was so startled she blurted out, "Wh-what are you doing?"

His blue-green eyes danced. They were still the most exotic color Emily had ever seen, and she knew she'd never be tired of looking into them.

In the middle of a crowded stadium, with millions watching on live television, suddenly, it was only the two of them. Her heart was pounding. She tried to take a breath. Mostly, she had a feeling she knew what he was up to. She hoped she wasn't wrong.

"Sugar, I love you with all my heart. I want to spend the rest of my life making you as happy as you make me. Will you marry me?"

His eyes twinkled. His smile dazzled. He was at his most irresistible, and she could only guess at why, out of all the women in the world, he'd chosen her.

"Say *yes!*" someone sounding remarkably like Amy shouted, followed by laughter and applause. Tears filled Emily's eyes. The amount of adrenaline coursing through her bloodstream left her jittery and trembling, but she'd never been so happy.

He waited patiently. It was the most private moment of their lives, and millions were witnessing it. If she was dreaming, she never wanted to wake up.

"McKenna, don't you know you need a ring when you ask a woman to marry you?" Shane said, and pulled the huge Super Bowl ring off his own finger. He pressed it into her hand. "Here's a loaner till the cheapskate buys you one."

She pulled Brandon's diamond ring from her jeans pocket. "I already have his ring."

"Well?" someone behind her said. The smile played around Brandon's mouth.

"Yes. Yes. I love you. Yes," she gasped out.

The crowd went crazy. Brandon took the ring she held, slid it onto the third finger of her left hand, and then gathered her into his arms. The trophy? Well, Emily managed to hang onto it and Brandon at the same time. Brandon kissed her, she cried, and he said into her ear, "We're still getting married February fifteenth."

All she could do was nod.

"I love you."

"I love you, too." She buried her face in his chest.

"Give Shane his ring back, sugar." There was laughter all over the stadium at that comment.

"Goddamn it, McKenna," they heard Damian say, "How do you expect me to follow that?"

Chapter Twenty-Six

EMILY OPENED HER eyes to sunshine streaming through Brandon's bedroom windows. Anyone who's ever lived in Seattle knows sunshine is a minor miracle, especially in February. All she wanted was a couple of hours more sleep. She was struggling with jet lag. They wouldn't be sleeping in this morning, though. It was their wedding day.

Brandon and Emily had returned home from New York the day before. The Met, it seemed, was fairly willing to overlook the fact she walked out on a performance. The international publicity that came after Brandon's proposal to the diva on live television caused an awful lot of people to buy tickets. The remaining performances of La Boheme sold out within twenty-four hours. Three days after the Super Bowl, Emily flounced onto the Metropolitan Opera's stage as Musette. Both the Hamilton and McKenna families were in the audience. She'd achieved her goal. It was better than she ever dreamed.

Brandon kissed the back of her neck. "It's time for the bride to wake up."

She let out a groan. "Already?"

"I want to give you your gift before we have to leave for the church."

Emily rolled over to face him, and twined her arms around his neck. "You already gave me my gift several times last night."

"I sure did." He looked pleased with himself, as he pulled her up and onto his chest. "Defensive ends are the real men of any football team, sugar."

"We've got all kinds of time," she coaxed. "We don't have to get out of bed yet."

"Your mom and Amy are supposed to be here in less than an hour."

"I'll call them," Emily said. "They can't have a wedding without us, can they?"

"Not so fast."

Okay, someone had his cranky pants on. So they started their honeymoon a bit early. It wasn't a crime. Truthfully, they had started the honeymoon two weeks ago, but who was counting? He was trying to be stern with her, but failing in a big way. It probably had something remotely to do with the amusement in his eyes.

"We have to get out of bed for at least one morning," he told her. "I've ruined you, and now we must marry."

"You've been reading the back covers of the romance novels in the grocery store again, haven't you?"

"That's where I get my best ideas." He wriggled his eyebrows in an attempt to look evil. Emily burst out laughing. He rolled her off him, and onto her back.

"I can't wait till later to find out what you've discovered," she said. "Fur-lined handcuffs?"

He pinned her wrists over her head with one hand, while he reached into the bedside table with the other.

"I never knew opera singers were so depraved."

"Well, excuse me, Mr. MVP," she said. "You just wait till later. I'm going to wear you out."

"Those lessons on trash talking are evidently paying off." He smirked. "I wonder if they'd miss us if we didn't show up."

He caught her mouth in a kiss that she could only describe as incendiary. Finally, though, he pushed himself off her, dropped the Tiffany box he held onto her belly, and said, "If you don't get dressed, sugar, you can't wear these."

"Tease," she shot back, but she dutifully sat up. She tugged at the white satin ribbon, pulled the robin's-egg-blue box open, and let out a gasp. A strand of pearls, stud earrings, and a bracelet were nestled inside. "They're beautiful. Thank you."

"Almost as beautiful as you are." His eyes twinkled. She threw herself onto him again, only to be escorted into the bathroom. "Shower time, young lady."

"But I haven't given you your gift yet," Emily protested.

He flipped the shower taps on, lightly smacked her bottom with his open hand, and said, "Later."

"I'll—I'll get you for that, bruiser."

"Promise?" He laughed, and then left the bathroom, shutting the door behind him.

Emily grinned to herself. He would pay for this, over and over again. In the meantime, she got in the shower.

She heard Brandon's voice through the bathroom door a short time later as she wriggled into undergarments and thigh-high silk stockings. "Sugar?"

"Yes, lover man?"

She heard Amy's laugh ring out somewhere in the background. She hoped her sister wasn't monitoring their conversation.

"The moms and Amy are here. I'll see you at the church."

Emily grabbed a robe off the hook on the bathroom door and slipped it on as the door opened a crack.

"You just wait, you little minx," he said in a low voice.

"Bring it."

Brandon let out a snort, shutting the bathroom door as he walked away. Amy opened the door a few minutes later.

"Okay. The coast is clear. Wait till you see him," her sister said.

"I've seen him in a tuxedo before—"

She cut Emily off. "Not like this. We helped him with the tie."

"It's not orange or powder blue, is it?"

"Uh, no. Let's get you dressed and ready." Amy pulled her out of the bathroom.

After what seemed like a never-ending amount of time

getting hair and makeup done, Amy helped Emily into the wedding gown she bought during her Meg-and-Suzanne-mandated shopping trip. Even in February, it was perfect for a morning wedding. Brandon's pearls went on last.

The moms stood in the doorway watching as Amy pinned the tiara and veil into Emily's hair. Suzanne clutched their mom's hand.

"She's so beautiful, Meg." Suzanne let out a loud sniffle, and pulled a lace-edged hanky out of her tiny evening purse.

Tears glistened in Meg's eyes. "I knew this day was going to come. I wasn't expecting it so soon."

Amy let out a snicker. "Ma, we're adults. When did you think this was going to happen?"

Tears or no, it wouldn't be a family occasion unless Amy said something completely sarcastic. Emily was surprised, though, to see Amy's chin tremble. She wasn't as unaffected as she appeared.

"Brian must be meeting us at the church."

"He can't make it today." Amy turned away from her and picked up the tote bag with various items Emily was warned all brides needed desperately, like an extra pair of hose, bobby pins, industrial-strength mascara . . . Something was wrong, but Amy wasn't going to tell her what it was in front of their mom. Emily would get it out of her later.

"We're going to be late for the pictures if we don't move our asses *now*," Amy told them.

"Amy Margaret Hamilton, I didn't raise you to use that kind of language."

Suzanne put a comforting arm around Meg's shoulders. "I can't even tell you how many times I washed Brandon's mouth out with soap for saying bad words when he was a little boy. He is just like his father . . ." The two of them followed Amy and Emily down the hallway, chatting away about their children's various misdeeds.

The bridal party hurried out to the waiting limousine for the trip to the church. Meg smoothed the skirt of her gown. "Are you nervous, honey?"

"No. I want to get there." Emily twisted her hands in her lap.

It took only a few minutes to drive to the little church on the hill with the floor-to-ceiling windows that overlooked Lake Washington. They all piled out of the car.

"Hey, it's not too late to drive over to the burger place and get a shake," Emily joked, but her stomach was full of butterflies. Her heart was beating a rat-a-tat-tat inside her chest. The moms bustled around them, and hurried inside the church.

Amy held Emily's train up so it wouldn't brush the sidewalk. She smoothed the skirt on her dress as well. "This is it, Em." Her sister's eyes swam with tears, and she took Emily's hand.

"Don't you start, or I'm going to start," Emily warned.

"It'll never be the same," she said, her voice quavering.

"It's going to be better," Emily said. They hugged each other. "You're not losing me, you're getting a brother."

Amy let out a snort.

"Fine, if you think that's going to make me feel better."

Emily burst out laughing. They pulled away from each other, and Emily touched the pearl bracelet around her sister's wrist.

"Where'd you get this?"

Amy rolled her eyes.

"Brandon tried to buy me off earlier with something from Tiffany." She rolled her eyes. "He probably thinks I'll fall for it."

"It's beautiful."

"I see you got pearls, too." Amy observed. "I love him, even if he is a freak. You do realize you're going to have to feed him. How many times a day does he eat?"

Just for a moment, Emily was six again, and Amy was five. They walked, hand-in-hand, to the first day of school. This was a different kind of school. Emily was going to learn how to build a family, and hopefully Amy would learn the same lessons, too.

Mark Hamilton waited in the foyer with Jack and Suzanne McKenna. Emily couldn't hear what was being discussed, but Jack took her arm. "Are you sure you want to marry my son?"

"Jack McKenna, you behave yourself," Suzanne told him with an indulgent smile.

"Never." He winked at Emily. "My offer still stands," but he kissed his wife's cheek. "Ready, Mrs. McKenna?"

Jack accompanied Suzanne up the aisle and made sure she was seated, and then it was time for Mark and Meg to make their way up the aisle. She gave Emily one last hug, and took both her hands.

"I love you, honey. I'm so happy for you."

Emily's fingers brushed metal. Wait a minute. There was a ring on the third finger of her mother's left hand.

"Mom?" Emily pulled her hand up to see. "What's this?"

"I asked your mother to marry me again the night before last, and she said yes," Mark Hamilton told his daughters.

Emily was frozen in shock for a moment. Her mother's face was radiant with happiness as she held out her left hand for Emily and Amy to see her new ring. A few minutes later, though, it was a bunch of Hamiltons, hugging and crying on the best day of Emily's life. Their parents finally pulled away, though. "We need to get this show on the road."

Emily watched her father loop her mother's hand through his arm. They beamed at each other, and made the slow walk up the aisle.

Amy stepped into place as well. The string quartet in the choir loft swelled.

Emily's breath caught as she watched Amy's progress. The ballroom skirt of her dress swished as she walked the aisle. Just buttoning the back of the gown took half an hour. The copper silk shone like a new penny as the sun hit it. She was incandescent.

Amy reached the altar, turned to face Emily, and mouthed, "Hurry up."

The wedding coordinator and her assistant shut the sanctuary doors, preparing for Emily's grand entrance. She'd seen far enough into the sanctuary to note it was standing room only. The physical contrast between Brandon's teammates and the rest of the guests was a bit startling, too.

Emily's father patted her hand. "Ready?"

Her voice came out in a whoosh: "Yes."

"Nervous?"

"Not at all."

She shook like the leaves in her headdress. Her palms were sweaty. She swallowed the tiny bit of moisture in her mouth. Her heart pounded, the adrenaline raced through her body, and she whispered, "Do you have any advice?"

A few seconds later, the sanctuary doors opened with a flourish. The organist and trumpeters launched into Purcell's "Trumpet Tune." Emily saw her mom stand up in the front row. The rest of their guests got to their feet and turned toward the back of the church.

Brandon and Emily had invited people on very short notice, but everyone they loved was here. Emily and her father took measured steps over the threshold and into the sanctuary.

"It's a hell of a time to ask for advice, punkin." Mark Hamilton held his eldest daughter's hand a little more tightly. "Brandon asked me the same thing this morning."

"You're kidding."

"Sure, he did. I'm going to tell you exactly what I told him, too. Love each other. Think about the things that would make him happy, and do at least one of those things every day. Put each other first. Take it one day at a time." Her father nodded at someone he knew as they passed by. "If there was one more thing I could tell you, maybe you should learn from your mom's and my mistakes."

"Dad, everyone makes mistakes."

"There's a difference between those who learn from it when they screw up, and those who keep doing it over and over." Her father's mouth twitched into a grin. "Punkin, this could never be a mistake. You and Brandon are always going to love each other."

The end of the aisle was in sight, and Emily's eyes locked on Brandon. He looked more handsome than she'd ever seen him. His curls were styled. He wore a black morning coat with a white silk pocket square, subtly striped tuxedo pants, a pearl-gray vest, and a soft gray cravat. He took whatever breath she still had away. She was so absorbed in staring at him that she was barely listening to her father.

Brandon stepped forward at the end of the aisle. His lips curved slowly into a smile, and he held out his hand to her. Her father stopped, and Brandon walked to them. Emily's dad shook Brandon's hand, and they hugged each other clumsily.

"Here she is, son. You can walk with her the rest of the way." Mark Hamilton pulled his daughter's veil up enough to kiss her cheek. "We love you."

"I love you, too, Dad."

He settled the veil back over her face, put her hand in Brandon's, and stepped aside.

Brandon and Emily took a few more steps, and they stood at the altar. "Nice dress," he whispered into her ear. "I can't wait to take it off you." She let out a laugh. The rest of their lives started now, and Emily could hardly wait.

An Excerpt from

RUSHING AMY

THE WEDDING WAS over, and Amy Hamilton stood amongst the wreckage.

Every flat surface in the Woodmark Hotel's grand ballroom was strewn with dirty plates, empty glasses, crumpled napkins, spent champagne bottles—the outward indication that a large group of people had one hell of a party. A few hours ago, Amy's older sister, Emily, had married Brandon McKenna, the man of her dreams.

Three hundred guests toasted the bride and groom repeatedly. Happy tears flowed as freely as the champagne. The dinner was delicious, the cake, even better. The newlyweds and their guests danced to a live band till after midnight. The hotel ballroom was transformed into a candlelit fairyland for her sister's flawless evening, but now all that was left was the mess. The perfectly arranged profusion of flowers were drooping. So was she.

Amy arranged flowers for weddings almost every

weekend. Doing the flowers for Emily's wedding, though, was an extra-special thrill. She'd seen it all over the past few years, first as an apprentice to another florist, and then opening her own shop a little over a year ago. It was long hours and hard work, but she was determined her business would succeed.

Amy took a last look at the twinkling lights of the boats crossing Lake Washington through the floor-to-ceiling windows along the west wall. She couldn't help but notice she stood alone in a room that had been packed with people only an hour or so ago. She'd been alone for a long time now, and she didn't like the feeling at all. She picked up the black silk chiffon wrap draped over yet another chair, and the now-wilting bridal bouquet Emily had tossed to her. Obviously, she'd stalled long enough. She wondered if the kitchen staff would mind whipping up a vat of chocolate mousse to drown her sorrows in.

HEAVY FOOTSTEPS SOUNDED behind Amy on the ballroom floor, and she turned toward them. The man she'd watched on a hundred NFL Today pregame broadcasts strolled toward her. Any woman with a pulse knew who he was, let alone any woman hopelessly addicted to Pro Sports Network.

Matt Stephens was tall. The body sculpted by years of workouts was showcased in a perfectly tailored navy suit, but that didn't tell the story. The wavy, slightly mussed blue-black hair, the square jaw, the olive skin that seemed to glow, and the flawless, white smile were exactly what

Amy saw on her television screen each week during football season. Television didn't do him justice. After all, on her TV screen he didn't prowl. He locked eyes with her as he crossed the ballroom.

She glanced around to note she was still alone in the ballroom, and he was making a beeline toward her. She couldn't imagine what he wanted, but she would be finding out in a few short moments.

She knew a lot about him. Matt was a former NFL star, and a good friend of her new brother-in-law's. When Matt got tired of playing with the Dallas Cowboys (three Super Bowl rings and six visits to the Pro Bowl later) he'd played in Seattle for the last two years of his career, afterward embarking on the wide world of game analysis and product endorsements. Guys wanted to be him, and women just plain wanted him.

Well, women who were still on the playing field wanted him. She was putting herself on injured reserve. After all, once burned, twice shy, and every other cliché she'd ever heard that reminded her of salt being poured on the open wound that was her heart.

Mostly, guys that looked like Matt weren't looking for someone like her; she was a woman more interested in being independent than being some guy's arm candy.

Matt stopped a few feet away from Amy. The deep dimples on either side of his lips flashed as his mouth moved into an irresistible grin.

"Hello, there."

"You're late." The words flew out of her mouth before she realized she'd said it aloud.

His smile cajoled. The man was completely aware there wasn't a woman on the planet that could hope to resist him. She could, though. She would. She wasn't going to fall for someone like him. He slipped one hand into his pants pocket.

"Oh, I'm definitely not late," he said. "As a matter of fact, I'm right on schedule."

She let out a gasp of outrage.

His eyes slid over her from head to toe. Slowly. They made a few stops along the way, too. Amy dragged a shallow breath into her lungs. She resisted the impulse to smooth the wrinkles out of her dress, shove the hairpins back into what was most likely the wreck of her updo, and press her lips together in any attempt to salvage lipstick eaten off hours ago. Until she reminded herself that she was dealing with yet another male. Even worse, this one evidently believed the rules in life applied to everyone else but him.

"Were you actually invited to this event?" she asked.

He looked a bit wary. Even if Matt was the most gorgeous man she'd ever met, he was not getting away with this. She was busting his chops. After all, someone had to do it.

"Yes, I was invited." He tried to look sheepish, but she wasn't buying it. "McKenna's going to kick my ass."

"Why do I think it won't be the first time that's happened?"

Matt lifted one eyebrow, seemingly unused to any woman who didn't collapse into a quivering mass of flesh whenever he chose to make any effort at all. She saw his mouth twitch into a smile.

"It seems we've gotten off on the wrong foot. Maybe we should try this again." He took a couple of steps toward her and extended one hand. "Hi. I'm Matt Stephens."

Amy tried to surreptitiously wipe what she was sure was a sweaty palm on her dress before her hand vanished into his much larger one.

She nodded a bit and tilted her chin up, as if she were introduced to guys who made *People*'s "Sexiest Man Alive" issue every day. "Matt, huh?"

"And your name is?"

Her mouth evidently had a mind of its own. For some perverse reason, she blurted out, "I'm Fifi."

"Fifi." He looked a bit skeptical.

"Yes." She squared her shoulders. "My parents were . . . imaginative."

"Is that so?" He glanced around for a brief moment, and his eyes moved back to her. "I'm a little thirsty. Are you thirsty, Fifi? Let's have a drink."

Amy deliberated for about half a second. Despite the fact she was fairly sure she'd just met the most arrogant man in the world, she was dying to see what he was going to do next. Broken heart or not, she was in.

About the Author

JULIE BRANNAGH has been writing since she was old enough to hold a pencil. She lives in a small town near Seattle, where she once served as a city council member and owned a yarn shop. She shares her home with a wonderful husband, two uncivilized Maine Coons, and a rambunctious chocolate Lab.

When she's not writing, she's reading, or armchair-quarterbacking her favorite NFL team from the comfort of the family room couch. Julie is a Golden Heart finalist and the author of four contemporary sports romances.

Visit www.AuthorTracker.com for exclusive information on your favorite HarperCollins authors.

Give in to your impulses . . .
Read on for a sneak peek at four brand-new
e-book original tales of romance
from Avon Books.
Available now wherever e-books are sold.

ALL I WANT FOR CHRISTMAS IS A COWBOY
By Emma Cane, Jennifer Ryan, and Katie Lane

SANTA, BRING MY BABY BACK
By Cheryl Harper

THE CHRISTMAS COOKIE CHRONICLES: GRACE
By Lori Wilde

DESPERATELY SEEKING FIREMAN
A BACHELOR FIREMEN NOVELLA
By Jennifer Bernard

ALL I WANT FOR CHRISTMAS IS A COWBOY

by *Emma Cane, Jennifer Ryan, and Katie Lane*

What's better than Christmas?

Christmas and Cowboys.

**From Emma Cane, Jennifer Ryan, and Katie
Lane come three wildly romantic holiday
stories featuring snowstorms, proposals,
a sleigh ride . . . and, yes, cowboys.**

The Christmas Cabin by Emma Cane

Sandy and her five-year-old son, Nate, are Christmas tree–
hunting when a snowstorm strikes and an old ranch hand
points them to an abandoned cabin. Little does Sandy know,
the hand sent cowboy Doug Thalberg to the same place. It's a
Christmas all of Valentine Valley will remember.

Can't Wait by Jennifer Ryan

Before The Hunted Series began . . .

Though she is the woman of his dreams, Caleb Bowden
knows his best friend's sister, Summer Turner, is off limits.
He won't cross that line, which means Summer will just have

to take matters into her own hands if she wants her cowboy for Christmas.

Baby It's Cold Outside by Katie Lane

Alana Hale hits the internet dating jackpot when she finds Clint McCormick. He's sensitive and responsible—not to mention wealthy. When he invites her to spend the holidays on his family's ranch, she readily accepts. But on the way there, a blizzard strands her with a womanizing rodeo cowboy who could change everything . . .

An Excerpt from

SANTA, BRING MY BABY BACK
by Cheryl Harper

A bride abandoned at the altar . . . just in time for
Christmas? 'Tis the season for second chances at
Cheryl Harper's Elvis-themed Rock'n'Rolla Hotel.

There was something about Grace Andersen that made him want to help, even after decades of trying to guard his mother and her money against personalities and stories like hers.

He wouldn't mind being Grace Andersen's hero.

To avoid doing something stupid, Charlie turned to go but stopped when she added, "Oh, Charlie, could you do me a favor?"

She shuffled toward him, the rustle of the wedding dress sweeping the floor loud in the silence. "Could you unzip me? I thought I was going to dislocate a shoulder getting it zipped in the first place." She turned and bent her head so that all Charlie could see was the smooth, pale skin of her shoulders and the loose dark hairs that tickled her neck.

When he didn't move quickly enough, she turned her head to look at him over one perfect shoulder.

Remembering to breathe became a struggle again.

He forced himself to step closer. He grasped the zipper with one hand and slid the other under the fabric. The zipper made a quiet hiss as it slid down the curve of her back, every centimeter showing more beautiful skin.

And out of the blue he wondered if unzipping Grace Andersen would ever get old. Finished, he took two steps away to keep from smoothing his hands over her shoulders like he wanted, or tracing a finger down her spine just to see goose bumps.

She turned her head. "Thanks."

As he pulled the door closed behind him, Charlie tried to remember the last time he'd seen anyone as pretty as she was in real life. Never. But she wasn't his type. He preferred career women who wore glasses and looked like they could reel off stock prices or legal precedents. He liked women with sharp minds and sturdy savings. He'd had enough excitement growing up with Willodean McMinn Holloway Luttrell Jackson. Now all he wanted was a comfortable home, an easy, companionable, stable relationship, and maybe a baby to keep things interesting. Maybe.

Grace Andersen looked like . . . magic.

He propped his hands on his hips and shook his head as he looked out at the guitar-shaped pool that was covered for the season.

Magic? He hadn't been in the hotel for a full twenty-four hours and already his mind was going. Something about being that close to her had melted it. But Grace Andersen was just a woman. She'd been left at the altar but didn't seem too broken up about it. He hoped her new plan, whatever it was, included checking out of the hotel immediately. Beautiful Grace Andersen might have the ability to wreck his goals along with his logic if she stayed.

An Excerpt from

THE CHRISTMAS COOKIE CHRONICLES: GRACE

by Lori Wilde

(Originally appeared in the print anthology
The Christmas Cookie Collection)

New York Times bestselling author
Lori Wilde returns to Twilight, Texas, for
another delightful holiday installment of
her *Christmas Cookie Chronicles*. And this
time, a young couple are thrilled to expect
the greatest gift of all: a new baby!

Flynn MacGregor Calloway put a palm to her aching back, wrapped her other arm around her pregnant belly, canted her head, and studied the spindly-branched, lopsided Scotch pine. After much wrestling and a few choice words, she'd managed to get it set up in a corner of the living room in the cottage she shared with her husband, Jesse.

She'd wanted to surprise him, so she'd waited until after the morning wedding of Jesse's father, Sheriff Hondo Crouch, and his bride, Patsy Cross, before she'd slipped down to the Christmas tree lot and, using Jesse's pickup truck, drove the tree home. Jesse had volunteered to drive the newlyweds to DFW airport to catch a plane bound for a Hawaii honeymoon, so he had taken their sedan because three people and luggage fit in it better, giving Flynn plenty of time to get it done.

The glow from the icicle lights dangling on the eaves outside slanted through the window and shone through some of the more meager limbs.

Okay, so it wasn't quite a Charlie Brown tree, but it was close and clearly not what Maven Styles, the author of *How to Host the Perfect Christmas*, had in mind when she declared that an impeccable holiday began with the perfect tree.

Then again, Maven Styles probably wasn't on a newlywed student's tight budget that required her to wait for Christmas Eve, when they marked down the trees. Flynn had picked this one up for five dollars, and she was proud of her bargain. Maybe not proud, but it was a real tree, not artificial, and seven feet tall. She should get points for that, right? All it needed were a few decorations to spiff it up.

She couldn't regret cutting corners. The baby had been a surprise, a very welcome surprise to be sure, but their finances had taken an added hit because of it. Between scraping together money for her college tuition, the cost of rebuilding Jesse's motorcycle shop after the fire, exorbitant health insurance for the self-employed, and getting ready for the baby's arrival, they hadn't much money left to spend on holiday celebrations. Their situation was a temporary setback, she knew that, but part of her couldn't help feeling wistful that their last Christmas with just the two of them was going to be as sparse as that scraggly Scotch pine.

Stop feeling sorry for yourself, she scolded. *Plenty of people have it much worse.*

By tightly pinching pennies all year and keeping an eagle eye out for sales, she'd managed to save just enough to buy Jesse a new leather jacket to replace the one he'd worn since high school. She couldn't wait to give it to him on Christmas morning. For now, it was wrapped and stowed in the trunk of their car. He'd had so little growing up that she ached to give him everything his heart desired. Which was why she'd checked *How to Host the Perfect Christmas* out of the library, hoping she could pick up a few pointers.

A cardboard box filled with decorations from her childhood sat on the floor. Flynn peeled back the tape and opened the flaps. Her mother had had the habit of either buying or making one special ornament to commemorate each Christmas.

As she removed them from the box, each decoration stirred a memory—the candy canes made out of bread dough and shellacked (crumbling a bit now with age) that she and her younger sister, Carrie, had helped their mother bake in 1992. The twin wooden toy soldiers her mother's best friend, Marva Bullock, had given her after the twins, Noah and Joel, were born; and the last ornament her mother had ever purchased, a delicate red glass ball inset with a tiny nativity scene.

Air stilled in her lungs. Although her family hadn't known it at the time, the red glass ball represented the last perfect Christmas before her mother had been diagnosed with amyotrophic lateral sclerosis.

Tears misted her eyes. *Oh, Mama. You'll never know your grandchildren.* With a knuckle, she wiped away the tears. Should she put the ornament on the tree? It would stir painful memories every time she looked at it. And yet the ornament was a shining reminder of that one perfect Christmas when her family was last together and whole.

An Excerpt from

DESPERATELY SEEKING FIREMAN
A Bachelor Firemen Novella
by Jennifer Bernard

From *USA Today* bestseller Jennifer Bernard
comes the steamy story of a sexy bachelor fireman
and the woman who will turn his life around.

Wayside Chapel, San Gabriel, California

The groom's side of the aisle was packed with an astonishingly high number of gorgeous men. Nita Moreno, standing near Melissa McGuire—soon to be Melissa Brody—surveyed the pews with widening eyes. There was enough testosterone in the building to fuel a small nation's army. Enough handsome, manly faces to fill an issue of *Playgirl*. Enough brawny muscles to . . .

Oops. Busted. From across the aisle, two steps behind Captain Brody, a pair of amused, tiger-striped eyes met hers. An unusual mixture of gold and green, surrounded by thick black eyelashes, they would have made their owner look feminine if he weren't one solid hunk of hard-packed male. A smile twitched at the corner of his mouth. Even in this context—the so-called Bachelor Firemen crowding the wedding of their revered fire captain—he stood out. First there was that breath-taking physique. Then there was his face, a study in contrasts. His features were so strong they almost qualified as harsh. Firm jaw, uncompromising cheekbones. A man's man . . . until one looked into those golden eyes, or noticed that he possessed the most beautiful mouth Nita had ever seen on a man.

She narrowed her own eyes and met him look for look. Hey, she wasn't checking out the available men. She had one of her own. Very deliberately, she let her gaze roam to the bride's side of the aisle and settle on Bradford Maddox the Fourth. Hedge fund operator, family scion, possessor of a killer business instinct and an only-slightly-receding hairline, he was hers, and she could still scarcely believe it. Maybe soon she and Bradford would be making their way down an aisle like this. Out of unconscious habit, she took the inside of her cheek between her teeth and worried it at. She loved Bradford, and she knew he felt the same. He must.

Bradford, who seemed lost in thought, startled when he realized she was looking adoringly at him. He gave her a faint smile, then pressed his finger to his ear. Lovely. He wasn't lost in thought, he was listening to his Bluetooth. She sighed, telling herself to let it go. It came with the territory when you dated a hotshot financier. Of course he couldn't focus his *entire* attention on the wedding of two people he didn't even know.

The right side of her body felt suddenly warm, and she realized the man across the aisle was still watching her, as if she fascinated him.

Really? *She* fascinated *him?* That seemed unlikely. She

raised a questioning eyebrow at him. He smiled, the expression transforming his face from the inside out. Goodness, the man was gorgeous, in a totally different way from Bradford. Dark instead of blond, tough instead of charming. Virile and primitive, the kind of man who would toss you over his shoulder and have his way with you.

He jerked his chin at her, as if signaling her to meet him in the chancel.

She frowned at him, scolding. *Excuse me?* How inappropriate.

He did it again, more urgently this time.

What did the man want? She lifted her hands, palms up—a frustrated question—as he mouthed something to her.

"Bouquet."

Aw, crap.